IN THE
NAME OF
TRUTH

IN THE NAME OF TRUTH

VIVECA STEN

TRANSLATED BY MARLAINE DELARGY

SANDHAMN MURDERS

 AMAZON **CROSSING**

Previously published as *I sanningens namn* by Forum in Sweden in 2015. Translated from Swedish by Marlaine Delargy. First published in English by Amazon Crossing in 2020.

Published by Amazon Crossing, Seattle

www.apub.com

Amazon, the Amazon logo, and Amazon Crossing are trademarks of Amazon.com, Inc., or its affiliates.

ISBN-13: 9781542015325
ISBN-10: 1542015324

Cover design by Damon Freeman

Printed in the United States of America

To Helen, because you're always there

The children were asleep. The sun hadn't yet risen above the grass surrounding the red cabins, and the dew still sparkled on the dinghies that had been lifted out of the water.

Every cabin contained two dormitories, and each dormitory housed eight children. Eight girls and boys, some with rounded cheeks and slender bodies, others with the first downy hairs of puberty and budding breasts beginning to show.

He'd waited a while behind a tree, but now he pulled down his cap and looked around. It was getting lighter very quickly, and the birds were singing more and more loudly.

He moved closer.

The window of the nearest cabin was ajar. Inside he could just see sleeping figures with tousled hair and tan faces. Foreheads damp with sweat, arms dangling over the side of the bed.

He examined the door carefully. It didn't appear to be locked; he couldn't see a catch in the gap between the door and the frame.

He turned his head and scanned the area. The instructors' accommodation was a few hundred yards away among the pine trees. They'd stayed up late; it had been after midnight when the lights in their cabin finally went out.

A soft splash caught his attention as a tern plummeted toward the smooth surface of the water. Circles spread outward from the point of contact, then disappeared.

It would take no more than a moment; he knew exactly what he was going to do.

Chapter 1

Thursday, June 12, 2014

"Don't look so miserable, Benjamin." Åsa Dufva tried to smile encouragingly at her son. "Plenty of kids would be delighted to have the chance to go to sailing camp."

Benjamin didn't answer. He was sitting on the bed with his head down, staring at his phone. A faint electronic melody came from the game he was playing.

Åsa folded another pair of jeans and put them in the bag on the floor. She'd already packed several T-shirts and a hoodie, along with his sailing gear and a life jacket she'd borrowed from a friend.

"I'm sure you'll soon make new friends—maybe some of your classmates will be there?"

Still no response; Benjamin's gaze was still fixed on the iPhone his father had given him.

Åsa's jaw tightened when she thought about Christian's birthday gift to his son six months earlier. Benjamin had been so thrilled he'd barely noticed that his father had stayed at his party for less than an hour, but Åsa had seen him leave long before everyone else, looking stressed. Desperate to get home to Ninna and the baby.

Benjamin glanced up. "Do I have to go?"

His voice lacked conviction; he would never refuse to comply with his father's wishes. Åsa opened her mouth, then closed it again. She should have told Christian that sailing camp was a dumb idea. Just because he'd loved camp life, that didn't mean it would suit their son. Benjamin wasn't sporty like Christian, nor was he particularly outgoing or sociable. He kept to himself, preferring to sit on the sofa and play computer games.

But as usual, Christian had gotten his way.

He'd already arranged everything before he revealed that Benjamin had been accepted on a weeklong sailing course. Åsa would pick him up the day before Midsummer's Eve. Tomorrow Christian and Benjamin would take the ferry over to Sandhamn, then continue to the island of Lökholmen, where the camp was taking place.

Åsa sighed. "Don't forget to brush your teeth after breakfast and before you go to bed when you're away," she said, folding one last sweater.

No response.

"Did you hear what I said?"

Benjamin looked up from his phone. "I'll be the smallest one there. All the others will be older than me."

This was true. He would probably be the youngest, and he was shorter than most of the others in his class at school. That was another way in which he differed from his father, who was tall and broad-shouldered.

Åsa sat down on the bed next to Benjamin. He had his back to the wall, knees drawn up. His light-brown hair had fallen over his forehead, but Åsa knew she had to resist the temptation to push it back, which would annoy him.

Without meeting her gaze, he went on: "I don't know how to sail."

"Well, that's why you're going to the camp—so you can learn."

Åsa did her best to sound positive, but it was a real struggle. If it had been left to her, she and Benjamin would have been going to stay with Grandma and Grandpa in Småland, as they always did in the week leading up to Midsummer. The camp was all Christian's idea, but it wouldn't help Benjamin if she made a sarcastic comment about his father's belief that he could buy his way out of his responsibilities.

"It's only a week, sweetheart. It'll soon pass. You know Dad really wants you to go." She couldn't resist ruffling his hair, but of course he pulled away.

She had to finish packing so that she could get started on dinner. Christian was due to collect Benjamin at seven thirty in the morning, and she was tired after a long shift at the hospital. As usual there had been too few midwives to cope with what was expected of them.

She got to her feet and took a pair of pajamas from the top drawer. They were made of pale-blue flannel; the fabric was soft and smooth beneath her fingertips.

The knot of anxiety in her stomach grew.

Christian had insisted on sending Benjamin to camp, but she was the one who had to console their son. Christian wasn't worrying about whether Benjamin would get upset or homesick.

"It'll be fine," she said, wondering whether she was trying to reassure herself or Benjamin. "You're going to have so much fun."

CHAPTER 2

Nora Linde closed the folder containing the interview transcript and pushed it away. The trial was due to begin on Monday—her last one before the wedding.

Nora smiled. At three o'clock on the afternoon of Midsummer's Eve, she and Jonas would be married in the chapel on Sandhamn. Little Julia was going to be a flower girl, and Jonas's daughter, Wilma, would be her bridesmaid. Adam and Simon were both acting as groomsmen.

She'd already started checking out various meteorological websites. Jonas laughed at her desperate attempts to convince herself that it wasn't going to rain. At the moment the sun was shining outside the windows of the Economic Crimes Authority, but the midsummer weather was notoriously unreliable.

Her gaze fell on the computer screen, and her smile vanished.

This morning she'd received another anonymous email regarding the trial. The content was the same as the previous messages—aggressive accusations aimed at her principal witness.

DON'T BELIEVE THAT FUCKER!

As always the tone was vicious, the sender anonymous and impossible to trace.

There was a knock on the half-open door. Nora looked up to see Jonathan Sandelin, chief prosecutor.

"Are you busy?" he asked as he took off his horn-rimmed glasses with their slim frame.

"It's fine—come on in." She gestured toward the visitor's chair. Her boss sat down, glancing at the folder on her desk as he did so: *B1216-14, The state versus Niklas Winnerman and Bertil Svensson.*

"I thought you'd be hard at work."

Nora nodded. She'd spent a lot of time during the spring preparing the upcoming case against Alliance Construction. The company's managing director had siphoned off so much money that the firm had ended up going bust. Nora had charged him with the crime of grave disloyalty to principal, and was aiming for a lengthy jail term.

"How's it going?"

"Fine."

The Economic Crimes Authority had suffered a number of well-publicized setbacks over the past few years. They had lost several major cases in both the county court and the crown court, and the media had been quick to point out this lack of success. Nora knew the general director was keen to improve the statistics.

"We're going to win this one," she added.

"You're not worried that Winnerman will wriggle out of it?"

As always, Jonathan had his finger on the pulse. Niklas Winnerman, the managing director, had denied any wrongdoing from the get-go, and his defense was very clear: the Economic Crimes Authority had misunderstood the whole thing, and they were trying to send down an innocent man.

"Shit happens," as Winnerman's lawyer had put it during an early interview. "Making a bad deal isn't a crime. Not yet anyway."

"The sales director's testimony will be key," Nora said, waving a hand in the direction of the relevant documents. "I've just read through all the transcripts again. Christian Dufva swears that Winnerman alone was responsible for the deal that led to the firm's collapse. It was thanks to Winnerman that they paid ten million kronor for planning permission that turned out to be worthless, then he managed to hide the money overseas before anyone realized what he'd done."

"Not a bad amount to tuck away."

Nora had to agree. "It was far too much for a company of that size," she said. "When the bills weren't paid, it didn't take long for Alliance to go under. If the official receiver hadn't begun to suspect something was wrong, Winnerman would probably have gotten away with it."

She heard the sound of a door closing, a key turning farther down the hall. The day was coming to an end; most of the offices would soon be empty.

"If I remember correctly, it was a pretty sophisticated operation," Jonathan said, crossing one long leg over the other.

Nora nodded. Winnerman had hidden behind a nonexistent company, and used an alcoholic by the name of Bertil Svensson as his patsy. Svensson spent most of his time sitting on a bench in the Hallunda shopping mall, and he, too, had been charged with complicity. For ten thousand kronor and a few bottles of schnapps, Svensson had happily signed all the documentation and fronted the deal, enabling Winnerman to hide his involvement.

"That's why Dufva's testimony is so important," she said. "With his help, I should be able to make the jury understand exactly what happened."

There had been no mistaking Christian Dufva's bitterness and frustration when he was interviewed, and Nora was convinced he would do his utmost to make sure his former business partner was convicted. They'd worked together for ten years, and this was the thanks he got, as he'd put it.

"The money still hasn't been traced?"

"I'm afraid not."

That had been a real blow. The ten million had immediately been transferred to an anonymous overseas account, leaving them with nothing but circumstantial evidence. Nora knew the defense would use the Economic Crimes Authority's failure to find the money as a stick to beat them with during the court proceedings. Leila Kacim, the energetic young detective who was working on the case, had turned over every stone, but to no avail.

"Any theories as to where it might have gone?"

Nora shook her head. There were no millions sitting in Winnerman's bank account. He lived in a heavily mortgaged three-room apartment in the inner city, and was joint owner of a summer cottage on the island of Ingarö with his sister. He had no other assets. Nora had given a lot of thought to the missing money, but hadn't been able to come up with a credible explanation.

Should she mention the anonymous emails?

She hesitated; she hadn't really attributed any importance to them until now. Most prosecutors encountered this kind of thing from time to time. Before she could make up her mind, Jonathan got to his feet.

"Anyway, it seems as if you've got everything under control. Good. By the way, you do know there's a vacancy for a deputy district chief prosecutor after the summer? A good result here . . ."

He raised his eyebrows meaningfully, and Nora couldn't help smiling. She'd been thinking about the post ever since she first heard about it, and had already started formulating her application in her head.

"Just to give you the heads-up, the general director is following the case," Jonathan added before he left. "Don't disappoint her."

CHAPTER 3

It was almost four o'clock, and the bakery would be closing soon. He'd had to hurry in order to buy bread.

When he emerged onto the steps with the bag in his hand, he caught sight of the little girl. The lilac hedge that separated the house next door from the bakery was in full bloom; the air was heavy with the scent of its clusters of blossoms. The white wrought-iron chairs where customers could sit and enjoy coffee and cakes were bathed in afternoon sunshine.

He was alone for now. The season wasn't fully underway, even though it felt like a hot day in July or August.

The girl was wearing a pale-blue cotton dress cut just above the knee, the shoulder straps tied in a bow at the back of her neck. Her flip-flops were almost the same color.

How old was she? Eleven, maybe?

That was exactly the right age—she was still a child. The spring sunshine had brought out a dusting of freckles over her nose; May had been an unusually fine month. He'd spent many afternoons on benches outside schools and day care centers. No one had paid any attention to an ordinary guy taking the time to enjoy the first sunny days of the year.

He moved closer.

The girl's brown hair was tied back in a high ponytail; a few strands had escaped. She had curly hair, which appealed to him. That was exactly how he liked it; he could almost feel its soft silkiness between his fingers.

His eyes lingered on the area where the soft curve of her breasts would soon begin to form.

She had no idea he was watching her; she was completely focused on a fat Labrador at the bottom of the steps leading up to the Sandhamn Inn. The leash was looped around the railing, and the dog was sitting there panting, its tongue hanging out. The girl went over and reached out to pet it. The animal stood up, delighted with the attention. It raised its head, tail wagging.

When she dropped to her knees and bowed her head, her shoulders and the nape of her slender neck were exposed. The inviting gesture didn't escape him. The sun was shining directly on the thin skin, paler than the rest of her body, smooth and pristine, because her hair had protected it.

He thought about that soft, bare skin, the feeling of the pale downy hairs beneath his fingertips, the arousing sensation of a young body.

He tightened his grip on the bread bag. He licked his lips and craned his neck to get a better view.

"Excuse me."

A tall woman in tight jeans tapped him on the shoulder.

"You're in the way."

He mumbled an apology, avoided looking her in the eye. He pretended to be sniffing the lilac blossom. The important thing was not to attract anyone's attention, which he now knew instinctively.

By the time the woman had pushed past, the girl had disappeared. The black dog was sitting alone on the grass.

However, he would be staying on the island for several days. And he would be back to buy more bread tomorrow.

CHAPTER 4

Thomas Andreasson had barely unlocked the front door of the apartment in the Söder district of Stockholm before Elin raced past him and into the bathroom. The fact that he'd had to use the key told him that Pernilla was still at work.

Admittedly the text message asking him to pick up their daughter from preschool on a day that wasn't his turn had given him fair warning, but this was the third evening this week she'd worked late. He'd hoped they would meet in the doorway at least.

He went inside, took off his well-worn denim jacket, and ran a hand through his blond hair.

"What's for dinner?"

Elin emerged from the bathroom and kicked off her pink shoes with Barbie on the toes.

"Have you washed your hands?"

She held up both hands, palms facing him. "Will Mommy be home soon?"

"I think the two of us will be having dinner on our own, sweetheart."

"It's not fair—I want Mommy!" Elin's little face crumpled.

Thomas picked her up and whirled her around. Tickled her under the chin until she started smiling again. "We can eat on the balcony if you like," he said.

He carried her over to the window; the balcony overlooked the courtyard where time had stood still since the apartment block was built in the early 1900s.

"How about Daddy's homemade burgers? You like those."

"I want Mommy to eat with us." She buried her face in his shoulder.

Thomas didn't know what to say; he patted Elin on the head and put her down, then went into the kitchen, which was in shade at this time of the day. He thought there was half a package of ground beef in the refrigerator; that should be enough for two.

He remained standing with his back to the counter.

Pernilla had been in her new post as brand ambassador for a Scandinavian telecoms company for ten months now. Elin was right; she seemed to be constantly working. When she wasn't at the office, she was on the phone, or writing lengthy emails on her laptop. Text messages came pinging in nonstop, and she checked her emails as soon as she woke up. She spent most of the weekend "preparing."

The sound of Thomas's cell phone interrupted his frustrated thoughts. He glanced at the display and saw Margit Grankvist's name. It was only a few hours since they'd seen each other at the police station in Nacka. He hoped it wasn't something urgent; he had to take care of Elin.

"I need a favor."

As usual, his boss didn't waste her energy on small talk.

"OK . . ."

"I want you to take morning briefing tomorrow. I've managed to get a dental appointment at eight o'clock; I'm having trouble with a wisdom tooth."

Come to think of it, Margit hadn't looked too good earlier on.

"No problem."

"Thanks. I should be in by ten. Unless the dentist kills me."

There wasn't much conviction behind the joke.

Thomas slipped the phone into his back pocket.

It was mainly thanks to Margit that he'd been able to return to Nacka after resigning last summer. He'd been tempted by a post with a private security firm, but he'd been back in his old job since April, and he knew that Margit had had to pull several strings in order to facilitate the move.

He took out the frying pan and placed it on the stove.

When Pernilla first told him she'd been offered her new role, he'd encouraged her to take it. He'd had no idea how completely it would swallow her up. And then there was the travel—back and forth between the Scandinavian capital cities. He was heartily sick of seeing her wheeled suitcase standing in the hallway.

They'd established a routine; Elin was picked up either by Thomas or his mother, who was happy to step in, fortunately. Thomas had gotten pretty good at cooking dinner for two, but without his mother's help they would never have coped with the challenges of everyday life. Luckily his job had been pretty quiet over the last few weeks.

He found the hamburger buns in the freezer, then chopped an onion and some tomatoes. He fetched the bottle of ketchup from the pantry.

In the kitchen window he caught sight of a forty-seven-year-old man with a grim expression on his face, deep lines running from nose to mouth. It took a moment for him to grasp that it was his own reflection.

Pernilla's job had come along at almost the same time as Thomas had been contacted by Erik Blom, a former colleague who'd moved to the private sector. Erik had painted an attractive picture, and the salary was significantly higher than Thomas's pay within the police.

Pernilla's enthusiasm for a fresh start had carried him along. Maybe it was time for a change? He'd told himself that he was stuck in a rut, that he needed to do something different.

However, while Pernilla had happily embraced her responsibilities, Thomas had felt trapped behind a desk. He'd written security reports, sat through meetings on budgets and quotes. Cost was key, profit margins needed to be carefully monitored.

After only a month or so, he hated going to work. He'd missed being a police officer more than he could ever have imagined: Margit's dry comments, the daily exchanges with Aram Gorgis and his other colleagues.

The feeling that he was making a difference.

It sounded banal, but all of that meant something. He hadn't realized how much until it was gone.

Eventually he'd picked up the phone and called Margit, asked if he could come back. He'd thought he longed for something else, but the answer didn't lie in the private sector.

Erik had been deeply disappointed, much to Thomas's surprise. They'd hardly spoken since. And Pernilla had told him he was crazy.

Don't come running to me when you're miserable again.

Maybe that was where it had started, the gap that had opened up between them?

Thomas took out the ground beef and slammed the refrigerator door.

"Are you mad, Daddy?"

Elin was standing in the doorway, staring at him.

"No, sweetheart." He bent down and stroked her cheek. "It's fine— Daddy just happened to push the door a little too hard. Nothing to worry about."

He glanced at the clock: five thirty. Pernilla probably wouldn't be home until eight, if then.

He was so sick of this.

CHAPTER 5

"Hello?"

Nora heard Jonas's voice almost as soon as the front door opened.

"I'm in the kitchen," she called out quietly so as not to wake Julia. It was nine thirty, and their four-year-old daughter was already asleep. Simon had gone off with his friends to celebrate the beginning of the summer break, and Adam was at his girlfriend's as usual.

Jonas came in and gave her a kiss. His brown hair was damp from the drizzle that had set in during the evening, and a few droplets lingered on the silver trim of his pilot's uniform. He loosened his tie and sat down opposite her. He nodded toward the papers spread across the table. "Wedding?"

"I'm trying to finish the seating plan. Do you have any idea how many possible combinations there are with forty-five guests?"

"Does it really matter where everyone sits? I'm sure it'll be fine."

"Oh well, here you go." She pushed the notepad and pen over to him. "Feel free to take over. You decide who sits next to your sister and her husband. Not to mention your aunt."

"OK, calm down." Jonas took Nora's hand and pressed it to his cheek.

When he smiled, she was lost, as always.

I love you so much.

"Sorry—I didn't mean to start as soon as you got home. It's all a bit much right now—the trial next week, and the wedding straight after. I need to cut myself in half if I'm going to get everything done!"

Something about the way Jonas straightened his shoulders made her suspicious.

She drew back her hand. "What is it?"

"What do you mean?"

"You look as if you have something to tell me." Nora sat back and waited.

Jonas had never been a good liar; he couldn't even look her in the eye. He took off his jacket and draped it over the back of the chair next to him. It was so obvious that he was stalling.

"Come on—I can see there's a problem."

"Crew Planning called."

He fell silent, but Nora knew what was coming.

"And?" She couldn't help the sharpness in her voice.

Jonas placed a hand on her arm. "They want me to fly to Bangkok on Saturday."

"But that means you'll be away next week! It's out of the question—you do know that? I'll be tied up with the trial from Monday to Wednesday, then we need to go straight over to Sandhamn to get everything ready for the wedding."

Jonas looked uncomfortable, and Nora realized he'd already said yes. Before he'd even spoken to her. He tried to explain.

"It's an emergency. They've already used all the pilots on standby; otherwise they wouldn't have contacted me. A lot of people are away because it's midsummer."

"But we're getting married!" Her voice had shot up to a falsetto.

They hardly ever argued—never, in fact. She and Henrik had bickered and quarreled the whole time, but Jonas was different. Over the past five years, the children had rarely heard raised voices at home.

However, his good nature had a negative side: he found it difficult to say no. If there was one thing he hated, it was conflict.

"It'll be fine," he said gently.

He got up and moved behind Nora, then began to massage her shoulders and neck. It was embarrassingly clear that he was trying to win her over.

"I leave on Saturday evening and land in Bangkok on Sunday morning. Two days' rest, then I fly home on Tuesday evening. I'll be back in Stockholm early on Wednesday, in plenty of time."

Nora stared at him. "Early on Wednesday? That's only forty-eight hours before the wedding!"

"But we're not leaving for Sandhamn until Thursday, are we?"

"What if something goes wrong? There's no safety margin!"

How could he be so insensitive? Being loyal to his employer was one thing, but this was ridiculous.

"You'll be exhausted when you get back—you'll be jet-lagged."

"No, I won't—I'm not away for long enough. I won't have had time to adjust."

Nora pursed her lips. The table was strewn with pieces of paper with the names of the guests on them. There was so much to do, so many details to finish up. Was she going to have to do everything herself?

"Sometimes we just have to step up to the plate. You must understand that, given how hard you work?"

The comment hit home, but Nora couldn't let it go.

"The Winnerman trial starts on Monday. What are we going to do about Julia if you're away? I'll be working twenty-four seven."

Jonas stopped massaging her shoulders and straightened some of the papers on the table. Then he fetched a cloth and cleared away the crumbs from Julia's place.

"Can't Adam help out? Or Simon? It's only a few days. I'd have asked Wilma, but she won't be home until Wednesday evening."

Jonas's eldest daughter had been working as an au pair in the US, and would be back just in time for the wedding.

Nora unclipped the barrette holding her hair in place, then refastened it. Adam wasn't due to start his summer job at the grocery store on Sandhamn until after Midsummer. Simon was around, too, so of course the boys could take turns picking up their little sister and watching her for a couple of hours.

However, Nora was still shaken, unwilling to rethink things. So much preparation had gone into this wedding—all the invitations, discussions with the Sands Hotel where the reception was to take place. She was already worried that something might go wrong.

The little voice in her head whispering that a major trial in the same week as her wedding wasn't a particularly good idea didn't help matters.

Jonas crouched down beside her and put his arms around her. "We don't need to fall out over this, do we?" he said softly, his lips brushing her temple. "Not when we're finally getting married, you and I."

Nora's anger melted away like a patch of snow in April, and she rested her forehead against his.

"Promise you'll be back on Wednesday morning. I don't want to be the jilted bride left at the altar." She gave him a wan smile. "Promise?"

CHAPTER 6

It was almost midnight. The lights in the opposite apartment building had been switched off one by one, but Niklas Winnerman couldn't relax.

There was no point in going to bed. Last night he'd lain there wide awake since the early-morning hours, his thoughts clawing away at the inside of his skull. Just as he'd done night after night for months.

Whatever happened, he couldn't face jail. He had no illusions about what would happen to him in there. The people he'd borrowed money from had been very clear about the consequences if he didn't pay his debts on time. They had plenty of contacts on the inside.

Niklas broke out into a sweat. How would he survive in an environment like that? More than once he'd toyed with the idea of ending his life. The company was gone, his life's work ruined. Every time he saw his boys, Albert and Natan, he felt guilty. They were far too young to cope with what he'd put them through. However, he knew it took a different kind of courage to go through with suicide. He was a coward, and despised himself for that, too.

Niklas stared at the black façade of the ugly building from the 1960s, which didn't fit in with the area's turn-of-the-century architecture at all.

He got up and went to the kitchen for a bottle of mineral water. He'd managed to stay away from the booze since last Monday. He knew he had to keep a clear head; there was a great deal resting on the events of the next few days.

He poured the water into a glass and drank greedily, the drops trickling down his chin. It didn't help; he was desperate for a proper drink.

Somewhere in the distance he heard the sound of an ambulance siren.

The trial was due to begin on Monday, and Christian's testimony would destroy him. He took out his cell phone and stared at it. He'd already called Christian so many times, begged him to retract his statement. The phone number was seared into his retina.

Should he try again? Christian never answered; he simply rejected Niklas's calls as casually as he might squash an irritating mosquito.

Niklas gripped the edge of the counter so hard that his knuckles glowed white in the dark kitchen. Then he opened the freezer. The bottle of vodka was on the top shelf, white with frost. As if it were waiting for him.

Condensation covered the glass as he poured. He knocked the first drink straight back and felt the calmness spread through his body at long last. He poured himself another and took a good slug before heading back to the living room. He sat down, stared at his phone again, and eventually allowed his index finger to key in Christian's number.

No answer, as usual.

He glanced at the laptop on the sofa.

He had to resist temptation. But the desire was so powerful, tugging at him and demanding his attention as it always did.

It was thanks to gambling that he was in this mess. He had to stay strong; he couldn't afford to lose any more money.

The laptop seemed to come to life before his eyes, pulsating with promise, drawing him in.

Anything is possible, whispered the voice inside the black case. *You can win back everything you've lost, enough to pay off your debts. You can have a fresh start.*

Go on, you know you want to.

He had to stop this—think about something else.

Niklas reached for the laptop and opened it up. Excitement coursed through his veins. *Just for a little while,* he thought. *Half an hour, no more. Then I'll log out and go to bed.*

"I'm in control," he murmured, then took another slug of vodka.

CHAPTER 7

Friday, June 13

Christian Dufva steeled himself before ringing the bell. There was a brief silence, then he heard footsteps approaching.

Åsa opened the door and pointed to a rucksack and a sleeping bag on the floor of the hallway.

"That's Benjamin's stuff," she said without a word of greeting.

Christian closed his eyes for a couple of seconds. He was so tired of Åsa's bitterness. He'd given her everything she asked for, she still lived in the spacious apartment in the Vasastan district of the city, and she was well provided for. He'd done his utmost to meet all her demands when they divorced, and yet she still looked at him with distaste.

"How are you?" he ventured.

"That's no longer your concern."

To his relief, Benjamin appeared. Christian gave him a hug.

"Hi, there—isn't this exciting? The sun's shining, and you're off to your very first sailing camp!"

Benjamin nodded, and Christian picked up the rucksack. He had no intention of letting Åsa spoil the day; he'd been looking forward to traveling out into the archipelago with his son. They spent far too little time together.

"OK, let's go. Can you grab your sleeping bag, Benjamin?"

Christian led the way into the elevator and pressed the button just as his phone rang. When he saw the name on the display, his good humor disappeared in an instant.

Why couldn't Niklas leave him in peace?

"Careful!"

His father's voice made Benjamin stumble and fall just as he was about to step ashore. Two older boys who were already on the jetty started to laugh, and Benjamin felt his face flush red.

I hope they're not going to the camp.

The boat to Lökholmen was packed with children on their way to the camp—that was obvious from their luggage, and many were carrying life jackets. Almost every child was accompanied by both parents.

"Come along, Benjamin—get a move on!"

Christian sounded impatient, just as he had during the drive to Stavsnäs, where they'd caught the Vaxholm ferry. Benjamin had been so pleased when his dad came to pick him up, but then his phone had rung and everything had gone wrong. There had been several more calls, all of which went unanswered, and each one had increased Christian's level of irritation.

Benjamin had curled up in the passenger seat and played a game on his own cell phone until he started to feel carsick and had to stop.

Christian was already some distance along the narrow forest path leading from Trollharan where they'd docked. Quickly Benjamin picked up his sleeping bag and ran after him. They passed a recycling center before reaching the pontoon bridge over to Lökholmen. There were several boats moored along the wooden jetty in the marina on the right.

Benjamin turned his head and saw the camp on the other side of the inlet. A dozen small sailing boats and dinghies had been pulled up out of the water and onto a broad ramp. Beyond the pale-green reeds lay a number of red cabins, and the Swedish flag fluttered from a tall flagpole in the middle of a patch of sandy grass.

A large motor yacht was making its way along the narrow channel, with a boy who looked to be a few years older than Benjamin on the foredeck. Presumably he was also on his way to the camp.

"Don't stand there daydreaming, Benjamin! Come on—it looks fantastic!"

Benjamin hurried to catch up with his father, who was striding across the extensive lawn in front of the island's restaurant, a white pavilion in front of a building that had been designed to resemble a mountain lodge. The path continued on the far side; they were nearly there. Benjamin stopped again. The place was heaving with kids. He hadn't expected so many.

Christian was already talking to a girl in denim shorts, asking where Benjamin would be sleeping.

"OK, so you're in Star," his father informed him. "That sounds nice, doesn't it?"

He led the way to one of the cabins and pushed open a white door that was already ajar.

"This must be it."

There was a big white-painted room on either side of a small hallway. Each room contained bunk beds; most had already been claimed, with bags and life jackets dumped on top of the mattresses, but there was an empty bed by the window.

Christian went over with Benjamin's rucksack. "This must be yours." He glanced out the window. "You've even got a bit of a sea view—it's the best spot in the room!"

Benjamin noticed dusty footprints on the gray-blue vinyl floor, and someone had thrown crumpled candy wrappers under his bed. This must be the worst place; otherwise someone else would have grabbed it.

"So what do you think?"

"It's OK," Benjamin replied quickly. His dad sounded so stressed.

"There's a shelf here for your things." Christian looked at his phone again; that was the fourth time since they'd arrived. Benjamin had been keeping count.

On the wall by the door was a sheet of paper, a list of eight names— one for each bed.

"Do you know any of these guys?"

Benjamin peered at the list.

Linus Andersson
Markus Grönvall
Lukas af Helsing
Sebastian Grandin
Samuel Karlberg
Oscar Hagander
Martin von Post
Benjamin Dufva

He shook his head. Why was his name at the bottom? Did that mean anything?

"It doesn't matter, you're bound to get along—that's what happens at camp, especially at your age."

Something softened in Christian's face; the lines on his forehead smoothed out, and he no longer looked so tired.

"I was only ten when I first came here," he continued. "It was the best summer of my life—I made so many new friends."

In his smile, Benjamin caught a glimpse of his old dad, the person he'd been before the divorce. There was a life *before* and *after* what had happened. A *before* and *after* dad.

He looked at the sheet of paper again:

Instructors: William Sjölund and Isak Andrén

He didn't recognize their names either; he hoped they were nice. His dad's phone rang again, echoing around the room. Immediately Christian's features hardened, his mouth no more than a thin line. For a second Benjamin thought he was going to reject the call, but this time he answered, said he couldn't talk right now.

"Do you hear me?" he suddenly yelled, making Benjamin jump. "Stop fucking calling me—leave me alone!"

He pushed the phone into his back pocket, his face white with anger. Without any warning, he slammed his right fist into his left palm; Benjamin almost felt as if he'd been slapped. He stared at his father; he'd never seen him like this and didn't dare make a sound, let alone ask what had happened. He became aware of the hum of conversation from outside, a cacophony of voices in the sunshine.

Everyone seemed so happy.

Benjamin stood perfectly still and concentrated on a cobweb clinging to the wall.

"I guess it's time for roll call," Christian said eventually. He turned and left the dormitory with Benjamin trailing along behind him.

The bright sunlight was dazzling, and it took a moment for Benjamin's eyes to adjust. He searched for a familiar face, one foot scraping at the sand. Mom had said there was bound to be someone he knew, but that didn't seem to be the case. In fact, most of them seemed to be older, just as he'd feared.

A group of girls was giggling under the shade of a tall pine tree. Were they laughing at him?

"Over here," Christian said, pointing to a table with a large basket on top of it. The basket was full of cell phones, and Benjamin realized this was where he must leave his phone and money. Mom had explained last night: No one was allowed to keep their phone in camp. The candy store was open for only an hour a day.

A young guy with a brightly colored bandanna around his head climbed the steps, holding a gray megaphone.

"Time for group allocation and roll call—and to say good-bye to moms and dads." He raised his hand and waved exaggeratedly. "See you in a week. Don't worry, we'll take good care of your kids."

The children began to split into groups: Green, Blue, Red, Yellow. Benjamin was in Blue, which was for those who had some sailing experience. He knew it was wrong; he'd been out to sea with his father on only a few occasions, but Christian had decided it was the right level, and had ignored his son's protestations.

"OK, so you're over there by the blue flag. Don't forget to do whatever the instructors tell you."

He patted Benjamin on the shoulder. Benjamin wanted to fling his arms around him, beg him to stay—but that would be dumb, especially in front of everyone else. He suddenly noticed how gray his father's stubble was—and his hair was graying, too. There was hardly any brown left.

The sun was strong down by the water where Blue Group had gathered. Christian put on his sunglasses.

"Time for me to leave, kid," he said in a softer tone. "I hope you enjoy yourself this week."

His phone rang again, and the anger was back.

"Have fun." He turned away before Benjamin could say good-bye, then headed toward Trollharan, where the taxi boat was just arriving. His phone was pressed to his ear.

CHAPTER 8

When Niklas Winnerman arrived in the meeting room, Jacob Emilsson was already seated at the oval mahogany table, surrounded by open ring binders and piles of papers.

Niklas hoped the throat lozenge he'd just popped into his mouth would conceal the sourness of his breath. His head was pounding in spite of the fact that he'd taken two painkillers.

"At last," Emilsson said, forcing a smile even though Niklas was twenty minutes late. "We have a great deal to get through today."

One of Emilsson's paralegals hurried in, clutching yet more files. They'd met before; her name was Carin. Or was it Carmen?

Emilsson pointed to a tray with an elegant thermos and three cups and saucers. "Coffee?"

Niklas nodded. Just getting out of bed had been a huge effort. He hadn't bothered with breakfast; he'd simply stood in the shower letting the hot water cascade over him. His stomach heaved at the memory of yesterday evening. He'd stayed up until four, and the empty vodka bottle was sitting in the sink. And during those hours he'd . . .

No, he couldn't think about it. He just knew he was in deep shit.

It won't happen again, he promised himself, gripping the seat of his chair.

"I hope you're not going to turn up in court looking like that?" his lawyer said.

Niklas shook his head, which was a mistake. Someone seemed to be hammering nails into his forehead just above his eyebrows.

"I want you in a clean shirt and a smart suit," Emilsson went on. "And a tie—nothing too colorful, preferably gray or dark blue. And make sure you have a decent shave."

Niklas ran a hand over his chin; he'd cut himself this morning, and it had bled profusely. He'd stuck on a Band-Aid and given up on the rest of the shave.

The paralegal handed him a cup of coffee, and he knocked it straight back. He felt a little better as the caffeine began to take effect. He relaxed, closed his eyes.

"You have to take this seriously," Emilsson remonstrated. "Otherwise I can't help you."

"I know. I get it." Niklas wasn't an idiot, even if he had shown up late. "I'm just . . . It's kind of early."

It was ten thirty. Emilsson's expression didn't change.

"The prosecutor is going to do her best to secure a conviction. She's requesting a four-year jail term for grave disloyalty to principal. It will mean a significant loss of face for both her and the Economic Crimes Authority if she doesn't win." Emilsson folded his arms, revealing his expensive cuff links. "The biggest problem is your former associate, Christian Dufva. His testimony could send you down."

The room was suddenly too hot; Niklas felt his shirt sticking to his back. He saw himself through Emilsson's eyes and felt a wave of despair. The familiar fear gripped him by the throat. He couldn't go to jail. He was prepared to do anything to avoid that.

"Tell me what to say. I'll do whatever you want."

CHAPTER 9

Benjamin glanced at the other kids, who were busy getting their boats ready. They were on the wooden ramp by the inlet where Blue Group's sailing boats lay in a line.

Most of his camp mates seemed to know exactly what they were doing. Many had already fetched their sails from the storage shed and were busy pushing their boats toward the water.

He was sailing with Clara and Stina, who already knew each other. They were in the same class at a school in the city center, and were a year older than he was.

"So how's it going?"

Isak appeared beside Benjamin. He was wearing a baseball cap turned backward, with his sunglasses pushed so far up they were actually on top of the cap. Benjamin guessed he must be nineteen or twenty. He was almost as tall as Benjamin's dad.

"Good, I think . . ." His voice was too thin. He took a deep breath and pointed to a dangling rope. "I'm not sure what this is for."

Isak laughed, but there was nothing spiteful about him. Benjamin relaxed; Isak seemed to be OK.

"No problem—there's a lot to learn at this stage. You'll be sailing like a pro before the week's out."

The three boys in the next boat were almost ready to leave, and were looking impatiently at Benjamin. Samuel had been standing on the foredeck of the big motor yacht earlier; he was staying in Star, too.

"OK, let's get a move on," Isak said, glancing at Clara and Stina, who didn't seem to know what they were doing either.

Clara stared at Benjamin, then leaned forward and whispered something to Stina, who giggled. Stina was sweet, with her blonde hair tied up in a messy ponytail. Clara had short brown hair and seemed more self-assured.

"Time to go," Isak said encouragingly. "You sailed with the leaders this morning, and now it's your chance to go out on your own." He patted the nearest hull. "If you do exactly as we said during the briefing, everything will be fine. The instructors in the escort boats will always be there. Remember, we're not going to let you out of our sight. It's also very difficult to capsize one of these, but if it does happen, a little swim might be fun. Ready?" He gave a three-fingered salute. "When I ask if you're ready, you respond like this, with three fingers. That means 'always ready.'"

Stina gave Benjamin a nudge and grinned. Did she think the same as he did—that Isak talked too much?

"Come with me." Isak led the way to the shed. He helped them to pick out the right sails and put them up. It took only a few minutes; it looked so simple when he did it. He inspected all the crews.

"Everyone wearing their life jacket? Everyone been to the restroom and drunk a glass of water?"

Benjamin nodded obediently.

"OK, one last head count, then we can go."

Isak counted them all the time, whenever they changed activities or gathered for something to eat.

Benjamin clambered into the boat after Stina and tried to do whatever she did. Clara sat down in the stern with her hand on the tiller, as if it was obvious that she would be the one to steer.

"You'll be fine," Isak shouted after them.

CHAPTER 10

There had been no sign of the girl when he returned to the bakery. He wandered around the harbor area trying to spot her.

He'd already walked along the Royal Swedish Yacht Club's jetties and drunk a cup of coffee at the Anchor Café, searching for that blue dress. But she was nowhere to be seen, not even on the shore over by Fläskberget. There were just a few sun worshippers lying on their beach towels.

She'd definitely been interested in him. The coquettish way she swung her ponytail had told him that, along with the movement of her slender hips.

This was something he'd learned over the years; he could always tell if they were willing. It didn't matter if it was a girl or a boy; he just knew. The signals were there in the sway of their body, the secret invitation when they licked their lips.

It was almost four o'clock in the afternoon, and the June sun was still high in the sky. It hardly got dark at this time of year; the sky merely took on a deeper shade of blue for a few hours around midnight. Sometimes he stayed up until it grew light again, or surfed the websites that offered what he needed until the desire died down.

But it was much too long since he'd been with someone for real.

He decided to grab a hot dog from the kiosk. If he couldn't find her after that, he'd have to take the boat over to Lökholmen.

His little motorboat was hidden away in the inlet. He was practically alone in the marina, which suited him perfectly. That was the advantage of the low season; he'd never liked crowds. Nor did he want to be recognized, even though the risk was small. He'd served his time near Gothenburg and moved to Stockholm for a more anonymous existence.

There was no line at the kiosk by the steamboat jetty; he paid for his hot dog and a drink, then moved a short distance away.

He saw a little girl walking toward the grocery store—was that her?

Someone honked behind him—he was blocking the path of a red quad bike and trailer that had come to collect goods from the cargo ferry *Oliver*.

When he looked back, he realized it was a different child. This girl was nowhere near as pretty. She was older and had shorter hair.

He finished his hot dog and dropped the wrapper on the ground. The taxi boat would be leaving soon; he might as well head for the departure point by the Sailors Hotel.

Why hadn't she shown up? Sandhamn was pretty small; it couldn't take more than ten minutes to walk through the harbor area. He should have spotted her somewhere. If she was still on the island.

He remembered her bare shoulders as she bent forward to stroke the dog, pictured the flat stomach beneath the blue dress, the hollow of the navel.

He'd wanted to wind her hair around his fingers.

But there were other possibilities. The first sailing camp of the season was underway on Lökholmen; he'd seen the children gathering this morning, then all the moms and dads had left.

How many children were attending the camp? Seventy, maybe eighty? There couldn't be more than twenty instructors, and they didn't look very old.

They had a lot of kids to keep an eye on.

CHAPTER 11

They'd left the inlet and were sailing toward the open sea, toward the Svängen lighthouse outside the channel leading to Sandhamn.

Clara was on the tiller, shouting orders as if she'd been steering all her life. Benjamin and Stina were sitting by the mast. One of the escort boats passed them; the instructor waved and Benjamin waved back. This wasn't so bad after all. He even managed to smile at Stina.

After an hour or so, the wind grew stronger. It was coming diagonally from behind, and the mainsail bellied more and more. Benjamin struggled to hold it steady.

The other boats were no more than dots in the distance now. A bank of clouds had come rolling in, and the sky was gray. The temperature was dropping as the waves grew higher.

He glanced at Clara; why were they so far from the other boats? She also seemed surprised.

"What happened to everyone else?" she shouted. "I thought we were supposed to stick together!"

Benjamin peered at the horizon. Where was the escort boat? There were two escorts for ten boats; that had seemed plenty when the sun was shining, but now he wished there were more.

"I don't know," he said. His legs were freezing, and he hadn't brought a sweater with him.

"Look out!" Clara yelled as a huge wave came from nowhere, crashing against the hull. Benjamin almost lost his balance. The water caught all three of them, but Clara took the worst of it. She was dripping as she wiped her face with the back of her hand.

"Shit!" she hissed, giving herself a shake. It didn't help. Her shorts were drenched, her hair hanging like rats' tails. "What do we do now?" she said. "I'm fucking soaked!"

Benjamin tried to suppress his fear. Clara was supposed to be in charge; he'd thought she had everything under control. Stina was no help at all; she was just staring anxiously at the two of them and chewing her thumbnail.

"Shouldn't we turn around?" Stina said. "It's too windy. What if we capsize?"

The sky was the color of lead now, and the sea was getting choppier by the minute.

"We're not allowed to go back without permission," Benjamin pointed out. Isak had made it very clear that no one should split from the others; it could be dangerous. He looked around, hoping to spot one of the escort boats. Isak had promised there was nothing to worry about—the escorts would stay close by the whole time.

Lökholmen was barely visible now; it had melted into the surrounding islands and skerries. To the east he could see nothing but gray sea. During the briefing the instructor had told them they'd end up in Estonia if they kept sailing eastward; there were no more islands after Sandhamn.

Stina was on the verge of tears. "I want to go home."

Clara narrowed her eyes. She looked so mad that Benjamin decided to keep quiet.

"We're turning back," she decided. "Benjamin, are you ready to let go of the sail? Stina?"

Stina nodded, and Benjamin prepared himself for the maneuver. He didn't dare to disagree with Clara, even though he knew they shouldn't be doing this.

"Now!" Clara yelled. Benjamin let go of the rope, and the white sail started flapping wildly. The boom swung back and forth like the tail of an angry tiger.

Suddenly the boat lurched, listing dangerously. Everything happened so fast; the wind was way too strong.

"Take in the sail!" Clara shouted.

The water was pouring in over the port side and into the footwell. Benjamin gasped when it reached his knees, but Stina threw herself across the boat and leaned back over the starboard side, which had risen up at an alarming angle.

"Help me, Benjamin!" Stina cried. "I can't do this on my own!"

Benjamin was frozen to the spot. He stared at her, his arms and legs refusing to move.

This isn't happening, he thought, screwing his eyes shut. *We're going to sink on the very first day.*

"BENJAMIN!"

He opened his eyes. For a few seconds their fate hung in the balance. The port side was almost underwater, the mast was down, and the sail was dipping into the waves. Clara scrambled over the tiller to get to Stina.

A new white-capped wave came surging toward them. Then time seemed to stop.

Benjamin stared uncomprehendingly as the boom swung across and the boat righted itself. Suddenly the horizon was where it was meant to be once more.

He grabbed the mainsail rope and pulled as hard as he could, his wet fingers struggling to get a grip. The sail responded, billowing out in the wind as the boat moved forward. Somehow, they were heading in the opposite direction.

Back to Lökholmen.

Benjamin slid down into the footwell; he was sitting in several inches of water. He was soaked to the skin, every muscle was aching, and he'd cut his knee. The blood seeped into the water, forming pale-red rings that gradually dissipated.

Stina was crying, and Clara's eyes were almost black.

"I hate this fucking camp!" she snapped.

CHAPTER 12

Thomas was sitting next to Aram Gorgis, fingering his coffee cup. He knew he was stressed. When Margit called a meeting at short notice, it was rarely good news. Almost everyone was there; the room was full.

A great deal had happened during Thomas's absence, even though he'd been gone for less than six months. The biggest restructuring of the police in modern times had begun; a lot of balls had been thrown up in the air, and not all of them had been caught.

Even Margit was stressed in a way Thomas hadn't seen before. All senior posts had been advertised, and everyone had to reapply, regardless of qualifications or years of service.

Adrian Karlsson walked in. He was the latest addition to the team; in his previous role as a rank-and-file officer, he'd been involved in several major cases on Sandhamn.

The door opened again and Kalle Lidwall, sporting a full beard, came and sat down beside Thomas. All of a sudden the boyish appearance was gone; Thomas had always thought of him as something of a junior colleague, when in fact he was fast approaching the age of forty.

Margit got to her feet, pain still etched on her face; it seemed as if the visit to the dentist hadn't really helped.

"We've received more information about the new structure," she began. "There will be a number of changes for the Nacka district, and I suspect you're not going to like them."

Aram put down his cup and pushed it away.

"Nothing's been finalized yet, but it looks as if our department will be relocated to Flemingsberg."

Thomas could see his own shock reflected in the faces of his colleagues.

Karin Ek, the administrative assistant, was the first to pull herself together. "We can't stay here? Are you kidding?"

"According to the latest proposal, the whole department will move. Nacka will be reduced to a local station only as of 2015."

"Surely they can't do that!" Aram objected.

"I'm afraid they can."

Flemingsberg, Thomas thought. It was in the Huddinge area of the city, and it had already been decided that the police training academy would be relocated there. The Södertörn District Court was in Flemingsberg, and had been dealing with more significant cases of late. It was quite a distance from Nacka.

"But why . . . ?" Aram muttered as Kalle made a careful note in his leather-bound book.

"What about our jobs?" Adrian wanted to know, running a hand over his light-brown hair. He'd been a detective inspector for seven months, so the last-in first-out principle would hit him hard.

"It's too early to say," Margit informed him. "All department heads have to reapply for their posts, but I think, or hope, that the rest of you will simply transfer as you are. I've been temporarily appointed to something called New Division 1." She winced. "At my age, for fuck's sake."

Thomas sighed. Nacka was one of the best divisions in the country, with excellent closing statistics. Why anyone would want to break up a unit that worked so well was beyond his comprehension. On a personal level, it meant he would spend hours sitting in traffic. Dropping off and picking up Elin would be considerably more difficult, at least if Pernilla continued her current working pattern.

He hadn't expected such changes when he asked to come back. This would give Pernilla even more grist to her mill; she'd been far from happy when he left the private security firm.

"It's business as usual until we know more," Margit said in conclusion. "I'll get back to you as soon as I hear anything new."

CHAPTER 13

Nora stretched her arms out in front of her and turned her head from side to side a few times. Her back and shoulders were stiff from hours spent reading through the trial documentation once again.

She couldn't shake off the feeling of unease.

On Monday she would begin the fight to convict Niklas Winnerman, but the money was still missing, and the self-confidence she'd shown in front of Jonathan was dwindling.

She got up and walked down the hallway to Leila Kacim's office. She was still hoping that Leila would find some clue as to where the money had gone. The door was open, and she went in.

"Am I disturbing you?"

Leila was rummaging in her purse. She was fifteen years younger than Nora, and had been with the Economic Crimes Authority since 2012. She'd spent many hours on the Winnerman case. She beckoned Nora in, still rummaging.

"I'm looking for a tampon." She pulled a face. "Wrong day of the month."

There was a photo of Leila's dog on the desk—a brown Newfoundland weighing almost a hundred and fifty pounds. There was never any mention of a boyfriend, but Nora had heard a great deal about Bamse.

Leila put her purse down on the floor with a sigh of relief.

"Back in a minute," she said as she disappeared clutching something white.

Nora's thoughts returned to the case. You could never tell which way the court would go. Many judges regarded the Economic Crimes Authority as troublesome and overcomplicated. The narrow designations were difficult to apply to modern financial transactions, which were also tricky to explain with clarity in the courtroom.

"Let's hope Emilsson doesn't have anything new up his sleeve," Leila said when she returned.

Jacob Emilsson was known for going in hard when he was defending a client; on the other hand, one member of the bench also had a certain reputation. Barbro Wikingsson was an experienced judge who didn't tolerate any showboating. She had no hesitation in yanking battle-scarred lawyers if she thought it necessary.

Or prosecutors.

Nora believed Winnerman was guilty; otherwise she wouldn't have brought the case. However, she couldn't help worrying. She'd been sure they would have found the money by this stage, and the upcoming post Jonathan had mentioned was freaking her out slightly.

"Have you heard anything from the tax office?" she asked.

With the help of the tax office, they'd been trying to find out about the holder of the bank account in the Cayman Islands into which the missing ten million had been transferred. There was an agreement between Sweden and the Cayman Islands that was supposed to facilitate this kind of information exchange, but it was taking forever. The overseas authorities responded politely, but nothing happened. Nora still had no concrete proof that it was Winnerman who'd used that account.

Leila shook her head. "I'm afraid not. They're working on it, but they have no leverage to speed things up over there. I called them again this morning," she said with an ironic smile. She was only thirty-two, but she already knew the score. "You'll have to put the thumbscrews to Bertil Svensson—if he's sober," she added.

This wasn't the first time they'd come up against a deal with a drunken "goalkeeper," which was the term used when someone exploited an addict to front a company.

Svensson couldn't remember any details, and of course he had no idea why the money had immediately been transferred to the Cayman Islands.

"Do you know how many times he's told me his memory isn't too good these days?" Leila said. "It's almost funny."

Nora glanced at her watch; it was high time she left. Jonas and Julia were picking her up at the Slussen subway station so they could go straight to Sandhamn. There was no point in traveling home to Saltsjöbaden first. Jonas was coming back to the city on Saturday to fly to Bangkok. She still wasn't happy about the idea.

"I have to go."

Leila raised a hand in farewell and reached for an apple on her desk.

Nora still felt stiff, and she rubbed the back of her neck with two fingers as she quickly checked her emails before shutting her computer down for the weekend.

As soon as she saw the vicious words in the subject line, she knew what it was about. She sat motionless for a few seconds before she clicked on the message and began to read. The tone was the same as before; there was no doubt that it came from the same source.

Another rant about her key witness, Christian Dufva. A few lines halfway down were particularly disturbing:

HE'S LYING, THE FUCKER. HE'S LYING ABOUT
EVERYTHING, AND ANYONE WHO BELIEVES HIM
WILL BE SORRY. INCLUDING YOU!

She ought to report this to the security department. Until now she'd simply opened the messages, then ignored them; she hadn't even mentioned them to Leila.

She looked at her watch again; she was already late. She would deal with this on Monday.

CHAPTER 14

"What the hell is wrong with you?" Isak said.

The expression on his face made Benjamin want to shrivel up and disappear. He didn't dare look at Clara and Stina. Isak had taken them to the dining hall. It was strange to be alone in the big room that had been filled with eager chatter not so long ago. A thin beam of light shone in through the nearest window.

"Are you crazy? You know the rules: the group stays together, we all sail in the same direction. Didn't you listen to my instructions?"

"We were soaking wet," Stina ventured, her lips trembling just as they had when it seemed as if the boat was about to capsize. "And there was no sign of the escort boats . . ."

"We went through all this before you left! No one is allowed to sail off on their own—it's too dangerous. How are we supposed to keep an eye on you if you do something so dumb?"

Benjamin stole a glance at Clara. He knew she was angry, but she didn't say a word. It had been her idea to turn back, but Benjamin had no intention of telling on her.

Isak wasn't finished. "Anything could have happened!" He pushed his hands deep in his pockets. "Besides, the escort boats weren't far away; another group needed help, and their situation was more critical than yours. That's how it works at sea. You're old enough to realize that." He softened a fraction. "Anyway, let's put it behind us—but I hope you've learned a lesson. Never, ever do something like this again. No more stunts for the rest of the week—is that clear?"

We just wanted to get home, Benjamin thought.

Clara lifted her chin. She looked absolutely furious.

"Is that clear?" Isak repeated.

CHAPTER 15

"We're going to miss the boat to Harö if we don't leave soon," Thomas called out from the bedroom as he pushed a change of clothes and a couple of pairs of underpants into a bag. Pernilla was still sitting at the kitchen table with her laptop. It was after five, and it would take them a good hour to drive to Stavsnäs in the rush-hour traffic. The last boat left at twenty past six.

"Coming—I just need to send this email."

Thomas had left work early to pick up Elin and get back to the apartment. He zipped up his bag and went into Elin's room.

As usual there were Barbie dolls all over the place. Elin was sitting on the floor playing on her tablet; the 1950s ideal woman side by side with the Internet. Barbie's continued popularity was remarkable.

"Time to go, sweetheart." He picked up her rucksack. "I'll take care of this so it doesn't get lost." He tucked the tablet among Elin's clothes while she grabbed her favorite doll and obediently followed him.

"We're leaving now," he informed Pernilla.

She glanced up. "Almost done . . . There." She closed the computer, pushed it into her roomy purse, and got to her feet. "That wasn't so bad, was it?" She took Elin's hand. "We'd better hurry up so Daddy doesn't get even more grumpy."

Thomas sighed. He hated it when she communicated with him through their daughter. "Don't drag Elin into this."

"You started it."

He swallowed a sharp retort, picked up the car keys and the bag of groceries, and walked out the door.

CHAPTER 16

Nora joined Jonas in the glassed-in veranda at the Brand villa. He was sitting in the old wicker chair by the window; it had been there as long as Nora could remember. Aunt Signe used to sit there reading in the evenings. When Nora inherited the house from Signe Brand, there had been no question of getting rid of her beloved armchair.

The clouds were edged with gold, and the last rays of the sun had painted the sky pink.

Signe would have loved this beautiful sunset. Nora could almost hear her voice: *Sit down and enjoy it, girl.*

"I wish you didn't have to go to Thailand tomorrow," she said, wrapping her arms around Jonas's neck. "Are you sure they can't find someone else?"

"Don't worry, I'll be back in plenty of time. I've had to wait a whole year since I proposed—I have no intention of missing our wedding."

Jonas pulled her onto his knee, her back against the armrest. She tried to relax.

"I guess I'm just a little nervous about the trial," she said after a while. "Jonathan said the general director's following the case."

"You'll be brilliant."

"He also mentioned the vacancy for a deputy district chief prosecutor."

Jonas didn't say anything. Instead he traced the line of her throat with two fingers, continuing down toward the V-neck of her T-shirt.

"Maybe we should go and have a lie-down? So you won't miss me too much?"

Nora shook her head. She'd just put Julia to bed, and didn't want her to come marching into their bedroom in the middle of something. Her daughter didn't always fall asleep just because the light had been switched off. Besides, she couldn't stop thinking about Monday. She was restless and distracted; she'd lost the thread of the conversation more than once during dinner.

"I'm still wondering about the millions Winnerman took," she said. "Things would be so much easier if we could track them down."

"Have you seen how fantastic the sunset is?"

Jonas clearly wasn't interested in her problems. The weather forecast for the next five days was on the TV in the living room: plenty of sunshine. No danger of rain on her bridal crown.

"The money that disappeared," Nora persisted. "The theory has always been that Winnerman's hidden it away until the court case is over, but when I went through his finances, something else occurred to me."

"Oh really?"

Jonas's gaze was fixed on a point in the distance where the splendor of the clouds was reflected in the water. It was still light enough to read outdoors. The scent of lilac crept in through an open window. Nora knew she ought to be savoring this fine evening instead of brooding over a cheat.

"He's already borrowed a significant amount to buy the apartment, but I discovered that he's taken out fresh loans online, with sky-high interest rates."

"Lots of people do that; otherwise they wouldn't keep advertising them on TV."

"Yes, but what if something else is going on? What if we can't find the money because he's already spent it? He might be a gambling addict, for example."

Jonas's fingers began to wander over her bare arms. She felt a tingle in her stomach as he caressed her skin. She inhaled his aftershave, a subtle blend of green apples and pine needles. It reminded her of the sparse forest on the island where she often went walking. She loved the narrow paths, the sunlight filtered through the treetops.

"Shouldn't that have come up during the preliminary investigation?" Jonas murmured.

So he had been listening after all.

"Not necessarily."

It had been discussed at an early stage, but set aside because there was no evidence. When Winnerman's property was searched, there was no evidence of a gambling habit. No betting slips, nothing from the horse racing at Solvalla. They'd seized his office computer, but again, there was nothing to suggest an interest in gambling. There had been no sign of a personal computer; Winnerman had claimed that the one at work was all he needed.

Leila had concentrated on his banking history, and had interviewed all those involved. "Follow the money" was the Economic Crimes Authority's guiding principle.

"Let it go," Jonas whispered in her ear. "It's Friday night!"

"Mommmeee!" came a little voice from upstairs. "I need to pee!"

CHAPTER 17

Benjamin couldn't settle. If he'd had his phone, he'd have been able to play a game for a little while just like he did at home. He wished he was there, in his own bed. He missed his teddy bear; he always hugged Teddy until he fell asleep.

He pictured his mom's face, hot tears scalding the inside of his eyelids. He hadn't called her this evening; he was too ashamed after Isak had bawled them out.

The boys in the other beds all went to the same school except for him. He was the odd one out.

After dinner in the dining hall, he'd sat by himself in a corner; no one had come to talk to him. In the end he'd returned to the dormitory and crawled into his blue sleeping bag. That was another mistake—the others had all brought their own sheets and pillowcases.

The boy in the bed above him let out a loud snore. His name was Oscar; he'd just about managed to say hi to Benjamin.

One of the other beds creaked, then the silence was broken by a quiet voice.

"Sebbe? Are you awake up there?"

Benjamin wasn't sure, but he thought the sound came from the lower bunk opposite him. That was where Samuel slept; he was the boy who'd rolled his eyes when it took Benjamin and the girls so long to get their boat ready in the morning. Apparently Samuel's father had some kind of involvement in the organization; he was very rich, and knew the director. Samuel had been boasting during dinner about what a big shot his dad was, how much money he donated to the camp.

Benjamin opened his eyes, but the room was dark and it was hard to make anything out.

"Sebbe?"

"What?" someone whispered sleepily from the bunk above Samuel.

"What do you think of our beginner? The kid who took so long to do everything earlier on?"

"He's OK, I guess."

"I heard he panicked—started crying when he thought they were going to capsize."

Benjamin stiffened. They were talking about him!

"Shh—what if he hears you?"

A snort. "He'll be fast asleep. Did you see his life jacket? It's like something from the Stone Age!"

Benjamin hadn't paid much attention to his well-used life jacket until he arrived at camp and saw the fine gear everyone else had brought along. Theirs resembled padded vests; his was bulky and stained.

Silence fell. Benjamin needed to pee, but he didn't dare get up in case the others were still awake.

The first voice spoke again. "I bet he cried himself to sleep. How fucking embarrassing is that?"

Benjamin's mouth went dry. He was homesick and unhappy, but he hadn't cried. He hadn't.

"Just leave it—I need some sleep." This was followed by a loud yawn.

"OK—good night."

Oscar let out another snore and turned over. There was a soft thud as he bumped against the wall.

"For fuck's sake," the first voice said, then silence fell once more.

Benjamin held his breath; he didn't want them to realize he'd been listening. Tears pricked at his eyes once more, but he gritted his teeth. He couldn't let them hear him crying—anything but that.

CHAPTER 18

Isak sank down on the red sofa in the instructors' common room. It was after ten thirty, and he'd just checked on Blue Group to make sure they'd all gone to bed.

He'd really looked forward to this job. Just like most of his colleagues, he'd also attended sailing camp as a child. His parents had a summer cottage on the island of Ingarö, and learning to sail was part of life. They were on the go from seven in the morning until midnight, but he loved the spirit of the camp, the opportunity to make new friends. People who didn't know what he'd been through.

Mom and Dad had been proud when he told them he'd been accepted as an instructor; Dad's face had actually lit up, and the disappointed expression he so often wore when he looked at Isak had disappeared.

David Rutkowski, the senior instructor, walked in. He was two years older, and a close friend of Isak's brother. Presumably his brother had put in a good word; otherwise they wouldn't have taken him on.

It was time to review the day and plan tomorrow's activities. As usual David was carrying his black notebook, with a rubber band around it to stop any loose sheets of paper from falling out.

The door opened again as several more instructors arrived. The room was getting hot and crowded as the sofas along the walls filled up. Maja, who was also new, came and sat down beside Isak. She kicked off her knee-high sailing boots and massaged one foot, her face contorted in pain.

"Blisters," she explained. "New boots, no socks. Big mistake."

She had lovely teeth, white and even. When she smiled, her eyes reminded Isak of a cat's.

"So how did it go today?" he asked, discreetly checking out her breasts. She was a bit like Tina, his ex, who'd dumped him when he got sick.

"It was so windy this afternoon—where the hell did that come from? It wasn't forecast."

Isak nodded. "My group had a few problems. A few of the kids panicked, and one crew turned back before we managed to catch up with them. I had to give them a talking-to afterward."

Maja smiled again, tucking her blonde hair behind her ears. She seemed so natural—not the kind of girl who had to be messing with her appearance the whole time.

"You're in Yellow Group, aren't you?" Isak continued.

The children in Yellow Group already had some experience. They worked on navigation and plotted their routes according to charts.

"That's right—we had a great time, in spite of the weather. We were up north, so we were protected from the worst of it, but sailing back was pretty challenging."

By now the room was crowded, with several people sitting on the floor. The door had been propped open to let in some air, but it wasn't really helping.

David clapped his hands. "OK, let's get started. The forecast for tomorrow is promising—sunny in the morning, slightly overcast in the afternoon, wind speed moderate."

Isak stole a glance at Maja, who was half lying on the sofa with one hand beneath her cheek. As if she sensed that he was looking at her, she turned her head and winked.

He wondered whether to take a sauna when the meeting was over; it would be good to clear his head for a while. The sauna was his favorite place whenever he wanted to wind down; the heat entering his body always calmed him. It was much better than the medication.

Maybe he could ask Maja to join him?

David went through the details for the following day—which islands they would be sailing to, and which instructors would be on duty during Saturday evening.

"Unfortunately we haven't managed to find replacements yet, but we're working on it."

Two group leaders had been delayed due to illness. Wille, who was supposed to be sharing the responsibility for Blue Group with Isak, was one of them. His absence made Isak nervous, but he hadn't said anything to David. He didn't want to start the season by appearing unsure of himself, not now that his recovery was virtually complete and he had this fantastic opportunity. There were still around twenty leaders to seventy-five kids, and David thought Wille would probably be back tomorrow or the day after.

Isak just had to make sure he didn't mess up in the meantime.

"Don't forget these kids are at the very worst age," David added. "Young teenagers are hard work."

Maja sat up straight. "I found a cell phone in the dormitory in Tern," she said. "The girls were so busy posting pictures on Instagram, they didn't even notice when I walked in. The owner's name is Lisa Gunnarsson."

It meant nothing to Isak; he'd only gotten to know his own group so far.

"Didn't she hand in her phone when she arrived?" someone asked.

"Yes, but apparently her parents gave her a second one—just to be on the safe side."

David didn't seem particularly surprised. "You might well find more phones during the course of the week," he said. "Some of these kids are seriously spoiled. This is probably the first time anyone's asked them to make their own bed or clear the table after they've eaten." He closed his notebook. "Please make sure you keep an eye on them. We don't want any trouble. No *Lord of the Flies* on our watch."

CHAPTER 19

Niklas was in bed when a sound from the stairwell startled him. His heart started pounding, and he broke out in a sweat.

After a few seconds he realized it was the elevator on its way up.

He had to pull himself together, stay calm. He couldn't go to pieces every time he heard an unexpected noise.

He glanced over at his cell phone on the nightstand, its black case gleaming in the moonlight that had found its way in through a gap in the curtains.

The last text had arrived late the previous night, at around this time.

Time to pay.

Three words that turned his stomach inside out; he'd had to run straight to the bathroom to throw up.

He realized he was clenching his jaw so tightly that his teeth were aching. He opened his mouth wide, tried to ease the tension. Turned his head to the right and then the left until the bones cracked. He shifted position, knowing that sleep was far away.

His thoughts went back to the meeting a month ago, when, against his better judgment, he'd sought out the man known as Artūras.

The bank was threatening to take the apartment, throw him out onto the street. He couldn't lose his home; how would it look in court if he had nowhere to live?

The interest Artūras charged was crippling, but Niklas had no choice. He'd agreed to the terms, even though he knew it was foolish. The debt was due to be repaid within thirty days, as soon as the trial was over.

Artūras, smartly dressed in chinos and a V-neck sweater, had sat in silence as sweat trickled down the back of Niklas's neck. There was a faint blue glow from the screen of Artūras's laptop, and he had a photograph of a blonde-haired woman holding a little boy in her arms on his desk.

Just like any banker.

And yet Niklas shuddered when Artūras slowly drummed two fingers on the shiny surface of the wood.

Get the hell out of here, a voice screamed inside his head.

Artūras signaled to his assistant just as Niklas began to think he'd be leaving without the money.

The well-built guy, who hadn't said a word so far, went over to the safe in the corner and took out several bundles of notes, a mixture of euros and dollars. He'd pushed them into an ordinary grocery bag and handed them to Niklas.

"There you go," he'd said with a noticeable accent—unlike Artūras, who spoke almost perfect Swedish. "Don't forget where it came from."

As he sat there in the armchair, so low down that he'd had to lift his chin in order to look Artūras in the eye, Niklas had promised himself that he would find a solution. Everything would sort itself out. If all else failed, he would have to persuade his sister to sell the summer cottage on Ingarö.

But nothing had gone according to plan, and now the debt was bigger than ever.

Just like the fear.

Chapter 20

Saturday, June 14

David Rutkowski turned on the kitchen tap and rinsed his face with cold water. It had been past one o'clock by the time he went to bed, and the alarm on his phone had gone off at six thirty. His body felt slow, his eyes gritty, but it was always like this when the camp had to be kick-started.

Wille had just called to say he was still sick, which was a real blow. Bearing in mind that Isak was new, he'd really hoped that Wille would be well enough to join them this morning.

He went into the dining hall and spotted Isak at one of the long tables, where the last few kids were finishing their breakfast.

The sun was shining in through the wide doorway overlooking the water. The old red-painted repair shed that had been converted into a dining hall was west-facing. The walls were made of untreated wood, as were the beams. Here and there old life jackets and life buoys hung from simple nails.

With water dripping from his forehead, David went over to Isak, who was sitting with a bowl of cereal in front of him.

"I just had a message from Wille. I'm afraid he's still sick—he won't be in today either."

Isak frowned slightly, but didn't say anything.

David placed a hand on his shoulder. "If anything comes up, bring me in—I can lend a hand with Blue Group if necessary. I'm sure Wille will be here tomorrow."

Isak nodded.

"You're going to Alskär today, aren't you?" David continued.

"That's the plan."

"We've just decided to send Yellow Group out there, too. It would be good if you could help take out the provisions."

"No problem."

Isak immediately looked happier. David suspected it had something to do with Maja; he'd seen the two of them together the previous evening. He smiled and headed off to the jetty where the boats were waiting: Laser class, C55, and Hobie Teddy. As he left he heard Isak urging some of the boys along:

"Finish your breakfasts now—see you down by the water in ten minutes."

Benjamin and Stina were already rigging the sail by the time Isak appeared. The reeds were swaying in the gentle breeze, and the sun glinted on the waves beyond Trollharan.

This was going to be a better day, Benjamin thought. It had to be.

"Just the two of you?" Isak said. "Where's Clara?"

Benjamin looked around. "I don't know."

He hadn't seen her; he'd just assumed she was on her way. He'd started rigging as soon as he reached the boat; he had no desire to be the last to leave after yesterday's humiliation.

Stina merely shrugged.

"I'm sure she'll be here soon," Benjamin said.

The others were almost ready to leave; twenty children were divided among seven boats, several of which were already in the water.

Isak ran a hand through his hair. "I'll go and check the dormitory—you carry on with the rigging."

Benjamin and Stina finished the task together. Should they try to push the boat down the ramp, or wait until Clara showed up? He glanced hesitantly at Stina, who didn't seem to care. He decided it was too heavy, and sat down on the jetty with his feet dangling over the edge.

Isak reappeared, looking worried. "She wasn't there. Stina, when did you last see her?"

"At roll call. Before breakfast."

As usual the group had gathered behind the dining hall just before eight. Isak had counted them before they were allowed in.

"And you haven't seen her since?"

Stina shook her head.

"Benjamin?"

"No."

Benjamin was starting to feel uncomfortable. Was he somehow responsible, as they were on the same team? Then again, it wasn't his fault if Clara was late. None of them had spoken after Isak had scolded them yesterday; the three of them had just slunk off in different directions.

Isak blew his whistle, and everyone stopped what they were doing.

"Has anyone seen Clara since breakfast?" he asked.

No one said a word.

Isak checked the diver's watch on his left wrist. "Come on, guys. Has no one spoken to her?" He turned to the nearest crew. Lova, Tindra, and Sofie were half lying on the jetty with their life jackets unfastened. "Girls, any idea where Clara is?"

"I haven't seen her," Lova said, plucking at one of the cords on her jacket.

"Tindra? Sofie?"

They both shook their heads.

"OK, you'll all have to wait here until I find her. I'll be back soon. Benjamin, can you give me a hand? If you check the showers, I'll take the dining hall." He looked at his watch again. "The rest of you, stay here. I don't want anyone else doing a disappearing act."

CHAPTER 21

Christian Dufva was sitting at the kitchen table with the morning paper spread out in front of him. The window was open, but there was no draft. The cramped apartment already felt too warm; by the time the sun moved around in the afternoon, it would feel like a sauna.

He couldn't help missing his former home; no doubt Åsa was relaxing on the generous balcony right now. There were also plenty of windows to let in the fresh air.

He sighed and focused on the business section; his eyes skimmed a substantial article on dubious practices in the construction industry. Some expert from the Royal Institute of Technology had given his opinion on the matter.

There were smart alecks in every walk of life.

Ninna had Emil on her lap and was feeding him porridge. He was waving his little hands around, and had already messed up his mother's shoulder-length blonde hair.

"How did it go with Benjamin yesterday?" she asked.

Christian had hoped the baby would take up all her attention. He had too much going on in his head right now; he couldn't cope with making small talk.

"Fine." He turned the page.

"I hope he enjoys himself at the camp." Ninna rescued her coffee cup from Emil's fingers.

Benjamin—the source of Christian's ever-present guilty conscience. He knew he ought to get in touch more often, but Åsa's constant whining whenever he tried drove him crazy. She had refused to discuss joint custody, and in the end he'd given up. These days he only saw Benjamin for the odd weekend—plus, of course, Ninna's apartment was so small that there was barely room for two adults and a one-year-old, let alone a growing boy.

Benjamin had looked unhappy when Christian left him at the camp, but it would be good for him to make new friends, good to get away from Åsa's toxic outbursts against his father. She suffocated the kid, just as she'd done throughout their marriage, when everything had been about her son rather than her relationship with her husband.

The recollection of her sour expression when he'd collected Benjamin yesterday morning sent his spirits plummeting.

"He doesn't want to go," she'd hissed in the stairwell as Benjamin stepped into the elevator. "He's only going to please you!"

Christian hadn't bothered to reply. He couldn't do anything right, according to Åsa, so there was no point. From the moment she'd found out about Ninna, her aim had been to make life as difficult as possible for him.

Ninna pushed the last spoonful of porridge into Emil's mouth, then got up to grab a paper towel to wipe his face.

"You're very quiet," she said over her shoulder. "Are you worried about the trial?"

Christian mumbled something inaudible.

"It must be terrible for you, having to testify against your former partner. I don't understand why he isn't behind bars." She held Emil out so that Christian had no choice but to take him. "Can you have him while I eat my breakfast?"

Ninna took a piece of bread, spread it with jelly, then added a slice of cheese. She tightened the belt of her pale-green robe, which was covered in old and new baby food stains; Christian noticed the swell of her voluptuous breasts, and something stirred within him.

"I still don't know how Niklas could have done that to you," she went on, her mouth half full. "I hope they lock him up and throw away the key."

The scent of Emil's hair reached Christian's nostrils.

Little Emil, who was still too young to realize what people were capable of. Life was simple when it was all about food and sleep.

He didn't want to think about Niklas right now. The guy kept on calling him, like some crazy stalker. Two days to go; Christian was due to testify on Tuesday.

He'd found it difficult to sleep again last night. He reached out and covered Ninna's hand with his. What would he have done without her over the past twelve months? Her arms had been his refuge when he was at his most desperate, sick and tired of Åsa's demands.

When they started seeing each other, she'd been working as head of human resources with one of their suppliers. She always wore tight-fitting skirts and high heels, and was careful about what she ate.

These days she couldn't care less about her weight, and she was more beautiful than ever.

"You never know who you can trust," he murmured, his lips resting on Emil's head.

CHAPTER 22

Isak ran across the grass to the dining hall. There wasn't a soul in sight. A blue T-shirt lay on the ground, and the door to one of the cabins was wide open.

The dining hall was empty except for one of the housekeepers, who was busy wiping down the tables.

"Have you seen one of my girls?" he shouted above the whirr of the dishwasher. "Clara Rosman, thirteen, Blue Group."

The housekeeper, who was a year older than Isak and whose name was Katja, shook her head. "Have you tried the other side? Maybe she's waiting at the wrong jetty?"

Clara knew exactly where she was supposed to be, but Isak nodded and headed off into the bright sunshine.

Yellow Group was just leaving. He could see Maja in one of the escort boats, and farther away, just off Telegrafholmen, the catamarans Red Group was using.

He paused on the veranda and forced himself to look carefully at everything within sight. The old mines displayed on white bases, the gray rocks on the left. The wooden decking that continued as far as the storage shed just a few yards away from him.

There was no sign of Clara.

His irritation grew. She was penalizing the whole group with her stupid behavior. Presumably she was hiding away somewhere, hoping they'd leave without her. Was this some kind of childish revenge because he'd yelled at her crew yesterday? David was right, kids of this age were no fun at all.

Where the hell was she?

He turned and hurried up the forest path leading to the showers, which was behind a hill above the dining hall. Benjamin was coming toward him.

"Have you found her?"

"No, there was no one there." Benjamin seemed nervous.

"Are you sure you looked everywhere? Did you open the toilet-stall doors?"

"I swear the place was empty."

Isak checked his watch. Twenty past ten—all the others had left. His group was seriously late, and he had no idea where Clara could possibly be.

"OK, let me think for a minute."

Should he contact David, let him know that Clara was missing? No, she couldn't be far away. If he took another walk around, he was bound to find her. He hadn't tried the sauna—maybe she was in there?

He made an effort to sound calm; Benjamin already looked terrified. "We'll check all the buildings one more time. You take the boys' dormitories, I'll take the girls' and the sauna. We'll start with the cabins closest to the dining hall."

They were on an island, for fuck's sake. Clara couldn't be far away. But where had she gone?

CHAPTER 23

David was sending a text message when Isak rushed into the instructors' common room. It was twenty past eleven.

"We haven't found her," Isak said, trying to catch his breath. He'd spent the last hour running all over the place, calling out Clara's name with increasing desperation. "We've looked everywhere."

His fingers were tingling just like they used to do last year when he'd started to go downhill, and his T-shirt was drenched in sweat. So far he'd managed to keep the angst at bay, but he could already hear his father's reproachful voice telling him he wasn't up to the job, that they should never have let him go after what had happened.

Everyone who was left at camp had joined in the search. Some had gone to the youth hostel, while Sofie, Lova, and Tindra had asked around in the marina. Benjamin and Stina had been sent to Trollharan.

The instructors at sea had confirmed that Clara wasn't with any of the other groups.

"Let's go through it once again," David said in a strained tone Isak hadn't heard before. "You counted the kids before breakfast. What time was that?"

"Just before eight."

Everyone had assembled as instructed behind the dining hall, on the benches placed in a squared-off U-shape. It had been a perfectly normal morning.

"Are you absolutely certain Clara was there then?"

Isak took exception to the question. "Yes—I've already told you! Do you think I'm lying?"

Calm down.

"I know my group," he added, hating the apologetic note that crept into his voice. David gave him a look that made his heart pound even more.

If only he'd handled things differently. He could have had a word with Clara and Stina before breakfast, asked if they were OK after the previous day's scare, given them some encouragement instead of criticism. If only he'd spent five minutes with Clara instead of heading straight into the dining hall.

Why had he been so hard on them yesterday?

"How did she seem?" David wanted to know. "Was she angry, upset? Are you absolutely certain you saw her?"

Isak searched his memory. Clara hadn't drawn attention to herself in any way. He couldn't even remember what she'd been wearing.

The children in the other groups had passed by while he was checking his group. There had been a couple of sleepy latecomers; he'd counted several times, but eventually made it to twenty.

Had he made a mistake? No, they'd all been there before they went in for breakfast.

"She was there, she was behaving perfectly normally."

He sounded less certain than he would have liked. David's forehead was shiny with perspiration.

"What are you going to do?" Isak asked him.

It was almost eleven thirty now, and no one had seen Clara for nearly three and a half hours.

David stared at his phone. His sweaty fingertips had left smudges on the screen.

"We have to call the police."

Chapter 24

Pernilla poured coffee into a thermos, then placed it in the picnic basket.

"There you go," she said to Thomas, closing the lid on the sandwiches and pastries she'd already packed. "All done."

Her voice was unexpectedly gentle, as if she'd decided this was going to be a good day after the frosty atmosphere yesterday evening. They'd barely exchanged a word during the drive to Stavsnäs, and had gone to sleep with their backs to each other.

Thomas didn't want to fight either. He patted her on the cheek and picked up the bag containing their swimming gear and Elin's beach toys. It was the perfect day for a trip to Alskär. Elin loved the little island to the northeast of Sandhamn, with its fine white sand. The long, shallow stretch of water along its shoreline was perfect for wading to the skerry opposite to explore.

The plan was for Nora, Jonas, and Julia to join them. Elin had no siblings, and Julia was much younger than her two brothers, so the two girls had grown very close over the past year. They were always excited at the prospect of playing together.

Thomas went down to the jetty and put the bags into the boat—a Buster that was getting pretty old. He checked the fuel and made sure the anchor was in place. Some old busybody always came hurrying over if you pulled the boat out of the water and obstructed the shore.

He heard Pernilla's voice through the open kitchen door. "Thomas, your phone's ringing."

He hurried back, and she handed him the phone. He went around the corner of the house when he saw Margit's name on the display.

"Hi."

"Are you on Harö, by any chance?" She sounded stressed.

"I am."

"I'm so sorry to disturb you, but there's a problem at the sailing camp on Lökholmen. It seems as if a thirteen-year-old girl has disappeared. Could you possibly go over there and take a look, just to be on the safe side?"

"How long has she been gone?"

"A few hours."

The police didn't normally launch a full investigation if a teenager had been missing for such a short time, unless there was a known threat or some underlying issue. However, it was always a worry, particularly when a case involved young people near the water.

Thomas couldn't help glancing over at Elin, who was sitting on the shoreline playing with a pile of pebbles. She was wearing her life jacket.

"Any suspicion of a crime?" he asked automatically.

"It's too early to say. The girl was last seen at around eight o'clock this morning, and according to the guy who's in charge of the camp, everything was fine then. They've searched everywhere, but there's no sign of her."

Thomas glanced at his watch; it was almost midday. The sun was high in the sky; a motorboat chugged past the jetty, and the Buster bobbed up and down as the swell rolled toward the reeds.

"OK, I'll go over there. We're just about to leave for a day out on Alskär; I'll drop off Pernilla and Elin, then head for Lökholmen."

"Thank you so much. The girl's only thirteen . . ."

"Has the coast guard been informed?"

"Yes, and her parents. They've been told to stay home in case she contacts them. Unfortunately she doesn't have her cell phone; participants have to hand them in when they arrive at camp."

There was a brief pause, then Margit continued: "This isn't just any sailing camp. It was the local chief of police who called me. One of the big shots whose kids are at the camp knows her."

"I understand. I'll be in touch as soon as I've checked it out."

Pernilla appeared, carrying the picnic basket in one hand and a white sun hat in the other. "I thought we were going to Alskär?"

"We are—I'll drop you and Elin, then I have to go over to Lökholmen. I won't be long."

Pernilla's face darkened. "But it's your day off! Surely someone else could deal with whatever it is?"

There had been so many occasions during the spring when Pernilla had sent a text to say she was going to be late, or had to deal with something that had come up at the last minute. And yet she thought it was OK to take a swipe at him.

Thomas sighed. "You're not the only one who has a job to do."

CHAPTER 25

It was twelve thirty by the time Thomas reached Lökholmen. There were several empty berths by the sailing camp's jetty, and he quickly secured the Buster and stepped ashore.

A young man in his early twenties with wavy hair and glasses was coming toward him along the wooden footbridge linking the jetty to the island itself. Thomas could see the tension in his jawline from some distance away.

He held out his hand. "Thomas Andreasson, Nacka police. I believe a young girl has gone missing?"

"David Rutkowski—I'm camp leader this week. Thank you for coming so quickly."

His face was covered in red blotches. He led the way to the cabins, filling Thomas in on the situation and the search they'd carried out during the morning.

Suddenly a boy wearing a backward baseball cap came running up. He was holding a cell phone in the air, his words spilling out so fast that Thomas had trouble understanding what he was saying.

"I think we've found her! The Vaxholm Ferry Company just called—they've spoken to a member of the crew from the morning crossing, and he said there was a young girl on board who matches Clara's description!"

"Are we talking about the ferry from Sandhamn?" Thomas asked.

The boy nodded eagerly.

"This is Isak Andrén," David explained. "Clara's a member of Blue Group—Isak's their instructor."

Isak was so excited he couldn't stand still. "She told them she'd left her travel card at home, and was going to her grandmother's house in Stavsnäs. The crew felt sorry for her and let her travel without paying."

"Idiots," David muttered.

Thomas took the opportunity to ask a question while Isak was catching his breath. "Was she alone? Did she have an adult with her?"

"I don't think so."

Thomas didn't bother pointing out that this was a good sign. If she'd been abducted against her will, she would hardly have made a song and dance about not having any money.

"Do they know where she went?"

"No, the guy just said she disembarked in Stavsnäs." Isak suddenly looked worried; the news from the ferry company had obviously made him forget that Clara was still missing.

"So what time would that have been?" Thomas wondered.

David was quick to answer. "The morning boat leaves Sandhamn at eight fifteen, and the crossing takes about an hour."

Something wasn't right.

"And how did she get from here to Sandhamn?"

"She must have snuck on board the taxi boat."

"I took roll call at eight," Isak said, rubbing his forehead. "She must have run straight to the taxi boat; it arrives at five past eight. She would have barely made it."

And she would have barely made it to the ferry, Thomas thought. "The question is, where is she now?"

"Do you think she could have talked her way onto a bus into the city?" David said. "I need to call her parents again; she might be heading home."

Thomas gazed around. He might as well take a look, since he was here anyway. Just in case there was something else going on. He turned to Isak. "Meanwhile maybe you could show me where she was staying?"

Isak led the way to one of the cabins. A life buoy on the wall informed everyone that this was Eider.

"Here you go. She was on the starboard side. On the right."

The dormitory contained eight beds, and was a complete mess. The floor was covered in clothes, towels, odd shoes . . . Thomas wondered if Elin's room would look like this in a few years.

"You know what teenage girls are like," Isak added apologetically. It was meant as a joke, but he couldn't hide the strain in his voice. Thomas noticed how pale he was.

He's only a kid himself, he thought.

He placed a hand on Isak's shoulder. "So how are you doing?"

Isak looked as if he was on the verge of tears.

"It doesn't feel good, losing a child you're responsible for." He took off his cap and twisted it in his hands. "I told her off yesterday because of something that happened when we were out sailing. If I hadn't been so hard on her, then maybe she wouldn't have taken off . . ." His voice died away.

Thomas wasn't convinced that Isak should be left holding the bag for this. "She's old enough to realize that it's not OK to run away without saying a word to anybody."

David appeared in the doorway. "Clara's OK! I spoke to her father—she's just arrived at home!"

Thomas was relieved, but not surprised. There was nothing to suggest that a crime had been committed; there hadn't even been time to file a formal missing-person report.

"She's home?" Isak exclaimed.

"She managed to get a free bus ride," David said. "Then she took the subway, again without paying. Everything's fine."

"Thank God." Isak sank down on the nearest bed.

Thomas patted him on the shoulder once more. "In that case I'll say good-bye. But someone needs to have a word with that girl."

CHAPTER 26

Something had been going on at the camp all morning. The instructors had been running around shouting a name; the escort boats had returned, then set off again.

At lunchtime three girls came to his boat and asked if he'd seen someone named Clara. He'd shaken his head, tried to look sympathetic. Promised to let them know if he heard or saw anything. The trio had moved on. From his vantage point in the stern, he'd watched them go from one boat to the next. Two were blonde; the third had Asian features.

Now they were coming back across the footbridge. What did they want this time?

It was almost one o'clock, and he'd just made himself some lunch— sausage and eggs. Several boats had left, but new ones had arrived. Hopefully on Monday things would settle down, and he'd be more or less on his own in this part of the marina. It was usually pretty quiet both here and in Trollsundet before midsummer.

The taller girl, the one who'd done most of the talking before, stopped in front of his boat. Sofie, that was her name.

"Hi, sorry to disturb you again!"

He peered at her; his cap was pulled well down over his eyes, but he wasn't wearing sunglasses. He'd stupidly left them in the cockpit; he didn't want anyone to remember what he looked like.

He decided to shade his eyes with one hand.

"Back again?"

"We just wanted to let you know Clara's been found. Everything's fine."

He nodded in a thoughtful, kindly way. "Good to know. Where was she?"

"She'd gone home without telling anyone. She's back in the city." Sofie rolled her eyes.

"You mean she ran away?"

"Yes," said the Asian girl, tossing back her dark hair. She was wearing very short shorts, and her nails were painted bright pink.

"We have to go," Sofie said. "We just came to tell you she's OK."

She almost seemed to curtsy before she turned away. It was an appealing sight, those soft, skinny knees bending for a second.

"Bye then." He waved good-bye and sat down, then decided to fetch a cold beer from the refrigerator. The cap came off with a satisfying hiss and disappeared overboard.

It was just as he'd suspected; the instructors weren't really keeping an eye on the kids. Yesterday he'd taken a stroll through the forest, past the red cabins. The area wasn't fenced off, and the cabin doors weren't locked—in fact, some had been wide open.

It wouldn't have been difficult for Clara to run away, but the fact that she'd made it all the way into the city did surprise him. He thought she'd have hidden somewhere.

Lökholmen was bigger than you might think; it took almost an hour to walk around the island through the pine forest and the undergrowth.

The sun was blazing down; he watched the girls until they were out of sight. They weren't to his taste—too tall, and their attitude was too grown-up. They didn't have that inexperienced look that appealed to him.

He took a swig of his beer and thought things over. Clara's disappearance had caused an enormous fuss; he'd seen it with his own eyes. They'd brought in the police; he was pretty sure the man who'd shown up in the Buster at lunchtime was a cop. There was something about the posture—they all looked the same.

The atmosphere around the camp was somehow subdued now; he couldn't quite work it out. No doubt the instructors were exhausted by the tension of the morning, conscious that they'd failed in their duty of care.

A drama that had ended in an anticlimax.

He carried on drinking, enjoying the bitter aftertaste. Toyed with the idea of what would happen if another child went missing from the camp.

Presumably there wouldn't be quite the same degree of panic, nor would they be in such a hurry to call the police.

They'd already cried wolf.

They wouldn't want to do it again.

CHAPTER 27

Isak gazed at Blue Group, who'd gathered on the wooden decking. Since Thomas Andreasson left the island, Isak hadn't let a single one of them out of his sight; he'd watched them like a hawk, been on edge whenever anyone asked to go to the restroom.

He'd already counted them four times; every time he reached eighteen, his mouth went dry.

David had drawn him aside at lunch and suggested he should take a couple of days off—go home, get some distance from what had happened. Isak had refused. Going home would make him feel even worse; the angst could easily sink its claws into him for real.

He knew how his father would react. He might not even let Isak return to camp.

Besides, Wille was still out sick.

"OK, so we're going to have a quiet afternoon," he told the group, trying to sound as upbeat as when they'd first arrived.

He felt as if a heavy weight had settled on his chest. He slipped his hand into his pocket to make sure the bottle of pills was still there. He always carried it with him, just in case.

"We're going to sail through Korsö Sound," he continued, "then we'll meet up with the other groups for a picnic on the shore at Trouville. It's Sandhamn's best-known beach."

A few of the kids nodded in recognition, but Isak wondered what they were really thinking. Had they lost their respect for him when they realized he hadn't been on top of things?

Clara wasn't coming back, and Stina had been so upset that she'd asked to leave as well. Her parents were on their way to pick her up.

Benjamin raised his hand. "Who am I with?"

Isak had forgotten that Benjamin no longer had anyone to sail with. Samuel and Sebbe were the only ones who didn't have a third crewmember. They were older and came from the same school; it was obvious that shy little Benjamin was cut from a different cloth.

The two fourteen-year-olds were lying on the jetty looking bored. They had plenty of attitude—Isak had noticed that right from the start. Then again, maybe it would be good for the three of them to get to know one another. If it didn't work out, they could always swap around tomorrow.

"You can join Samuel and Sebbe," he announced.

Samuel gazed at Benjamin through half-closed eyes. "Do we *have* to take him?"

"Can't he go with someone else?" was Sebbe's contribution.

Benjamin kept his eyes fixed on the ground.

Isak opened his mouth to tell the older boys off, but remembered what had happened after his encounter with Clara and Stina. He mustn't go in too hard.

He rubbed his forehead, tried to come up with a solution. The kids were getting impatient. The girls had started whispering, and Sofie suddenly sniggered.

"I'm afraid the three of you will just have to try to get along today; we'll review the situation in the morning."

There was a pleading note in his voice; that wasn't good.

"And I don't want any foolish behavior out at sea," he added. "Is that clear?"

Samuel smirked and nudged Sebbe.

"OK, let's get these boats rigged, then we can be on our way," Isak said.

Chapter 28

It was almost two o'clock as Thomas approached Alskär. From a distance he could see Elin and Julia playing on the shore with Nora. They'd built an impressive sandcastle with a deep moat. The sound of the girls giggling with excitement reached him across the water.

Several towels were spread out, but there was no sign of Pernilla.

Nora spotted him and waved, then waded out to help pull the boat ashore.

"Is everything OK? Pernilla said there was some trouble at the camp—a missing girl?"

Thomas rolled up his pant legs and jumped into the sea to push. The water was cold, no more than sixty degrees. Typical for June.

"It was a false alarm. She'd gone home. Smart cookie—she made it all the way into the city without any money."

"Thank goodness she's safe." The relief was clear on Nora's face. "It's hard to imagine anything worse. You send your child to camp, then you get a call to say she's disappeared."

Simon was due to go to sailing camp in July.

"I felt sorry for the instructors," Thomas said. "They were really worried until they heard she was OK."

He fastened the bowline to a tree; there were two kayaks and a small yacht farther away. A few fluffy clouds drifted across the sky. He looked around. "Where's Pernilla?"

"She wanted to go for a walk. I'm sure she'll be back soon." Nora glanced at him. "Is everything all right between the two of you? Pernilla seemed kind of down."

Thomas brushed a little sand off the prow. "You know how things can be sometimes."

He knew that wasn't going to satisfy Nora. He could usually talk to her about anything, but for some reason it was impossible to discuss his relationship with Pernilla. And yet he felt an overwhelming desire to put his cards on the table, tell her how difficult their everyday life had become, that he was seriously wondering whether they had a future together.

His gaze fell on Elin, the daughter they'd waited such a long time for.

"Is she mad because you had to work today?"

"Something like that."

Nora tucked her arm under his as they set off toward the girls. "You're not the only one. My husband-to-be is flying to Bangkok this evening. You just missed him."

"But you're getting married on Friday."

Nora gave herself a little shake—a gesture with which Thomas was very familiar. "He's promised to be back on Wednesday, but the timing is crap. I've got a major trial from Monday to Wednesday—a managing director who's stolen millions from his company." She kicked at the sand with her foot. "Jonas had to step in for a colleague who's sick. You know what he's like; he can't say no."

She sounded irritated, but as soon as she mentioned Jonas's name, her expression softened.

Thomas felt a stab of envy. It had been a long time since Pernilla had looked at him that way.

CHAPTER 29

Benjamin was sitting on a bench by the wall in the dining hall, which had been transformed into a disco for the evening. The tables had been pushed aside, and loud music was pouring out of tall black speakers. Bowls of popcorn, chips, and cheesy puffs had been laid out.

He leaned back, wishing he had his phone; at least then he'd have something to do. He couldn't go back to the dormitory yet; he would attract attention to himself if he left too early.

Samuel and Sebbe wandered in. Benjamin stiffened. The afternoon had been torture. Samuel had taken the tiller and refused to speak to Benjamin, issuing orders via Sebbe.

Tell him to take in the foresail.

Doesn't he realize we need to turn around?

Benjamin had no idea why he'd behaved like that; it wasn't as if he'd done anything to Samuel. They hardly knew each other. He should have spoken up as soon as the older boy started messing around, but he couldn't do it, not when they were sitting three feet apart. Instead he'd just cowered in his seat, kept his mouth shut like an idiot. Stared at the horizon, counting the minutes until the trip was over.

Benjamin knew that Samuel despised him for his failure to fight back. He despised himself.

He just wanted to go home.

However, he hadn't said anything to Mom when he spoke to her after dinner. He knew she'd worry, and there was nothing she could do.

Five days left.

He caught a movement out of the corner of his eye; suddenly Samuel and Sebbe were standing in front of him.

His stomach contracted.

Sebbe leaned over him, sniffing loudly. "It definitely stinks of pig around here. No wonder Clara couldn't stand being in the boat with you. I guess she couldn't take it anymore—that's what everyone's saying." He shoved a handful of cheesy puffs in his mouth. Yellow powder stuck to his lips, making him look like some kind of evil clown.

Samuel took over. "No one wants to sail with you. Why don't you run off home to your mommy? Smelly little babies like you don't fit in around here."

Benjamin tried to ignore him; he fixed his gaze on the nearest speaker.

Samuel trod on Benjamin's sneaker, crushing his toes. His stomach was inches away from Benjamin's face.

Benjamin pressed his back against the wall in an attempt to increase the distance, but Samuel was still much too close.

Most of the girls were dancing to Justin Bieber; the floor was vibrating with the pumping bass line. Benjamin hoped one of the instructors would come in, but they were all out on the terrace; he'd seen them when he came in. Isak had been sitting with Maja from Yellow Group.

Samuel gave his shoulder a hard shove. It really hurt, but Benjamin made an effort not to show it. He had a lump in his throat.

I'm going to do it, he thought wildly. *I'm going to stand up and punch him.*

Instead he just sat there, his cheeks burning.

At that moment Isak appeared in the doorway.

Come over here, please come over here.

As if he'd read Benjamin's mind, Isak crossed the room.

"Are you having a good time?" he asked, putting his arm around Samuel's shoulders. "How's it going, man? Have you had a dance yet?" He nodded appreciatively in the direction of the crowded dance floor. "The girls seem to be going for it," he added with a wink.

"It's cool," Samuel said, as if they'd been chatting like friends do.

Benjamin got up and slipped away before anyone could stop him.

David was perched on the rocks outside the dining hall, with the music thumping in the background. He could just make out Sandhamn's quayside across the water in the warm glow of the evening; in spite of the distance, it was possible to see people strolling along the promenade.

What a fucking day.

The conversation with Björn Ekholm, the director of the organization that ran the sailing camps, had been no fun at all. Ekholm hadn't minced his words; he'd wiped the floor with David, and had been highly critical of Isak. However, David intended to keep that to himself. There was no point in telling Isak what Ekholm had said, not when he was still so upset by Clara's disappearance.

The volume of the music increased.

David sighed. He was going to have to ask them to turn it down. They were alone on this side of the island, but even so . . .

When he got to his feet, he saw Isak sitting at the far end of the jetty with Maja; they seemed to be deep in conversation.

She was a good girl, calm and stable. She was new this year, but she'd come with excellent references from the Vitsgarn sailing school. Maybe she could help Isak to get over this? David knew he was fragile.

He'd heard about the circumstances surrounding Isak's breakdown last year from his brother, Linus.

Had it been a mistake, taking him on as an instructor?

David didn't want to think that way, but he was very relieved that Wille would be joining them tomorrow.

CHAPTER 30

Sunday, June 15

Benjamin was sure he'd chucked his life jacket under his bed, but it wasn't there, and he was afraid he was going to be late. Isak would yell at him again if he didn't get there on time.

He lay down on his stomach and peered under the bed, even though he'd already looked there more than once. Nothing. He mustn't be late—but he couldn't show up without his life jacket either.

The stress made his heart race.

I want to go home.

He got to his feet, repeating the words over and over again in his head as he rummaged through his bag.

Where had it gone? Had someone dumped it in the lost and found?

Even if his life jacket wasn't there, maybe there was another one he could borrow in the meantime. He hurried out the door with a sigh of relief.

Isak was waiting on the jetty, legs wide apart, when Benjamin came running across the grass.

"Where have you been?" he yelled. "Everyone's had to wait because of you! I was just about to come and look for you."

Benjamin had never seen him so mad, not even when he'd shouted at them on Friday.

"Nobody knew where you were!"

"I couldn't find my life jacket," Benjamin gasped.

"You know perfectly well you have to keep all your belongings shipshape."

"Sorry. It won't happen again."

Isak still looked annoyed. Suddenly Samuel spoke up.

"That's Clara's," he said, pointing to a label on the life jacket Benjamin had found. Benjamin hadn't noticed it, and he went cold all over. Was it against the rules to borrow from lost and found?

"You've taken someone else's life jacket instead of looking after your own?" Isak sounded incredulous.

Benjamin was sure one of the instructors had said it was OK to borrow stuff, but he didn't dare protest.

"Sorry," he mumbled again.

Isak shook his head, then held up a chart. "OK, let's get a move on. We're sailing to Harö today, and it's going to take a while."

Benjamin waited for Isak to assign him to a different crew, as he'd promised yesterday. Did he dare say anything? Isak was in such a bad mood. Samuel grinned behind Isak's back. That did it.

"Excuse me?" Benjamin ventured, tugging at Isak's sleeve. "Wasn't I supposed to be sailing with someone else today?" He tried to keep his voice down so that Sebbe and Samuel wouldn't hear.

At first Isak didn't seem to understand what he was talking about. "Why?" he asked, much too loudly. "Didn't you get along with Sebbe and Samuel? I saw you chatting at the disco." He rolled up the chart and sighed. "Fine, you can swap over with Tindra if you like, which means you'll be with Sofie and Lova. Maybe it's best to mix the crews up a little." He placed a hand on Tindra's shoulder. "OK with you?"

Benjamin's knees went weak with relief as she nodded, but Samuel caught his eye and wrinkled his nose.

"Jesus, you stink," he mouthed. Then he grinned again.

Chapter 31

The evening sun had warmed the flat rock Benjamin had discovered on the northwestern side of the island. A mother duck and her young were bobbing up and down on the water. Benjamin was lying on his back, listening to the lapping of the waves, staring up at the sky with his hands clasped behind his head.

He'd snuck away after dinner. The theory class was out of the way, and everyone could do whatever they liked until bedtime at ten o'clock.

It hadn't been a bad day after all, he thought. The girls were nice. Sofie had offered him some gum, and the sailing had gone pretty well.

He closed his eyes, felt sleep creeping up on him.

Suddenly a shadow blocked out the sun. When he opened his eyes, he was looking straight into Samuel's face.

How had he found his way here? He must have followed Benjamin from the dining hall.

Benjamin sat up and saw Sebbe on the other side of the triangular rock, closing off his escape route.

"What are you doing here?" he said, doing his best to sound unconcerned.

"What are you doing here?" Samuel mimicked.

"Nothing."

"Nothing."

"Stop it."

"You stop it."

Benjamin tried to get to his feet, but Samuel gave him a hard shove. He looked around for someone who could help him, but they were all alone. That was why he'd come here, to be by himself.

Samuel came closer, and Benjamin shuffled backward. Samuel gave him another hard shove, and Benjamin shuffled again; he was dangerously close to the edge now. The water was several feet below; there was no sandy seabed here, just pebbles.

His lower lip trembled; he was going to cry at any moment.

Samuel stepped forward, but Benjamin didn't dare move any farther.

"There's a disgusting smell around here," Samuel said, sniffing the air. "What's the matter with you—don't you take showers?"

Benjamin wanted to protest—of course he showered. Every single day.

"We want to help you. To keep clean."

Benjamin didn't understand.

"Take off your clothes."

"What?"

"Take off your clothes and give them to me."

Samuel punched him on the shoulder, and when Benjamin didn't obey his instructions, he delivered a vicious kick to the younger boy's leg. Benjamin's eyes filled with tears; that really hurt. He managed to remove his shirt with fumbling fingers, and Samuel grabbed it.

"And the rest."

Benjamin took off his sneakers and pants. The granite was cold against his thighs; he wrapped his arms around his body.

"Don't forget your boxers."

"Please . . ."

A blow to his ear made his head spin. He managed to ease off his boxers, snot dripping from his nose. He was completely naked, and had no way to cover himself.

Samuel picked up the pile of clothes and sniffed it again. "They really stink," he said, turning to Sebbe. "Have you ever smelled anything worse?"

Sebbe grinned, pinching his nose between his finger and thumb.

"Fucking rank," Samuel said, holding the clothes at arm's length. With a flick of his wrist, the whole lot disappeared over the edge of the rock.

"Say thank you," Samuel went on. "It's important to thank people when they try to help you."

Benjamin had no choice. "Thank you," he whispered. When Samuel bent down to pick up his sneakers, he couldn't stop himself from begging. "No, please don't . . ."

"Maybe this will get them clean." Samuel hurled them into the sea.

Benjamin stared at his clothes floating on the water. His T-shirt was already on its way to goodness knows where, and his sneakers were sinking fast.

"Look, Sebbe!" Samuel shouted. "The kid has to wash his clothes in the sea! What a fucking loser."

Sebbe sniggered.

"I guess you'll have to go for a swim if you want them back," Samuel added with a smile. "That might get rid of the stench."

CHAPTER 32

A few minutes after Thomas had turned off the bedside lamp, Pernilla's cell phone pinged on the nightstand.

"I thought you'd switched that off?" he mumbled without turning over. As usual it hadn't taken him long to drift toward sleep.

Pernilla sat up and turned on her lamp. "Sorry, I just need to check something."

Thomas listened to her tapping away, composing a new message.

"Oh . . . Something's happened at work. I'm going to have to fly to Copenhagen on Tuesday; I might be away for a few days."

"Do you have to sort this out now?" Thomas muttered. "Can't it wait until tomorrow?"

"Don't start."

Thomas wasn't in the mood for an argument; it was too late. He adjusted the pillow. "Can't we get some sleep?"

"I won't be long."

Pernilla slid out of bed. Thomas heard her go into the hallway, and after a few seconds she was back. Judging from her movements, she had her laptop on her knee.

Another ping, from the computer this time. Then her phone beeped.

"Seriously, Pernilla . . ." He turned over so he could see what she was doing. He no longer felt drowsy.

"Sorry, I'll turn off the sound. I have to read a couple of emails. You go to sleep."

Pernilla might as well have been talking to Elin. Thomas didn't usually have a problem with her working in bed, but this time he couldn't suppress his irritation.

"I need the light off. I have to get up before six for work tomorrow."

"Why are you so grumpy?"

"I'm not grumpy."

"Honestly, Thomas, what's the problem?" Her tone suggested that he was the one being difficult, not her. "I'm just going to read through these emails and send a quick reply. It'll only take a few minutes."

How many times had he heard that before?

After his trip to Lökholmen, she'd sulked for the rest of the day. Thomas had had to watch what he said, but of course it was fine if she had to work in the middle of the night.

She'd already put on her glasses, and the rapid movement of her eyes told him she was absorbed in the contents of a message.

Enough.

"If you must work, I suggest you go into the living room or the kitchen. This is a bedroom, not an office."

There was no reaction at first, but after about five seconds Pernilla closed her laptop, grabbed her robe, and left the room, slamming the door behind her.

Thomas reached across and turned off her bedside lamp, then settled down and pulled the covers up to his chin. He was determined to get to sleep, in spite of the fact that he was now wide awake.

Ninna was fast asleep, just like little Emil in his crib by the window. Christian Dufva stared out into the darkness with burning eyes.

Niklas had tried to contact him again, and as usual he'd rejected the call. However, his pulse increased every single time; the mere sight of Niklas's number on the screen was enough to send his stress levels soaring.

They'd once been good friends, he and Niklas. For the first few years, they were colleagues at one of Sweden's largest construction companies. They'd gotten along well from the outset, worked well together and seen through several major projects. Gradually they'd begun to talk about starting up something of their own. They'd call the firm Alliance Construction—a kind of private joke. They'd formed an alliance with each other—now and forever.

Ninna let out a little snore.

How he envied her ability to fall asleep in seconds. He'd been tossing and turning for hours, aware of every crease in the sheets. It was way too hot in the bedroom, but he didn't want to risk waking Emil by opening the window.

He couldn't stop thinking about the past.

Their first office on the outskirts of Stockholm had been nothing more than one room with two desks, but those had been good times—a positive atmosphere, high energy levels, lots of laughs every day.

Their families had hung out together; their wives had become friends, and Benjamin liked playing with Niklas's sons, even though Albert and Natan were a little older.

Christian closed his eyes.

They'd been the best of business partners, the best of friends—almost like brothers.

Then everything went wrong.

Chapter 33

Nora knew she ought to get some sleep before the trial, but gave up shortly before midnight. She switched on the bedside lamp and opened up her laptop.

When Jonas was home she didn't usually work in bed, but of course he wasn't here. She hadn't even bothered to remove the bedspread on his side, just folded it over.

She hadn't logged in all weekend, so she went straight to her emails. Her eyes were immediately drawn to the threatening subject line. Her stomach contracted, but she couldn't help clicking on the message.

The capital letters screamed out at her.

> FUCKING WHORE! YOU SHOULD BURN IN HELL IF YOU BELIEVE CHRISTIAN DUFVA! HE'S LYING TO SAVE HIS OWN SKIN! HE'S LYING ABOUT EVERYTHING!!! HOW CAN YOU TRUST HIS TESTIMONY?!? YOU'RE GOING TO PAY, JUST LIKE HIM . . .

Nora shuddered. She stared at the words, blinked.

If Jonas had been here, it would have been different. She could have shown him the message, and he would have calmed her down, dismissed it as nonsense. Now the vicious words crept under her skin. This was the first time she'd received a personal threat since she took up the post as prosecutor.

She and Julia were alone in the apartment tonight; Adam and Simon had spent the weekend with their father and wouldn't be back until tomorrow. She couldn't help glancing at the bedroom window, where the roller blind was half drawn.

They lived on the third floor; it was impossible for anyone to see in. Nevertheless, she got out of bed and pulled the blind all the way down, pushing the bottom against the sill so there wasn't even the slightest gap.

Threats against prosecutors weren't unusual; more than one in three had experienced something like this at least once. A few years ago a bomb had been planted outside a prosecutor's front door when she went after several members of a biker gang. However, it was cases involving violent crimes or drugs that usually evoked this kind of response rather than financial wrongdoing.

Nora's pulse was still racing; logic had no impact. She clutched her computer in a viselike grip, tried to swallow, but couldn't produce enough saliva.

The front door was locked; she'd checked before she came to bed. But there was no security chain; a good kick or two would smash it open.

There was a scratching noise outside the window, and Nora stiffened. Was someone spying on her, even though she'd just drawn the blind? She quickly closed her laptop and turned off the light, then sat there motionless, waiting.

She heard a click from somewhere in the apartment; she gave a start, then realized it was the refrigerator. She listened hard, her throat constricting as the seconds passed.

Julia. Julia was alone.

Nora pushed back the covers and crept over to her daughter's room. She opened the door as quietly as possible and tiptoed in.

Julia was fast asleep, her forehead damp with sweat and the covers pushed aside. Everything seemed peaceful, but Nora went over to the window and pulled down the blind. She stood there for a moment pressed against the wall, listening for any strange noises.

Her arms were covered in goose bumps.

After a few seconds she lay down on the narrow bed and wrapped her arms around Julia, who didn't move.

The faint rasping sound came again, then there was silence.

CHAPTER 34

Benjamin had gone to bed before Samuel and Sebbe and pulled the sleeping bag over his head, hoping they wouldn't notice him. When Isak poked his head around the door to say good night, he'd pretended to be asleep, even though he didn't dare relax until the others had dropped off.

Somehow he must have dozed, because when he opened his eyes, it was dark. He could hear soft snores from Oscar in the bunk above.

His thoughts immediately turned to Samuel. Why was he behaving like this? Benjamin hadn't done him any harm, hadn't made a nasty comment or taken his stuff. OK, so he'd borrowed the life jacket, but it had been in the lost and found. He hadn't meant to steal it; he'd just wanted to use it for a few hours. Clara had gone home anyway.

He stifled a sob.

He'd managed to retrieve his clothes by slithering down into the cold water. One of his sneakers had disappeared; he'd dived several times, but there was no sign of it. In the end he'd clambered out, pulled on his soaking wet T-shirt and jeans, and run barefoot back to the camp.

One of the instructors had caught him before he made it to the dormitory.

"Did you fall in?" she'd asked with a smile. "You'll have to be more careful in the future."

Benjamin hadn't told her the truth.

He wanted to run away, just like Clara—but what would his father say? Christian thought sailing camp was the best thing in the world. And Mom would be upset, too.

Samuel snuffled in his sleep, and Benjamin stopped breathing.

Did he dare speak to Isak?

No, that wasn't a good idea; Isak was already mad at him. Isak had changed since Clara's disappearance; he'd become bad-tempered and volatile. Benjamin had only been a couple of minutes late earlier today, but Isak had really gone for him. Isak wouldn't take his side.

Benjamin glanced in Samuel's direction.

There was no point in speaking to any of the instructors. If Samuel found out he'd told on him, it would make things so much worse.

CHAPTER 35

Monday, June 16

It was long after midnight when Niklas Winnerman started fumbling with his key. The entry code for the main door stopped working at ten; after that residents needed a key to get in.

He shouldn't have drunk so much. He remembered all the other times when he'd thought exactly the same thing. The trial was due to begin in a few hours, and he had to be at the top of his game. It was no good turning up with a hangover.

However, the pressure on his chest had eased as soon as he walked into the bar. The music and the hum of conversation calmed his nerves. After a couple of drinks, he was almost able to relax, imagine that he was going into the office tomorrow instead of to court.

Just being among people who knew nothing about him made everything seem better.

The lock refused to cooperate. He tried to insert his key, but dropped it. He heard the clink as it hit the ground and bounced away. Where had it gone? He bent down, groping around in the darkness; the exterior light seemed to be broken yet again.

"Useless fuckers," he muttered. How hard could it be for the housing committee to make sure the bulb was changed?

Someone was walking toward him, moving fast. The hard blow to his side came out of nowhere; he didn't have time to react. He lost his balance and pitched forward, his chin hitting the pavement. His glasses fell off.

"What the hell are you doing?" he gasped. "Are you crazy?"

He hadn't seen anyone as he approached the door. Where had this guy come from?

Another vicious kick; this time Niklas couldn't suppress a groan.

Yet another kick, even harder.

Niklas curled up with his arms wrapped around his belly to protect himself. The last kick had struck his ribs, and the pain was unbearable.

The next delivered a direct hit to his chest, knocking the air out of him.

He whimpered, trying to brace himself for a fresh onslaught, but slowly he began to breathe again. Oxygen was reaching his lungs, even though it hurt every time he inhaled.

He could sense the other person in the darkness.

Don't kill me, he thought as he felt the cold night breeze on the back of his neck.

A fresh kick to the base of his spine numbed his entire nervous system like ice-cold water, then the pain exploded.

"Please, stop. I haven't done anything," he panted.

The silence made it worse.

"What do you want? Take my cell phone, and my wallet—anything, as long as you stop!"

This time he got an answer.

A hoarse voice whispered in his ear, so close that he could feel the warm breath on his skin.

"Have you got our money?"

Niklas immediately recognized the accent that had given him the creeps the first time he heard it.

Artūras's man.

Slowly he became aware of the cold ground beneath his body, the gravel digging into his flesh where his shirt had ridden up. His heart was racing, his pulse throbbing through his body as if every beat were its last.

He swallowed over and over again as he tried to find the right words, the words that would persuade this Lithuanian hit man to stop beating him up.

"I'll pay back everything I owe, I promise," he said with such conviction that he believed it himself. "I'll swear on anything you like. Tell your boss he'll have the money by the end of the week."

"You've got three days. Wednesday at the latest."

"Please . . . You'll get it all, with interest. Just let me go . . ."

For a second he thought it was going to work. The man was going to leave him alone.

Then came one final kick, delivered with such force that Niklas flew backward and hit his head on the steps.

He saw a shower of sparks, then everything went black.

CHAPTER 36

The adrenaline compensated to some extent for the lack of sleep, but Nora still felt shaken when she arrived at the courthouse and went through the security barrier.

Even though the threatening message seemed less alarming by the light of day, she had still made a point of looking around before she left home. She couldn't stop thinking about the rasping sound outside the window, and had given Julia an extra big hug before leaving her at preschool.

Nora paused in front of the electronic information board to find the right courtroom. Her briefcase was heavy, but she couldn't help wondering if she'd brought everything she needed.

An impersonal voice came over the loudspeaker, calling Nora's case.

"The state versus Niklas Winnerman and Bertil Svensson: all parties and their representatives to court five."

Nora headed upstairs. The accused and their defense attorneys were waiting by the door. Niklas Winnerman appeared to have been in a fight. He had a Band-Aid over one eyebrow, and his chin was badly grazed. He was clearly in pain, possibly from his ribs, and grimaced every time he moved.

Beside this vision of wretchedness, Jacob Emilsson looked even smarter than usual in his three-piece suit.

Judge Barbro Wikingsson was already seated. Threads of silver glinted in the parting of her shoulder-length dark hair. On her right were the law clerk, Dennis Grönstedt, and a juror by the name of Annika Sandberg, a stout woman whose hair had been sprayed into rigid submission. The other jurors, a man in his sixties and a middle-aged dark-skinned man, were on Wikingsson's left.

They were in one of the oldest rooms in the courthouse, with a high ceiling and dark wood-paneled walls.

Nora took her place to the left of the bench. The judge welcomed the participants and dealt with the formalities, then nodded to Nora. "Prosecutor Linde will now outline the charges."

In spite of the fact that Nora had served as a prosecutor for almost five years, her heart always beat faster when the focus turned to her. She remained silent for a few seconds, her gaze sweeping the courtroom and resting on Winnerman.

"Niklas Winnerman is charged with grave disloyalty to principal, and Bertil Svensson with aiding and abetting Winnerman. The prosecution asserts that Winnerman abused his position of trust as managing director of Alliance Construction, thereby causing the company serious harm. Bertil Svensson assisted him in this enterprise."

She allowed her words to sink in, glancing at the bench. Annika Sandberg and the two men were leaning forward, which was a good sign. Two smooth wedding rings shone in the light as Annika rested her chin on her hand.

"Winnerman facilitated the transfer of ten million kronor from Alliance Construction to a company known as Vine Holdings to secure planning permission on a plot that was completely worthless. As soon as Vine received the money, it was forwarded to a bank account in the Cayman Islands, thanks to Bertil Svensson. Christian Dufva,

Winnerman's former business partner, will testify that Winnerman went behind his back and demonstrably abused his position of trust."

Winnerman, who had kept his head lowered until this point, gave a start at the mention of Dufva's name.

"Winnerman expected his deception to be regarded as nothing more than a bad business transaction, but in fact it led to the collapse of Alliance Construction. Bankruptcy. Thanks to the meticulous work of the official receiver, it became clear that the situation was entirely caused by an unscrupulous owner who was unable to distinguish between his own funds and those of the company."

"Perhaps the prosecutor could save the summing up until the end?" Barbro Wikingsson said dryly.

Nora knew she'd gone too far, but she'd made her point. Annika Sandberg looked unimpressed with the defendant, and the middle-aged juror, Martin Nbeke, was shaking his head. Out of the corner of her eye, she saw Jacob Emilsson place a reassuring hand on his client's arm.

She addressed the bench once more. "During this trial I will show how Niklas Winnerman set up a company with the sole aim of siphoning money from Alliance Construction. He deceived his coworkers, he deceived his partner, and he manipulated Bertil Svensson in an attempt to conceal his own involvement."

The judge was frowning; Nora needed to rein it in if she was to avoid another reprimand. However, she had decided from the start that she was going to plead her case in the strongest terms, and to repeat the sum of ten million kronor as often as possible.

She knew that would provoke a reaction from the jury.

Should she say that the money was still missing? Sometimes it was an advantage to bring up a weakness before the defense could do so, but why wake a sleeping bear?

She decided to keep that detail to herself for the time being.

"Winnerman has cheated both the state and Alliance Construction of ten million kronor," she said in conclusion. "He deserves to be handed down a lengthy jail term."

Winnerman was now sitting bolt upright, staring at her with bloodshot eyes.

"Thank you, prosecutor," the judge said. "Over to you, herr Emilsson."

CHAPTER 37

Thomas sat down at his desk and switched on the computer to type up his report on the morning's activities. He'd drunk several cups of coffee, but still felt slow and unfocused.

The window was ajar, but the humid air drifting in from outside didn't help at all.

He'd lain awake for far too long last night, even after Pernilla came back to bed. Nothing more had been said before he left this morning; she hadn't moved when he got up.

So much was unresolved between them, but Thomas didn't know how to tackle the situation. Maybe things would improve when the pressure eased for her at work. She often said this was only temporary, although he wasn't convinced.

After morning briefing Thomas had taken a statement from a young man who'd been assaulted. The nineteen-year-old had been smoking outside a bar when he received a single punch to the chin. The blow had been so powerful that he fell to the ground and broke a rib. His jaw had been swollen for a week.

"It was totally unprovoked," he'd insisted. "I'd never even seen the guy before."

It wasn't the first time Thomas had heard about this kind of thing, but on this occasion there were witnesses: two girls had seen a drunken thirty-year-old deliver the punch with no warning.

The younger man had been reasonably composed when Thomas spoke to him, but he was pale and clearly still shaken. His hair was lank and greasy, and he didn't look good. He said he was scared to go out in the evenings, and didn't think he'd ever be able to go back to that same bar.

Thomas intended to charge his attacker with assault. He didn't have a criminal record, so would probably receive a suspended sentence along with an order to pay compensation of seven or eight thousand kronor, the usual price tag for an injury like this.

He doubted whether the payment would ease the victim's nightmares, or that he would ever feel as safe as he had before the attack.

"Are you busy?"

Aram was standing in the doorway with a cup of coffee in his hand. Thomas gratefully seized the opportunity for a diversion.

"Come in," he said, gesturing toward the visitor's chair. "I'll finish this later."

"Rough weekend? You look as if you've been partying half the night."

Were the dark shadows beneath his eyes so noticeable? Thomas waved a dismissive hand. Even though he and Aram occasionally spent time together outside work, they weren't close enough for Thomas to discuss his marital relationship with him—especially since Pernilla got along well with Aram's wife, Sonja.

He could hear the discussion around the table in the Gorgis household in Hagsätra if he told the truth: Pernilla's job took up so much of her time that they hardly saw each other these days. And they found it difficult to hold a civilized conversation when they did meet.

"You know what it's like when you have small kids," he said instead.

"I'm very happy that's all behind me," Aram said, finishing his coffee and tossing the cup in the trashcan. "We're definitely done!"

Aram's daughters were eight and eleven.

Thomas wondered if he was being unfair. He and Aram had worked together for more than five years, and his trust in his colleague was absolute. He couldn't imagine anyone better. He and Margit had been a good team in the past, but since her promotion he and Aram had become a pretty solid unit. And yet he couldn't open up to him, just as he'd been unable to confide in Nora.

"So what do you think of the restructuring?" Aram asked. "I never imagined we'd end up in Flemingsberg."

Before Thomas had time to answer, his cell phone beeped. He took it out of his pocket: a brief text message from Pernilla.

Flying to Copenhagen today. Sorry. You'll have to pick up Elin. P

He wasn't even annoyed; as soon as Pernilla mentioned the trip yesterday evening, he'd gotten used to the idea of being alone with Elin over the next few days. He just felt even more exhausted. Pernilla dropped everything and took off as soon as work called.

Thomas was under no illusions that his job came before hers; he'd learned that during the years they'd spent together. Almost twenty by this stage, not counting the period of their separation. She also earned significantly more than he did; his police salary wasn't much to shout about.

But she could have at least asked if he was able to pick up Elin, rather than just telling him what to do. He sighed.

"Bad news?" Aram said.

"It's just Pernilla—she has to go away on business at short notice." Thomas put down his phone and clasped his hands behind his head. "That's what happens when you live with a career woman." He didn't like the way it sounded, but it was too late now to take it back.

CHAPTER 38

It was time for Winnerman to take the stand.

Nora leaned back in her chair. Jacob Emilsson might describe the situation differently, but she was the one who'd set the agenda. She knew she'd gotten the members of the jury on her side; Annika Sandberg in particular had nodded approvingly several times.

The phases of a criminal trial were set in stone. The whole process was like a formalized drama in a series of acts. The prosecution opened, the defense responded, the facts of the case were laid out, the accused and the witnesses were questioned and counter-questioned, then there were the closing statements followed by the verdict.

Just as she'd expected, both Niklas Winnerman and Bertil Svensson had pleaded not guilty. Now they would have the opportunity to appear in the best possible light, led by their own attorneys.

Emilsson was already preening on the other side of the room.

"Niklas," he began. "How did it come to this?"

The question was purely rhetorical.

"Let's go back to the start of this sorry tale, Niklas, so we can get a clear picture of the course of events." He bestowed a warm smile on judge and jury. "The prosecutor has depicted my client as a cunning

businessman whose only aim was to line his own pockets. Which is why
I think that you, Niklas, should tell us what really happened."

Emilsson had used Niklas's name three times in sixty seconds.
Nora thought he sounded like a bad imitation of American courtroom
practice, but he usually knew what he was doing.

"When did you start thinking about this deal, Niklas?" he asked.

Four times, Nora thought wryly.

Winnerman raised his chin, the nasty graze showing clearly. He still
seemed uncomfortable, and his posture was odd.

"It was back in December 2012," Winnerman said. "I was contacted
by representatives from Vine Holdings; they told me the company had
access to a very attractive plot with planning permission. I immediately
felt that Alliance would be able to use this to our advantage."

"How does planning permission work? Could you explain for the
benefit of those of us who are not in the industry?"

"It's called planning permission, but it's more of a land allocation—
an agreement between a local authority and a property developer,
giving the developer the sole right to build on land owned by the
authority."

"And what determines the value of such an agreement?" Emilsson
asked.

"There is a whole range of factors—the geographical location of the
land, transport links, whether there are any stores nearby."

"So planning permission for a plot of land in Solna, close to inner-
city Stockholm, would be worth a lot more than a plot of the same size
in, say, Lapland?"

"That's correct."

"And how did you assess the worth of this particular agreement?"

"I compared it with similar plots. We were already working with
local authorities throughout Stockholm; it wasn't difficult to come up
with a reasonable price level."

Emilsson was making it sound like an ordinary conversation, Nora thought, but every time he got Winnerman to open his mouth, he planted fresh information.

"In this case you agreed on a price tag of ten million. Could you tell us how you justified this amount?"

"It was a good deal, because the agreement spanned a period of almost five years, which gave us plenty of time to develop the project. We were intending to build apartment complexes. Everybody's crying out for housing in Stockholm, so it would have been extremely profitable."

"You wanted to make a profit?"

Winnerman nodded, with a slightly frantic edge. "Absolutely. I might have been a little too keen, but I was convinced that we could make a real killing if we got in quickly."

You certainly did, Nora thought. *Ten million in your own pocket.*

"How did Vine Holdings contact you?"

"I received an email."

"Had you done business with them before? How did you know the firm was a serious player?"

Winnerman shuffled uncomfortably. "There are plenty of reliable companies in the construction industry, just like us."

Just like you used *to be,* Nora added silently.

"Then what happened?"

"We exchanged a series of emails, and eventually we arranged a meeting. I met their lawyer, who brought all the relevant documentation with him."

"Where did you meet?"

"In a conference room at the central station."

"So not on their premises?"

"No—their head office was in Örebro, so they suggested a venue in the city. I thought it was a good idea, as it meant I didn't have to travel."

Jacob Emilsson was listening attentively, as if every word his client uttered was completely new information. In fact, it was all in the transcripts of the interviews Leila had conducted. Nora had read them many times.

"Were there just the two of you at this meeting?"

"Yes. Their managing director was supposed to be there, but he had the flu and couldn't come."

"What was the next step?"

"I went home and studied the figures in detail. I decided we ought to close the deal—it was just too good to turn down."

"Was that when you spoke to your partner?"

"No. It was just before Christmas; Christian was away with his new family. I decided to talk to him when he got back in January, but I had mentioned it earlier."

"Please tell the court about your discussion with Christian Dufva."

"I explained the proposal, showed him all the documentation and my calculations. He agreed that it was an interesting deal, and well worth pursuing."

"He claims that he strongly advised you to have nothing to do with it."

Winnerman's cheeks flushed red. "I don't understand why he's saying that. He agreed that we should go ahead."

Emilsson stroked his chin, his expression pensive. "But it was only you who signed all the documents. Dufva's signature is nowhere to be seen."

"We were both supposed to sign, but on the day, Christian came down with gastric flu. We couldn't afford to wait; Vine Holdings had received a counteroffer, and the deal could have slipped through our fingers."

Nora wondered if the jury had picked up on Winnerman's defensive tone. The older man, Sven-Åke Hult, was busy making notes.

"Christian and I should have signed the contract together," Winnerman conceded. "But we have signed separately in the past."

His uncertainty was showing now.

"We all know this kind of thing can easily happen, don't we?" Emilsson turned to the jury. "I'm sure we've all bent the rules now and again." He smiled indulgently. "Please go on, Niklas."

"I sent everything over to Vine by courier, and arranged for the payment to be made."

"Ah yes—let's talk about the payment. It was a significant amount; I presume you were very careful before authorizing the transfer."

Winnerman spread his hands wide. "It sounds like a lot of money, but in fact it really isn't, under the circumstances. We've had projects with a turnover of fifty million or more."

Nora could see immediately that neither Annika Sandberg nor Sven-Åke Hult was convinced by Winnerman's comment. Ten million was a hell of a lot of money, particularly if it ended up in a con man's pocket.

"Needless to say, I was always careful with the company finances," Winnerman added.

It was too late. Even the law clerk couldn't hide his disapproval. What did he earn—twenty-five thousand a month, maybe? It would take him over thirty years to earn ten million. Before taxes.

Emilsson immediately realized things were heading in the wrong direction. "Then you had some bad luck," he prompted.

"You could say that." Winnerman pressed a hand to his ribs.

"What went wrong?"

"There shouldn't have been any problems with a payment of that size, but at the same time we hit unexpected difficulties on another project, and suddenly the company's liquidity was under pressure."

"Couldn't you have gone to the bank, requested a temporary overdraft?"

"We already had one. The bank refused to increase our overdraft limit when it emerged that the land allocation agreement was worthless. They pulled the rug from under us; if they'd taken a different approach, Alliance Construction would have survived."

Winnerman wiped his brow. His hair was noticeably thinning, the pale skin of his scalp visible through the strands of gray.

"Making money from us when things were going well wasn't a problem," he continued, "but as soon as we ran into difficulties . . . We would have made it if they'd given us a loan for a few months."

Nora almost heard him grunting to himself.

"When did you realize something wasn't right with the agreement?"

"When I contacted the local authority shortly after signing the contract. They sent over additional documentation showing previously unknown limitations to the validity of the planning permission."

"Previously unknown—what do you mean by that?"

"No one had shown me these documents before."

"Shouldn't you have checked?"

"I really wish I had." Winnerman lowered his eyes. "There are a lot of things I wish I'd done differently."

Maybe his scruffy appearance wasn't a careless oversight, but a deliberate strategy? It wasn't impossible, given Emilsson's approach to questioning his client, allowing him the opportunity to justify his actions and to correct himself.

Nora had to admit that Emilsson was good.

"I thought the contract was solid," Winnerman continued quietly. "There were guarantees in place, and as I said, the agreement covered a five-year period."

"Guarantees? What kind of guarantees?"

Nora noticed that both the judge and Annika Sandberg sat up a little straighter.

"The vendor expressly guaranteed that five-year period. I assumed everything was OK—it usually is. By the time I found out the truth, the money was already gone."

"Didn't you try to get it back? Couldn't you have contacted Vine's lawyer?"

"I couldn't get ahold of him."

"Why not?"

"He wasn't answering his phone. I sent emails but got no reply. Vine's address was a postbox number in Örebro. Suddenly everyone had disappeared."

Winnerman was spinning a decent story. Nora waited for him to go on; all the jurors were leaning forward.

Emilsson contemplated his client. "Just like the money," he said. "That had disappeared, too."

"I've no idea where it is."

"No—even the prosecutor doesn't know." Emilsson turned to the bench, emphasizing every word. "My client denies the charge, and the prosecutor has no proof whatsoever that he has taken the money."

CHAPTER 39

He stopped behind a lush shrubbery above the path between the sailing camp and the pine forest. It was a good spot, just on the edge of the trees, but well hidden. He couldn't be seen from the marina, and the bushes concealed him from the camp.

And yet he was no more than twenty yards from the back of the red cabins.

There wasn't a soul in sight.

He looked around carefully, but no one was mending a sail or tinkering with a boat, no housekeeper was clattering pots and pans in the kitchen.

It was just before lunchtime; the children were out sailing, and all the escort boats were at sea. Presumably the rest of the staff had gone along for a picnic lunch; it was a beautiful day for a trip.

It was a beautiful day for a lot of things.

He took off his sunglasses and spotted an open window in the nearest cabin. All the buildings were constructed on concrete plinths with large gray stones underneath.

The place appeared to be deserted; he couldn't see anyone moving around inside.

From his vantage point he had a clear view of the whole area, yet still he hesitated, even though his body was trembling with excitement. Should he risk it?

He paced back and forth, going through the pros and cons. In this weather they'd be out sailing all day. If anyone showed up, he could always say he was lost. No doubt it wouldn't be the first time someone from the marina had wandered into the camp.

There was always an excuse.

Just to be on the safe side, he waited another minute or two before crossing the path. The sign on the cabin told him this was Star. The green door wasn't locked, exactly as he'd expected. It only took a second to push down the handle and slip inside. He paused and gazed around.

So this was where the children slept. The thought excited him, made his heart beat faster.

The list on the door gave him their names. Eight boys sharing a dormitory. Some of them must surely be the right age, eleven or twelve, before puberty kicked in.

He couldn't help smiling as he imagined the naked bodies in these beds. Tan arms, white skin where their clothes had protected them from the sun.

Boys or girls, it didn't really matter. Those who wanted the same thing as he did were interested anyway, regardless of gender.

He'd hoped to find some pajamas lying around, items of clothing he could touch, but he couldn't see any. Most of the beds were properly made up with sheets, but on the one by the window lay a crumpled sleeping bag; maybe it belonged to someone younger?

He went over and picked it up. Inhaled its scent, made it his own. *He's young,* he thought happily.

There were none of the smells associated with puberty to assault his senses, no teenage sweat to spoil the feeling. Inside the sleeping bag he found a neatly printed label: *Benjamin Dufva.*

"Benjamin," he murmured. "Your name is Benjamin."

His mouth went dry, and he had to lick his lips several times.

He felt the familiar throbbing sensation down there. The desire to share his joy, his love. It had gone wrong only once.

He remembered his hands closing around the other boy's slender neck when the screams grew too loud. The lifeless eyes when he finally fell silent.

He turned his attention to a couple of discarded items of clothing that had been underneath the sleeping bag. He picked up a creased pale-blue T-shirt that was inside out. The size told him all he needed to know; the owner had to be ten or eleven years old.

Quickly he checked that he'd closed the door properly. There was still no one around outside, no one to hear or disturb him. He leaned forward and shut the window.

The T-shirt smelled exactly the same as the sleeping bag.

Benjamin, he thought again as he dropped to his knees by the bed and bowed his head.

With a contented sigh he pushed one hand down his pants while clutching the sleeping bag with the other.

He breathed deeply into the shiny fabric and let out a groan of sheer pleasure.

CHAPTER 40

The court had reconvened after breaking for lunch. The food coma was bound to kick in shortly. Dennis Grönstedt, the law clerk, was already yawning.

Jacob Emilsson had presented Winnerman in the best possible light during the morning; now it was up to Nora to see what she could do.

Winnerman was slumped in his seat next to his attorney. He wasn't required to take the stand during questioning.

"It was interesting to hear all the details about this affair," Nora began. "But of course that throws up a whole lot of fresh questions."

Winnerman's chin looked even more swollen now; his entire body was out of alignment. His two teenage sons were sitting in the public gallery, but he wasn't paying any attention to them.

"So you were contacted by a representative from Vine Holdings who suggested you should do business together."

"Yes."

"Via an email from a sender you didn't know?"

Winnerman shuffled. "That's not unusual in our industry. The initial contact is often made through an email."

"I understand. How did you prepare for that first meeting? Did you check out the company in any way?"

"No."

"You didn't take references? Ask for a credit check?"

"No."

Nora raised her eyebrows. "You also indicated that you were surprised when you learned there were problems regarding the land allocation agreement. Didn't you speak to the local authority before you signed the contract?"

"No."

"Sorry?"

"No, I didn't."

"Why not? Wouldn't that have been normal procedure?"

"Maybe." Winnerman loosened his tie.

"I'm afraid you're going to have to explain this a little more clearly," Nora said. "Is it difficult to get in touch with the local authority? I believe they have set times when you can phone. And yet you didn't do it. Was that deliberate?"

"No, I just . . ."

"You just . . . ?"

"It was almost Christmas, there was a lot going on. Plus there were clear guarantees written into the contract, as I said. The agreement was valid for five years." Winnerman glanced at his attorney. "I thought everything was in order."

"So you said."

Nora allowed a few seconds to pass before she asked the next question; she wanted to be sure she had the court's full attention.

"This lawyer you mentioned—what was his name?"

"Anders Johansson."

"That's a very common name. In fact, those are the most common first names and surnames in Sweden."

"Really."

"And guess what—there's no Anders Johansson registered with the Swedish Bar Association practicing in Örebro."

Winnerman didn't manage to look quite surprised enough.

"But you already know that, of course."

"How am I supposed to know that?"

"How indeed."

Nora let the question hang in the air. Judge and jurors were listening closely, and Dennis Grönstedt's fingers were flying over the keyboard.

"Presumably because he doesn't exist," Nora went on. "Because everything you've told us is a lie, fabricated to conceal the fact that you arranged a nonexistent deal and siphoned ten million kronor from Alliance Construction."

"Wait a minute—"

Nora didn't give him the chance to protest. She raised her voice and looked him in the eye. "Let me summarize what you're asking the court to believe. First of all, you were contacted about a multimillion-kronor deal, and made no effort to look into the details more closely, nor did you speak to anyone at the local authority. Second, you met a lawyer who doesn't actually exist, according to the Bar Association. And third, it's pure chance that all the documentation was signed only by you, since your partner *happened* to be suffering from gastric flu." Nora folded her arms. "Do you even believe it yourself?"

Chapter 41

Benjamin adjusted the sail a fraction and ventured a smile at Sofie, who was sitting in the stern with her right hand resting on the tiller.

The sun was shining, and the morning sail had gone well. He didn't think he'd messed up, and Sofie and Lova were happy to have him along.

They'd stopped off at Alskär and had lunch on the shore—fried sausage and potatoes with an egg on top, which was one of his favorites. Now they were heading east along with the other boats in Blue Group. They were roughly in the middle, sailing off the island of Korsö.

Sofie gave an enormous yawn. A few strands of brown hair had escaped from her ponytail and were protruding from beneath her blue cap. From time to time they caressed her cheeks whenever there was a gust of wind. Sofie was her own person; she didn't seem to care what anyone else said or thought. Benjamin wished he could be like her.

"So what's going on with you and Samuel?" she suddenly asked.

Benjamin gave a start. The knot of anxiety in his stomach came back as soon as he heard the name.

"What do you mean?" He hoped his discomfort didn't show.

Sofie gazed at him steadily. "Samuel doesn't like you." She wrinkled her nose. "He's so horrible to you, he's always making nasty comments."

Benjamin didn't know whether to be pleased because Sofie had noticed Samuel's behavior, or embarrassed because it was so obvious.

He didn't want to be a victim of bullying.

"I haven't done anything to him," he mumbled, feeling his face flush red. He turned away, pretending to check the sail.

Another boat had caught up with them; they were sailing side by side approximately twenty yards apart. Fortunately it wasn't Samuel and Sebbe's boat.

"He's vile," Sofie said. "He can be really vicious when he takes a dislike to someone. Just so you know."

Lova waved to the two girls and the boy in the other boat. "We know him," she said. "We were at the same junior high. He was very difficult; sometimes he just lost it, screamed the place down. His eyes used to go kind of weird—almost black." She nibbled a fingernail, then inspected it with interest. "And he always used to cheat when the teachers weren't looking—in exams, or when he was playing football. Everyone knew."

The knot in Benjamin's stomach was getting bigger.

Sofie nodded. "But nobody dared say anything, because he was crazy. Plus his dad knew the principal."

"He's got ADHD," Lova explained. "He had his own teaching assistant in elementary school, but he gets mad if anyone mentions it."

She sounded very serious, as if this were something he really needed to know. Benjamin realized the girls were worried about him.

The waves foamed in their wake.

"Try and stay away from Samuel," Sofie advised. "He's capable of just about anything when he loses control."

Chapter 42

Nora took a few sips of tepid water. The daylight seeped in through the leaded windows. It was time for Bertil Svensson to take the stand.

His defense lawyer should have told him to smarten himself up. Admittedly he'd had a shave, but his jacket was scruffy, and his jeans were crying out for a washing machine. His grubby tie was knotted so carelessly that it reinforced the impression of a man who was down on his luck.

Appearance mattered; the judge and jurors were only human. A well-groomed individual gained more points when it came to trustworthiness than a moth-eaten wreck, however unjust that might seem.

Fanny Ferlin was going to have to work hard for her client.

Nora had read Svensson's file, and was familiar with his background. He'd once worked as a truck driver, traveling the length and breadth of Sweden. His record had been blameless for over twenty years, and he'd been in a stable relationship. Then a patch of black ice and an eighteen-year-old who'd just gained his driving license changed Svensson's life. When he was cut free from the tangled wreckage after many hours, his back was damaged beyond repair.

Early retirement and constant pain made for a devastating combination. The relationship broke down, he lost his apartment, and life became a never-ending quest for booze and pills.

Nora had been far from convinced that he would actually turn up sober, but Fanny Ferlin had somehow managed to talk him into doing so.

Barbro Wikingsson made a note, then looked up. "Fru Ferlin."

Svensson's defense lawyer cleared her throat. She was wearing a long-sleeved blouse, but a colorful butterfly tattoo was just visible below the cuff. Nora realized how much had changed since she'd passed the bar. Back in the day it would have been unthinkable for a young, ambitious legal practitioner to get a tattoo—one that could be seen anyway.

However, Ferlin was fifteen years Nora's junior—a different generation in many ways.

"Bertil," she began, her tone warm and familiar. "Let's talk about these papers you apparently signed."

Svensson straightened up a fraction, but his back was still bent. He looked defeated.

"Do you have any form of training in economics?"

"No—no, I don't."

"Have you ever studied economics?"

"Not exactly."

"Have you worked in the financial sector?"

"No."

"That's what I thought."

Nora understood the tactic. Ferlin was hammering home the message that Svensson knew nothing about finance, and hadn't understood what he was signing.

"So how could you have known that those documents would lead to criminal activity?"

That was a leading question, to say the least. Not allowed, because this wasn't a cross-examination. The judge didn't intervene; maybe she was giving Ferlin a little leeway because Nora had pushed her luck.

"I had no idea," Svensson said.

"Bertil, think carefully before you answer my next question. Did you intend to assist in the execution of a criminal offense?"

"Absolutely not."

Svensson came to life and looked straight at the judge. It seemed as if Ferlin's coaching had had some effect.

"If I'd realized, I never would have signed," he said, his voice trembling. "I swear."

"I believe you," Ferlin assured him. "And I'm sure everyone here feels the same." She tilted her head to one side. "But in that case, why did you agree to be named as the managing director of an unknown company without finding out more about it?"

"I was drunk, of course."

Dennis Grönstedt hid an involuntary smile with his hand.

"And I needed the money," Svensson continued. "It was the beginning of January, and winter was setting in. The payment meant I'd be able to rent a room when the snow came."

Annika Sandberg shook her head sadly.

Ferlin's tactic seemed to be paying off, although Nora thought echoes of Winnerman's testimony still lingered. Ferlin might be young, but she'd done her job much better than Nora had expected.

"Have you finished, fru Ferlin?" Barbro Wikingsson asked.

"Yes, ma'am."

Ferlin put down her pen. Her smile revealed that she was pleased with her contribution.

"In that case, it's over to the prosecution. Fru Linde."

Nora straightened her papers and waited until she'd made eye contact with Bertil Svensson.

"Let's go back to January 11, 2013—the day you met Niklas Winnerman. He approached you in the Hallunda shopping mall and offered you a sum of money in return for taking on the role of managing director of a company by the name of Vine Holdings. Have I got that right?"

Svensson's back was even more bent now, if that were possible.

"I just signed some papers," he said. "It only took a couple of minutes. I don't know what it was all about."

"Didn't you find it strange that someone wanted you to be a company director? That's pretty high-level stuff."

"I don't know."

"Do people often pay you to sign papers?"

"No," Svensson mumbled, almost inaudibly.

Nora frowned. "So you say, but you have a conviction for a similar offense."

She held up the document showing that Svensson had been convicted of accountancy irregularities within a company some years earlier. On that occasion, too, he had been summarily appointed to the board just before the crime came to light. It had cost him several months in jail.

He looked uncomfortable.

"You know what I think? I think you were prepared to sign anything as long as you got paid."

"That's not true."

Nora ignored his response. "So tell me exactly what happened when you met Niklas Winnerman."

Svensson scratched the back of his neck. "I was sitting in the mall with some of the other guys. It was late morning, we'd had a couple of beers." He glanced at Winnerman, who refused to look at him. "He came over and wanted to talk. It sounded simple—all I had to do was sign a couple of documents."

"And he said he'd pay you ten thousand kronor."

"No."

Nora was taken aback; Svensson had already admitted this. Was he about to retract his statement?

"Sorry?"

"At first he offered me eight, but that's not enough for three months' rent, so I told him I needed ten thousand five hundred, or no deal."

Svensson was babbling; Fanny Ferlin's mouth was set in a rigid line.

"So he went and took out more money."

"From the cash machine?"

"No, it was out of order, so he went to the bank."

Another surprise; this was new information. Nora was sure he'd never mentioned this during his interviews.

"The bank?"

"Yes, the one in the mall. Not Nordea, the other one."

It was time to round things off; both the jurors and Dennis Grönstedt were starting to look bored. Even the judge seemed to be having difficulty concentrating. However, Nora hoped she'd made her point: Bertil Svensson was a man whose signature could be bought.

"I believe you knew exactly what you were doing," she said in conclusion. "But you didn't care about the consequences, because you were well paid by the man who approached you—Niklas Winnerman."

CHAPTER 43

Niklas Winnerman sank down onto the toilet seat and buried his face in his hands. He immediately felt a stab of pain; it was impossible to find a position in which his broken ribs didn't hurt as soon as he moved. The emergency medic had prescribed painkillers, but they weren't helping much.

The X-rays had revealed significant cracks in two ribs, but no other fractures, thank God. However, he had bruises all over his body, and had suffered a slight concussion.

"You'll probably feel at your worst after a week or so," the doctor had said, his expression sympathetic. "I'd recommend a week off work and plenty of rest."

Rest.

Niklas had almost laughed out loud, but that would have hurt too much.

The court had taken a twenty-minute recess. Twenty minutes before he had to go back to that stuffy room.

The restroom door opened; Niklas didn't recognize the voices. They sounded young, two guys talking about a friend who'd been accused of assault.

"It was only one punch, for fuck's sake—and the guy deserved it! Asse could wind up in jail for this—it's not right!"

Niklas closed his eyes, tried to get a little more comfortable. He was trembling from a lack of sleep; it had been after four in the morning by the time he got home from the hospital.

Jacob Emilsson had already asked him several times how he was feeling, but Niklas hadn't told him what was going on. No one knew about his gambling debts, and he was in no doubt about how Emilsson would react if he told him.

If the truth came out.

It would be the final nail in the coffin if it somehow reached that bitch of a prosecutor. A perfect motive, which she wouldn't hesitate to present to the court.

His left side was hurting even more, and a dull headache had begun to throb at his temples.

He rubbed his face with both hands. He had no idea how he was going to get through the rest of the day.

CHAPTER 44

Leila Kacim was waiting for Nora outside the courtroom as requested. Nora had discreetly sent her a text message, even though phones were strictly forbidden in court.

She was sitting on a bench under the window checking something on her phone, but she put it in her pocket as soon as Nora emerged, just behind Winnerman's ex-wife and two teenage sons.

Nora quickly summarized her interaction with Bertil Svensson.

"He's now saying that Winnerman took out money from a bank in the Hallunda shopping mall. Were you aware of this?"

Leila shook her head, her long black braid swinging to and fro. "No, but he was never sober when I spoke to him—not once. It was like questioning a goldfish—no memory at all."

Just as Nora had suspected.

"Which bank was it?" Leila asked.

"He didn't know—just that it wasn't Nordea. How many can there be?"

Nora could see that Leila's interest had been aroused; her dark-brown eyes were shining.

"We must be able to Google it." Leila retrieved her phone.

"The bank must have CCTV," Nora said. "Maybe we can find an image of the person who made the withdrawal?"

"If they still have it after such a long time."

Almost a year had passed since Alliance Construction went under. The case had been with the official receiver for months before it was referred to the Economic Crimes Authority, where it had languished until someone got around to it.

It was unlikely that the CCTV footage still existed, but not impossible.

"It's worth a shot," Leila said.

If they could prove that Winnerman had taken out money at approximately the same time as Svensson was handed ten thousand five hundred kronor in cash . . .

Nora couldn't help glancing toward the other end of the hallway; Jacob Emilsson was on the phone, pacing up and down and waving his free hand around. She'd like to hear him explain away photographic evidence of his client in the bank.

A short distance away Fanny Ferlin was sitting with Bertil Svensson. He was drinking from a can of Coke, his hands shaking.

Leila looked up. "According to Google, there are two banks in the Hallunda mall—Handelsbanken and Nordea."

"Can you check with Handelsbanken as soon as possible?"

They didn't have much time; the trial was due to conclude on Wednesday.

"I'll contact them right away."

CHAPTER 45

Nora was the last to take her seat; she directed an apologetic smile at the bench.

Barbro Wikingsson simply raised her eyebrows. "Herr Emilsson, do you have any questions for Bertil Svensson?"

The defense attorney adjusted his tie—a perfect Windsor knot. The sun shining in through the window made him look as if he'd acquired a halo.

"Bertil," he began in a casual tone. "The prosecutor claims that you met my client in early 2013—on Friday, January 11, to be precise. How can you be sure it was Niklas Winnerman who sought you out on that day?"

"I think it was him." Svensson leaned across Fanny Ferlin and pointed to Winnerman. "Him over there, the guy with the glasses."

"You say you *think* it was him." Emilsson slowly stroked his chin. "You're not sure?"

"He said his name was Niklas."

"Did he give you both names? Did he actually introduce himself as Niklas Winnerman?"

"I don't remember. He definitely said Niklas."

"Did he show you any ID?"

"No."

"Did you have any contact at a later date when he perhaps confirmed his identity?"

"No."

"And yet you've pointed him out in this courtroom." Emilsson's voice deepened. "Do you understand the significance of this allegation? We're talking about a serious offense that could mean many years in jail for my client."

Svensson's eyes were darting all over the place.

"Answer the question," Ferlin whispered.

"I think I recognize him . . ."

"What was he wearing when you met?"

"I don't really remember . . . The same glasses, with brown frames. And a baseball cap. He looks like the guy who spoke to me."

"He looks like the guy who spoke to you." Emilsson turned to the judge, his expression skeptical.

Nora shifted on her seat. Svensson wasn't doing too well.

"He had brown hair," Svensson mumbled. "And he was tall."

"In that case let me inform you that Niklas Winnerman is exactly six feet tall. Do you know what the average height is in Sweden?"

"No."

"It's five eleven. You can ask Statistics Sweden if you don't believe me. I can also tell you that one-third of all men in Sweden have dark-brown hair, just like my client. So there are tens of thousands of men who are the same height and have the same hair color." He slowly drummed his fingers on the table. "Bertil, do you remember what you said when your lawyer asked you why you signed the papers?"

Svensson looked from Emilsson to Ferlin and back again. He chewed his upper lip. "Not exactly."

"You said you were drunk."

"Yes?"

"How drunk were you?"

"Pretty drunk."

"Could you be a little more specific? How much had you had to drink?"

"I'd had a few beers with the guys. And some vodka."

"What does that mean? Quarter of a bottle? Half a bottle?"

"More than a quarter, I guess."

"In other words, you'd consumed a considerable amount. Your blood-alcohol level would have been significantly raised. It would have been enough to see you convicted of drunk driving."

"But I wasn't driving!" Svensson protested.

"I'm not saying you were. I'm merely trying to put your alcohol consumption in some kind of context." Emilsson nodded to the judge and jurors. Annika Sandberg was frowning.

Nora hoped it would soon be over. Bertil Svensson's testimony was turning into a disaster.

The clock struck four.

"Most people wouldn't be able to walk or even stand up if they'd drunk as much as you did," Emilsson continued. "And yet you claim that Niklas Winnerman was the man who approached you that day."

Nora knew exactly what he was doing. This was all about sowing the seeds of doubt. He didn't have to disprove anything; there was no need for him to present a case of his own, or to bring in new witnesses.

It was Nora's responsibility to prove that Winnerman had paid Svensson to sign the contract, and had squirreled away the money.

One juror who wasn't convinced by her argument—that was all it would take.

Chapter 46

Dinner was over, and the area outside the dining hall was crowded with kids waiting to hear about the evening's activities.

They'd been told to gather at six fifteen. Most were already there; small groups had formed on the steps of the cabins. A few latecomers were hurrying along.

Benjamin had sat down on a bench in a spot where the sun still lingered. Distractedly he poked at a pine cone with his foot; he felt quite drowsy after a meal of spaghetti Bolognese.

Samuel had left him alone all day, and Sofie had beckoned him over to sit with them for the theory class. They'd shared a chart while plotting courses as part of their navigation training.

It was warm in the sun, nice to rest for a while. Benjamin would have liked to skip the evening program; he had no desire to move. He also had a slightly sore throat, no doubt as a result of being forced into the water to retrieve his clothes the previous day.

"Hi, everyone!"

Isak had appeared along with Wille, the new instructor who was also responsible for Blue Group. Wille had cropped red hair and was taller than Isak.

Benjamin straightened up, trying not to belch.

Wille waved a bundle of papers. "OK, guys, listen up. We're going to have a quiz this evening, and there's a great prize for the winning team!"

Isak took over. "We're going to divide you into teams of three. The questions are distributed all over the island, and you'll be given a map to help you find them."

Sofie groaned. "Do we have to? Can't we just chill?" She was sitting on the ground with her back against a tree trunk, and seemed to have eaten as much as Benjamin.

"This will be so much fun!" Wille said, beaming at her.

Isak tucked in his shirt at the back and gazed at the group for a few seconds. "So let's sort these teams."

Samuel stepped forward. "Benjamin can come with me and Sebbe."

Benjamin stared at him. What was he up to? There was no way Samuel would want to spend time with him voluntarily, not in a million years. Samuel came and stood beside him, ignoring his stunned expression. Sebbe joined them.

Benjamin looked around for Sofie, but he was too late. Isak handed over the answer grid, a small map, and a pencil.

"There you go. You've got two hours to find the questions and fill in the answers. When you've finished, come back here, and we'll work out the results before suppertime." Isak gave them an encouraging wink. "Don't get lost—the island's bigger than you might think." Then he divided the rest of the group into teams.

Benjamin saw that Sofie and Tindra were together, while Lova ended up with two other girls. One by one the teams set off toward the forest.

Benjamin swallowed, trying to figure out what Samuel had in mind. He definitely wasn't trying to be nice.

The previous evening Benjamin had finally found his life jacket, stuffed away at the back of a closet. He knew he hadn't put it there.

Sofie's words echoed inside his head:

143

Try and stay away from Samuel.

Just as he was about to ask if he could be on a different team, Isak raised a hand in farewell.

"Off you go, boys—no point in hanging around here. See you later!"

He and Wille headed for the instructors' common room. Maja was coming from the other direction; Isak's face lit up and he hurried to meet her.

"Are you any good at quizzes?" Samuel said, poking Benjamin in the side with his elbow. "I'm fucking useless."

Benjamin shrugged.

"You're OK about yesterday, aren't you?" Samuel went on. "We were only messing around."

Isak disappeared indoors.

"Look at that!" Samuel said suddenly, pointing up at the sky.

When Benjamin tipped his head back to look, Samuel punched him on the chin.

"Ha ha—just messing around again!"

Sebbe laughed, as he always did when prompted by Samuel. Benjamin forced himself to smile; the blow had been too hard to be a joke. He needed to pee, but Samuel was already on the move.

CHAPTER 47

Nora had left the courthouse as soon as the proceedings ended for the day. She wanted to get away from the stuffy atmosphere and the sense of failure following Emilsson's questioning of Bertil Svensson.

On top of all that, there was a delay on the subway; it took an eternity to reach Slussen, where she changed to the Saltsjö line. It felt as if the train was crawling along, and it was six thirty before it finally reached her stop. She hurried home carrying her heavy briefcase; she was sweating as she unlocked the front door.

"Hello?"

"Mommy!"

Julia came racing from the living room. Nora could hear the sound of a children's TV show in the background.

"I talked to Daddy!"

Julia had a ketchup stain on her T-shirt.

"Daddy called?"

"He's flying!"

Nora bent down and picked up her daughter. Adam emerged from the kitchen clutching a half-eaten sandwich.

"Hi, Mom," he mumbled with his mouth full.

"Hi, sweetheart—did Jonas call?"

"About fifteen minutes ago."

Such a small amount of time.

Adam tickled Julia under the chin and made her giggle, then turned back to the kitchen. "By the way, we're out of milk," he announced.

"Wait a second—come back here."

Nora had to stand on tiptoe to kiss his cheek. He'd graduated from high school two weeks ago, specializing in natural sciences. The family had celebrated by putting up a huge photo of Adam as a ten-month-old baby, lying on a towel fresh from his bath.

She'd always liked that picture; she could still remember the moment when she held his little body to her breast. That special baby smell, gone forever.

You were so tiny, and now you're so tall . . .

She'd been different then, a younger Nora. More naïve, but also more excited, with no idea of what taking care of a newborn actually involved. Feeling simultaneously terrified and fiercely protective.

Nothing like the woman who gave birth to Julia at the age of forty-two.

With each passing year she saw more and more of Henrik in their son, although his character had evolved into a mixture of her ex-husband's unshakeable self-confidence and her own slightly reserved approach. Sometimes his gestures were so like Henrik's that it was positively eerie.

Suddenly she felt dizzy. She carefully lowered Julia to the floor and sank down on the stool next to the mirror in the hallway. Julia ran back to her TV show.

It had been such a long day.

Nora closed her eyes and rested her head on the wall. Then she took out her phone and rang Jonas. A voice said something in Thai that she didn't understand—presumably that her call couldn't be put through. She would have loved to talk to him for a while, tell him about the trial.

Hear his voice.

She was used to Jonas being away on long-haul flights, and yet she couldn't help feeling anxious, even though his employer was one of Europe's most reliable airlines in terms of safety.

I'm just tired, she thought. *My mind is playing tricks on me.*

She gazed at her engagement ring, white gold with three inset diamonds. The stones sparkled as they caught the light.

The proposal had taken her by surprise last summer. They'd been sitting on the glassed-in veranda at the Brand villa, Nora wrapped in a blanket, shaken and upset after a devastating fire that had broken out on the island.

Jonas asking her to marry him was the last thing she'd expected at that moment, but the answer had never been in doubt, even though she'd promised herself she would never remarry and risk the kind of pain she'd felt after the divorce from Henrik.

She ought to eat something. And change her clothes. She stayed exactly where she was, blinking several times to clear her vision.

She tried Jonas again, but the same voice simply relayed the same message.

CHAPTER 48

Niklas Winnerman rubbed his eyes, exhaustion weakening his body like a fever. As he reached for the bottle of beer, he felt a stab of pain in his left side; he couldn't suppress a groan.

Hearing Nora Linde paint him as the villain of the piece had been a horrible experience, especially in front of Albert and Natan. He hadn't even been able to bring himself to look at them after the first half hour. Although they'd waited for him outside when proceedings were over, he'd hurried away without speaking to them.

They mustn't come to court tomorrow; he couldn't cope with them being there to witness his public humiliation.

He pushed away the plate of bacon and eggs he'd cooked, and laboriously got to his feet to toss the food in the trash.

His cell phone rang.

"You called?"

Jacob Emilsson never wasted time with small talk on the phone. Niklas didn't usually mind, but this evening he would have appreciated a little more warmth.

"I just wondered . . . How do you think it went?"

Emilsson had rushed off straight away; Niklas hadn't had the chance to speak to him. After a few beers he'd left several messages asking his attorney to contact him.

"It was the first day."

Not helpful.

"But what did you think?" Niklas persisted. He could almost hear a sigh on the other end of the line.

"The prosecutor took a pretty aggressive approach."

It was nice to know he wasn't the only one who'd thought that fucking bitch had gone in too hard with her theatrical attempts to frame him. She thought she was something special, just because she was a prosecutor. Everything had sounded so much worse coming from Nora Linde.

"What do you think Christian's going to say?" Niklas hated the fact that he sounded so anxious.

Emilsson let out a bark of laughter. "You should know that better than I do."

Christian was due to give his testimony tomorrow. The very thought made Niklas feel sick.

Emilsson cleared his throat. "I'm sorry, but I have to go—you know how it is. I'll see you in the morning—five to ten outside the courtroom." He was gone before Niklas could ask another question.

Niklas sank down in his armchair and sat there with the phone in his hand. As if in a trance, he scrolled through his address book until he reached the letter C.

Only Christian could help him. Without his damning testimony, the court wouldn't be able to convict Niklas—Emilsson had more or less said so. The prosecutor needed Christian to confirm that a crime had been committed—it was that simple.

"Getting caught making a bad deal isn't illegal," Emilsson had stated.

Niklas had already called way too many times, begging Christian not to give evidence against him. At first, he'd mainly picked up the phone when he was drunk, but over the past few days, he'd been trying twenty-four seven.

He got up and fetched another beer from the refrigerator.

He gasped as he sat down again; the pain was agonizing. He reached into his pocket for his painkillers and swallowed a white pill, rinsed it down with a swig of beer.

He stared at the screen, the thoughts going around and around in his mind. He kept reaching the same conclusion.

He had no intention of ending up in jail because of Christian Dufva.

CHAPTER 49

Benjamin trailed along behind Samuel and Sebbe, even though he was pretty sure they were heading in the wrong direction. They were on the north side of the island, far away from the camp. Question seven had been displayed on the last board, but that was at least fifteen minutes ago. They'd searched for the next one, but had failed to find it.

Samuel was striding along resolutely.

Benjamin looked up; the pine forest was much denser here than in the south. They'd passed Heinecke's Tower and continued in a straight line.

Where had all the others gone?

The only sound was their own footsteps, the pine cones crunching beneath their feet. They should have come across the other groups by now.

Samuel stopped in a small clearing where the ground was covered in yellow needles.

Benjamin desperately needed to pee; he wondered if he could go behind a bush. But what would Samuel and Sebbe do if he pulled down his pants in front of them? He decided to try and hang on for a while.

"Don't you think we should turn back?" he ventured. "There won't be any questions this far out."

Samuel shook his head. "The next board must be here somewhere. I vote we keep looking." He glanced at Sebbe, who was busy scratching a mosquito bite until it bled. "What do you think? Shall we search around here?"

"Yes . . . good idea."

Benjamin felt more uncomfortable with every passing minute. He didn't trust Samuel, didn't trust his assertion that he'd only been "messing around" yesterday. He stared at his Wellington boots and thought about the sneaker that was at the bottom of the sea somewhere.

"But none of the others are around," he said tentatively, not wanting to provoke Samuel. "I don't see how there can be any questions so far away from the camp."

Samuel waved the map in front of his nose. "Are you trying to tell me I don't know how to read a map?"

"That's not what I meant. I'm just saying maybe we should look somewhere else."

Samuel came closer. "Like where?"

"I don't know—nearer the camp?" Benjamin stepped back and bumped into a tree.

"Are you saying we've gone the wrong way? Did you hear that, Sebbe? Do you agree with him?"

"Calm down, OK?"

Sebbe was trying to sound cool, but Benjamin could tell he was getting nervous. It was still daylight, but the tall pines were blocking out the evening sun. The forest was gloomy, and the temperature was dropping.

Benjamin shivered.

Samuel moved so that he was blocking the path leading back to the camp. He stood with his legs apart, arms folded.

"So you don't like my map-reading skills. Anything else you don't like?"

At close quarters it was clear how strong he was, broad-shouldered and muscular. His nails were bitten to the quick.

Benjamin just wanted to get away. Maybe he could sneak past Samuel? He didn't know what the older boy had in mind, but the expression in Samuel's eyes scared him.

Sebbe said nothing; he just continued to pick at the open sore around the mosquito bite.

"Go on, tell me," Samuel insisted.

Benjamin remembered when his father had stopped the car to avoid running over a rabbit. It had looked so feeble in the beam of the headlights, absolutely terrified. That was exactly how he was feeling right now.

"So where do you think I went wrong?" Samuel was almost spitting out the words. "We need to sort this out. You know what the instructors say when a 'conflict situation' arises. It's important to talk to each other."

Benjamin's tongue was thick and uncooperative. "Can't we just go back?" he whispered, knowing that wasn't going to happen.

Samuel laughed, and Benjamin realized how much he was enjoying the situation.

He's crazy.

Samuel looked different now, almost excited.

"Of course we can. If you ask me nicely enough." Slowly he undid the buckle of his brown leather belt and slid it out of the loops. "But I don't think you'll be able to manage that." He held the belt in his hand and flicked it menacingly at the ground.

Something warm and wet ran down Benjamin's legs, turning his jeans a darker shade of blue.

"Oh my God, he's pissed himself!" Samuel exclaimed, eyes shining.

Benjamin could no longer hold back the tears. "Please let me go," he sobbed.

Samuel flicked the belt again, and Benjamin sobbed even harder.

"Stop it," Sebbe said suddenly.

"What the hell's wrong with you? Are you too chicken?" Samuel snapped.

Sebbe rolled his eyes. "I don't give a shit about him, but we need to finish the quiz before it gets too late; otherwise we'll be in trouble with the instructors."

Samuel tightened his grip on the belt. "I'm sure we'll have time to do that as well."

CHAPTER 50

Benjamin closed his eyes, waiting for the blow. All at once he heard an unfamiliar voice.

"What are you boys up to?"

He opened his eyes and saw a man wearing sunglasses and a baseball cap, standing by the blueberry bushes a short distance away. Benjamin ran over to the man and babbled:

"We're from the sailing camp, we're doing a quiz but we can't find the boards with the questions on them, can you help us?"

His heart was pounding so hard he could hear the blood rushing in his ears. He grabbed the man's left arm, desperate to stop him from leaving.

"What's your name?"

"Benjamin."

The man smiled warmly and placed a hand on his shoulder. "What a great name."

Benjamin was determined not to leave the man's side as long as Samuel and Sebbe were around.

"And how old are you?" said his savior, his hand still resting on Benjamin's shoulder.

"Eleven—I'll be twelve in November."

"That's a great age to go with a great name."

Out of the corner of his eye, Benjamin saw Samuel and Sebbe begin to move backward, then they turned and ran in the direction of the camp.

The man repeated his name; he almost seemed to taste it, which was a little weird, but Benjamin was so relieved he didn't care.

"Benjamin. And are you OK, Benjamin? It looked as if you might have been having problems with those other boys."

"It was nothing," Benjamin mumbled, hoping he wouldn't ask any more questions.

It was even darker in the forest now. Something rustled in a bush behind them, but no animal appeared. The man bent down and contemplated Benjamin's jeans. The dark stain was unmistakable, and Benjamin lowered his head.

"Would you like to come to my boat for a Coke?" the man said without commenting on the mark. "We could play a computer game—I've got Wi-Fi on board."

The kindly voice almost made Benjamin burst into tears again. He really wanted to go with the man, avoid returning to the camp and seeing Samuel and Sebbe again, but he didn't dare. Isak would go crazy if he was late again.

"I have to go," he said reluctantly.

"Surely you've got time for a short visit? You look as if you need to take it easy for a little while."

He couldn't see the man's eyes behind the dark glasses, but Benjamin felt the warmth of his concern.

Everything seemed better now. It was nice to meet an adult who cared about him. He hesitated; a little while would be fine, wouldn't it?

The sound of voices interrupted his train of thought. Sofie and Tindra appeared farther down the path.

"Benjamin—are you OK?" Sofie shouted as they ran toward him.

"We have to get back," Tindra added. "We don't want to be late."

The man frowned, then quickly patted Benjamin on the cheek. "Stop by tomorrow if you like. My boat's in the inner harbor; it's a white Aqualine with a blue cabin. Just pop in anytime."

Before Benjamin could reply, the man turned and disappeared among the trees.

CHAPTER 51

Niklas Winnerman was sitting on the sofa listening to the phone ring. His headache wouldn't let up, and it was impossible to find a comfortable position because of his injured ribs.

Three, four, five rings, then voice mail kicked in and Christian's dry voice asked him to leave his name and number.

Christian hadn't picked up since he'd yelled at Niklas on Friday. There was no point in leaving a message; Christian was never going to call back. However, Niklas had to make him listen; the guy was in the process of destroying his life. The least he could do was speak to him.

This was all because of that bitch Nora Linde. Niklas hated her so much he couldn't think straight.

What could he do to make Christian answer?

He searched through the apps and found the symbol for "number withheld." Worth a try.

He waited ten minutes, then tried again. Once again the phone rang three, four times, but then he heard a familiar voice.

"Hello?"

"Christian!"

"So it was you."

Those few words told Niklas that Christian had hesitated before answering, but it was too late now.

"Please don't hang up," he said, aware that he was on the verge of tears. "Just give me a couple of minutes."

"What do you want?"

Niklas forced himself not to give way to panic. He had to remain calm; the rest of his life depended on this conversation.

"I'm so sorry things turned out the way they did," he said, keeping his voice steady. "I've tried to tell you that, many times."

"What do you want?" Christian said again, speaking very quietly.

Niklas searched for the right thing to say; he had to move Christian, stop him from letting his anger take over in court tomorrow. Niklas was angry, too, filled with bitterness that his former partner had turned against him after all these years, but he knew Christian would hang up immediately if he showed his true feelings. He had to come crawling, even though the shame and humiliation threatened to choke him.

If he was sent to jail, he would never get his life back, never be able to pay off his debt to Artūras. He didn't dare think about what Artūras and his henchmen would subject him to behind bars.

He clenched his fist, his nails digging into the fleshy part of his palm.

"I want to ask you . . . I just wish . . . ," he began, but he was immediately interrupted by a joyless laugh. He couldn't go on.

"I wish I'd never met you," Christian said after a long pause. "I wish we'd never set up the company together."

Niklas could almost see Christian shaking his head, as he always did when he was disappointed. Once again he was overwhelmed by a sense of shame, but he couldn't give in to it.

"You can't testify against me tomorrow," he said, clutching the phone. "If you do, you'll ruin me. I'll go to jail, Christian. They'll lock me up for years."

He waited for a reaction; nothing.

"Hello?" he said eventually.

There was a strange sniveling noise; was Christian crying?

He heard a door opening in the background, high heels crossing the floor, a baby whimpering. Then a woman spoke:

"Christian, Benjamin's on the landline. He wants to talk to you right away."

"Is he calling from Lökholmen? From the sailing camp?"

Christian's voice was muted; presumably he'd put his hand over the microphone.

"You need to take it—he's really upset," the woman said.

"I have to go."

Christian's name disappeared from the display as he ended the call. Niklas slowly placed his phone on the table. There was no point in trying to contact Christian again, no hope of any support from that quarter.

Tomorrow he would be a dead man.

He grabbed the bottle of beer and hurled it at the wall behind the TV with as much force as he could muster. Broken glass went everywhere; beer splashed over the walls and carpet. He covered his face with his hands and sobbed.

He had to stop Christian from taking the stand, and he was prepared to do whatever was necessary.

He dragged himself to his feet, his ribs more painful than ever. He was pushing another pill out of its blister pack when he was struck by a fresh idea.

Maybe it was time to fight fire with fire?

CHAPTER 52

Benjamin shifted from foot to foot as he waited. He hadn't gone to the debriefing in the dining hall, but had crept along to the instructors' common room where there was a phone on the wall. With his heart in his mouth, he'd called his dad. The cell phone was busy, but he remembered the number for Ninna's apartment.

He froze when she answered; for a few seconds he couldn't say a word.

"Is Daddy there?" he managed eventually.

"Benjamin, is that you?"

"Is Daddy there?"

His little brother, Emil, was wailing in the background, but Ninna ignored him. She seemed to realize that Benjamin was upset.

"Are you OK, sweetheart?"

It was hard to control his voice. "Can I speak to Daddy?"

"Just a minute. He's in the living room on his cell phone."

Benjamin was trying to keep watch through the grubby window. He didn't dare sit down on the sofa in case the door opened. There was a dead fly smeared across the inside pane.

The receiver felt warm and sticky in his hand.

Why didn't Daddy come?

Footsteps outside made him grip the phone even harder. A twig snapped.

Please, Daddy.

Suddenly he saw David walking along the path from the dining hall. Benjamin stared at the phone, his eyes filling with tears.

Please, Daddy, please.

David mustn't find him; kids weren't allowed in here without permission.

Isak would be furious.

Benjamin slammed down the receiver and looked around; he had to find somewhere to hide, but there was no other way out, not even a closet or bathroom to duck into. He couldn't crawl under the sofas, and if he crouched down in the kitchen area, David would see him in seconds.

"David?"

Someone was calling outside, and David stopped just yards from the door. It was Maja, waving and holding up a sheet of paper. David turned and went to join her.

Benjamin's entire body was shaking.

Should he try to contact his father again? He'd already called his mother, but her cell phone was switched off. She was probably at work; she wasn't allowed to have her phone with her when she was at the hospital.

The thought of his mother made him want to cry again. He reached out for the receiver, then thought better of it. David might be back at any minute; it was too risky.

His jeans were cold and wet with pee; he had to change before anyone saw him. He opened the door and ran.

CHAPTER 53

The surface of the water was smooth and shining, apart from the odd ripple caused by a stickleback darting along.

He was sitting in the stern of his boat enjoying a beer; he'd decided to stay outdoors for a while, even though the mosquitoes were becoming active. They didn't really bother him; he rarely got more than a couple of bites.

Maybe they didn't find him sufficiently attractive? Maybe his blood wasn't sweet enough?

The thought amused him.

This evening he'd met Benjamin for the first time.

Benjamin.

He repeated the name, remembering how he'd felt when he placed his hand on the boy's shoulder. The warmth of Benjamin's body through his T-shirt, the sweet little mouth with those pink lips.

The two older boys had been picking on Benjamin, that much had been obvious. But the bullies had played right into his hands; Benjamin had been so relieved when he appeared.

A knight in shining armor.

This was a new role, which also made him smile. The teenagers didn't know what a favor they'd done him. Sometimes it was hard to win children's trust, persuade them to come along voluntarily, but this time everything had been handed to him on a plate.

It was almost like the previous occasion, which had ended so badly. He would make sure this was different.

By now Benjamin would be back in camp, getting ready for bed. Soon he would brush his teeth and take off his clothes before sliding into his blue sleeping bag.

Did he keep his underpants on, or did he sleep naked?

His breathing grew heavier as he imagined Benjamin on the way to bed. The boy slept nearest the window, which was usually left open despite the mosquitoes; otherwise it would be too warm with all those children in one room.

A little splash attracted his attention. A silver flash disappeared beneath the boat, leaving faint rings on the water. When he looked up, he saw a small yacht approaching. A woman was standing on the foredeck with a rope in her hand, ready to moor up for the night.

He wasn't pleased. The other boats had left the inner marina during the morning; he'd hoped to be alone here for a few more days.

He finished his beer. Maybe he'd take a stroll after sunset, wander past the camp.

Say good night to Benjamin.

CHAPTER 54

Isak opened the door of the common room and put down the box David had asked him to take to the evening meeting. It was ten thirty; they were all due to gather in fifteen minutes.

His cell phone rang.

As always he felt a faint sense of unease when he saw *Dad* on the display. Those three letters were enough to make him wonder what he'd done wrong this time. He just hoped his father hadn't found out about Clara running away.

He couldn't cope with yet another lecture about his defects in comparison with his older siblings—Mia and Linus, who had never doubted their own ability. Mia had already completed her law degree, and Linus was at the Royal Institute of Technology.

Isak was so sick of having the two of them held up as role models.

He dreamed of studying cinematography, but his father assumed Isak would apply to the Stockholm School of Economics, just as he'd done. Isak was destined for a career in banking and finance—a real profession.

But Isak's grades were nowhere near good enough to get in, especially after all the time he'd had off sick. His fingers found the bottle of pills in his pocket. He couldn't help touching it, just to reassure himself that it was still there.

His father had never accepted that he was actually ill when he was diagnosed with depression and the darkness took over. He simply stated that Isak was tired; he just needed to pull himself together and everything would be fine.

Isak realized that he found his son's condition embarrassing. It would have been better if Isak had broken his leg or contracted pneumonia—something that could be explained within his father's social circle.

No one talked about depression.

His phone rang for the third time. Isak briefly considered rejecting the call, but he couldn't do it.

"Hello."

"When will you be back from camp?"

His father never bothered with a greeting.

"Why?"

"When will you be home?"

"Thursday night."

"I need to go into town early on Friday to pick up some chairs for the Midsummer party. You'll have to come with me to help."

Isak wanted to protest; one of the other instructors was having a party at his summer cottage on a different island, and Isak had arranged to go with David. Maja would be there, too. Isak had been so pleased to be invited; he'd felt he belonged, for the first time in what seemed like years.

But it was impossible to say no to his father.

"When will we be back?" he asked, hoping his disappointment was obvious.

"Twelve at the latest. The guests are due at three, and we need time to set up everything."

That would be too late for David.

"Sorry, that doesn't work for me," he ventured. "I need to leave by eleven—I'm going to another party."

"Don't be difficult, Isak. I'll see you on Thursday."

The call ended abruptly. Isak stared at his phone, recognizing the familiar angst that had nowhere to go. The blackness he must try to resist.

At least his father didn't seem to have heard about Clara. Isak attempted to calm his breathing.

The phone on the wall rang, and Isak answered.

"Lökholmen sailing camp—Isak speaking."

"Hi, Isak, this is Christian Dufva, Benjamin's father. I'm sorry to call so late."

"No problem."

"I'm hoping you can help me out. I was thinking of dropping by tomorrow evening with a couple of things Benjamin left behind, but I'm not sure which cabin he's in."

"It's Star—the first red building you reach if you're coming from Skothalarfladen."

"Of course, I remember now."

Christian Dufva laughed with a warmth Isak had never encountered in his own father.

"By the way, which is Benjamin's bed? I can just leave his things there if he's out sailing when I arrive."

Isak thought for a moment. "It's on the starboard side—the bottom bunk by the window on the right."

"Great—thanks for your help!"

Isak put down the phone. His father would never have traveled over with anything Isak had forgotten. He would have said that Isak had only himself to blame, and that would have been the end of the matter.

CHAPTER 55

In some strange way everything was calmer after the phone call. Niklas Winnerman allowed his shoulders to drop. The next day no longer seemed like a deep black hole, ready to suck him in at any moment. The favor he'd just requested would cost him dear, but it was worth every penny. He was in debt anyway, and if his only way to pay back what he owed was to increase the sum temporarily, then so be it.

A few glasses of vodka had also helped to steady his nerves.

The doctor had said that the painkillers he'd prescribed mustn't be taken in conjunction with alcohol under any circumstances—but what did he know?

Niklas licked his lips as he went into the kitchen to pour himself one last drink. Then he must go to bed, gather his strength for tomorrow.

"Couldn't you smarten yourself up a little?" Emilsson had said when they met outside the courtroom. Tomorrow he would show that smug bastard. He'd already laid out his best suit, with an elegant shirt and tie that complemented each other perfectly. Armani, bought from his favorite store in Östermalm.

He glanced at his watch: almost eleven thirty. Then his eyes strayed to the laptop on the table.

It was like a chemical reaction in his blood. From zero to a hundred—that was how fast it happened when the urge hit him, a tingling feeling that wouldn't go away.

A dragon had to be given the right food.

There were those who would call it an addiction, but he refused to see it that way. He'd looked up the symptoms on a website, read about people who spent all their time gambling, whose social life withered to nothing because human contact became meaningless.

Dependence manifested itself through stress, lies, and mental health issues, none of which applied to him. He wasn't obsessed, and he hadn't spoken to anyone. Neither the boys nor his ex-wife was aware of what he did, but he'd never lied to them. On the contrary—he certainly hadn't lost control, despite the year from hell. OK, so he'd had to take out a fresh loan on the apartment and sell his shares, and when the payday loan hadn't been enough, he'd had to resort to other measures. And in the end he'd contacted Artūras.

But it had been his own choice.

His stomach flipped at the thought of the Lithuanian.

Niklas hadn't had much success recently, but something told him that his luck was about to change, that it was his turn at last. If he could win it all back, he would be able to fix his life, pay off his debts, including the one he'd incurred this evening.

He poured himself a vodka and sat down. It took only a second to open up the computer and log in. His energy level shot up as he typed his password.

His blood was positively fizzing and singing. He was going to recoup his losses; he could feel it in every fiber of his body. He usually visited various sites depending on his mood, but this time he was in no doubt.

This was a night for craps.

CHAPTER 56

Tuesday, June 17

The sun was shining in through the window when Isak opened his eyes. Wille was still fast asleep in the bed opposite, lying on his back with his mouth half-open.

Isak smiled.

The feeling came from nowhere; he just knew that the anxiety had left his body for the first time since Clara ran away. He'd slept properly for once, rather than lying awake worrying about the things he should have done differently. After the incident with Clara, he'd been terrified of being sent home, terrified that everyone, especially his father, would see that he wasn't up to the job.

But now it was all fine. He was in control, and Wille was here.

Today he would call his father and make it clear that they would need to go into town earlier on Friday morning if he wanted Isak to help with the chairs. He was determined to stick up for himself for once. He wanted to celebrate Midsummer with Maja.

Last night he'd chatted for a while with the boys in Blue Group. The atmosphere seemed to have improved; they'd gotten to know one another a little better. Only Benjamin remained on the periphery. He'd been curled up in his sleeping bag when Isak arrived, so Isak hadn't had the chance to tell him his father had been in touch.

Maybe it wasn't surprising that the older boys didn't really bother with Benjamin; he was only a few years younger, but it made a huge difference. It was good of Samuel and Sebbe to take him with them for the quiz.

Isak turned over in bed. It was twenty to seven, but the room was already warm.

The birds were singing outside the window.

It's going to be a good day, he thought as he stretched luxuriously. He would see Maja at breakfast, and the weather was going to be glorious. Everything was better.

A sense of anticipation spread through his body.

Roll call took place before breakfast as usual. Blue Group had assembled in the clearing behind the dining hall, waiting impatiently for Isak to count them.

Fifteen, sixteen, seventeen.

There were supposed to be eighteen children.

He counted again. Still only seventeen.

He felt panic begin to stir in his belly, but pulled himself together.

"Has anyone seen Benjamin? Samuel, do you know where he is?"

Samuel looked offended. "How should I know? I'm not his fucking mother."

Sebbe sniggered, but Isak didn't have the energy to reprimand them. He rubbed the back of his neck. Wondered what to do.

"I'm hungry," Tindra announced.

"OK, guys, go and have breakfast while I look for Benjamin."

Isak set off for the showers. Over and over again he'd stressed the importance of keeping an eye on the time, but it just went in one ear and out the other.

Maja was standing on the steps outside one of the girls' cabins as he went by. He'd noticed her on the way to the showers earlier. Today she was wearing deck shoes instead of Wellington boots, and the sight of her tan legs made him want to whistle. Maybe he could persuade her to join him in the sauna this evening.

"Where are you going?" she asked.

There was something of an invitation in her tone of voice.

"One of my kids was missing during roll call—Benjamin, the youngest one. He's a real dreamer—always has his head in the clouds."

Maja's blonde hair was shining in the morning sunlight.

"Have you checked the toilet stalls?" she said. "He's probably sitting in there with a comic, no idea what time it is."

"I was just on my way to take a look."

Maja gathered her hair into a ponytail and ran down the steps. Suddenly they were standing very close to each other. He gazed into her blue-gray eyes.

She'd just brushed her teeth; he could smell peppermint. He placed the palm of his hand against her cheek; her soft skin was cool beneath his fingertips.

"You're so lovely," he murmured.

She took his hand and drew him into the empty cabin. "Everyone's at breakfast—there's no one here."

She led him into one of the dormitories, wrapped her arms around him, and pressed her body to his.

Eyes like a cat's.

He ought to go and find Benjamin, but Maja was probably right: the kid was sitting on the toilet. He wouldn't miss breakfast.

Maja parted her lips; they tasted every bit as good as Isak had imagined.

CHAPTER 57

Christian Dufva had just knotted his tie in front of the hall mirror when his cell phone rang. He'd slept badly, had to force down a cup of coffee and a sandwich for breakfast.

Number withheld.

Niklas, making one last attempt to dissuade him from testifying?

He left the phone lying on the table. He would have to set off for the courthouse very soon. At least the end was in sight.

Voice mail took over, but after a few seconds the phone started ringing again. Nora Linde's number was also withheld; maybe she was trying to reach him? Christian hesitated, then decided to answer.

"Hello?"

"Listen very carefully."

The man had a strong accent, and his voice was so menacing that Christian's mouth went dry.

"Who are you?" he managed to force out.

"That doesn't matter. All you have to do is listen."

There was a lot of noise in the background, as if the man were on a busy street. Christian thought about ending the call, but something stopped him.

His tie was too tight, and he tried to loosen the knot with one hand. That didn't work; he had to insert a finger between his neck and the collar to get some air.

The unknown voice explained what would happen if Christian didn't do exactly as he said.

Through a fog of confusion, Christian confirmed that he understood, that he would follow the instructions he'd just been given.

He wasn't to contact the police—if he did, then the worst would happen, and his family would suffer the consequences.

There was a click as the man hung up.

"Wait, please wait! Don't hang up!"

The conversation had lasted no more than a minute, but it was enough.

He looked in the mirror and saw a gray face staring back. He wanted to smooth down his hair, but his hands were shaking too much. He couldn't fix his tie either.

He should have let the call go to voice mail, or switched off his phone.

A wave of nausea came over him, and he rushed into the bathroom. A slimy mixture of coffee and a cheese sandwich splashed down into the toilet. He retched until there was nothing left but bile.

He sank down on the floor and rested his head against the wall.

"Are you OK? What are you doing in there?" Ninna called from outside the door.

There was a horrible taste in his mouth; he tore off a couple of pieces of toilet paper and wiped his face.

"Christian?"

"I'm coming. Leave me alone."

Ninna mustn't find out what was going on, no one must find out.

Don't contact the police.

The words rang in his ears.

He had no doubt that the man was capable of carrying out his threat. That couldn't be allowed to happen, not at any price.

He saw little Emil in his mind's eye. Ninna.

Benjamin.

He didn't dare think of the consequences if he failed.

CHAPTER 58

"See you later."

Maja kissed Isak on the lips, adjusted her T-shirt, and disappeared in the direction of the dining hall, where Yellow Group was waiting.

Isak looked at his diver's watch: almost nine o'clock. He'd have to miss breakfast; it would soon be time to talk the students through the day's program. He also needed to make sure Benjamin had shown up.

He ran a hand through his hair and just managed to get out the door before two girls from the dormitory came along to pick up their stuff.

Isak couldn't hold back a foolish smile.

There were kids all over the place now. Half an hour earlier they'd been in the dining hall, but now they were running around gathering everything they needed.

Isak hurried down to the wooden jetty. Some of the girls had already opened up the storage shed and were busy carrying out ropes and sails.

"Has Benjamin turned up?" he asked Sofie and Lova as they emerged with their arms full of equipment.

In his head he was still with Maja.

"No—he's supposed to be helping!"

The girls went over to the nearest boat and set to work.

Isak counted his group again—still only seventeen. His fingers started tingling in the old familiar way.

He spotted Tindra by one of the other boats. "Have you seen Benjamin? Was he at breakfast?"

She shook her head. "I haven't seen him all morning. Ask the boys."

A heavy weight had settled in Isak's belly, even though there was no reason to fear the worst. Benjamin had forgotten the time, just as Maja had suggested. However, he was beginning to wish he hadn't gone into the dormitory with her; he should have focused on finding the boy.

Wille was coming toward him with the charts.

"I can't find Benjamin," Isak said immediately, without going into details. "Have you seen him?"

The expression on Wille's face gave him the answer. His stomach contracted.

"I'll go and look for him," Wille said. He didn't seem particularly bothered, which was reassuring. Isak decided he was probably worrying about nothing. What were the odds that another kid would run away?

He still broke out into a sweat as he followed the same procedure as a few days earlier, when Clara disappeared. He shook his hands to try to get rid of the numbness.

Part of him wanted to organize the kids into search parties, but on the other hand that would cause unnecessary panic, and the parents wouldn't be happy when they found out.

David would go crazy, not to mention the head office.

Everyone would realize that Isak wasn't in control of his group, and it would confirm his father's view that Isak wasn't up to the job.

His heart was pounding, just like last time. He was gasping for air.

He'd already checked both the dining hall and the showers. The dormitory was empty.

Where the hell could Benjamin be?

CHAPTER 59

Nora entered court five and sat down to the left of the bench. She had dressed carefully this morning, choosing a tailored jacket with a pencil skirt, and she'd put on more makeup than she normally did. It was a kind of armor that boosted her confidence.

Jacob Emilsson was opposite her, with his tiepin and three-piece suit as usual, despite the warmth of the early summer's day. Nora had already greeted Emilsson, Fanny Ferlin, and their clients outside the courtroom.

Winnerman was clearly still in pain, and the scrape beneath his chin was even more noticeable, but he'd made more of an effort with his appearance than the previous day. His tie was an elegant dark blue, his shoes were well polished, and there was a fresh confidence about him; Nora could see the successful company director he had once been. He looked worryingly calm.

Nora smoothed down her skirt and arranged her papers in neat piles. Everything must go like clockwork today; Christian Dufva's testimony was vital. They'd been due to meet fifteen minutes before the session began, but he hadn't shown up. She assumed he'd just been delayed for some reason, although the sweaty palms of her hands indicated a creeping concern.

The door opened and Christian Dufva walked in. Nora gave him an encouraging smile, but he refused to meet her eye. She understood; this must be difficult for him. Most people were intimidated the first time they found themselves in court. Testifying against an old friend and business partner wouldn't be easy.

Barbro Wikingsson explained the procedure: Dufva would be required to take the oath before they began, and everything would be for the record.

Christian nodded and obediently recited the oath. "I, Christian Dufva, do solemnly swear that the evidence that I shall give shall be the truth, the whole truth, and nothing but the truth."

He ran a hand over his hair and fiddled with his glass of water. He seemed very nervous, and Nora gripped her pen tightly as she realized he truly wanted to be somewhere else. So much depended on what he was about to say; he had to deliver.

She planned to begin with a few simple questions about the relationship between him and Winnerman, get him to relax before she moved on to the tricky part.

"Could you tell us how long you and Niklas Winnerman have known each other?"

Dufva was perched on the edge of his seat. The gray suit hung loosely on his body; he must have lost a lot of weight recently.

"Twelve, thirteen years. We were colleagues before we decided to start up Alliance Construction together. That was around ten years ago."

"Were you friends as well as coworkers?"

"I guess so. We used to meet up socially, with our families."

"With your families. The way good friends do."

Nora noticed a little shake of the head from Annika Sandberg. The reaction was exactly what she wanted: indignation. The close relationship between the two men, the trust and warmth, had been brutally set aside.

"So how did you acquire the capital you needed? It must have taken a significant amount of money to get underway."

"We both took out bank loans. I used my apartment as security, and I think Niklas did the same."

"What percentage of the company did you own?"

"We each owned fifty percent."

Nora behaved as if this information was new to her, even though the golden rule in court was never to ask a question to which you didn't already know the answer.

"Did things go well?"

Dufva's strained expression softened. "Extremely well. The company grew year after year, and we were able to take on more and more employees." He almost managed a smile.

"So you must have made a good profit?"

"Yes, but we folded virtually everything back into the company. Niklas thought we should wait before we paid ourselves a dividend, leave the money where it was. Invest in our future, as he always said."

The light in his eyes died.

"And what's your financial situation at the moment?"

"I don't have a job, and it's hard to get a new one when . . ." Dufva gripped the edge of the table. "When things are the way they are. Most of my capital was in the company. I got divorced a few years ago, and I had to pay off my ex-wife so that I could retain my share of the business."

"That can't be easy," Nora said sympathetically.

"No. No, it isn't."

Dufva reached for his water and took a sip. He put it down, but was unable to let go. His fingertips were pressed against the glass.

Nora decided to change tack. "How come the two of you decided to set up a joint enterprise?"

"We worked well together, we complemented each other. We didn't want to be wage slaves for the rest of our lives; we liked the idea of having something of our own, something that would enable us to earn good money."

"To earn good money," Nora repeated, almost in passing. "Did that interest Niklas?"

"I'd say he was the driving force, out of the two of us."

"Why?"

"Niklas has a different lifestyle from me and my family."

"Could you perhaps clarify that?"

Dufva looked uncomfortable but answered anyway. "Niklas lives in Östermalm, one of the most expensive areas of Stockholm. He's always liked going to clubs and bars, and he drives top-of-the-line cars. My tastes are a little simpler." He touched the lapel of his jacket. "My suits aren't exactly designer labels."

Nora raised her eyebrows. "And were you really making enough to support that lifestyle?"

"We were getting there. We'd talked about our exit strategy, selling the company in ten years when we both turn fifty-five. It would have been worth a significant amount by then."

"How much are we talking about?"

"It's hard to say, but if it had continued to grow at the same rate, probably several million."

"But now there's nothing to sell."

The two jurors to the left of Barbro Wikingsson had disapproval written all over their faces, and Annika Sandberg stared skeptically at Winnerman.

"The company doesn't exist anymore." Dufva's shoulders slumped. "It's gone for good." He swallowed hard, his Adam's apple bobbing up and down.

Nora took her time picking up a sheet of paper; she wanted his words to linger.

"Alliance Construction doesn't exist anymore," she said slowly. "Let's discuss the events leading up to the collapse."

She saw Dufva clench his fists. She understood his anger, and knew it wasn't directed at her.

"The court has already heard that Niklas Winnerman purchased a worthless land allocation agreement from a company known as Vine Holdings for ten million kronor. Is that correct?"

Dufva responded with a brief nod.

"Could the witness please answer for the record," Barbro Wikingsson said.

"Yes." Dufva cleared his throat. "That's correct."

He'd been definite during his interviews with the police: he'd specifically advised Winnerman against the deal, because the company's cash flow wouldn't be able to withstand the strain. There simply wasn't enough money in the pot.

And yet Winnerman had gone behind his partner's back.

Malicious intent according to the letter of the law; Nora could see no other interpretation. She couldn't help glancing at the bench. Dennis Grönstedt was leaning forward; that was usually a good sign.

She just needed to hammer a few more nails into the coffin.

"Niklas Winnerman claims he thought it was a good deal. He insists the two of you were in agreement."

Dufva seemed unwilling to look at her.

"Isn't it true that you objected strongly when he proposed entering into an agreement with Vine Holdings?"

"I don't really remember."

Nora stared at him. The floor gave way beneath her feet for a second.

"A little while later you brought the matter up again," she said, trying to keep her voice steady. "Didn't Winnerman assure you that you had nothing to worry about?"

Jacob Emilsson raised his hand. "Your Honor, that sounds like a leading question to me."

Barbro Wikingsson agreed. "Sustained. Please express yourself with a little more care, fru Linde."

Nora took a deep breath. She'd crossed the line, but the man in front of her was a different person from the one who'd sat in a police interview room, complaining bitterly about his ex-partner.

"My apologies," she said, even though she had the urge to yell at Dufva. "If Niklas Winnerman hadn't done this deal, would that have made a difference to Alliance Construction's financial situation?"

"Of course."

"In that case, let me put it this way: Did you advise Winnerman against purchasing the land allocation agreement or not?"

"I don't remember." Christian Dufva directed his gaze somewhere above Nora's head. "I trusted Niklas to take care of his responsibilities just as I took care of mine."

What the hell was going on? Nora searched through her papers, found the transcript of the interviews, and held it up. "That's not what you said when you were questioned by the police. It's printed here in black and white."

"Maybe it is." The response was barely audible.

Nora turned to the judge. "May I have the court's permission to read an extract from the interviews conducted by the police with this witness?"

"You may."

"You said," Nora read aloud, "that you strenuously advised Niklas Winnerman against this deal, and he assured you he wouldn't proceed if he had any concerns about its validity. You also said that he lied to your face when you asked him about the matter at a later date."

She waited for a reaction from Dufva. The seconds passed. When he didn't speak, she leafed through her papers. The clock ticking on the wall sounded unnaturally loud.

"You said your financial director came to you when funds were running low, but Winnerman refused to admit what was going on."

It was against the rules to stand up in the courtroom, or to approach the witness. All Nora could do was lean across the table as far as possible.

"Have you forgotten *all* of this?" she asked.

A barely perceptible smile played across Jacob Emilsson's lips.

"There must have been some kind of misunderstanding." For the first time, Christian Dufva turned his head and looked at Winnerman. "Niklas made a bad deal," he said quietly. "I've done it myself over the years. We can't condemn him for that."

Chapter 60

Isak ran past the dining hall and out onto the jetty. David was at the wheel of one of the escort boats, ready to shove off.

"Wait," Isak gasped. "I have to talk to you."

The last of the white sails heading north filled the inlet; several yawls had already rounded Telegrafholmen. All the groups were completing a longer trip today.

"There's a child missing," Isak shouted over the sound of the engine. "I've counted over and over again; there are only seventeen."

"Calm down. What's happened?"

Isak realized he was yelling. His fingers were almost numb. He had to pull himself together. He ran his hands through his hair and spoke more slowly. "Benjamin's missing from Blue Group. I don't know where he's gone. I've searched everywhere."

David frowned as he absorbed the information. He switched off the engine, slipped the key in his pocket, and stepped ashore. "OK, start from the beginning. When did you last see him?"

"I haven't seen him at all today. He wasn't at breakfast, and I've been looking for him ever since." Isak broke off. He couldn't possibly tell David that he'd been with Maja instead of trying to track down Benjamin from the start.

"So he's disappeared—are you absolutely certain?" David sounded calm, but his face was flushed.

There was a weird buzzing noise in Isak's ears. He'd lost another child. He was completely fucked.

"He's not here. I've been searching for nearly an hour." His voice rose to a falsetto. "What if he's run away, just like Clara?"

"What makes you think that?"

"I don't know! But he's gone!"

Isak was having difficulty getting enough air into his lungs. His legs had started tingling, too. The angst was on its way to the surface. Why had he applied to be a sailing instructor?

David pressed two fingers to the bridge of his nose and rubbed up and down.

"What are we going to do?" Isak said. "Should we contact the parents?"

"He's probably hiding somewhere. We'll give it an hour. Has your group left yet?"

"No."

Wille was with Blue Group. It was ten past ten; they should have been underway long ago.

It's just like last time, a voice screamed inside his head.

"In that case we'll split them into pairs," David said decisively. "Get them to search the island systematically, just like we did when Clara went missing. If you organize that, I'll call the Vaxholm Ferry Company. I'll check with the harbormaster in Sandhamn, see if Benjamin's taken the taxi boat over there." He already had his phone in his hand and was scrolling through the address book.

Isak's breathing was still labored, even though it was a relief that David had taken charge.

David placed a hand on Isak's arm. "We'll find him. Don't worry."

CHAPTER 61

She was losing ground. Was the panic showing in her eyes? Nora had been involved in other trials where witnesses suddenly changed their minds in court, but not in a way that jeopardized the whole case. Not like this.

She had been totally convinced that there was enough evidence to secure a conviction, but now it was clear she'd relied too heavily on Christian Dufva's testimony.

And the worst thing was that she had no idea what to do.

The case was slipping through her fingers by the minute. Instead of questioning her witness with calm effectiveness, she sounded like a broken record. Every sentence was stilted; she was stammering and repeating herself.

Had she really thought she could apply for the post of deputy district chief prosecutor?

Her shirt was sticking to her sweaty armpits.

"Have you really forgotten what you said during your interviews with the police?" she tried again.

"Perhaps it's time to finish up, fru Linde?"

Barbro Wikingsson's neutral expression didn't help matters. The courtroom didn't look any different, the fan was humming away, but everything was wrong. Nora had never felt so helpless.

Soon they'd be breaking for lunch. However she angled or rephrased her questions, she could get nothing out of Dufva apart from the assertion that Niklas Winnerman had been caught making a bad deal.

Even the few people in the public gallery had started yawning. Dennis Grönstedt was making notes without a trace of enthusiasm, and Fanny Ferlin was drawing a series of little circles on her notepad.

Nora couldn't end the morning so poorly.

"You are aware that you're under oath?" she snapped.

Emilsson's smile grew even broader. Nora's words revealed her desperation, but were unlikely to make Dufva change his testimony. If he did so now, he would risk being charged with perjury.

And yet she had to ask.

"I am," he replied in the same monotone.

He must have been subjected to some form of pressure; that was the only possible explanation.

"The maximum sentence for influencing the outcome of a trial through perjury is eight years."

"I understand."

The stuffy atmosphere of the courtroom felt more oppressive than ever, and the hot sun added to the unpleasantness.

Only Emilsson seemed totally unconcerned.

I have to give it one last shot.

"How can you have changed your mind so fundamentally about Winnerman's actions since you spoke to the police?" she said.

"I can't be held responsible for the way the police interpreted our conversation."

"Interpreted? This is a transcript of everything you said, which was read back to you."

"I didn't write it down."

"So you're claiming the police are lying?"

"I didn't say that."

"But if you think the transcript is wrong, then the police must have made it up. Why would they do that?"

"I've no idea."

Hopeless. Nora held up the transcript once more. "So Leila Kacim, the officer who conducted the interviews, made this up?"

"I didn't say that. You're putting words into my mouth."

Nora managed to suppress a comment about who was putting words into whose mouth. "Well, you need to come up with some kind of explanation," she said instead. "I don't understand why you would say one thing to the police, and the opposite in court."

Dufva didn't answer, but Nora was determined to wait him out.

Eventually he cracked.

"I admit I was very bitter when the company went bankrupt. I blamed Niklas, refused to accept any responsibility myself."

Nora wanted to grab him by the shoulders and give him a good shake.

"But you've seen these transcripts before," she said, hating the fact that she couldn't hide her frustration. "Why didn't you point out the inaccuracies then?"

Dufva shrugged, then took out a handkerchief and wiped his forehead.

"This is an important case," Nora went on. "It would be nice if you took it a little more seriously."

She regretted the words as soon as she'd spoken. That attitude would win her no sympathy from the jurors, especially when it involved a witness called by the prosecution. Ground rule number one: don't remonstrate with your own witness.

Emilsson raised a hand and addressed the judge. "My apologies, Your Honor, but it feels as if we've heard these questions over and over again. Perhaps it's time to adjourn for lunch to give the prosecutor time to consider her approach?" He bestowed a warm smile on the court, and Nora's cheeks burned red.

Barbro Wikingsson consulted her jurors. Annika Sandberg nodded with such enthusiasm that her double chin wobbled.

"This court is adjourned for one hour. We reconvene at one o'clock."

The judge gave Nora a look that could be construed as sympathetic. It didn't make her feel any better.

Chapter 62

"Phone, Åsa."

Jamila, the new junior nurse, called to Åsa Dufva from the office as she closed the door of room three behind her, leaving a twenty-two-year-old mother-to-be in tears when she realized that Åsa was unable to stay with her. Åsa already had three women in labor; she had no choice.

It was only the middle of June, but there were already problems because of understaffing. What it would be like as the summer wore on was too much to think about.

"I haven't got time," Åsa shouted back. "Take the number and I'll contact whoever it is later."

"He says it's important—he's calling from a sailing camp on Lökholmen."

Benjamin.

He hadn't been in touch for two days. He'd sounded so small and lost on Sunday, but in spite of repeated attempts to find out what was wrong, he'd just kept mumbling that everything was OK.

Åsa had found it hard to relax that evening. She'd considered calling Christian, but had changed her mind at the last minute. The risk of Ninna answering was too great. She refused to discuss Benjamin with that woman.

She hesitated outside room four, where a mother in the throes of delivering triplets was struggling with the pain. But Benjamin knew it was hard for her to talk when she was at work; it must be important.

She turned and hurried to the office, where Jamila was tapping away on the computer, the phone by her side.

"Hi, sweetheart." Åsa made an effort to sound cheerful so that Benjamin wouldn't realize she was worried. "How's it going? Is the sun shining over there on Lökholmen?"

"This is David Rutkowski," an unfamiliar voice informed her. "I'm the senior instructor at the sailing camp, and I'm calling about your son."

Åsa reached out her hand and leaned on the wall for support. "Has something happened to Benjamin?" she asked, her voice so shrill that Jamila looked up.

"I'm just wondering if he's with you."

"With me?"

David might be the senior instructor, but Åsa could tell from his voice that he wasn't very old. *I want to speak to an adult.*

"What do you mean?"

Jamila came over and placed a hand on her arm. "Is everything OK?"

Åsa shook her head and turned away. She could only listen to one person at a time. "Are you saying you can't find him?" she said. "He's supposed to be with you all week."

"Has he tried to contact you? Has he called you today?"

"I don't know, I'm at work. I'm not allowed to have my phone on."

"Could you check, please?"

"Wait a minute—my phone's in my locker."

She hurried to the staff room, opened up her locker, and took out her purse. She rummaged around with awkward fingers until she found her phone. It took forever to turn it on; her hand was shaking so much she couldn't press the button.

"It's switched off," she muttered to David.

"No problem, take your time."

Reception inside the hospital wasn't great, but eventually two bars appeared in the top corner. She waited as the seconds passed; no messages appeared in her inbox. She kept staring at the screen, kept hoping.

"I don't think he's tried to contact me," she said at last.

"OK. If he does, could you let me know right away?"

Åsa rested her head against the door of her locker and closed her eyes. Only a few days ago, Benjamin had been sitting on the bed while she packed his bag. She'd seen how unhappy he was, but had simply babbled away, pretending everything was fine.

And now he'd disappeared.

"He can't be missing," she said, fighting to stop herself from breaking down. "He's only eleven. He wouldn't be able to find his own way home from the camp."

"I know."

"Plus he doesn't have a phone—you said all phones had to be handed in."

"I really wish I knew where he's gone," David said, sounding far more concerned now. "We've searched everywhere. We're still searching."

Åsa stared at her iPhone as the sense of unreality grew. "Has anyone spoken to his father? Have you called Christian?"

"I wanted to check in with you first."

"It was Christian who wanted Benjamin to go to camp."

Without any conscious thought, Åsa opened the staff-room door. The hallway looked exactly the same as it always did. The lights outside rooms three and five were flashing, and a food trolley stood outside the kitchen.

"Have you contacted the police?"

David didn't answer her question. "Is there any way he could have gotten back home without letting you know? Or gone to a friend's place? Is there anyone else we should call?"

"I need to go home, see if he's there. I'll do it right away—and I'll speak to Christian."

Åsa realized she was already moving toward the elevators. She handed the phone to Jamila as she passed by, then broke into a run with her purse under her arm, still in her white uniform.

"You're needed in room four!" Jamila shouted after her.

"Not now."

Benjamin is missing.

CHAPTER 63

When Thomas stepped ashore on Lökholmen, he almost expected someone to tell him they'd found the boy at home, just like last time. But he didn't like what he'd heard so far; no one had seen Benjamin for half a day.

Margit had given him and Aram a quick briefing before they left Nacka. Benjamin Dufva was eleven years old and small for his age. His parents were divorced.

Aram followed him off the police launch that had given them a ride to the island. He paused on the jetty and looked around, then said, "I guess you've been here pretty often." He gazed at what appeared to be the ruins of some kind of medieval fortress up on Trollharan. A yellow flag adorned with a sea eagle fluttered above tall walls and a stone tower. "What the hell is this? Disneyland?"

"Come on, we need to find the senior instructor," Thomas said.

They set off across the grass, where a group of twelve- and thirteen-year-olds were sitting with nautical charts spread out in front of them. It was obvious they knew about the disappearance; as soon as they saw the two detectives approaching, the whispers began.

David Rutkowski came to meet them; his expression was grim, his eyes darting from side to side.

"Is there somewhere we can talk in private?" Thomas asked.

"We'll use the instructors' common room."

David led them to a spacious room with well-used sofas and armchairs lining the walls and a black soapstone stove in one corner. Another instructor, whom Thomas recognized from his previous visit, was waiting for them. His face was gray.

"Hi," Thomas said. "Isak, isn't it?"

The young man nodded.

"So how are you doing? Is your group involved again?"

For Isak's sake, Thomas hoped this wasn't the case, but another nod confirmed his fears.

"OK, let's start from the beginning."

Aram sat down, took out his pen and notebook, and opened it to a clean page with narrow blue lines.

"Tell us what's happened today."

"We can't find Benjamin," Isak said, as if he were sleepwalking.

"We've called his parents, but he hasn't been in touch," David added. "Not with his mother anyway. We haven't managed to contact his father; his cell phone is switched off."

"When did you last see Benjamin?"

"Yesterday evening," Isak mumbled. "I checked the boys around midnight; they were all asleep in bed."

"How come no one's seen him today?"

Isak ran a hand through his already messy hair. "I didn't notice he was missing until breakfast time."

David glanced at his colleague. He opened his mouth to say something, then closed it again.

"What about the other boys in his dormitory? Surely they know if he was in his bed this morning?"

"No one remembers if he was there or not," David said. "We wake them at seven thirty; it's pretty chaotic with everyone getting up and dressed at the same time."

"Who woke them?" Aram turned to Isak. "Was it you?"

"Yes. I banged on the door and shouted that it was time to get up. That's what I usually do." His voice broke. "But I didn't go into the room."

If only he'd gone in and noticed that Benjamin was missing . . . Thomas could hear the questions going around and around inside Isak's head. He was an expert in that kind of self-reproach when it was too late.

If only he'd woken up on the night Emily died in her sleep, at the age of three months. Eight years had passed, but he still wondered if he'd have been able to save her.

If was a dangerous word.

"So what steps did you take during the morning, before you called the police?" Aram asked.

"We searched the camp, the forest, and the whole island," David explained. "We also sent small groups of children to ask if anyone in the marina had seen him." He rubbed his forehead, which was beaded with sweat.

They'd done their best, but Thomas knew there were plenty of hiding places on Lökholmen.

"Anywhere in the camp he could be hiding?"

"It's not very big. There are the dormitories, the dining hall, and this common room. We've checked all the boathouses and the showers, plus the instructors' accommodations."

"What about that fortress?" Aram said. "Could he have gotten himself locked in there by mistake?"

David shook his head. "The tower's locked. It's used by a sailing club called the Sea Eagles."

"That explains the flag," Thomas commented.

"There's a cellar beneath the tower, but we've searched that, too."

"I'm wondering about the youth hostel," Thomas said. "The last time I visited Trollgården, there were lots of places where a child could tuck himself away."

David took out his phone and started texting as he spoke. "We've already been there, but I'll ask someone to run over and take another look."

Thomas tried to picture Benjamin. It took a great deal of courage to break the rules and head off on his own. The girl who'd disappeared a few days earlier had been older; why would an eleven-year-old run away from a sailing camp?

Had something happened to him?

"Was Benjamin enjoying camp?" he asked.

Isak had one hand in his pocket. Thomas could see the outline of his fingers against the fabric; he was clutching something.

"I think so," he said. "He was shy, but things were improving each day."

"Who did he hang out with?"

"He got along well with some of the girls—Sofie, Lova, and Tindra. They're in Blue Group, too. Two of the older boys in his dormitory took care of him, too—Samuel and Sebbe. Sebastian."

Aram made a note of the names. "What did you do yesterday evening? Did anything happen that might have made him want to run away?"

"I don't think so," David said. "We did a quiz, combined with orienteering."

"Benjamin was in a team with the two boys I mentioned," Isak offered. He took his hand out of his pocket and scratched his arm, which was covered in red marks. "He was late for the debriefing afterward—apparently he'd had to go to the restroom." He closed his eyes, tried to pull himself together. "I don't know if that's important."

"There could be something else behind his disappearance," Thomas said hesitantly. Aram had mentioned the possibility as soon as they got in the car. "This is an island, after all," Thomas went on. "We're in the middle of the archipelago."

"You think he's drowned?" Isak exclaimed.

David placed a hand on Isak's shoulder. "Benjamin can swim. All the children have to be able to swim to take part in the camp."

"I understand that, but accidents can happen," Thomas persisted. "It's easy to slip on a jetty, or lose your balance and bang your head."

"Have you searched around the jetties?" Aram asked.

Isak scratched his arm even harder.

"We've focused mainly on dry land," David admitted.

"Could you send out some boats to travel slowly around the island? Check under the jetties in the marinas, too," Thomas said.

David covered his face with his hands for a couple of seconds, breathing heavily through his nose. "Yes, I can do that."

"Could we have a chat with the friends you mentioned?" Thomas's chair creaked as he shifted position. "Are they around?"

David pointed through the window. "Blue Group is down by the inlet. We kept them in camp because you were coming. Everyone else is out at sea."

Aram put down his notebook. "Can we stay in here? It'll be a while before we're done."

"No problem." David got to his feet and gave Isak a nudge to push him along. "I'll go and fetch the girls."

Aram watched the two men as they left the room. "How old do you think they are? Nineteen, twenty?"

"Something like that."

"Not very old to carry so much responsibility."

CHAPTER 64

Thomas and Aram waited for David to return with Benjamin's friends. They exchanged a worried look; neither of them was comfortable with the situation.

Thomas was still hoping that Benjamin had run away; if that was the case, then statistically they had a good chance of finding him very soon, heading for home. However, if a tragic accident had occurred and he'd fallen in the water, it could take a long time to find his body, particularly in view of the currents around the island.

He clasped his hands behind his head as he thought things through. Could there be another explanation? There was a faint chance that Benjamin hadn't left the camp voluntarily.

He hadn't mentioned it to David and Isak; he didn't want to alarm them even more, especially given the state Isak was in. However, children were abducted, though such cases were rare and usually linked to a custody battle.

The parents were divorced, so it was worth following up.

There was a knock on the door, and three slender girls in shorts appeared with David.

"Come on in," Thomas said warmly.

"Sofie," the tallest girl murmured as the three of them sat down on the sofa. They stuck close together, although there was plenty of room. The girl with Asian features giggled nervously, while Sofie peered at Thomas from beneath her bangs.

David introduced the other two as Lova and Tindra, then briefly explained why the two detectives were on the island.

As if they don't already know, Thomas thought. *Kids aren't stupid.*

"I believe you're friends with Benjamin," he began. "We'd like to ask you a few questions, if that's OK."

Technically a parent or guardian ought to be present when minors were questioned, but Aram and Thomas had decided that they could get around that by having David sit in. After all, he was responsible for the children while they were in camp, and Thomas didn't want to have to wait until parents arrived.

Sofie nodded, her expression serious. She seemed more mature than the other girls, who were both chewing gum with their mouths open. Lova's dark hair shone beside Tindra's white-blonde ponytail.

"Could you tell us when you last saw Benjamin?" Aram took the lead; his oldest girl would soon finish junior high, and he perhaps had a better understanding of how to talk to girls near puberty. Elin, too, would be a teenager one day, but Thomas found it impossible to imagine.

Sofie spoke first. "We saw him in the dining room yesterday evening. There was a quiz, then there was a debriefing at suppertime."

"And how did he seem?"

"He was kind of down," Tindra said. "He didn't have many friends; everyone in Star already knew one another before camp."

"But you were friends," David interjected. "Surely things can't have been that bad?"

Thomas frowned. It would be better if the girls were allowed to talk freely.

"Why are you here?" Sofie demanded. "Do you think Benjamin's run away?"

"We don't know yet, but we are trying to locate him."

Lova's eyes narrowed.

"It's important that you tell us everything you know," Thomas added. "Anything at all—for Benjamin's sake."

It wasn't easy to understand loyalty among young people. It might seem self-evident to him that something should be passed on, yet it might be unthinkable to a teenage girl.

However, these girls surprised him.

"I don't think he wanted to be with Samuel and Sebbe," Sofie said. "He was scared of Samuel."

David gave a start and was about to speak, but Thomas held up his hand.

"Why?"

Lova tugged at her lower lip. "They were horrible to Benjamin. Especially Samuel—he's sick in the head."

Sofie nodded. "He used to call Benjamin names when the instructors weren't around."

David leaned forward, and Thomas quickly said, "Did he do anything worse than that?"

Sofie rubbed her hands up and down her thighs. "He hid Benjamin's life jacket; that made Benjamin late for morning briefing, and Isak told him off. I heard Samuel bragging about it."

Aram stopped taking notes for a moment and said, "Thank you for telling us this. I realize it's not easy."

He sounded exactly the way he did when he was talking to his daughters—warm and kind, but Thomas could see that he was upset. Few things affected Aram more than children suffering; he was concerned about the way schools were developing these days, particularly in major cities.

"If we can go back to yesterday evening," Thomas said. "You saw Benjamin in the dining hall?"

Sofie licked her lips. "We saw him in the forest before that, during the quiz."

"Were Sebbe and Samuel with him then?"

"They'd left him, even though they were on the same team. We saw them running along the path back to camp, and we went to look for Benjamin."

"So Benjamin was alone?"

Sofie shook her head. "No, he was talking to someone in a clearing."

Aram paused with his pen in the air. "Are you sure?"

All three girls nodded.

It might not mean anything, Thomas thought. *It could be anybody, a dog walker or a sailor, maybe a tourist.*

Then again . . .

Aram turned to a fresh page. "Man or woman? Tall, short, fat, thin? Can you give us a description?"

Sofie tilted her head to one side. "He was, like, an old man."

She had the perspective of a thirteen-year-old; anyone over thirty was old.

Thomas took over. "Let me put it this way: Was he more David's age, or did he remind you more of your dad, or your granddad?"

"My dad, I guess, or a bit younger. Older than David." Sofie frowned. "But I can't really tell you what he looked like—he was wearing a baseball cap and sunglasses."

"They were horrible," Tindra announced. "Not cool like Isak's."

Thomas had to smile. He turned to Lova. "Did you see this man, too?"

"Yes."

"Can any of you remember what he was wearing? Jeans? A T-shirt? What color were his clothes? Did you notice any kind of logo or brand name?"

No one said anything, but why would they remember?

"Nothing?" Thomas prompted them.

"It all happened so fast," Sofie said apologetically. "He walked off in the opposite direction as soon as we called out to Benjamin."

Tindra opened her mouth, then closed it again.

"Anything you'd like to tell us, Tindra?" Thomas said gently. "Even if it's only a tiny detail, it could help us to find Benjamin."

"I'm not sure . . . It was just . . ."

"Tell me what's on your mind."

She tugged at her ponytail, which was fastened with a red rubber band. "The man who was talking to Benjamin. In the forest."

"Yes?" Thomas resisted the urge to hurry her; it would be better if she went at her own pace. However, he was starting to feel impatient; it had been over an hour since they'd arrived on Lökholmen. Very soon they would have to make a decision about the next step.

Should they put out a call for Benjamin and bring in forensics and a dog team to search the whole island, or wait and hope the boy turned up at home?

Several long seconds passed. "Tindra?"

"He reminded me of a guy we spoke to in the marina on Saturday. When we were looking for Clara."

"You're right!" Sofie exclaimed. "It was him!"

Tindra's face lit up.

"So was he on his boat?" Aram asked.

The girls nodded.

"He had a white motorboat with a blue cabin," Tindra said.

"And he was drinking beer when we saw him," Sofie added. "He was wearing a cap then, too, but no sunglasses."

"Would you recognize him again?"

"Don't know," Lova said.

"I don't think so," Sofie added with a shrug.

"Maybe when we're done here you could show us where the boat's moored."

Aram finished making notes. "OK, thank you for talking to us. If you think of anything else, please get in touch. David's got our number."

The girls got to their feet, but Tindra lingered.

"It looked as if Benjamin had wet himself yesterday," she said, blushing slightly.

"Sorry?"

"When we saw him in the forest. His jeans were kind of dark-colored around the zipper and down his legs."

Lova giggled nervously, and Sofie looked uncomfortable.

She noticed it, too, Thomas thought. *But she didn't say anything because she's trying to protect him.*

"He pretended everything was OK," Tindra went on, "but it was exactly the same as when my little brother doesn't make it to the bathroom in time. He's only five, though."

Thomas didn't like the feeling in the pit of his stomach.

A boy who'd wet himself, despite the fact that he could have gone behind a tree for a piss anywhere in the forest. An unknown man who left as soon as the girls showed up.

Something wasn't right.

And time was passing.

CHAPTER 65

Nora had gone into a side room to be alone when she called Leila. The sun was on the other side of the building, so the heat was less oppressive than in the courtroom, making it easier to breathe. However, Nora still felt somehow cracked and chipped, like a plate at a flea market.

"Come on, come on," she muttered, even though the phone had only rung once.

Leila answered on the second.

"Any luck with the bank?" Nora asked.

"Not really."

Nora leaned against the wall and closed her eyes.

"I've spoken to the manager at Handelsbanken, and nobody seems to know whether the CCTV footage is still available. He promised to check it out and get back to me."

"When?"

"I said it was urgent; he'll be in touch by the end of the day."

Something clicked in the background; Nora assumed Leila was on her way into the building on Hantverkargatan where the Economic Crimes Authority was housed. It was only a stone's throw from the courthouse—no more than a five-minute walk.

"How did it go this morning?" Leila said.

"Not too well."

Nora briefly summarized Christian Dufva's testimony and his new assertion that Winnerman had simply been caught making a bad deal. It was enough for her heart to start fluttering like a hummingbird's wings.

"It sounds as if someone's gotten to him," Leila said. "No one changes their mind like that. I remember exactly what he said when I interviewed him."

Nora agreed. "There's only one person who could be behind this, but I don't know how to prove it."

She went over to the window. There was a large horse chestnut outside, its leaves fresh and green, its flowers well past their prime.

The threatening emails. She'd received another one last night. Niklas Winnerman must have sent them, and now he'd persuaded her witness to change his mind. However, there was no way of proving his involvement; she could hardly bring it up with Dufva in court. If he was prepared to perjure himself because of Winnerman, he wasn't about to admit the truth to Nora.

"Do you think someone's threatened Dufva?" she asked.

"Sounds that way." Leila was aware that Dufva's testimony was key.

"But why would he be afraid of Winnerman?"

"Maybe he's not—maybe he's been bribed," Leila suggested.

Nora remembered what Dufva had said about his financial situation; Winnerman had ten million kronor at his disposal. In the park a woman was pushing a stroller across the neatly raked gravel path.

"I'll keep pushing the bank," Leila promised.

"The trial ends tomorrow." Nora sank down on a chair by the window. "Then it'll be too late."

CHAPTER 66

Thomas got up from the sagging sofa and opened the door to let in some fresh air. The ground outside was covered in pine cones and needles. A short distance away he could see some granite stones at the foot of a tall pine tree, with a few moss-covered rocks here and there.

David had gone to fetch Samuel and Sebastian. The plan was to talk to the boys, then head over to the marina to look for the man from the forest.

"I'm wondering if we ought to put out a general call for Benjamin," Thomas said over his shoulder.

Aram clicked his ballpoint pen several times. "Maybe we should speak to the boys first. You know what happened last time, when Clara disappeared: a lot of fuss about nothing."

Before Thomas could reply, David reappeared with two teenage boys trailing behind him. The sun shining in through the doorway filled the room with bright light.

David made the introductions. "Samuel Karlberg and Sebastian Grandin. They're in the same dormitory as Benjamin."

Thomas hadn't been told their age, but he could guess. They were tall, but not fully grown. They had the adolescent's typical outbreak of zits scattered across their foreheads, and the uncoordinated gait showing they'd shot up a little too quickly.

Benjamin was a child, much smaller than these two.

"Samuel—pleased to meet you," said the first boy, holding out his hand.

"Sebastian, but everyone calls me Sebbe."

Samuel was wearing a blue checked shirt with the sleeves rolled up and a pair of pale khaki shorts. Thomas wondered if he ought to recognize the small logo on the shirt pocket.

The boys might have different surnames, but they could have been twins with their fresh appearance and identical short haircuts.

Two well-brought-up young men.

"We need to speak to you about Benjamin Dufva," Aram began. He folded his arms, his approach more formal than it had been with the three girls.

"How well did you know one another, you and Benjamin?" Thomas asked.

"We're not, like, friends," Samuel replied. "But we're in the same sailing group and the same dormitory."

Sebbe nodded.

"I believe you were on the same orienteering quiz team yesterday evening."

"Maybe," Samuel said.

"Mmm," Sebbe added.

Thomas was irritated. He'd wanted to form his own impression rather than being influenced by what Sofie had said, but of course the boys had no idea they'd been portrayed as a couple of bullies.

"Was that a yes?" he snapped.

"I guess so," Samuel said with a yawn.

"How come you volunteered to be with Benjamin if you weren't friends?"

"He didn't have anyone to hang out with."

The answer came so glibly that Thomas would probably have bought it. If it hadn't been for Sofie.

"Is that the truth? Only we've heard that you two were pretty nasty to Benjamin."

Samuel no longer seemed quite so self-assured. He shifted position on the sofa and poked at the frayed fabric on the armrest. "Who said that?"

"It doesn't matter, but don't bother lying; we want you to be honest. Is that clear?" Thomas allowed his words to sink in. "Tell us what you did in the forest yesterday evening."

"There was a quiz—we had to search for the questions."

Samuel still sounded unconcerned, but Thomas saw him glance at David, who was sitting to one side as before. David didn't say a word. After the interview with the girls, Thomas had asked him not to get involved.

"If I've understood correctly, the two of you took off and left Benjamin alone in the forest. Do you think that was fair?" He knew he sounded brusque, but he wanted to see how the boys would react. Aram looked at him; *take it easy.*

Samuel stared at the floor, one foot constantly bouncing up and down.

"Nothing to say?" Thomas turned to Sebbe. "How about you? Would you say you were kind to Benjamin yesterday evening?"

Sebbe was fiddling with the cord of his gray fleece hoodie, which had grass stains on one sleeve.

"No," he mumbled. "Maybe not."

He wouldn't be as brave without Samuel. Should they question the boys separately? Next time, perhaps. The fact that the parents weren't here was still a stumbling block. If anyone decided to complain, it would look better if they'd spoken to the boys together; this could hardly be regarded as a formal interview.

"Look, we need your help. If we're going to find Benjamin, we need to know what happened yesterday evening."

Thomas got the feeling that Sebbe was softening—but not Samuel.

"He was fucking disgusting!" Samuel suddenly burst out. "We were looking for questions when he pissed himself! I mean, we had to leave him—who wants to hang around with a kid who stinks of piss?"

Sebbe let go of the cord. "Disgusting," he repeated obediently.

There was no doubt that Samuel set the tone and Sebbe followed. Thomas recognized the pattern; it was the herd mentality that ran through any group, whether it was a gang of criminals or a couple of pimply bullies. The leader made the decisions, and the entourage fell into line.

Thomas focused on Sebbe. "Was that really what happened? It sounds pretty weird to me."

"Don't know." Sebbe's eyes were darting all over the place.

"Besides, we didn't just take off," Samuel insisted. "Benjamin started talking to some old guy, and in the end we got tired of waiting for him."

That must be the same guy, Thomas thought, resisting the urge to run straight down to the marina. The boys would have been closer than the girls, and therefore have had a better view of the man's appearance. Maybe they could give a clear description?

"What did the old guy look like?" Aram asked.

"I'd never seen him before," Samuel replied.

"Can you describe him?"

Samuel shrugged, but Sebbe said quietly, "He had brown hair. He was wearing a green sweater and a baseball cap with *Stadium* on it. He was about the same height as my dad—just over six feet."

Thomas was surprised but grateful.

"That's pretty detailed," Aram said.

Sebbe didn't look at his friend. "I like watching crime shows. I know accurate descriptions are important."

"Did he mention his name?"

"No."

"What did you do after you left Benjamin?"

"Nothing special. We went back to the dining hall for supper; the instructors were going through the answers to the quiz."

"Did you speak to Benjamin later that evening?"

Both boys shook their heads.

Thomas leaned forward. "I want to know exactly what happened between the two of you and Benjamin yesterday."

David was looking anxious, but Thomas continued: "Did you do anything to Benjamin that might have made him run away?"

Sebbe altered his position again, but Samuel was determined to defend himself.

"We didn't do anything, I swear! I never said another word to him!"

"Are you sure?"

"He'd gone to bed when we got back to the dormitory," Sebbe said. "He was asleep."

"And how about during the night? Were you so mean to Benjamin that he didn't dare stay around?" Thomas was going in hard, but something told him it was the only way to get anything out of these two.

"We didn't do anything to Benjamin yesterday," Samuel assured him, the picture of wide-eyed innocence. "Ask anyone."

Thomas wasn't remotely convinced, but reminded himself that teenagers' brains weren't like adults'. The frontal lobe needed to keep on growing for many years to come; important parts of the empathy center were still missing. In their world, everything was about them.

Aram took over. "OK, let's move on to this morning. Was Benjamin there when you woke up?"

"I don't remember," Samuel said.

Thomas turned to Sebbe, hoping his good memory would help them out again. "How about you? Try to picture the dormitory when you woke up. Sometimes it helps to close your eyes."

Sebbe scratched his head. "I don't remember seeing him . . . I think his bed was empty, but I'm not a hundred percent certain."

Eight boys who'd just woken up, rummaging around for their clothes. One ran off to the restroom, another tried to grab five minutes' more sleep.

Why would they remember whether one of the others was there or not?

Isak had stated that Benjamin was asleep in his bed just before midnight, when he did his final check. When Sebbe got up just after seven thirty, the boy was apparently missing.

At least that gave them some kind of time frame. If Benjamin had run away, he must have gotten up early, before anyone else, and crept out. The first taxi boat to Sandhamn left at five past eight, but he hadn't been on board that one, or the next one an hour later. The boat had room for some sixty passengers, and the driver stood right at the back with a good view of everyone. There was nowhere to hide.

Which suggested that Benjamin was still on the island.

But what if he'd simply woken early and gone for a walk, slipped on a jetty, or lost his footing on a rock covered with early-morning dew . . . In seconds it would have been too late.

There wasn't a trace of concern in Samuel's eyes; he was just waiting for permission to leave. Thomas stared at the two boys and couldn't help wondering whether the bullying had in fact gone too far.

CHAPTER 67

The noise level was painfully high in the crowded restaurant around the corner from the courthouse. Not that it mattered to Christian Dufva; in a way it was a relief to let the racket fill his head.

He had rushed out of the courtroom and into the bathroom as soon as the judge broke for lunch, but as he bent over the toilet bowl, nothing came up but foul-tasting bile.

His head was throbbing; he had to get ahold of some painkillers if he was going to survive the afternoon. Many hours of torture remained before his time on the stand was over.

He remembered the prosecutor's shock when she couldn't persuade him to change his mind, and the smug expression on Niklas's face.

Christian closed his eyes and felt the sweat break out yet again. He used his napkin to wipe his forehead, and saw the woman at the next table grimace in disgust. The diners were way too close together in this place.

He'd ordered oven-baked cod with egg sauce, but barely touched it. The sauce had congealed into an unappetizing sludge; the sight of it was making him feel sick.

He finished off his glass of water. He was so tired, so worried that they would carry out their threat.

How did things end up this way?

He'd lain awake on so many nights, trying to make sense of the chaos that had been his life ever since Alliance Construction went under. When he scraped together the shards of the past ten years, he couldn't believe it had come to this, after all the years he and Niklas had worked together, side by side.

Niklas, whom he'd once regarded as his best friend.

But Niklas had shown a different side of himself when Christian divorced; he'd openly taken Åsa's side, criticizing Christian's actions and his choice of a new life partner.

Everything had changed from that moment.

And now he was sitting here.

He heard a shrill signal behind his back; someone's cell phone, a few tables away.

Just the way his phone had rung in the hallway this morning.

The memory of that muffled voice made him shiver, in spite of the stuffy atmosphere in the restaurant.

Ninna and Emil were on the way to her parents' summer cottage. His instructions had been very clear: Ninna mustn't answer the phone to anyone but Christian.

He couldn't think about Benjamin right now.

He'd been forced to say things that weren't true in order to survive, in order to save the life he had with his family. But he had to protect those who were closest to him.

He took out his phone. It had been switched off all morning in court. With trembling fingers he turned it on, and immediately saw that Åsa had tried to reach him several times. He hesitated, then turned his phone off again. He couldn't cope with talking to his ex-wife until the trial was over.

CHAPTER 68

Sofie led the way across the narrow wooden bridge to the marina. Her shoulders were hunched, and occasionally she wiped her eyes. The other girls had stayed in camp for a quick snack before they carried on searching.

Thomas and Aram followed her down a slope that ended at a wide wooden jetty running along the sheltered inlet. Opposite lay the uninhabited island of Kroksö, a popular tourist destination. The islands were almost joined together; the sound between Kroksö and Lökholmen, known as Lopphålet or the Flea Hole, was only a few yards across.

In the distance they could just see the tower on Korsö, the military base that had once been the home of Sweden's Coastal Rangers.

Sofie pointed to one of the white guest buoys. "That's where the boat was."

Thomas looked around. A few yachts were moored farther in, but there was no sign of any motorboat. Could Sofie be mistaken?

"Are you sure?"

"Yes, it was just by that rock—I swear."

"We believe you," Aram reassured her. "We'll ask around, see if any of the other boat owners have seen him. Someone might know when he left."

"Or ask at the marina office."

The office was by the bridge between Trollharan and Lökholmen; it wasn't much more than a kiosk, but with a bit of luck, the supervisor would have a good memory.

"Good idea." Thomas turned to Aram. "We'll check there after we've spoken to the owners. The office should have a record of who uses the moorings; there's a fee for staying overnight. Our man might have paid by credit card, which would give us an ID."

"Thanks for your help," Aram said to Sofie. "We can take it from here."

But Sofie didn't move. "What happens if you don't find Benjamin? I mean, it didn't take this long to track down Clara." Her eyes were shiny with unshed tears.

The fact that the motorboat was gone didn't necessarily mean anything, but the feeling that something was wrong was growing stronger by the moment.

"Don't worry, we'll find your friend." Aram gave her an encouraging pat on the arm. "He hasn't been missing for that long—it just seems that way."

Thomas wasn't convinced, but there was no point in frightening the girl; the atmosphere in the camp was already tense. If they didn't locate Benjamin within the next couple of hours, all hell would break loose, especially when the parents were informed.

"It'll be fine," he said to Sofie as he set off toward the boats.

"But what if it isn't?"

Her faint whisper was barely audible, then Sofie turned and walked away with her head down.

When Aram and Thomas reached the marina office, the door was open, but no one was inside. Thomas looked around; an elderly man with a gray beard was sitting on a boat moored nearby.

"Excuse me, have you seen anyone in the office?"

"Kia was there just now," the man replied. "She won't be far away."

It was almost one o'clock; they didn't have time to hang around.

At that moment they saw a girl approaching along the jetty. She was wearing turned-up shorts and a dark-blue T-shirt with the marina logo on the right-hand side. A name badge revealed that she was indeed Kia. She appeared to be about the same age as the sailing instructors, nineteen or twenty.

Thomas went to meet her and held up his police ID. "Could you help us out with some information about a motorboat that we think has been moored here over the past few days?"

"Sure." She hesitated. "Has something happened?"

There was no point in keeping quiet about Benjamin's disappearance—the news would soon be out in any case.

"One of the boys from the sailing camp has gone missing," Aram explained. "His name is Benjamin Dufva."

"Oh no! Some of the girls were asking about him this morning, but I didn't realize the police were involved."

"We're hoping it's nothing serious, but if you do see him, please contact us."

Thomas showed Kia Benjamin's passport photograph. It was old; Benjamin couldn't have been more than eight or nine. A shy child staring into the camera. If he didn't turn up soon, they would have to get ahold of a better picture.

"He's eleven now," Aram went on, "but not very tall."

The two detectives followed Kia into the office, where a narrow desk sat alongside an ice-cream cabinet. A selection of notices was displayed on the walls: the taxi boat ran between eight in the morning and nine in the evening; the depth of the channel leading into Kroksöfladen was six feet; use of the sauna was free.

"We don't see much of the kids from the camp," she said. "They tend to stick to their own area."

Through the window Thomas could see the ramp with the small boats drawn up out of the water on the other side of the inlet. How deep was it? No more than three feet at its shallowest, but significantly deeper farther out.

Small children could drown in eighteen inches of water; an eleven-year-old who'd banged his head wouldn't need much more.

A motorboat with two instructors on board was just setting off, and Thomas hoped David had gotten the search underway.

Kia sat down at the computer.

"We're looking for the owner of a small motorboat," Thomas said. "Unfortunately we don't know the make, but it's white with a blue cabin. We think there was only one person on board, a man in his late thirties or early forties. Does that ring any bells?"

It was still low season, so it was unlikely there had been many temporary moorings. The other two sailors currently in the marina hadn't noticed either Benjamin or the man.

He hoped Kia would be able to help.

"I'm afraid I haven't been at work since Friday, so I don't know which boats were in over the weekend, but let me check." She logged in, then paused. "How far back do you want me to go?"

"Last Thursday," Thomas decided. The camp had started on Friday.

Kia's fingers flew across the keys. She stared at the screen, muttered, "It's so slow!" and pressed "Enter" again.

Thomas's cell phone vibrated in his back pocket: a text from Margit.

Spoke to Benjamin's mother. She's called his friends—no luck. Benjamin hasn't been in touch. Father still not answering his phone.

They were losing valuable time.

"Finally!" Kia said, turning the screen so that Thomas and Aram could see. "This is everyone who's paid a mooring fee over the past six days."

Thomas scanned the list of forty names and boats. "Recognize any of them?" he asked Aram.

"No—do you?"

None of the names rang a bell with Thomas. Most were men; equality hadn't gotten very far when it came to owning a boat. Most were typically Swedish names like Andersson and Karlsson.

"I can't see a Gorgis or Danho," Aram said ironically.

Thomas gave a wry smile and leaned in to get a better look. The right-hand column showed the fee paid—two hundred kronor, two hundred and fifty, three hundred, while in some cases there was a blank space.

"Why do people pay different amounts?" Aram asked.

"It depends on the size of the boat." Kia held up a laminated sheet:

< 30 feet	200 kr per night
30–42 feet	250 kr per night
43–49 feet	300 kr per night
> 50 feet	400 kr per night

"If you're a club member, it's free for the first five days," she added.

The girls had said the man's boat was pretty small—Sofie had guessed at around twenty-five feet. Thomas looked at the list again; if he discounted the large boats, the number of owners who were of interest shrank by a third, which would save some time.

"Could you print off a copy?"

"No problem—just let me know if I can help with anything else."

"Could you email it to me as well?" Thomas said, jotting down his address on his card and handing it over. It would be a good idea if someone back at the station in Nacka got started checking the names right away.

His eyes were drawn to the water once more. He was increasingly certain that Benjamin wasn't hiding away somewhere on the island. Which left only two alternatives.

CHAPTER 69

Nora went back into the courtroom. Her briefcase had never felt heavier. She was determined not to show any reaction to the testimony Christian Dufva had given before lunch, but the expression on Jacob Emilsson's face turned her stomach.

Only a man who was sure of victory would smile like that.

His job was to punch holes in the evidence, and she'd given him every possible assistance.

Dufva would be here in a minute, and this would be Nora's last chance to get the truth out of him. She had to use the time to elicit sensible answers, make him revert to what he'd said during his police interviews.

However, no flashes of inspiration had struck her during the lunch break. Nor did she feel any more energetic, despite the fact that she'd forced down an overcooked portion of spaghetti Bolognese. She just wanted to put her head down on the table and close her eyes, snap her fingers, and wake up somewhere else.

That wasn't an option, so she opened her briefcase, took out her files, and arranged them in front of her, then carefully placed two blue ballpoint pens beside them.

On the bench Barbro Wikingsson was exchanging a few words with Dennis Grönstedt, whose forehead was already shiny with sweat.

Nora couldn't bring herself to look at the three jurors. She, too, had sat up there as a law clerk, and knew exactly what happened when a case was adjourned for lunch. That was when the events of the morning were discussed in detail. She could hear their comments as clearly as if she'd been sitting next to them:

Well, she certainly wasn't expecting that! Or: *The prosecutor ought to have better control over her witness.*

No doubt Barbro Wikingsson would have agreed, with a tight little smile indicating that the prosecutor was in over her head. Someone had probably said that the Economic Crimes Authority needed to take a good look at its procedures. Nora Linde should think carefully before she decided to prosecute next time.

There was no chance that she would get the post of deputy district chief prosecutor now.

The door opened and Christian Dufva entered the room. The harsh sunlight accentuated the deep lines running from nose to mouth. His lips were narrow and colorless, his complexion almost gray, without any hint of a tan.

He went over and sank down on his chair. Nora saw him glance at Niklas Winnerman. The more she thought about it, the more she was convinced this was about money. It wouldn't be the first time a witness had allowed himself to be bought; she'd seen it before, in other contexts.

Winnerman must have agreed to share the missing ten million with Dufva. That would give him enough capital to get back on his feet, maybe even start up a new business.

They hadn't gone through Dufva's finances with a fine-tooth comb, as they had with Winnerman's. Nora toyed with the idea of asking Leila to take a closer look, but the chances of finding something were probably minimal. Winnerman had managed to hide the ten million so successfully that neither she nor Leila had found any trace of the money. He would hardly transfer a sum to his former partner in a way that was easy to track down.

Yesterday she'd finally sent copies of the threatening emails to the security department, but this morning she'd been informed that it was impossible to locate the sender without a significant surveillance operation. The prospects of success were negligible.

The way the case was going, it didn't really matter.

Nora realized she was staring blankly at Niklas Winnerman. He noticed before she could turn away. He gave a faint smile, then an almost imperceptible wink.

CHAPTER 70

The idyllic inlet outside the marina office was peaceful, a vacation paradise ready for Midsummer. From time to time the water sparkled as a stickleback popped its head above the surface, then disappeared.

It was just after one thirty. Thomas and Aram were on their way back to the camp with the list of boat owners. It was still possible that Benjamin was hiding somewhere, but surely he should have emerged by now, driven by hunger if nothing else. Or tried to contact his parents.

Thomas stopped by the white pavilion that served as an outdoor café.

"If Benjamin's run away, he ought to have been in touch with someone by now," he said, taking out his phone. "Especially in view of all the fuss last time. We have to put out a call. It's been more than twelve hours since anyone saw him, and we've no idea where he's gone."

Aram was staring at the list Kia had given them. "Do you think the boat owner's involved? Could Benjamin have been abducted?"

"It's too early to say, but I'd really like to speak to the guy, or at least find out who he is so we can eliminate him from our inquiry."

It was so still that the red buoys appeared to be standing at attention. The water was clear, but it was impossible to see more than eighteen inches or so beneath the surface. Thomas couldn't help wondering if there was an eleven-year-old boy lying down at the bottom.

"We have to bring in more resources," he said decisively.

Beyond Korsö Tower a plane was drawing a white line across the bright-blue sky.

He called Margit. "Put out a call for Benjamin Dufva. There's no sign of him out here, and we don't think he's taken off on his own."

"Consider it done."

"Have you managed to speak to his father?"

"His phone is still switched off. I've tried his wife, Ninna, but she's not answering on the landline in their apartment or on her cell."

Margit must be in the staff kitchen; Thomas could hear the sound of the coffee machine grinding beans.

"We'll give them a few hours," she went on. "They might be busy."

A yacht was heaving to by the marina office, and the dark-blue taxi boat was on its way to Sandhamn.

"We need help," Thomas said. "Dog teams, and maritime police who can drag the waters around the island. Contact the coast guard, too. This is going to take time."

David Rutkowski was waiting on the steps of one of the red cabins when Thomas and Aram reached the camp.

"How did it go? Did you find the man the girls mentioned?"

"I'm afraid not. The boat was gone."

"What happens now?" David's voice was thin.

"We're putting out a call for Benjamin," Aram told him. "We're also bringing in dog teams and more officers to search the island. We'll probably need a search party on Sandhamn, too, just in case Benjamin's somehow managed to get over there."

"A specialist team will also be dragging the offshore waters; it's possible Benjamin might have fallen in," Thomas added.

David clasped his hands behind his head and rocked back and forth on his heels. "What should we do with the other kids? What do we say to them?"

"You should inform them of the situation. We're going to want to speak to everyone from Benjamin's dormitory, and everyone in Blue Group." Thomas glanced at his watch. "When are they due back?"

"Not until this evening—they're on a long trip today."

"I think you'd better bring them in. We'd like to question them as soon as possible."

David nodded. "I'll take care of it."

"Can we use the common room again?" Aram asked.

"No problem. What about the parents?"

"They should also be informed, and you need to contact your boss, if you haven't already done so—make sure he's up to speed."

"His name is Björn Ekholm."

"This is going to hit the media very fast—you do realize that?" Aram said.

It wouldn't take the press long to sniff out a story like this. A child going missing from a sailing camp, particularly a camp favored by the upper echelons of society, was a gift for any tabloid editor.

The phones would start ringing at any minute.

"I'll do that right away." David's voice sounded even hollower now.

"Good idea."

Thomas moved to one side to call his mother and ask her to pick up Elin. It was going to be a long day out here.

While he was waiting for her to answer, he couldn't help glancing at the water. A tern plummeted toward the surface and grabbed a fish. The rings spread outward, then vanished.

As if nothing had disturbed its fragile tranquility.

CHAPTER 71

"Your witness, herr Emilsson," Barbro Wikingsson said.

Nora felt battered and bruised, as if she'd just finished a full-on stint at the gym. Nothing new had emerged, whichever way she'd phrased her questions to Christian Dufva. Her efforts since lunch couldn't be regarded as anything other than a total fiasco.

At one point she'd considered confronting him, coming straight out with the allegation that Winnerman had paid him to change his testimony, but she knew that Emilsson would immediately accuse her of harassing the witness.

Now it was his turn.

Dufva waited, his eyes sunken. He'd emptied his glass of water and refilled it from the pitcher in front of him. He was facing Emilsson, but after a little while, he moved his chair a fraction, as if he sensed that Nora was watching him. The leg of the chair scraped along the floor.

Emilsson adjusted his tie.

"It must have been your worst nightmare," he began. "Seeing the company go bankrupt, losing everything you'd worked for."

"It was terrible. That's exactly what this last year has been—a nightmare."

"The prosecutor has pointed out that there are certain . . . let us call them discrepancies between your testimony today and your original statement to the police. Perhaps we could clear that up once and for all?"

Dufva nodded.

"How did you feel when Alliance Construction collapsed?"

"It was hard to understand—one minute the business was doing well, the next it was a disaster. Things just got worse and worse, however hard we tried to salvage the situation. Then the police got involved . . . I never thought we'd end up here."

He spread his hands wide, but Nora couldn't summon up a scrap of sympathy.

"How did you react? You must have experienced a range of powerful emotions—bitterness and sorrow, maybe even anger? Personally, I would have been furious!"

"I was very upset."

"Did you want revenge?"

"I'm sorry?"

"Did you want to get even?" Emilsson shook his fist. "Under circumstances like these, we all want to blame our misfortune on somebody else, wouldn't you say?"

He paused, offering Dufva the opportunity to agree. Dennis Grönstedt waited for the answer with his arms folded, and Barbro Wikingsson raised an inquiring eyebrow.

"You don't need to be ashamed of feeling that way," Emilsson went on encouragingly. "It's a perfectly normal, human reaction."

"Yes."

Even though the room was quiet, Dufva's voice was barely audible. A fan hummed in the background, but had little or no effect on the stuffy atmosphere. Nora felt as if the oxygen wouldn't last the day.

"Christian, isn't it the truth that you took out your frustration on your partner? That you let out all those feelings when you were questioned by the police, without giving a thought to the consequences?"

The corner of Dufva's mouth twitched. "I expect it was a relief to hit back, metaphorically speaking. To blame this whole mess, if I may call it that, on Niklas Winnerman. It had to be someone's fault, and Niklas was the easiest target."

Nora couldn't help noticing that two of the jurors nodded in recognition.

The case was going downhill fast.

"Isn't that what happened? You needed—no, you longed for a scapegoat, and your business partner was right there. Despite the fact that you'd been good friends for so long, despite the fact that you'd built up the company together."

Dufva buried his face in his hands. "I thought it was Niklas's fault that we'd lost everything."

"And then it was too late to take back what you'd said, wasn't it? Once it was all written down and you'd signed the statement the prosecutor was waving around this morning."

Emilsson was firing off one leading question after another, but who was going to stop him? Dufva was Nora's witness, so Emilsson had the right to cross-examine him.

"You couldn't revoke what you'd said," Emilsson continued smoothly. "It was easier to carry on accusing Niklas instead of admitting the truth."

"That's right."

Emilsson leaned forward. The handkerchief in his top pocket, an exact match with his tie, fluttered a fraction.

"In that case I must repeat what the prosecutor said earlier." His voice had taken on a new, serious tone. "You understand that you're under oath? That you could be charged with perjury if you don't tell the truth, the whole truth, and nothing but the truth?"

"I understand."

"Can we believe what you're telling us now? What you said to the police wasn't true, but today you're being completely honest?"

"I am."

Nora wondered if she was getting a fever; her skin was prickling, and her legs were sweaty beneath her pencil skirt.

"So there was no deception on the part of Niklas Winnerman, as you previously alleged."

"No."

"Is it true to say that Niklas Winnerman acted with good intentions, and that his aim was to secure a good deal for the company?"

"Yes."

Emilsson took a moment to make eye contact with each juror in turn. Annika Sandberg was sitting with her head tilted to one side.

"In your opinion, is Niklas Winnerman guilty of the offense known as grave disloyalty to principal, by defrauding Alliance Construction of the sum of ten million kronor?"

"No," Christian Dufva said. "No, he isn't."

CHAPTER 72

Isak was sitting outside the sauna when Maja found him. The sun was hot, and Isak had moved into the shade, his back against the wall. He couldn't even bring himself to look up as Maja approached.

"I thought you'd be here," she said, sitting down beside him. "I heard what had happened, so I came back in one of the escort boats." She took his hand and stroked it.

Her sympathy was more than Isak could bear. He shook his head, turned away.

Maja leaned forward. Her sunglasses had left pale rings around her eyes. Her face was suddenly much too close, and he pulled back.

"How are you feeling?"

What a stupid fucking question.

"How do you think I'm feeling?" he said with such force that a blob of saliva landed on her cheek. "The police are here and Benjamin's missing!"

Maja's eyes widened. "Listen, I know it's not easy, but nobody blames you."

"You know nothing!"

He'd seen it in the eyes of the two detectives, those accusing looks when they were asking about Benjamin's last few hours in camp.

He was the instructor who couldn't keep tabs on his kids. First Clara, now Benjamin.

He deserved their contempt.

He'd been naïve enough to think that Benjamin running away was the worst thing imaginable, but now he realized there was another, much darker scenario.

What would he do if Benjamin had drowned? If the little boy was lying at the bottom of the sea with his skin turning blue?

It was obvious that it was all his fault. He'd neglected his duties. He should never have taken this job; he should have realized right from the start that he would fail, just as he'd failed at everything else in his life.

Maja wasn't about to give up. "Why don't you come and have something to eat? The housekeeper's put out some sandwiches in the dining hall. I'm sure you'll feel better with something inside you."

"I'm not hungry."

The cramps in his stomach were coming in waves, as they'd done all day.

"Come with me anyway. Isak?"

Maja waited for his reaction.

"David's wondering where you are," she said eventually, reaching out to stroke his cheek.

Isak knocked her hand aside. "Don't touch me."

"I'm only trying to help."

"Leave me alone!"

"Isak, please . . ."

Her eyes shone with tears, but he didn't have the energy to consider her feelings.

How bitterly he regretted the time they'd spent together that morning.

"I was on my way to look for Benjamin when you stopped me," he said nastily.

"When I stopped you?" Maja pushed herself backward, away from him.

"If it hadn't been for you, I might have found him."

It was unfair and he knew it, but it was too late now.

Maja leaped to her feet and wiped her nose with her hand. "Fuck you!" she shouted, and ran away.

Somehow Isak had thought he'd feel better if he made her feel bad, but instead his sense of guilt was overwhelming now.

He reached into his pocket, touched the bottle of pills. How many were left? No more than a dozen.

He clawed at his arm, which was already red raw. He stared after Maja, who had disappeared among the trees.

"I'm sorry," he whispered. "I didn't mean it."

CHAPTER 73

The sailing dinghies were approaching Lökholmen. Thomas was standing outside the dining hall watching them come in, one after the other with the wind at their backs, sails billowing. The sound of cheerful voices drifted through the air, accompanied by the odd burst of laughter in the warm afternoon sun.

He'd just spoken to his mother, who'd collected Elin and taken her back to his parents' house. It was best if Elin slept there tonight; he didn't know what time he'd be back on the mainland. He didn't bother contacting Pernilla; she wasn't home anyway.

It was almost four o'clock, and Benjamin was still missing without a trace.

He heard a dog barking not far away. Two dog handlers had arrived an hour earlier, along with other officers to help with the search. Thomas had quickly outlined the situation and formed a plan of action. The fire department on Sandhamn had also been called in.

The dogs would pick up Benjamin's scent all over the camp, but if he was hiding somewhere on the island, they would find him.

The maritime police had already started dragging the offshore waters.

"Hi, Thomas."

Kalle Lidwall was coming toward him in sunglasses and a dark-blue baseball cap. Thomas raised a hand in greeting. He was very pleased to see his colleague; Kalle had developed into an excellent interrogator, and had recently completed specialist training to further hone his skills. Interviewing children and adolescents was a delicate balancing act. It was essential to convey the seriousness of the matter, while at the same time creating a sense of security in a frightening situation. Scared children had difficulty remembering things, and right now the police needed all the information they could get.

Aram and Thomas had already discussed where they should begin, and how the questions should be put.

"Any news on the father?" Thomas asked. "Has he been located yet?"

Kalle shook his head as he rolled up the sleeves of his pale-blue shirt. "No one seems to know where he is, including the ex-wife. Margit's spoken to her. There's no answer from his apartment, and his cell is switched off. Same with the new wife."

That wasn't a good sign, but right now they had to prioritize the search for Benjamin.

"What about the list of boat owners we sent over?"

"Adrian and Karin are working on it, but there are quite a lot of names to go through—you know how it is."

Thomas nodded. Everything took time, and a systematic approach was essential. And yet he couldn't help feeling frustrated. He glanced at his watch; five past four.

The first of the dinghies were mooring at the fixed buoys down below the dining hall. A catamaran with a neon-yellow foresail glided up to the ramp.

"Thomas!"

Aram was hurrying along the path with an agitated look on his face.

"One of the dogs has signaled—down by Skothalarfladen."

Thomas and Kalle quickly followed Aram to the grassy area in front of the dormitories. Aram pointed to the jetty at the bottom of the hill, just beyond the camp itself. Thomas knew that the instructors and visitors often used the mooring; he'd done so himself last Saturday.

"Over there."

Thomas immediately recognized the gray-haired handler at the far end of the jetty. He'd met her seven years earlier on a bitterly cold February day on Sandhamn. On that occasion her German shepherd had found the place where the dismembered remains of a nineteen-year-old had been hidden. In spite of the fact that six months had passed since the girl had been murdered, the dog had signaled without hesitation.

He hoped there would be no further similarities with that case.

"We've met before," Sofia Granit said as soon as Thomas reached her. Today she was accompanied by a Belgian shepherd.

"We have—it's been a while. So what have you found?"

Sofia was holding a blue T-shirt belonging to Benjamin, which she'd used to give her dog the scent. The small garment made Thomas think of Elin, and his heart turned over. Pernilla had taken off because of *her* job. He was searching for a missing child while she was discussing brand-marketing strategies.

He couldn't bury his head in the sand any longer. They had to sit down and talk when she got home.

"This is Jackson," Sofia said, interrupting Thomas's train of thought. "He's only four, but he's already very good." She produced a dog biscuit from her pocket and held it out.

"What happened to . . . ?" He couldn't think of the name.

"Raja?"

"That's it."

"Tumors." There was a deep sadness in Sofia's eyes. "She's crossed the rainbow bridge, as they say." She bent down and patted Jackson. "You're a clever boy, aren't you?"

Jackson wagged his tail.

"So you've found something?"

"Jackson's signaled in several places." Sofia pointed to a vacant berth between the jetty and the shoreline. "The missing boy has definitely been on board a boat that was moored here. There are traces farther out; Jackson was on his way into the water when I stopped him."

It didn't take much to leave a scent trace—a hand grabbing a gunwale, a leg brushing against the side of a boat.

Thomas peered over the edge. The water was shallow; he could see the bottom all the way to the shore. If Benjamin had fallen in here, they would have found him. A body shouldn't have drifted away so quickly.

"Anything you can tell us in terms of a timescale?" Aram asked.

Sofia gave a wry smile and said, "Recently." She moved her hand, and Jackson immediately lay down at her feet. "He's a good dog, but he doesn't have a digital time reader in that nose."

Thomas rubbed his chin. The outlet to Sandhamn was opposite the pontoon, no more than a hundred yards away. Beyond lay the Sandhamn Sound, and the shipping lane to Stavsnäs and the mainland. A boat setting off from here would be gone in seconds.

"The mother still hasn't heard anything from Benjamin," Aram said.

Åsa Dufva was at home, waiting by the phone. She'd repeatedly assured Margit that there was no way her son would fail to contact her if he'd run away. They were very close; it seemed that Benjamin didn't have quite such a good relationship with his father.

Thomas turned to look in the other direction, toward the marina at Kroksöfladen. How far was that—maybe three hundred yards?

It wasn't such a long way, but the uneven terrain made it difficult to take a direct route, especially at night when it was dark. There were rocks and undergrowth, and no lighting. However, for a boat owner who was already in Kroksöfladen, it would be a simple matter to come around and moor at this jetty.

If someone had an errand in the camp. If someone wanted to take a little boy from his bed.

Was he moving too fast? It was important not to jump to conclusions based on the dog's first signal. They still had so little to go on; they hadn't even gotten ahold of Benjamin's father.

Aram had followed his gaze. "Are you thinking of the guy on the boat? Could he be involved?"

"If he moored here with the intention of abducting Benjamin, and carried him back to the boat . . . It's the perfect spot." Thomas knew this was pure speculation.

"There could be plenty of reasons why he's no longer here," Aram pointed out. "His vacation is over, he was heading somewhere else for Midsummer . . ."

Aram was right, but the probability that Benjamin had run away was getting smaller by the minute. The coast guard was also out searching, but had found nothing so far.

They would have to ask David if the kids were in the habit of coming down here, if there was any reason for Benjamin to be on this particular jetty. Otherwise there might be a completely different explanation for the scent traces.

The fact that Benjamin hadn't left the camp of his own free will.

CHAPTER 74

When David came out of the common room, he saw a group of police officers standing on the jetty with the dog handler. Should he walk over, ask how things were going?

The head office had just called and asked the same question as before: *Have you found Benjamin yet?*

Every time he said no, his tongue felt thick and unmanageable.

Björn Ekholm, the director, was on his way over to help out. David's cell phone rang constantly, and there was a never-ending stream of text messages as the news spread.

He noticed Sebbe sitting on the steps of Star, flipping through a magazine.

David hadn't been able to stop thinking about Samuel and the way he'd bullied Benjamin right in front of the staff without anyone noticing. He knew Samuel had a bad reputation, he'd heard the whispers, but hadn't seen any real indication that they were true.

Until now.

When Sofie and the other girls had told the police what they knew, he'd clenched his fists. He was supposed to be in charge of the camp, but he hadn't had a clue what was really going on.

Any residual sense of shame was driven out by anger. Enough messing around, enough pandering to these spoiled brats whose parents simply dumped them at camp!

"Sebbe! Get over here now!"

Sebbe put down the magazine and got to his feet. He brushed the dust of his shorts and ambled across the grass. "What?"

"Where's Samuel?"

"No idea. I think he said he was going sailing."

David grabbed hold of Sebbe's arm. "What did you and Samuel do to Benjamin?"

"I don't know what you're talking about." Sebbe looked away. He was four inches shorter than David, and a lot skinnier. A large zit on his forehead was about to burst.

"You know exactly what I'm talking about. You and Samuel have behaved like complete assholes toward a younger camp mate." David tightened his grip. There was no one else within earshot, and he realized he'd just made a decision. If Benjamin was missing because of this little shit and his friend, then he was going to get to the bottom of it. Whatever it took.

They had only themselves to blame.

That cop, Thomas Andreasson, had hinted more than once that Benjamin could have fallen into the water and drowned.

Or been pushed in.

The image of the boy's dead body floating in the sea came into his mind.

Had the bullying gone too far? David couldn't help wondering when he'd heard what Samuel had done, the way Sofie and her friends had described him.

Kids could be astonishingly cruel to one another. David had seen all kinds of behavior during his years at sailing camp; this was his fourth summer on Lökholmen, and his second as senior instructor.

Sometimes he thought it wasn't the kids' fault that they turned out as they did; some of the parents were far worse than their offspring, especially the nouveau riche fortysomethings who often had a really arrogant attitude.

He'd thought he had everything under control. He'd raised the issue of bullying on the very first evening, when the instructors first got together. Early puberty was the worst age for that kind of thing, and he'd stressed the importance of intervening at the first sign of any problem. The camp had an antibullying policy and clearly laid out procedures, but this time they'd failed completely.

Once again he wondered whether it had been a mistake to employ Isak, whether the situation would have been different if Blue Group had had a more experienced leader.

"Let go—I need to pee!" Sebbe said, trying to pull away.

David felt a surge of rage, and the change in his expression had an immediate effect on Sebbe. The boy was clearly terrified, and his body went limp.

Was that how Benjamin had looked?

The thought was devastating. No one had been there to protect him.

"You're going to tell me exactly what happened," David said in a voice he'd never used to a child in camp. "What did the two of you do to Benjamin?"

Sebbe visibly shrank. His voice was barely audible.

"It wasn't me. It was Samuel."

CHAPTER 75

Isak stared out across the water. If Benjamin had drowned, would he be held responsible?

The wind was blowing at around eleven knots; it was a good day for a longer sailing trip. Unfortunately the day's activities had needed to be interrupted. He'd seen the boats on their way back, making their way to the jetty down below the dining hall.

He remembered the contract he'd signed when he accepted the job as instructor. Clause after clause on obligations and responsibilities, the duty of care toward the children, the vital importance of carrying out the requirements of the post.

He hadn't shown that duty of care, hadn't done his job properly. He'd failed to fulfill his responsibilities.

Might he face criminal charges? He didn't think so, but the fear was gnawing away at him.

What if they found out he'd been with Maja instead of looking for Benjamin?

He'd been perfectly well aware that he was doing something wrong, but he hadn't cared. *It'll be fine,* he'd thought, because he wanted to be with Maja.

Despite the fact that Benjamin was already missing.

The thought made him let out a sob, and he rubbed his eyes. Benjamin's parents must be so worried by now, and it was all Isak's fault. He'd never be able to explain to his own father how Benjamin had disappeared on his watch. His father, who always insisted that failure was not an option.

"Grit your teeth and do your best," that was what he always said. For once he'd been proud of Isak.

"My son's going to be an instructor on Lökholmen," he'd boasted to anyone who would listen. "There were so many applicants, but Isak got the job!"

He wouldn't be proud now. Instead he would stare at Isak with the same frustrated expression he'd worn throughout last year, as if he'd always known that his youngest son would never live up to his expectations.

The cramp in his stomach had settled into a dull ache. He hadn't eaten since the previous evening. There was no point in trying to force anything down; he was thirsty, though.

But how could he go over to the dining hall and face the other instructors? David had run out of patience with him, and he'd pushed Maja away. She'd be better off with someone else.

His throat was bone dry. He got up and opened the door of the sauna to see if anyone had left a drink behind—maybe a bottle of water or a soda?

He looked around and spotted a half-full can of Coke in the outer room. It didn't taste too good, but at least it quenched the worst of his thirst. He continued into the inner room and sat down on the slatted bench, running his fingers along the rough wooden panels on the wall. He'd always enjoyed spending time in here after a day at sea, letting the heat penetrate his skin, feeling his muscles slowly begin to relax.

Now the place seemed totally alien to him.

He went back into the outer room. As he put down the empty can, he spotted a rope in one corner, neatly coiled. He bent down and picked it up. It must measure a good fifteen feet, if not more. Brand new—there was no sign of dried seaweed or brown kelp stuck to its surface.

Isak looked up at the ceiling. A sturdy hook had been fixed there one evening when they were playing a stupid game. Everyone had to knock back a beer, then haul himself or herself up a rope and hang there by one arm for at least ten seconds.

He ran his hand over the rope; it was cool against his palm.

Over by the wall was a wooden box that would bear his weight.

He looked up at the hook once more.

The silver-colored metal glinted in the sunlight, shining in through the window. Tiny dust motes danced in the air, forming a shimmering halo around the hook.

Maybe there was another way out?

CHAPTER 76

Thomas and Aram were about to go into the dining hall when someone came running up behind them.

"Hang on a minute," David shouted.

All the participants in the sailing camp had been called to a meeting that was due to begin shortly, at five o'clock. Children and instructors were approaching from all directions.

Thomas stopped by the ramp, where several boats had been hauled out of the water and carelessly dumped, sails still fluttering in the breeze. There hadn't been time to de-rig.

David scrubbed at his forehead with a clenched fist. "I've spoken to Sebbe again. I made him tell me what really happened in the forest."

Aram simply shook his head when David explained how Samuel had threatened Benjamin with his belt, how fear had made the little boy wet himself.

"That's not all," David went on. "Apparently the boys found Benjamin sitting on a rock by the water the day before yesterday, in the evening. They made him strip naked, then threw all his clothes in the water and ran away." His breathing was labored. "Little shits."

Thomas looked at David closely. His eyes were bloodshot, and he was blinking rapidly. He mustn't break down now; they needed his help. Thomas took a step forward and placed a hand on his shoulder. "Are you OK?"

David rubbed his hand beneath his nose. "Those two need to be sent home immediately!" he burst out.

Aram had taken out his notebook and turned to a clean page. "Did Sebbe say anything about last night?" he asked.

David shook his head, shuddered. "He swears they didn't touch Benjamin again. The last time he saw Benjamin was in the dining hall when everyone came back from the quiz. Benjamin was already in bed when they got back to the dormitory, and Sebbe fell asleep almost right away."

"In that case he can't possibly know what Samuel did," Aram pointed out. He turned to Thomas. "Eight hours is a long time to lie there waiting for more trouble. It's enough to make any kid take off."

Was that the explanation? Had Samuel frightened Benjamin so much that he simply ran away?

Or was it the other way around? Had Samuel waited until everyone was asleep, then attacked Benjamin again? Taken him outside and done God knows what?

Jackson had found Benjamin's scent down by the pontoon. The cabin where he slept was no more than a hundred yards away.

"Tell me something," Thomas said. "Do the children spend time on the pontoon?"

"No—we actually tell them not to go there, because that's where we moor the escort boats, and we don't want anyone messing around with them."

"Do you know if there were any boats there last night?"

"I'm sure there were. Blue Group's escort boats would have been there. And White Group's." David pointed to the jetty in front of them. "There isn't room for all the boats on this side."

Aram seemed to understand where Thomas was going. They had to find out whether Samuel had somehow forced Benjamin into one of the boats during the night.

"Is Samuel capable of driving an escort boat?"

David frowned. "I don't know for sure, but I guess so. Most kids of his age whose family has a summer cottage in the archipelago can handle a motorboat. Ours aren't complicated, but of course he'd need a key."

Thomas still had a bad feeling. They had to speak to Samuel again—as soon as possible. "Where are Samuel and Sebbe now?"

"They should be in there," David replied, pointing to the dining hall. "I haven't seen Samuel for a few hours; Sebbe said he was out in one of the boats. Maybe he was helping with the search, though I find that hard to believe. But everyone's supposed to be at the meeting."

Through the doorway Thomas could see something like a hundred people. Many were still wearing unfastened life jackets, having come straight from their sailing trip.

No doubt the news had spread by now. Blue Group already knew what had happened, and would have shared the story with their friends as they came ashore.

Out of the corner of his eye, Thomas saw the instructors gathering by the doorway. A blonde girl looked particularly upset; her eyes were puffy, her nose red. There was no sign of Isak; come to think of it, Thomas hadn't seen him for quite some time.

A nervous buzz of conversation could be heard. David glanced at his diver's watch. "We ought to get started."

Thomas nodded, still trying to spot Samuel. The group of instructors dispersed, and a few latecomers hurried in.

Kalle Lidwall arrived with two uniformed officers, causing the volume of chatter in the dining hall to increase.

Right now the CSIs were going over the dormitory in Star. Staffan Nilsson, Nacka's most experienced forensic technician, had also arrived.

"I want to speak to those two boys as soon as the meeting's over," Thomas said.

CHAPTER 77

Christian Dufva left the courthouse with no idea where to go. This had been one of the longest days of his life. He lived in Birkastan, yet an hour later he found himself in the Söder district, in the middle of Götgatan, where the rush-hour traffic was just beginning to ease.

He couldn't face the thought of going home, let alone traveling out to his in-laws' country home in Norrtälje, where Ninna was waiting with Emil.

When he came across a bar a couple of blocks past Medborgarplatsen, he went inside without hesitation.

"A double Cognac," he mumbled to the bartender. He paid with two one-hundred-kronor notes.

The decor was a parody of an American sports bar, with various team pennants on the ceiling and pinball machines along the walls. There was an enormous flat-screen TV above the bar with the volume turned down; two foreign teams were playing soccer.

The place was almost empty, and Christian found himself a quiet corner. No doubt Ninna was wondering where he was, but he couldn't bring himself to call her—not yet. She would demand an explanation for his behavior this morning, when he'd insisted that she and Emil must go to her parents' house. She would ask questions he couldn't answer.

He could already hear her moaning and complaining, and he knew he'd snap if she started on him, especially when he felt so wretched and powerless.

He ran his tongue over his teeth, felt how dirty they were. By this time his tongue should be black from all the lies he'd told.

His phone was still off. He took it out of his pocket, and his pulse increased as the black metal case glinted in the light.

A symbol for the misery in his life.

If he switched it on, he became accessible, just like this morning, and his world might come crashing down. Until then he could pretend that everything was fine.

Obliterate this day, as if it had never happened.

Christian emptied his glass and signaled to the bartender. One more drink, then he'd switch on his phone and call Ninna.

He wandered over to the jukebox and inserted a five-kronor coin. An old up-tempo number from the eighties began to play, drowning out the memory of that threatening voice. His head was pounding; he felt as if a steel band was slowly tightening around his skull. The painkillers he'd bought at lunchtime were useless. It couldn't have hurt more if someone had driven a steel spike into his cranium.

The door opened, and two men in their thirties walked in—typical hipsters with horn-rimmed glasses and close-fitting shirts, the kind of intellectuals who populated the former workers' district of Söder these days.

They glanced in his direction, but he ignored them and knocked back half of his second Cognac.

Then he froze.

Those two guys didn't belong here. A sports bar wasn't the kind of place they'd hang out in. He thought he detected a hint of a foreign accent as they each ordered a beer.

They must have followed him.

Christian broke out into a cold sweat. How had they managed to find him so fast?

They were sitting between him and the door. He was caught in a trap. The bartender leaned forward and asked them something—was he involved, too?

Perspiration trickled down the back of Christian's neck. His eyes darted around the room. There must be an emergency exit somewhere, a window he could climb through—where was the restroom?

As he got to his feet to make a run for it, the door opened again and a woman in a yellow summer dress came in. She went over to the two men, kissed one of them on the lips, and gave the other a warm hug.

Christian sank down on his chair and buried his face in his hands.

There was nothing shady about the trio; they were normal people out for a beer. He was haunted by his own demons, that was all.

Tears seeped between his fingers and dripped onto the table. He cursed the day he met Niklas Winnerman.

He emptied his glass and caught the bartender's eye to order another.

CHAPTER 78

David clapped his hands to get everyone's attention. He was still wearing his red baseball cap, which made his shocked face look even paler.

"Unfortunately I have some bad news," he began. He blinked several times, searching for the right words. "As some of you are already aware, one of our boys is missing—Benjamin Dufva from Blue Group. We don't know where he is; he could have run away, or fallen in the water. We're extremely concerned about him."

Whispers spread around the room like wildfire, and Thomas heard a sob. He spotted Tindra at a table not far away. She had tears in her eyes, and Sofie put her arm around her friend's shoulders.

"No one has seen Benjamin since last night," David continued. "We've informed his parents and are in regular contact with them."

That wasn't entirely true; they'd only spoken to his mother. Thomas was more and more uneasy about the fact that his father seemed to have vanished into thin air.

"No more sailing today. We'll be calling your parents to tell them what's happened, and we will also be returning your cell phones shortly. If anyone wants to speak to an adult here in the camp, your instructors will be around the rest of the day."

As soon as David stopped speaking, the noise level rose. He clapped his hands, but to no effect. Eventually a loud whistle sliced through the air.

"The police are on-site searching for Benjamin," David said, pointing to Thomas. "This is Detective Inspector Thomas Andreasson from Nacka, and he'd like to say a few words."

Thomas went and joined David. Behind them a staircase led up to the loft, where all kinds of equipment were stored. A couple of windsurfing boards were poking through the banister, and a life jacket was drying on a hook.

Confused faces gazed up at Thomas, but here and there he caught a glimpse of something darker, an enjoyment in the sensationalism of it all. This would be an exciting story to tell back in school when the summer was over.

Sebbe was sitting to the side, but there was no sign of Samuel. Thomas made eye contact with Aram and nodded in Sebbe's direction. There was a space around the boy, as if the other children had instinctively moved away when David explained that Benjamin was missing. Maybe the girls weren't the only ones who'd known about the bullying?

Thomas waited until the room fell silent.

"So Benjamin Dufva is missing, and we already have a large number of police officers searching for him all over the island and in the waters offshore. We've also put out a call to every police force across the country." He pointed to Aram and Kalle. "My colleagues, Aram Gorgis and Kalle Lidwall, and I will need to speak to all of you with any information about Benjamin as soon as possible. We need to find out if anyone's seen him since midnight. We'd also like to know if he indicated that he wasn't happy here, or hinted at where he might go. Even the smallest piece of information is important."

Several of the girls were crying now, and there was quite a lot of whispering, even though Thomas hadn't finished.

"Make sure you tell us everything you know, even if you think it might not be relevant," he emphasized, hoping he had gotten his message across.

He saw the glint of a phone case as one of the instructors took out his cell. These days no one was more than ten seconds away from the Internet. He would have to tell them to go easy on social media, before the whole story was all over Instagram and Facebook.

"If you know where Benjamin might be, it's essential that you tell us," he said again. "This is not a game."

He knew he had to mention the other possibility.

"One more thing. If anyone has seen anything unusual over the past couple of days, for example, a stranger in the vicinity of the camp, we need to know. We can't exclude the possibility that Benjamin has been abducted."

The murmur of voices died away, then rose to a crescendo.

The meeting was over, and the dining hall was beginning to empty. In spite of the height of the ceiling—around twenty-four feet—the air was oppressive beneath the corrugated metal.

"I saw Sebbe sitting on his own," Thomas said quietly to David; he didn't want the children who were still around to hear the conversation. "But Samuel wasn't there. Have you seen him?"

David shook his head. He seemed calmer now, but the color hadn't returned to his face.

Anxious voices could be heard from outside; small groups had gathered around the tables on the terrace.

"Could you please find him for us? Right away."

David nodded. "Anything else I can do?"

"We want to begin the interviews. I was thinking of using the instructors' common room; could Aram and Kalle each take a corner of the classroom?"

"No problem."

Thomas's phone rang: Margit. He hoped she'd managed to get ahold of Benjamin's father.

"I have to take this. Let me know as soon as you track down Samuel."

CHAPTER 79

The door of the common room closed behind thirteen-year-old Sabina. She barely remembered Benjamin despite the fact that they'd been in the same group, and she certainly had no idea where he might have gone.

Thomas straightened his back, trying to inject fresh life into his stiff muscles. The chairs in here weren't exactly ergonomic. His neck cracked unpleasantly when he turned his head from side to side.

He couldn't help wondering about Samuel Karlberg. What the hell was wrong with a kid of fourteen who was prepared to whip an eleven-year-old, who got a kick out of tormenting others? Lack of empathy was one thing, but what Samuel had done to Benjamin was utterly heartless, evidence of a cruelty that was hard to imagine in someone of that age.

According to David, Samuel was the youngest of three siblings, with a significant age gap between him and the other two. There were also two grown-up half siblings from his father's first marriage. Ragnar Karlberg was a well-known figure, the managing director of one of the country's largest business conglomerates, and he often featured in the business press.

Thomas glanced at his watch: almost six thirty. Where was David? Surely he should have found Samuel by now.

The door opened and Aram appeared. Thomas was pleased to see that he was carrying two cups of coffee.

"We're not going to finish tonight," Aram said. "We'll have to come back tomorrow."

"Do you think they'll all still be here by then?"

A number of parents were on the way to the camp; as Thomas had feared, the story had spread fast. He knew that Margit had had to deal with a lot of calls.

"It would be best if the kids could stay in camp for now," Aram agreed.

It was much easier to interview them on Lökholmen instead of driving all over the city to track them down, but they couldn't prevent worried parents from taking their children home.

"Anything from the offshore teams?"

Aram shook his head. "No news is good news, I guess. Under the circumstances."

Thomas had just spoken to the colleague who was responsible for the search parties on Sandhamn. Dog teams had been brought in, but found nothing. The best lead was still the spot by the jetty, where Jackson had picked up Benjamin's scent.

"I'm still waiting to speak to Samuel," Thomas said. "Have you seen David? He was supposed to be looking for him, but that was over an hour ago."

"I thought you'd already spoken to him."

Thomas's phone rang; it was David. "How's it going?"

"I'm afraid I can't find Samuel." David sounded as if he was on the verge of tears.

"What do you mean?"

"Nobody's seen him for hours, and Sebbe doesn't know where he is."

Thomas closed his eyes. Not another child. "When was the last time someone saw him?"

"Sebbe says they met up at about four o'clock, and Samuel said he was leaving."

"Who with?"

"Sebbe thought one of the escort boats was taking him somewhere, but none of the instructors I've spoken to has seen him."

Thomas put down his coffee. "Have all the instructors confirmed that Samuel wasn't with them?"

"All but two."

"Find them and check. I'll see you in the classroom in ten minutes."

Aram raised his eyebrows inquiringly as Thomas ended the call.

"Apparently Samuel has gone missing, too. We'd better go and join Kalle."

There were so many issues to deal with; Thomas hardly knew where to start. At that moment there was a knock on the door. The female instructor Thomas had noticed earlier was standing there.

"Sorry to disturb you, but there's something you need to hear."

"Unfortunately we don't have time right now," Aram said.

"It's really important." She chewed at her lower lip; Thomas realized she was very stressed. "Please, it'll only take a minute."

Thomas looked at Aram, who nodded. Thomas beckoned the young woman in, even though he was so restless he could barely sit still.

"What's your name?"

"Maja—I'm the instructor for Yellow Group."

As Maja came into the room, Thomas saw a small red-haired child behind her. The girl's face was covered in freckles that continued down her throat.

"This is Agnes," Maja said. "Tell these police officers what you told me just now."

"Hi, Agnes," Aram said calmly, as if they were in no hurry at all. "Come and sit down. So how old are you?"

"I'm eleven, but I'll be twelve at the beginning of December."

She was quite short, and still looked like a child. One front tooth was crooked, and her skinny legs were covered in mosquito bites.

Maja sat down next to Agnes. She placed her hand over the girl's and gave her a reassuring squeeze.

"Tell them about the man you saw outside Benjamin's cabin first thing this morning."

Chapter 80

Nora looked out the subway window. They'd almost reached Slussen. Her phone rang, but by the time she'd dug it out of her purse, it had gone to voice mail. When she saw that it was Jonas, she called him back immediately, but needless to say reached his voice mail instead.

Nothing was going her way right now.

It was only a few days to Midsummer's Eve, yet the disastrous events in court overshadowed everything else. She was incapable of looking forward to her wedding. She stared at her phone, then called Leila.

"How's it going?" she asked before Leila had time to speak.

"I was just about to call you. I've been in touch with a guy in the security department at Handelsbanken, and he has access to the CCTV footage from the Hallunda branch."

Something flickered in Nora's breast.

"The only problem is he's up north, in Kiruna. He won't be back until late tonight. I've arranged to meet him at ten o'clock in the morning."

An automated voice informed Nora that the next station was Slussen. She gathered up her things and got to her feet.

"That's when we're due to start summing up," she said. "Can't you move the meeting forward?"

She knew she was grasping at straws, but anything was better than what she'd achieved today.

"I'll call you as soon as I find something," Leila promised.

The doors opened and Nora headed for the Saltsjö line. The train was already in, so she broke into a run; departures were every twenty minutes, and she didn't want to miss this one.

Once she was in her seat, she decided to try Jonas again, and this time he answered.

At last. She couldn't help smiling; just the sound of his voice made her feel so much better. The image of Jacob Emilsson's supercilious smile disappeared, along with the memory of Christian Dufva's lies and Niklas Winnerman's face.

"Do you know how much I miss you?" she said.

"I miss you, too. How's the trial going?"

"Not too well. I can't bring myself to talk about it." She massaged her temple.

"Is it that bad?"

"I'll tell you all about it when you get home. What time will you be back tomorrow?"

"We were due to land at nine thirty in the morning." He paused. Cleared his throat. "The thing is, we have a bit of a problem."

In the background Nora could hear a voice over a loudspeaker giving information in Thai.

"We were supposed to take off in an hour or so," Jonas went on. "But there are a few technical issues."

"Like what?" Nora realized she was almost shouting. She took a deep breath and tried to tone things down. "What's happened?"

"There's no point in going into details; the technicians are working as hard as they can. I just wanted to let you know that I might be slightly delayed."

"What does 'slightly delayed' mean?"

"I don't know, I can't answer that question at the moment. We'll take off as soon as the problem is fixed."

"And if it isn't fixed?"

"I'm sure it's nothing serious. You know how it is, a couple of lights flashing red instead of green . . ."

Nora knew him well enough to realize when he was being evasive. She also knew what his schedule looked like. If the plane was delayed for more than five hours, he wouldn't be allowed to fly on that day, because he would have been on duty for too long. If the repairs took twenty-four hours or more, then the airline would keep the same crew rather than flying out a new one. Which meant he might not be home until Thursday.

Nora rested her cheek against the window and closed her eyes. *I can't cope,* she thought. *I can't deal with this as well.*

As soon as he'd mentioned the flight to Bangkok, she'd been worried that something like this would happen, that he'd be held up on the way back to Sweden.

"Honestly, Nora. I'm sure it'll be fine."

Nora opened her eyes and stared out at the weeping birches, still fresh and green. They'd passed Östervik; soon the line would split in two, heading toward Solsidan and Saltsjöbaden.

"In the worst-case scenario, I'll be back on Thursday morning," Jonas assured her. "And we're not traveling over to Sandhamn until the afternoon."

The train pulled into Fisksätra station.

"We'll get everything done exactly as planned, I promise."

"You promised you'd be home in time."

"And I will."

There were yellow dandelions growing along the railway track, ugly weeds that ruined lawns and stained your clothes.

"We're getting married on Friday, Nora. Nothing is going to change that."

CHAPTER 81

Thomas was like a coiled spring. A man outside Benjamin's cabin? He gave Agnes an encouraging smile.

"I woke up early this morning," she began quietly. "I needed to pee." She broke off and looked at Maja. "As I was coming back from the restrooms, I saw a man opening the door of Star, where Benjamin sleeps."

She fell silent again, and Maja gave her hand a little squeeze.

"I waited, and after a little while he came out again."

"How long was he in there?"

"Not long."

"Five minutes? Ten?"

"Five, maybe. Or less." Agnes tugged at her sleeve. "It looked as if he was carrying something. I thought he was one of the instructors who'd gone in to collect something—a sail bag, maybe."

Or a child in a sleeping bag?

Thomas tried to picture the dormitory and Benjamin's bed. When he checked the room, all the beds had been unmade, with the sheets in a tangle and clothes and towels all over the place. But Benjamin's bed had been empty—no sheets or blankets. If Benjamin had used a sleeping bag, it was gone.

"Did you see where the man went?" Aram asked.

"Down toward the water."

Agnes lowered her head, her hair falling over her face. The warm red color glowed in the sunlight.

The man must have been heading for the jetty—where a boat was waiting for him and his prey. Maybe he'd put Benjamin down for a moment, which was why the dog had signaled earlier.

There was little room for doubt now: Benjamin had been abducted.

They already knew there was no ongoing custody battle between the parents. When Margit spoke to the mother, she'd been adamant that Christian Dufva wouldn't have taken his son; he wasn't even that keen on spending time with him.

It didn't make sense.

From what Agnes had said, it didn't sound as if Benjamin had been struggling. Had he been drugged? He must ask Staffan Nilsson to check for any traces of a sedative.

"What did you do then?" Aram prompted Agnes gently.

"I went back to bed. But after David told us about Benjamin, I went to Maja."

"Well done—that was the right thing to do."

Agnes fingered her necklace, a small pendant on a chain.

Thomas knew they'd been lucky. If Agnes had woken five minutes later, there would have been nothing to see. They must be grateful for the fact that a young girl in pajamas happened to be on the edge of the forest when the door of Star opened.

Maybe they should be grateful that the stranger hadn't taken her as well.

Where was Samuel?

"Can you tell us anything about the man's appearance?" Thomas asked. "What color was his hair? How was he dressed?"

Agnes swallowed and frowned. "He was wearing a hat. I think it was black, or dark blue. A dark color anyway."

"Not a baseball cap?" Aram interjected. According to Sofie and her friends, that was what the guy in the forest had been wearing.

Agnes shook her head. "No, it was, like, knitted. Pulled right down over his forehead."

He didn't want to be identified, Thomas thought. *He was smart enough to think of that. Was he afraid of being recognized by someone in the camp?*

Once again he thought of Benjamin's father, but dismissed the idea. What about the man in the forest, the boat owner?

"So you didn't see his face clearly?"

"No."

The response was no more than a whisper. Agnes's lower lip was trembling, and Maja was beginning to look concerned. There was no point in pushing the girl too far, but Aram couldn't help asking one final question.

"Are you absolutely sure it was a man? It couldn't have been a tall woman?"

"It looked like a man."

The tears came, and Maja put her arm around the child.

"Thanks, both of you," Thomas said. "What you've told us could be really important."

Aram closed the door behind the two girls. Thomas looked at his watch; they should have been in the classroom long ago.

"The sail bag she mentioned," Aram said. "Do you think that was Benjamin in a sleeping bag?"

Thomas nodded. There was a ruthlessness about this whole thing that he found disturbing; a kidnapper who entered a room where eight children lay sleeping had to have strong nerves.

A kidnapper who'd done this before.

"The question is whether it was Benjamin he was after from the get-go," Aram went on.

Thomas leaned against the wall and gazed out the half-open window. The shadows were longer now, the stones on the ground golden yellow in the evening sunlight.

"How many people knew Benjamin was at the camp?" he wondered.

"We'll need to check that out, but surely the MO suggests he was targeting Benjamin? Otherwise it would have been easier to take one of the boys near the door."

Benjamin's bed was by the window, at the far end of the room, which meant the perpetrator had to walk past all the other boys in order to reach him.

"And how did the kidnapper know that was Benjamin's bed?" Aram added. He opened the door, then paused. "It doesn't sound as if Samuel was involved in Benjamin's disappearance."

But Samuel was still missing. Was this part of a wider pattern they couldn't yet see?

Two boys missing from the same dormitory could hardly be a coincidence.

Chapter 82

Benjamin woke up because he was cold. His body felt weird, alien, as if it no longer belonged to him. His fingers and toes were numb, and his face felt . . . tight. He had a sore throat.

He wanted to move, but his arms refused to obey him. He tried to stretch his legs, but there was something wrong with his feet. Eventually he managed to raise his head, but it hurt.

Slowly he became aware that his wrists and ankles were bound. He was no longer in his own bed; instead he was lying on a hard surface, and something was digging into his back.

A strange noise penetrated his consciousness—the throbbing of an engine. There was an odd smell, too, diesel or gas fumes, an oily odor that made him feel sick.

He was in danger.

This insight was worse than the cold and the darkness. The sudden panic made it hard to get enough air; his breathing grew more and more rapid until his whole body was shaking.

Someone had taken him. Kidnapped him.

He started sobbing. "Help me, please help me!" His voice sounded feeble, pathetic, bouncing off the blackness all around him, but he carried on until he realized it was pointless; no one could hear him.

He shuffled a little, trying to find a position that wasn't painful. The rope was cutting into his wrists.

His lips were dry and cracked; he tried to lick them, but his tongue stuck to the flesh. The nausea was getting worse, but he couldn't let himself vomit all over his clothes.

Benjamin closed his eyes. The tears continued to flow, and he sniveled as he breathed through his nose.

Nobody knew where he was. Even he didn't know where he was.

Chapter 83

Who crept into a dormitory in the middle of the night and abducted an eleven-year-old from a room full of children? Thomas had been asking himself that question all the way to the classroom. Why hadn't anyone heard, woken up?

But according to David, after a long day at sea, the kids slept like logs.

David was sitting at a table with a man in his fifties, while Kalle was leaning on a wall next to a whiteboard and flip chart.

There was a pile of a dozen or so mattresses in one corner.

When the man saw Thomas and Aram, he stood up and held out his hand. "Björn Ekholm. I've come over from the head office; I'm responsible for all our sailing camps."

After fifteen years with the maritime police, Thomas recognized a sailor. The sun-bleached hair and weather-beaten complexion spoke for themselves. The harsh fluorescent lights brought his lined face into sharp focus.

"Have you found Samuel?" Thomas asked.

"His father came and picked him up in their boat," Ekholm explained. "He was concerned when he heard what had happened."

It was a relief to hear that Samuel was OK, but the unnecessary worry the boy had caused didn't exactly improve Thomas's impression of him.

"Any progress?" Ekholm wanted to know. His posture was almost unnaturally erect; Thomas wondered if he had a military background.

"We'll be leaving on the police launch shortly. We need to have a meeting back at Nacka to assess the situation."

Kalle nodded; he, too, had received Margit's text message calling everyone in.

The search had moved into a different phase when Benjamin was no longer considered a runaway but the victim of a kidnapping. Priorities changed, activity intensified.

With every hour that passed, the chances of finding him diminished.

Thomas summarized the new information they'd received from Agnes.

"So we think we're looking at an abduction," he said in conclusion.

David inhaled sharply. "He's been kidnapped?"

"I'm finding it hard to get my head around this," Ekholm said. "We've been running sailing camps for over fifty years. I can't believe something like this could happen here." He held up his phone, looking slightly dazed. "The press are calling nonstop. I don't know what to say."

"As little as possible."

Thomas spared a thought for Margit, who had also been fielding calls. He suspected the news about Benjamin would soon be on TV.

"The board is holding an emergency meeting," Ekholm continued. "The company will issue a brief statement as soon as possible." He glanced at the logo on the wall. "This is a disaster for us."

"There's something I have to ask," Thomas said. "We can't rule out the possibility that someone in the camp is involved. It seems as if the kidnapper knew exactly where Benjamin was sleeping."

They couldn't exclude anything at this stage. Agnes hadn't recognized the man, but he could easily have had help on the inside.

"I'd be appalled if any of our staff were a part of this," Ekholm said after a brief silence.

"How well do you know your instructors? Do you carry out detailed background checks?" Thomas deliberately kept his tone neutral.

"We don't go that deep," Ekholm admitted. "But they all go through an extensive training program before they begin. We're very meticulous about that."

"Can you give us a little more information on the program?" Aram said.

Ekholm placed his hands on the back of the chair. "First of all, there's a practical course on key aspects of sailing, safety, and seamanship, plus basic teaching techniques. Once applicants have successfully completed those modules, they can work as instructors, maintenance staff, or housekeepers. Then there's an advanced course for anyone who wants to be a group leader, then stage three is for those aiming to be senior instructors, like David here." He cleared his throat. "We take the process very seriously—I hope you understand that."

"No one is saying otherwise," Aram assured him.

"But how well do you actually know them?" Thomas asked again. Ekholm hadn't answered his question.

"We know quite a lot about them, I'd say. Most are friends before they start working for us, and many have been active in the club for years. Almost all of our instructors regularly attended camp when they were younger."

Thomas did a quick mental calculation. The company ran at least six camps on Lökholmen every summer. With between sixty and eighty children participating, each one would require around twenty instructors. That meant a total of maybe a hundred, assuming that some instructors would work more than one camp.

One rotten apple was all it took.

"I'd like to believe they're decent young people," Ekholm added. "I know a lot of them personally; their parents are often involved, too."

"Which doesn't help us to figure out how the perpetrator knew which block Benjamin was in, and which bed was his," Aram pointed out.

"There are lists of the children in each dormitory," Ekholm said. "Maybe he got ahold of one of those?"

"Who has access to the lists?"

"Everyone at the head office, and the instructors of course. And they're up on the door of each building before camp begins so the children know where to go."

"So anyone can see where a particular child is—they just have to glance at the list," Aram said.

Ekholm nodded.

The camp wasn't fenced in, nor was there any security presence. During the day the place was virtually deserted. It wouldn't be difficult to slip in and check the lists.

"Are the doors always left unlocked at night?" Thomas asked.

"Yes, they have to be in case anyone needs to go to the restroom," David replied.

"That's always been the case." Ekholm sounded almost apologetic.

Thomas didn't think he had anything to reproach himself for. It was entirely logical to leave the doors unlocked; a child who woke up during the night had to be able to dash off to the restroom if necessary.

However, that also meant that anyone could get in.

CHAPTER 84

The police launch had arrived; it was time to leave. Aram had already gone down to the boat; Thomas headed over to Star to see Staffan Nilsson. Kalle was staying on the island to interview more children with the help of uniformed colleagues before the camp emptied completely.

Blue-and-white police tape cordoned off the door of the building. Discarded boots and sneakers still littered the steps. Thomas ducked beneath the tape, went up the steps, and poked his head into Benjamin's dormitory. The room smelled of dust and sweat.

A black forensics case stood just inside the door; apart from that the place looked just the same as earlier in the day, with unmade beds and clothes all over the place. An orange life jacket had ended up on the floor.

And yet it felt completely different.

Staffan Nilsson was leaning over Benjamin's bed, holding a shining metallic instrument in his hand.

"How's it going?" Thomas called out. "The launch is here—we need to go."

If there was one man who knew exactly where to look, it was Nilsson. He was nearing retirement age, but Thomas hoped he would stay on until he was sixty-seven, or even longer. They needed experts of his caliber, just as much as the new, young IT guys who played with the Internet as if it were their own personal pet.

Nilsson's skills had led Thomas and his colleagues in the right direction many times.

"No sign of a struggle," he replied without turning around. "No traces of blood, no clumps of hair. I don't think there was any physical violence involved in Benjamin's abduction."

Thomas had already reached the same conclusion. "So he was drugged?"

"Either that or he was so scared he didn't dare call for help."

Someone who took a child in the middle of the night wouldn't want to attract any attention. Once again Thomas wondered why none of the other boys had woken up, but then again it had probably happened very fast.

"Have you found anything to indicate the use of some kind of sedative?" Thomas asked, trying to see what Nilsson was doing.

With the right drug, it wouldn't take long to knock someone out, especially a small child with very little body weight. Less than a minute with a preloaded syringe, or chloroform, which had a pleasant odor and was therefore more frequently used.

"I'm working on it." Nilsson held up an evidence bag. "We need to analyze this. Could be ether."

A piece of cloth soaked in ether was highly effective, and the compound could easily be bought online from most Eastern European countries.

Thomas's attention was caught by the closed window; it was just as easy to see in as out.

"If he was drugged, then this was planned," Nilsson went on. "People don't just wander around with ether in their pockets." He placed the evidence bag in his case and unzipped his white crime-scene suit.

Thomas thought about the man in the forest. Had he met Benjamin there by chance, or was he checking out the area?

"We've secured a number of prints from the window ledge and the bed frame," Nilsson said. "They may or may not help us."

How many people had been in this room recently? At least eight boys, parents, instructors, police officers . . . There must be hundreds of prints on the doors and walls, maybe even more depending on how thoroughly the place was cleaned between camps.

They were treading water.

"We have to go," Thomas said. "Are you coming?"

Chapter 85

Isak was sitting on the floor of the sauna with his eyes closed when the door was suddenly flung open.

"There you are! Why aren't you answering your phone? I've called you over and over again!"

David was glaring at him.

"It must need charging," Isak said, though he'd purposely switched it off. He let go of the rope that he'd been clutching for hours and surreptitiously slid it behind his back, hoping David wouldn't notice.

"Maja said you'd be here," David explained, looking stressed. "Björn Ekholm has arrived, and he wants to speak to you right away."

Isak's legs had gone to sleep, but he managed to drag himself to his feet. He followed David through the forest, past the restrooms.

They met Sofie, hurrying along with her arms full of clothes from the drying room. Presumably she was packing, getting ready to leave. Isak didn't have the energy to wave at her.

Ekholm was on the veranda outside the dining hall. He was on the phone, but ended the call abruptly and got to his feet as soon as he saw David and Isak.

"How the hell did this happen?" he yelled at Isak.

David stared at the older man, but didn't say a word in Isak's defense.

"You can go—I'd like to speak to Isak alone," Ekholm said firmly.

David patted Isak clumsily on the shoulder, then turned and disappeared around the corner of the building.

"Do you realize how serious this is?" Ekholm began. "You were Blue Group's instructor. It was your responsibility to monitor those children."

"I did t-try," Isak stammered.

"Not hard enough, obviously. A boy has gone missing from camp. And the girl who took off on Saturday was in your group, too."

Isak lowered his eyes. "I'm sorry."

Ekholm pointed to his phone. "I've just had a call from Samuel Karlberg's father. Apparently his son has been accused of bullying; people are saying he was unpleasant to Benjamin Dufva. Samuel's beside himself; he was so upset that his father had to interrupt an important meeting in order to come and fetch him in their boat. What the hell have you actually been doing?"

"Benjamin just disappeared," Isak whispered. "He was in his bed when I checked at midnight."

"Don't try and wriggle out of this."

There wasn't enough saliva in his mouth; Isak didn't think his voice would hold. He kept quiet.

"Do you understand what this means? Not one single family will be prepared to entrust their children to our care in the future!"

Ekholm started pacing back and forth.

"You've single-handedly destroyed this company's reputation. Fifty years of hard work has gone up in smoke because you couldn't be bothered to fulfill your responsibilities."

He slammed his hand down on the table so hard that his phone jumped in the air.

"It would have been better if the boy had run away as well, then at least the parents wouldn't have been able to blame us. But the fact that a man walked in and took him . . . It's totally unacceptable."

Isak was sweating and shivering at the same time.

"Are you . . . are you saying Benjamin's been abducted?"

"That's certainly what the police think." Ekholm shook his head. "Plus all the parents and reporters who keep calling."

Isak swallowed and swallowed, but the hard lump in his throat refused to move.

"I want you to pack your things and leave as soon as we're done with the police. I've spoken to your father, and he's picking you up at nine o'clock tomorrow morning."

"You've spoken to my father?"

Isak tried to wipe his nose with his hand. He couldn't let Ekholm see that he was on the verge of tears. He turned away. The evening sun was sparkling on the water. He'd often sat here with the other instructors. At this time the decking was usually crowded with kids, full and happy after dinner.

"Clearly you're finished as far as we're concerned. You'll never work as an instructor for us again."

Isak just wanted to put his hands over his ears.

"I have to go," he mumbled, taking a step backward.

"I'm not done with you yet." Ekholm clenched his fists, the veins on the back of his hands bulging. "Have you told the police everything?"

Isak had—apart from the half hour he'd spent with Maja. The half hour that could have made all the difference.

The police had said that every minute was vital. That was why they'd asked him over and over again about the timeline, when he'd last seen Benjamin, what he'd done next, where he'd gone.

If Isak had sounded the alarm at eight in the morning, maybe Benjamin would have been found by now.

He took another step back. His head was pounding.

"I have to go."

Ekholm grabbed his arm; the director's voice seemed to come from far, far away.

"Are you involved in this?" His face was only inches from Isak's. "How did the kidnapper know where Benjamin slept? Did you tell him?"

He released his grip so suddenly that Isak almost fell over.

The only person he'd spoken to was Benjamin's father, when Christian Dufva called and said he couldn't remember the name of the building where Benjamin was sleeping. Isak had given him the information, told him that Benjamin's bed was by the window.

As if he hadn't already been in there when Benjamin arrived.

Isak started shaking as the realization dawned. It wasn't Benjamin's father who'd phoned. Isak had obligingly spilled every detail to a total stranger.

He thought about the rope in the sauna. The silver hook, glinting on the ceiling.

"Leave me alone!" he yelled as he turned and ran.

Chapter 86

When Benjamin woke up again, he immediately sensed that he was in a different place. It was just as dark, but the space seemed bigger, and the air wasn't as stuffy as before.

He was able to move his head without banging it, and his wrists and ankles were no longer bound, although they were still sore where the rope had been. His throat felt raw.

He listened hard, not daring to move.

It was quiet; the throbbing noise of the engine had gone. However, the dull sensation that his body didn't quite belong to him remained; he was a little dizzy, and the world was moving very slowly.

Somehow he was in his own sleeping bag. The smell was so familiar, the feeling when he rested his cheek against the silky fabric.

He tried to piece together the disjointed memories of his last few hours in camp.

The meeting in the dining hall, where he'd gone after failing to get ahold of his father on the phone. He'd slipped away before it was over, crawled into his sleeping bag. When the others came in, and when Isak did his final check, he'd pretended to be asleep. He'd kept his face to the wall, his body motionless.

But what had happened after that?

He must have fallen asleep for real, because the last thing he remembered clearly was Isak's voice from the doorway, saying good night to everyone.

A fragment drifted into view, then disappeared. A blurred recollection of a man dressed in dark clothing, bending over him. Strong hands, something being pressed over his mouth.

Benjamin couldn't remember any more. However hard he tried, the image slid away, became even more unclear.

He was so tired.

Someone had taken him; that much he understood.

He let out a sob. Why him? Had he done something wrong, something stupid?

If he could just go back home, he'd never argue with his mom again. Never complain or refuse to do stuff. He'd clear his plate away after dinner and make his own bed every single day.

If only he could go back home.

He clasped his hands together and said a prayer.

Then the darkness took him once more.

CHAPTER 87

Thomas walked into the large conference room on the third floor of police HQ. The lights were on; the room lay in shadow, even though it wasn't yet dark outside. Someone had put a photograph of Benjamin and a map of Lökholmen on the notice board.

It had taken no more than twenty minutes for the maritime police launch to get them to Stavsnäs where Thomas had left his car, and from there it was only a half-hour drive to Nacka.

Another ten minutes and they would have been in central Stockholm.

Thomas knew exactly how little time it took to leave Lökholmen and disappear into the crowded city. Benjamin could be anywhere by now. Too many hours had passed since Agnes saw a man carrying him away.

They were so far behind.

His thoughts turned to Elin. She would have had her supper by now, and would probably be sitting on Grandpa's knee watching one of her favorite shows on TV.

He'd called from the car to say good night to her. She'd sounded cheerful, happy to be staying over with her grandparents, and yet he still felt guilty.

To be on the safe side, he'd texted Pernilla just so she'd know where Elin was. He'd kept it brief and impersonal; there were too many unresolved issues between them.

He pulled himself together. He didn't have time to sit here brooding over his private life.

"Hi, Thomas."

Margit arrived and took her seat. She looked tired; her mascara was smudged beneath her eyes. Two analysts, a man and a woman in their forties whom Thomas vaguely recognized, joined the group. Additional staff had also been brought in to help log and organize information as it came through.

Thomas yawned. He'd been on the go since six o'clock this morning. Too long, with too little food. He functioned better when he ate properly, but had a tendency to forget about it.

Karin Ek appeared with a thermos. "You look as if you need a coffee."

She poured Thomas a steaming cup, then did the same for Aram as he sat down next to Thomas. The coffee was strong and delicious, without the metallic taste that came from the machine in the staff kitchen. Thomas knew that Karin had a far superior machine of her own in her office. She'd also brought a plate of ham and cheese sandwiches; Thomas took one and gave her a grateful nod.

Adrian was the last to arrive. He closed the door behind him and ran his fingers through his short light-brown hair. Under his arm he carried a bundle of papers; on the top sheet, several lines were highlighted in yellow.

"OK, let's get started," Margit said.

They would follow standard procedure: facts must be laid out, information analyzed, possible leads identified or dismissed.

They had to agree on a direction.

Certain elements merited more attention than others, more resources. Only when this had been decided could tasks be assigned. No one would leave this room without knowing exactly what was required of them.

As always there would be too much to do in too little time.

Thomas and Aram began with a brief summary of the interviews they'd conducted on the island.

Margit turned to Staffan Nilsson. "You were there, Staffan—what can you tell us?"

Nilsson shook his head. "I don't have any definitive answers yet. We'll start with the fingerprints, see what we can get from them."

"How long will that take?" Margit said with a hint of impatience.

Nilsson scratched his nose. "We'll do our best."

Margit leafed through her papers, back and forth, as if the answers were buried in there somewhere.

Thomas felt the weight of everything they hadn't achieved on Lökholmen. They should have spoken to more children, found more leads. Had they missed something?

However, there were no shortcuts. One step at a time, that was the key to effective police work.

"We still haven't gotten ahold of Christian Dufva," Margit said. "But I did manage to speak to his wife, Ninna. She sounded worried; he hadn't contacted her either. She said he was due in court in Stockholm today to give an important witness statement. Maybe that's why his phone is switched off."

"At this time of night?" Karin frowned. "Surely no court is still in session at eight o'clock?"

Margit turned to Thomas. "By the way, the prosecutor in the case is your friend Nora Linde."

Nora had mentioned the upcoming trial when they were on Alskär on Saturday; she'd said it was a major case, and that she'd put a lot into it. How strange that their paths should cross like this.

"Maybe you could give her a call after the meeting," Margit suggested. "See if she has any idea where Christian Dufva might be."

Thomas nodded. The coffee had made him feel better. Although he really preferred tea, he held out his cup to Karin for a refill.

"Do we know any more about the relationship between Benjamin's parents?" he asked.

"Strained. The divorce went through just before Christmas 2012; Dufva's new partner was already pregnant with their child. You can imagine what Benjamin's mother thought of that. She blames Christian for sending Benjamin to camp; apparently he didn't want to go."

"How's she doing?" Adrian asked. An engagement ring glinted on the third finger of his left hand; had it been there before? Thomas felt slightly ashamed; he ought to have a better idea of what was going on with his colleagues.

"She's shocked and frightened," Margit replied. "Benjamin's her only child."

Elin is an only child, too.

Thomas took another sip of coffee. He ought to ring Pernilla, but somehow it went against the grain.

"Åsa mentioned a guy she'd dated; apparently he turned nasty when she didn't want to see him again. We'd better check him out."

"And the father?" Aram said.

"Christian has an alibi. Ninna confirmed that he was at home with her all night."

There was nothing to suggest that Christian was involved, but Thomas thought it was very strange that no one could reach him.

Margit went over to the whiteboard and picked up a black marker. She wrote two words:

WHY BENJAMIN?

"Any ideas?" She waited a few seconds, and when no one spoke she added three more words:

BLACKMAIL
REVENGE
PRESSURE

"Cases like this are usually down to one or more of those," she said.

Thomas stared at the board. There were very few instances of kidnapping per year in Sweden, although it was a growing problem, as was the proliferation of organized crime. There were often links to extortion, the application of pressure because of an unpaid debt, or some kind of retribution. "Regular" kidnappings, where the aim was to get money out of the victim's family, were rare.

But they did happen. Ten years ago the son of a company director had been abducted and held captive; the ransom was set at ten million kronor.

"What's the parents' financial situation?" he asked. "Do they have money?"

Margit nodded to Karin.

"Christian Dufva is a consultant in the building industry. His last tax declaration shows an income of around twenty-five thousand a month. He lives with his new family—his wife, Ninna, and their one-year-old son, Emil—in a rented apartment in Birkastan. Ninna works in human resources at a property company, but has been on maternity leave since May 2013."

Karin adjusted her glasses.

"Dufva has been significantly better off in the past. When he was married to Benjamin's mother, he was sales director and joint owner of Alliance Construction, a building firm. He and Åsa lived in a large apartment in Vasastan, and declared an annual income of over a million kronor."

A million kronor.

That was a lot of money, well above the Swedish average, but not enough to put Christian Dufva on the radar of the kind of people who might consider kidnapping a child.

"So he's no longer with Alliance Construction?" Aram said.

"The firm went bankrupt just over a year ago, so he lost his job."

"Difficult," murmured the male analyst with a ponytail.

"What about the mother's finances?" Thomas asked.

"Åsa's effectively a single mom now. She works as a midwife at the Söder Hospital, and she still lives in the family's four-room apartment."

"It sounds as if Benjamin spends most of his time with her rather than his father," Margit interjected.

How much was an apartment like that in Vasastan worth? Thomas was no expert on the Stockholm housing market, but it had to be four or five million, if not more. It shouldn't be a problem to borrow money using the property as security, if necessary.

"Does she have any other assets?"

"She has a share portfolio worth almost eleven million."

Adrian let out a low whistle. "That hospital must pay pretty well these days—I wonder if they need a new security guard?"

Margit raised an eyebrow.

Åsa Dufva was more than comfortably off, but Thomas still didn't see her as the key. She didn't move in the circles where kidnapping occurred. A kidnapper usually wanted to scare someone or recoup a debt; the socioeconomic profile just didn't fit a midwife.

Could there be other links? The ex-boyfriend?

"We need to find out if there's anything suspicious in her background," he said. "Maybe the guy she was dating has criminal connections?"

Margit agreed. "We don't know enough about Benjamin's parents, and experience tells us that a case often begins and ends with the parents."

"I'll look into it, and check out Åsa's ex, too," Adrian offered.

"How's it going with the list of boat owners?" Thomas asked.

"We're working on it—nothing interesting so far."

Margit looked at her watch. "We'll keep trying to contact Christian Dufva, and in the meantime we'll keep digging into the home environment." She turned to Adrian. "Make the ex-boyfriend your first priority."

There was a sudden flash of lightning outside the window, followed a few seconds later by a deafening clap of thunder.

Then the rain came pouring down.

CHAPTER 88

Niklas Winnerman was lying on the bed in his underpants watching the storm through the window. The sky had been transformed into an inferno of lightning flashes, and the torrential rain hammering down on the capital was more reminiscent of a November day than a June evening shortly before midsummer.

However, the apartment had felt like a sauna when he got home; the rain and a drop in temperature were much needed.

He sipped his drink with an inner calm he hadn't felt for months. The fear of ending up in jail was finally beginning to fade. Christian had finished giving his testimony.

And he'd had to retract all those allegations.

When Niklas first read the statement Christian had given to the police, he'd found it hard to control himself. If Christian had been there, he would have killed him.

Their long friendship counted for nothing; the loyalty Niklas had believed he could rely on had gone straight out the window. Christian had dragged his name through the dirt without a second thought.

A dazzling flash lit up the sky, followed almost immediately by a loud clap of thunder, then everything went dark again.

The only light inside the apartment came from a lamp in the hallway, but Niklas found it quite restful after the tension of the day. It was a relief to lie here with his head on the pillow, to let everything go.

He ought to call Albert and Natan, tell them things had gone well today, much better than yesterday. Then again, maybe he should wait? It would be even more enjoyable to speak to them tomorrow, tell them there was no case to defend.

"Excellent," Emilsson had said before he rushed off as usual, his cell phone clamped to his ear. "I'll see you tomorrow; with a bit of luck, they'll dismiss the case in no time. That really would be something to celebrate on Midsummer's Eve."

The day had belonged to Niklas. His ribs were more painful than ever, but his heart was lighter than it had been for months.

Nora Linde's face when Christian did a complete U-turn and defended him! That had given the bitch something to think about.

Even Fanny Ferlin, who had treated him with such condescension, had looked at him with new respect.

But the best thing of all had been Christian's pathetic appearance, his humiliation as he sat there retracting everything he'd said. Niklas savored the thought of Christian waking up in the middle of the night, with anxiety like a heavy weight on his chest.

There was always a price to pay.

Another clap of thunder; a hell of a storm was going on out there.

Everything was heading in the right direction. Soon the trial would be over, after months of fear and worry.

What he'd done had definitely been worth the money—it had been the only way to get Christian to change his testimony.

The initial positive sign had come last night, when he'd started winning again for the first time in God knows how long. The dice had spoken his language, and he'd won a significant amount. Another night like that, and his troubles would be over.

The thought gave him a fresh burst of energy. He pulled on his robe and went into the kitchen. His laptop was on the table, exactly where he'd left it in the early hours of the morning. A few clicks would open the door to another world.

Niklas stroked the metal lid. Tonight his winning streak would continue; he could feel it in his bones.

Christian had already destroyed so much for Niklas, but tomorrow the case would be dismissed. If his luck held tonight, he would be able to pay off his debt to his Lithuanian lenders, and then he would be free to start a new life. The life he deserved, after all he'd been through.

Niklas opened up the computer and logged in.

Chapter 89

Thomas sat down at his desk. Pernilla, with Elin on her lap, smiled at him from the framed photograph next to his computer. It had been taken on the jetty in front of the house on Harö; the wind had ruffled Pernilla's hair, and she was kissing Elin's forehead.

How did we end up here?

His cell dinged—a text message from Pernilla. A single sentence:

Is Elin OK?

Was that all they had to say to each other? Thomas stared at his phone, then called his wife.

"It's me. Elin's fine. As I told you before, she's sleeping over with my parents tonight."

"But why?"

"I have to work."

He sounded more abrupt than he'd intended, and Pernilla's sharp intake of breath didn't exactly improve matters.

"What do you mean? Aren't you at home?"

"I had to deal with an urgent case."

"A case that's more important than your own daughter?"

Nobody could misunderstand him more effectively than Pernilla. After twenty years together, there was nobody who knew him better or could hurt him more.

He didn't want to get drawn into another argument, especially not on the phone; that wasn't why he'd called her.

"That's not fair."

"I'm only away for two nights—is it too much to expect you to prioritize Elin for forty-eight hours?"

Thomas could hear the hum of conversation in the background; it sounded as if she was in a restaurant. A song he vaguely recognized was playing.

So it was OK for her to go out and enjoy herself, but he wasn't allowed to do his job?

"Are you seriously starting on me, when you're the one who's gone away?" he said.

"You have a responsibility."

Thomas went over to the window, opened it wide, and let in the cool evening air. Tried to keep his temper. "So do you."

"Don't try to make me feel guilty, Thomas."

"An eleven-year-old boy has gone missing from the sailing camp on Lökholmen; we think he's been abducted. The situation is critical."

Pernilla sighed. "There's always something, isn't there? It was the same on Saturday. Why does your job always come before mine?" Someone laughed loudly right next to Pernilla. "Is it because I earn more than you? Is that why you have to believe your work is more important than mine?"

"Enough, Pernilla."

Thomas heard a man's voice proposing a toast.

"I can't talk now. Speak to you later."

The call ended and Pernilla's name vanished from the screen. Thomas stood there with the phone in his hand. Outside the window the last rays of the sun touched the red brick façade, and the scent of elder blossom reached his nostrils.

The glory of early summer didn't make him feel any better.

He went back to his desk and kicked the trashcan hard, scattering crumpled balls of paper and empty coffee cups all over the floor and leaving black trails of cold coffee. He sank down on his chair and closed his eyes for a few seconds, trying not to give in to the frustration that was so near the surface.

Not now.

Thomas massaged his forehead, ran his fingers along his eyebrows. After a minute or so he got up, went to the bathroom, and rinsed his face in ice-cold water. The paper towels had run out, so he grabbed some toilet paper and wiped his mouth and nose.

He went back to his office, picked up the trashcan, and tidied up as best he could. Then he called Nora, as he'd promised Margit.

"Hi, do you have a few minutes?" He explained that a child had gone missing from the camp on Lökholmen. "The boy's name is Benjamin Dufva. His father is Christian Dufva."

"Christian Dufva? He testified in court today, in the trial I told you about on Saturday. He's my key witness."

"I know. His wife told us he'd gone off to the courthouse this morning, but we can't get ahold of him."

"What do you mean?"

"He's not answering his cell, and no one knows where he is."

Thomas glanced at his watch; it was almost nine o'clock. Where the hell could Christian Dufva be at this hour? The fact that he still hadn't been in touch wasn't a good sign. Ninna had called again, wondering if they'd found him.

Was he also in danger? Had he been threatened?

Ninna had told Margit that he'd behaved oddly before leaving the apartment in the morning, that he hadn't been himself. He'd suddenly insisted that she must take Emil and go to her parents' place in the country, which wasn't like him at all.

"We have to contact him," Thomas went on. "The situation is serious. We suspect that his son was abducted during the night."

Nora inhaled sharply. "That's terrible!"

"That's why I'm calling you. We really need to speak to Christian. What time did you finish in court today?"

"We adjourned at four thirty."

Four and a half hours ago.

"You don't know where he went after that?"

"I've no idea."

"Did anything strike you as odd during the trial?"

At that moment Aram appeared in the doorway.

"Hang on a second, Nora."

"Margit wants us in Staffan Nilsson's office right away," Aram said. "She's already up there with Adrian."

They must have found something.

Finally.

Thomas got to his feet. "I have to go—speak to you later," he said to Nora.

"No, wait—"

"Sorry, I really have to go. But if Dufva calls you for any reason, please ask him to get in touch with us as a matter of urgency."

Nora started to say something, but Thomas was gone.

CHAPTER 90

There had to be a connection. Nora remained sitting at the kitchen table with her phone in her hand.

The brief conversation with Thomas had made her head spin.

She'd wondered whether Dufva might have changed his testimony as a result of a bribe, but what if someone had abducted his son in order to put pressure on him?

She poured herself a glass of water and tried to think logically. She was still thirsty after her run earlier in the evening. The exercise had eased her anxiety over the fact that Jonas was delayed, but now her pulse shot up again.

She went into the living room, sat down on the sofa, and switched on the TV. The nine o'clock news had just started.

A woman in her forties with her dark hair gathered into a loose bun was speaking to the camera, her expression grave.

"An eleven-year-old boy has gone missing from a sailing camp on the island of Lökholmen near Sandhamn in the Stockholm archipelago," she announced. Her face was replaced by images of the area, possibly taken by drone. Nora recognized the inlet by Trollharan, the red dormitory buildings around the grassy area. The flag was flying, but in her mind's eye Nora saw a flag at half-mast.

Those poor parents. Poor Christian Dufva; it was hardly surprising that he'd looked so strained.

A picture of a boy appeared. He looked younger than eleven.

"Benjamin Dufva vanished from his dormitory at some point during Monday night or the early hours of Tuesday morning. Anyone with any information is asked to contact the police as a matter of urgency; the number is on your screen now."

If that was my child . . .

Nora blinked several times. She grabbed a cushion and pressed it to her stomach.

When Thomas had told her about the missing girl on Saturday, the one who turned out to have run away, her heart had flipped over. The thought of sending her child off to summer camp and never seeing him again . . .

She bit her lip. Simon was due to go there in a month or so. Would she dare to let him after this?

She stared blankly at the television, where the news anchor had moved on to an item about genetically modified crops.

Niklas Winnerman.

He'd likely sent her threatening emails, and he seemed volatile, but could he really be behind the kidnapping of a child in order to influence a witness? A child who must have played with his own sons?

Nora didn't want to believe it.

CHAPTER 91

Åsa went into the kitchen, then stopped by the sink. Why had she come in here?

She couldn't think of a reason. Confused, she looked around for clues, but couldn't see anything that would help.

She picked up the dishcloth and tried to wipe the already spotless draining board. She was shaking so much that she dropped the cloth. She clasped her hands together and prayed.

Dear God, please let him come home. Please don't let anything bad happen to him.

After a while she poured herself a glass of water, stared at it, then tipped it away.

The detective had asked if she'd been threatened in any way recently.

Åsa had mentioned Gregor, the man she'd met online and dated a few times. He'd been furious when she said she didn't want to see him anymore; he'd sworn at her and called her a whore. Was this his way of punishing her?

She suppressed a sob.

Please don't let that be true.

She went back into the living room. The television was on, just in case there was anything about Benjamin. They'd talked about him on the nine o'clock news, shown a picture of him and said he'd gone missing from the sailing camp.

Benjamin.

Åsa swayed and had to lean on the doorframe for support, but her legs gave way and she slid down onto the floor. She sat with her back to the wall, arms wrapped around her legs. She pressed her mouth against her knees to stop herself from screaming, rocked back and forth until the scream turned into a low moan deep in her throat.

Slowly she became aware of a window banging. Her muscles were heavy and slow, but she managed to drag herself to her feet.

The noise was coming from Benjamin's room. A catch had slipped during the storm. Fat droplets of water were running down the glass, like the tears constantly running down her cheeks.

A gray curtain of rain dissolved the contours outside and darkened the sky. There was a flash of lightning, a clap of thunder, a remorseless storm.

The sky is weeping for my son, Åsa thought.

Benjamin's cuddly toy lay on his bed next to his pillow. He loved his old bear, even though the brown fur was shabby and worn away in patches. Benjamin didn't like going to sleep without Teddy, even though he would be twelve in just a few months.

Åsa drew back the covers. Benjamin's blue pajamas were tucked beneath his pillow. It was only five days since he'd worn them, the morning she'd woken him to get ready for camp.

They still smelled of Benjamin. Åsa lay down on the bed and pressed the pajamas to her lips.

Chapter 92

Thomas took the stairs up to Staffan Nilsson's office two at a time, with Aram right behind him.

They found Adrian and Margit sitting opposite Nilsson. She beckoned them in and pointed to a color photograph on the desk.

"Adrian's found an interesting name on the list of boat owners."

Adrian leaned forward, his expression grave. "This is a known pedophile by the name of Pontus Lindqvist. It seems as if his boat was in the marina from last Thursday onward."

The children had arrived at the sailing camp on Friday.

Thomas picked up the list and skimmed through it until he found Lindqvist. Just as he thought, Lindqvist had paid the mooring fee for a motorboat of less than thirty feet. The same size the girls had mentioned, the boat that belonged to the man in the forest.

Was Pontus Lindqvist the man who'd been lurking among the trees?

"What's his record like?" Aram asked.

"Not good." Margit pushed back her short gray hair. When Thomas started in Nacka, it had been streaked with bright red, but over the past year Margit had gone back to her natural color.

Adrian took over. "He's thirty-seven, and he's already been in jail several times for offenses involving child pornography and child rape.

His latest conviction followed the discovery of thousands of images on his computer, which he'd distributed through the file sharing program GigaTribe. Some of the pictures showed him having anal and oral intercourse with a young boy."

Thomas's stomach contracted. Benjamin was only eleven.

Margit glanced at Nilsson.

"I ran a check on the fingerprints we lifted from the dormitory," he said. "Several are a match for Pontus Lindqvist's prints."

"Are you sure?" Thomas said.

"I'm afraid so. I can't swear that he took Benjamin, but I can guarantee that at some point, since the dormitory was last given a thorough cleaning, he was next to Benjamin's bed."

"Fuck!" Aram exclaimed.

"Lindqvist's thumbprints were found on the bed frame," Nilsson went on. "Roughly on a level with the place where Benjamin's pillow would have been."

Thomas rubbed his chin. They had to get Lindqvist's picture over to the camp as soon as possible, see if the girls could identify him.

"We also found traces of ether in the room. It's just as I thought, Thomas: that's what the perpetrator used to sedate the boy."

A well-prepared kidnapper. Thomas had suspected as much from the start.

"Do we know if Lindqvist has done anything like this before?" he asked.

Margit took a deep breath. "It's a question of definition, really. As Adrian said, he was found guilty of child rape, but always denied the charges. The child couldn't be identified from the images on Lindqvist's computer, but because the visual evidence was so overwhelming, he was convicted anyway."

Adrian gave a mirthless laugh. "The idiot had filmed the whole thing, but forgot to erase the recording from a USB stick with his fingerprints on it. He left it behind when he moved out of his apartment; the new tenant found it and went to the police."

Margit shook her head. "It's impossible to say how Lindqvist got ahold of the boy on that occasion. There are many ways of gaining access to children in those circles, as you know."

The photograph on the desk showed a pleasant-looking man smiling at the camera. He had a small scar on one cheek, and his teeth were white and even. He obviously worked out; his muscles strained against the fabric of his short-sleeved T-shirt.

"He served his last jail term in Skogome outside Gothenburg, but he's also done time in Kristianstad."

There were six institutions that took sex offenders in Sweden; Skogome was the only one exclusively for such prisoners. This meant it was also the place other criminals despised the most; those who committed sex crimes were right at the bottom of the hierarchy.

Aram picked up the photograph between his finger and thumb, as a dog owner might pick up a bag of dog shit. Then he tossed it aside.

"When was he released?" Thomas asked.

Margit checked her notes. "Eighteen months ago," she said, unable to hide her frustration.

So he hadn't been able to control himself for longer than eighteen months. The re-offending rate among pedophiles was very high, despite the fact that all six institutions ran comprehensive rehabilitation programs.

"Does he have violent tendencies? Do we know if he's killed anyone?" Aram wanted to know.

"It doesn't seem that way," Margit replied. "None of his convictions contain evidence of that level of violence."

"There's nothing on the suspects' register either," Adrian interjected. "I checked."

Thomas studied the photograph of the smiling man; was he calculating enough to abduct a child in the middle of the night?

It was impossible to tell. He didn't have devil's horns growing out of his head to warn those around him, no external signs that this was a man with a serious personality disorder, a man who for many years had carried out sexual attacks on children in order to satisfy his perverted needs.

"If it is Lindqvist who's taken Benjamin, then at least that explains why his mother hasn't received a ransom demand," Thomas said, hating the implication behind his words.

Margit sighed. "He's not interested in money; that's not what drives him."

Nilsson looked at the photograph of that smiling face. He had several grandchildren; the oldest was a boy of ten.

"Get it out of my sight," he said, pushing it away so that it ended up under a pile of papers.

Sexual attacks on children were impossible to understand. Thomas could never see the person behind the crime, only the monster, even though he was well aware of the psychological mechanisms.

Most pedophiles rationalized their behavior and came up with explanations. They often claimed it was the child who had initiated the first sexual contact.

As a father, Thomas couldn't understand how an adult could engage in sexual activity with a child, even less his own child. Which also happened way too often.

"What do we know about Lindqvist's social situation?" Aram asked.

He sounded calm, but Thomas knew him well enough to realize how deeply this was affecting him.

"He trained as an elementary school teacher, but these days he works in IT," Adrian replied. "He's a freelance programmer. There's nothing wrong with his finances; he owns a three-room apartment in Farsta."

A pedophile who'd worked with children and knew his way around a computer. A perfect fit, unfortunately.

"We have his address," Margit said. "His apartment isn't far from the shopping mall—Ekebergabacken 5A, first floor."

Thomas pushed back his chair and placed a hand on Aram's shoulder. "Let's go."

CHAPTER 93

The door opened and Mom came into the room carrying a big breakfast tray. There was a wonderful smell of toast and strawberry jelly. Benjamin realized how hungry he was.

Mom had poured him a glass of freshly pressed orange juice and made chocolate milk, just the way he liked it.

She was smiling.

As he reached for a slice of toast, it disappeared, leaving nothing but the stale smell of the enclosed space.

Benjamin opened his eyes.

He wasn't at home. He was still in darkness, and Mom wasn't here.

Why did he have to wake up?

He began to cry, hot tears pouring down his cheeks.

It would have been better if he'd stayed asleep; at least then he didn't feel scared.

He licked his dry lips, trying to produce a little saliva. Swallowing was even more painful now.

He was so hungry, so thirsty. His stomach rumbled quietly.

He must have dozed off again; he didn't know for how long.

He reached out with one hand and cautiously felt around his body. He was still in his sleeping bag, but now it was on top of a mattress. The surface was rough against his palm, with the odd piece of horsehair sticking out. He moved his hand over the edge and encountered something hard, a stone or concrete floor.

The dust made his fingertips feel dry and flaky. Suddenly he touched something sharp, a piece of glass maybe, and the pain brought tears to his eyes again. He stuck his index finger in his mouth and tasted blood and earth.

His eyes had begun to grow accustomed to the darkness, and he was able to make out vague shapes. He was in a small room, maybe a cellar or storeroom.

He carried on groping around with his other hand and found something. He picked it up; it was a one-and-a-half-liter plastic bottle. When he unscrewed the cap and smelled Coca-Cola, he couldn't believe his luck. With trembling hands he lifted the bottle to his lips and drank in great big gulps. The Coke was lukewarm, but that didn't matter; it was wonderful to be able to quench his thirst. He'd never tasted anything so delicious in his entire life.

After a moment he stopped himself. This might be the only drink he'd get for a long time. He put the cap back on.

His finger was still bleeding; he put it back in his mouth, despite the horrible taste.

Where was he? Who had brought him here? His head was spinning, but he knew he had to get out.

Slowly he got to his feet. His legs were shaky, and he was weak and dizzy, but somehow he managed it. He sucked his finger to try to get rid of the blood; it was a really deep gash.

He shuffled along by the wall. He couldn't find any windows, but eventually he reached something that resembled a door handle.

"Please, please," he whispered as he tried to open the door.

But it was no good. He pushed and pulled, kicked and yelled and wept, but the door remained locked.

Chapter 94

There was a God after all. Niklas Winnermán stared at the brightly colored numbers flashing on the screen, and knew he'd been given a second chance.

He added it all up one more time and came to the same conclusion as before. Together with the previous day's winnings, he now had enough to pay off his debt to Artūras.

He went over to the window, flung it wide open, and roared with joy. The heavy raindrops landed on his face, mingling with tears of relief.

After a few moments he drew back and closed the window, then he went into the bathroom and dried his face with a towel. He looked at his reflection in the mirror and promised himself that he would never, ever get into a situation like that again. If necessary he would seek professional help or join a Gamblers Anonymous group.

Never again.

He was going to pull himself together and sort out his life. He owed it to Albert and Natan, who had already gone through far too much.

His boys had the right to be proud of their father again.

He went back into the kitchen. As soon as he saw the laptop, the desire was there, even though he knew he had to stay in control. He just couldn't give in and risk losing everything again. This time he had to stop while his luck was in.

And yet he stood there transfixed by the screen, his thoughts running away with him.

Would it be so bad to play just once more? He'd been doing so well. Just once more before he logged out forever.

One click, that was all it would take.

His fingers were already picking up imaginary dice. He licked his lips, reached for the mouse as he tried to make up his mind.

"No!"

He struck his cracked ribs. Hard.

The pain was so intense that he doubled over. He couldn't breathe; he almost saw stars.

But it worked. It made him think clearly and enabled him to find the willpower he needed.

He quickly typed in the details to allow the money to be paid into his overseas bank account, then immediately pressed the button to log out and resolutely closed the lid of his laptop.

Pay or go under.

Wednesday at the latest—that was what the man who'd been waiting for him outside the apartment building had said. Niklas remembered the fear, the gravel digging into his skin as he lay on the ground. He'd been convinced that he was going to die within the next few minutes.

He would transfer the money tomorrow.

He pushed away the laptop, and that small movement eased the pressure on his chest. Soon he would be free from all his problems.

Then he would make sure that Christian Dufva got what he deserved.

CHAPTER 95

The heavens had opened, great pools of water were forming on the freeway, and the rain was hammering against the windshield.

This time Aram was driving. The road surface gleamed as they entered the tunnel leading to the southern link. They passed one set of decorative lights after another, but Thomas was too busy to admire the shimmering blue patterns adorning the walls. He was trying to read Margit's notes, which wasn't easy given the speed at which they were traveling.

"Could Lindqvist have been dumb enough to have taken Benjamin to his own apartment?"

"Who knows," Aram said. He was hunched over the wheel, eyes glued to the road ahead, one hand on the gearshift.

Thomas's eyes darted from one paragraph to the next in an effort to take in the whole picture.

"The rape for which he was convicted took place in his home," he said. "The wallpaper in his bedroom was clearly recognizable in the images they found on the USB stick."

"I wonder if he's learned anything from that."

Thomas continued flicking through verdicts and reports. The more he read, the more disgusted he became.

The glow of the streetlights became straight lines as the car raced along.

At the bottom of the pile of papers was a new photograph of Benjamin that Margit had requested from his mother. It had been taken outdoors; there were trees in the background. Benjamin was smiling, but his thoughts seemed to be elsewhere. The expression in his eyes was distant, and his mouth was half-open. Maybe he was about to say something to the person behind the camera?

He was wearing a striped T-shirt, and his arms were skinny, but his cheeks still had a childlike roundness.

Unfortunately, Thomas had to admit that Benjamin's age and appearance fit perfectly with Pontus Lindqvist's known preferences—girls and boys who had not yet reached puberty. No doubt Benjamin's slight figure had caught Lindqvist's eye, while the boy's older companions hadn't interested him at all.

When it came to the kind of desire that Lindqvist represented, puberty brought safety.

They had turned onto Nynäsvägen and passed Tallkrogen; they were no more than ten minutes away from Farsta.

Aram put his foot down, ignoring the surface water. When they passed a truck, their windshield was drenched; even the wipers didn't help. Visibility was down to about three feet.

The clock on the dashboard showed 9:28. Thomas was painfully aware of the time; Benjamin had been missing for over thirteen hours.

Aram flashed his headlights repeatedly at a car in the left-hand lane until it moved. He sped up and overtook it, his back wheels sliding briefly before the tires regained their grip.

"The question is where he could have hidden Benjamin," Thomas mused. There were no other properties registered in Lindqvist's name—only the apartment in Farsta. "Could he have access to a storage room down in the basement?"

The idea had struck him while he was reading the notes. So far Benjamin's abduction had been preceded by meticulous planning. As far as they could tell, Lindqvist had arrived on Lökholmen well prepared, the day before camp began. He'd had plenty of opportunities to pick out his victim, and had even managed to make an initial contact with Benjamin.

With that level of forethought, he was hardly likely to take the risk of keeping the boy at an address that could easily be traced. But if he had access to a storeroom, or maybe an old cabin somewhere in the forest . . . There were plenty of places available to those who were willing to pay.

Thomas took out his phone and called Margit.

"I was just about to call you," she said. "Where are you?"

"Almost there. Can you check something out for me? I'm wondering if Lindqvist has a storeroom in the apartment building. I don't think he'd be dumb enough to take Benjamin to his—"

Margit didn't allow him to finish. "Listen to me. I've just had new information from Skogome. When Lindqvist was in there, he got involved in a fight with another prisoner on the same wing."

Aram turned off the freeway, ignoring a stop sign. The birch trees lining the road were swaying and bending in the strong wind.

"What happened?"

"Apparently Lindqvist did some serious damage to the other guy—he ended up in the hospital with a ruptured spleen."

"And Lindqvist?"

"Solitary confinement, and his sentence was extended, but not by very much. You know how these things work."

Thomas pressed the phone to his ear; it was hard to hear over the sound of the engine and the swishing of the tires.

"Skogome still regards Lindqvist as a risk in terms of violence," Margit informed him. Thomas's hand instinctively moved to his gun. "I'm sending a patrol car to meet you there. Don't go in until it arrives."

Aram glanced over at his colleague as Thomas ended the call. "Not quite as docile as we thought?"

Thomas shook his head. "Margit's sending backup. She wants us to wait."

He looked at the picture of Benjamin again. According to Margit, the first boy had never been identified, which meant they had no idea how Lindqvist had managed to get ahold of that child. He'd been convicted on the basis of the evidence on the USB stick, but nobody knew what had become of the boy. Or if he'd survived.

CHAPTER 96

Nora switched off the TV; she had no idea what she was supposed to be watching. She sat there in the semidarkness, with only the light from the kitchen seeping into the living room.

Should she try to contact Thomas again? It was just after ten, and he hadn't called her back.

The rain was lashing against the big windows opposite the sofa. It was impossible to see a thing through the cloudburst, and the wind was howling all around the house.

She remembered how frightened she'd been the other day, when the shadows crept up on her. Winnerman's email had really spooked her, and she'd lain awake half the night.

She was alone with Julia again this evening; Adam was with his girlfriend, and Simon was having a sleepover with a friend.

Nora shivered and swallowed hard, trying to get rid of the lump in her throat. Jonas should have been here now, then she wouldn't have been anxious and lonely.

Wouldn't have felt so abandoned.

How could he prioritize his job over her this week of all weeks? She would never have done that to him.

Her phone lit up with a new text message.

Jonas. But no, it was just Adam, telling her that he was staying at his girlfriend's. Nora blinked away the tears and forced herself to think about something else.

Why hadn't Thomas been in touch again? She wanted to talk to him about Winnerman and Dufva. She called his number, but his phone was off.

She thought for a few minutes, then called Leila. It was late, but she hoped Leila wouldn't mind.

"Hello?" Leila sounded a little dazed; had she already gone to bed?

"It's Nora. Sorry, did I wake you?"

"No, it's fine. Is everything OK?"

Nora explained the situation as quickly as she could. "I don't know what to do. I didn't have time to tell Thomas about Winnerman before he hung up the first time, and now he isn't answering his phone."

Leila thought for a moment. "Do you think Benjamin's been kidnapped in order to put pressure on Christian Dufva? Have you any evidence for that? Anything concrete? Abduction is a serious accusation."

"No, but Dufva changed his evidence so suddenly."

Leila sighed. "He could have been lying to us all along, just as Emilsson claimed. You know what he said—that Dufva was looking for a scapegoat when the business collapsed. Blaming his partner was the easiest option."

They were interrupted by the sound of loud barking. Leila shushed Bamse and told him to go back to his basket.

"I'm thinking of contacting Barbro Wikingsson first thing tomorrow morning to explain the situation," Nora said. "She needs to know about this."

Leila took a deep breath. Bamse was still whimpering in the background, but at least he'd stopped barking.

"Just be careful, Nora."

"What do you mean?"

"If you don't have any concrete evidence that Winnerman's involved in Benjamin's abduction, it could look bad. It might seem as if you're trying to save your case by coming up with new accusations against him. Do you really want to lay yourself open to that?"

Did she?

They ended the call, and Nora sat there staring at her phone again. Then she sent a text message to Thomas.

Call me as soon as you can.

CHAPTER 97

An entry code was required to get into the smart apartment building on Ekebergabacken. Thomas looked around; how the hell were they going to get in? The nearest windows were in darkness, the street was deserted, and backup hadn't yet arrived.

It would take hours to bring in a locksmith.

It was still pouring; he was already drenched.

"So what now?" Aram said. Suddenly a figure appeared on the other side of the frosted glass. The door opened, and a man in a dark-colored jacket slipped out with his head down.

Thomas gratefully grabbed the door and stepped inside, then realized that Aram wasn't following him.

"Shit—I think that was him."

Thomas spun around. The man was heading away from them, walking quickly. What had Sofie said about his hat being well pulled down?

"Hey, you! Stop!" Aram shouted.

The man was already about ten yards away. He stopped in the shadow of the apartment building next door, with his back to them.

He was wearing a woolen hat.

Was it Pontus Lindqvist? It was impossible to tell. The man looked back and the light from the streetlamp fell on his face.

It was Lindqvist.

"Police! We need to talk to you!" Aram yelled.

Big mistake. Lindqvist turned and ran.

It took Thomas and Aram a second to react, then they both broke into a run.

"Stop!" Thomas bellowed as loudly as he could.

Lindqvist ignored him and dodged in among the rain-sodden buildings.

They couldn't lose him.

Thomas's heart was pounding as he drew his gun. "Stop or I'll shoot!"

Lindqvist simply increased his speed; he was clearly fit, and the distance between them rapidly increased.

"Final warning!" Thomas roared, taking aim as he ran.

Lindqvist passed a bike rack, then jumped over a fence and into a small playground. He was still pulling away.

They were running across grass now, but the rain had transformed the surface into a treacherous mess. Thomas could feel the mud sucking at the soles of his shoes.

All at once Lindqvist darted between two buildings and disappeared.

"I will shoot!" Thomas shouted again, even though it was too late. He stopped and bent forward, hands on his knees. "Where the hell has he gone?"

The rain made it almost impossible to see. He blinked repeatedly, but it made no difference. Water was dripping from his forehead, and his eyelashes were sticking together.

Aram peered through the grayness. "There! Over there!" He pointed to a running figure about a hundred yards away, heading for an underpass beneath the freeway. "That must be him!"

Thomas became aware of the noise of the traffic, cars and trucks thundering along in close proximity.

"Come on!" Aram set off again.

They raced down a slippery slope; Thomas almost fell several times, but somehow regained his balance. They slithered down onto the road surface and ran along the narrow path leading to the tunnel, but when they emerged on the other side, there was no sign of Lindqvist.

"What the fuck . . ."

Aram stopped and pushed back his wet hair. They could see the lights of the Farsta shopping mall in the distance. Every time a vehicle sped by above them, the headlights lit up the area.

"He has to be here," Aram said.

They had been so close to picking up Lindqvist. And finding Benjamin.

"This is pointless," Thomas said through clenched teeth. "We've lost him."

CHAPTER 98

He'd tried to hold on for as long as he could, but in the end he just had to pee. There was something like a bucket in the far corner; Benjamin had groped his way across the room, pulled down his pajamas, and peed as best he could in the darkness. His aim wasn't perfect, and his stomach contracted. Would the person who'd taken him be mad because he'd made a mess?

He hesitated, but didn't know how to clean up. In the end he wiped the palms of his hands on his pajama pants and staggered back to the mattress.

He was shivering; the concrete was cold against his bare feet. He crawled into his sleeping bag and soon felt a little warmer. His finger was throbbing where he'd cut himself; the skin felt tight and sore over the knuckle.

Why? he kept thinking, over and over again. *Why did he take me?*

Samuel had been in the bed opposite, with Sebbe in the top bunk. There were eight boys in the dormitory—why had he chosen Benjamin?

He was so hungry and thirsty. He grabbed the bottle of Coke and took a few swigs. As he put it down, he realized it was very light; there wasn't much left.

His throat felt even worse after hours of yelling and screaming. In the end he'd given up; no one could hear him anyway.

He wanted to cry, but instead he curled up with his nose pressed against the fabric of his sleeping bag. As he inhaled the smell, he could pretend he was somewhere else, on the boat with Mom and Dad.

When everything was the way it used to be, before the divorce.

Mom had been much happier back then.

They would go for picnics on different islands, sitting on a blanket with the food all laid out on plastic plates. Mom made pancakes with jelly, and Benjamin was allowed to eat them with his fingers.

The image of those sunny days faded away.

He couldn't block out the reality of his situation. No one was going to come and rescue him.

He was all alone here in the darkness.

CHAPTER 99

Isak was lying on his bed fully dressed, waiting. Soon everyone would go to sleep and the camp would settle. No one would be looking for him.

He had drawn the blind before he switched on the bedside lamp, so that it was impossible to see in. He was alone. Wille's sailing jacket was draped over a chair to dry, but there was no sign of his roommate. Wille was probably avoiding him, just like the rest of the instructors. David was no longer supporting him, and Isak himself had driven Maja away.

The instructors would be in the common room now. The children ought to be in bed by now—those who were still on the island. Most were going home tomorrow.

Someone sobbed; was it him?

I'm totally fucked.

He was worthless, just as he'd known from the start. Why had he believed that things would go his way this time?

The expression on Maja's face outside the sauna. She had been disgusted by him; she'd left him just like his ex-girlfriend had done when the depression took over. He understood perfectly; he disgusted himself. Maja would be so much better off without him; he didn't deserve a girl like her.

He scratched his arm; the skin was beginning to break.

David. He'd actually thought that he and David could be friends. So naïve. David hadn't defended him, hadn't come to his rescue when Ekholm started on him. David didn't want to be his friend. Nobody wanted to be his friend, and he knew exactly why.

He was a freak.

He didn't deserve friends; he deserved nothing but contempt. He'd actually told the kidnapper where to find his victim.

As soon as he closed his eyes, Benjamin's terrified face appeared. He could have done things differently, made different decisions. Then everything would have been all right.

Instead he'd gotten it all wrong.

He'd helped the kidnapper. He'd spent time making out with Maja instead of facing up to his responsibilities. He hadn't even realized that Benjamin was being bullied.

David had told him about Samuel, about how he and Sebbe had given Benjamin a hard time from day one.

How could he have been so blind?

Isak was utterly crushed by the knowledge that Benjamin had been so unhappy in camp even before he was taken. Isak knew all about being unhappy.

He stared at the white wall and felt the hysteria swirling around his body. His chest burned when he tried to get some air.

He mustn't give in. Not yet. The coping mechanisms his psychologist had taught him were no use by this stage, but he had to hold it together, just for a few more hours.

The last time he'd been in a psychiatric ward for over a month. He'd watched the other patients shuffling down the hallways, unable to grasp that he belonged in the same place. The drugs had made him dull and apathetic, even more depressed, until life seemed as black as night. The doctor had explained that it would be several weeks before they took effect. His depression would get worse before it got better. There was no other way; that was how the medication worked. Everyone went through the same thing.

He was never, ever going back there.

He pressed his clenched fist to his mouth to stifle another sob. He just wanted to go to sleep and never wake up again, disappear so that he couldn't make any more mistakes, mess up anyone else's life.

Everyone would be better off if he wasn't around anymore. Especially Mom—she'd finally be able to stop worrying about him.

Only the rope could help him to achieve this.

How long did it take to stop breathing with a noose around your neck? He'd tried to Google it, but had switched off his phone before the results came up. He didn't really want to know; he just hoped it would be quick.

He'd read somewhere that people often wet themselves at the last minute. That was almost the worst part; he didn't want to be found like that, didn't want Mom to remember him that way.

To be on the safe side, he hadn't had anything to drink for several hours. He hadn't eaten either, but that didn't matter. He wasn't hungry, even though the cramps had stopped and his stomach had begun to settle.

Only a few more hours, then he would go to the sauna. He would never have to feel anxious again.

Worthless, worthless, worthless.

The words reverberated inside his head, grew and filled his mouth like a lump of food that was impossible to swallow.

Isak closed his eyes tightly to shut out the world.

Chapter 100

"You're telling me you lost him?" Margit snapped. "He walked straight past you, and you lost him?"

Thomas was still cold and wet, and Margit's fury didn't make him feel any better. He was well aware that Pontus Lindqvist had disappeared from right under their noses.

"I explained what happened. What else can I say? He just vanished." Thomas's tone was sharper than usual, which was hardly surprising.

"In that case I suggest you get back out there and find him."

Officers were already searching for Lindqvist in the darkness. Dog teams had been brought in, and the CSIs were on their way to his apartment.

"By the way," Margit added, "Adrian checked out Åsa Dufva's ex-boyfriend, and he's been in Greece since last week. It's good that someone's doing their job properly." She ended the call without saying good-bye.

Thomas shook his head. He knew Margit was feeling the stress of the ongoing restructuring program, but hadn't realized how badly she'd been affected.

He'd moved out of the way while the locksmith was working on Lindqvist's door, and now he heard Aram call out to him.

"Thomas, we're in!"

Thomas hurried upstairs to find the apartment door wide open.

The hallway was in darkness. He groped around for the switch, and when the light came on, he saw a narrow corridor with closed doors on either side. The kitchen was on the right.

Aram had already drawn his gun. Thomas followed suit and flicked off the safety. The apartment was probably empty, but he had no intention of taking any more chances. Not tonight.

He switched on the kitchen light; no one there. Aram flung open another door.

"The living room's clear!" he called out.

The next door revealed the bedroom. A wide bed, neatly made, took up most of the space. On the square nightstand was a pile of colorful porn magazines in various foreign languages.

Thomas put on his latex gloves and picked up the top one. He opened it at random and was faced with a dark-haired Asian girl who looked suspiciously young. She was lying on a table with her legs spread, eyes lowered.

He felt a fresh wave of frustration.

Letting Lindqvist go when they'd had the chance to catch him was unforgivable. He checked the time: ten thirty already.

A call had gone out, but the guy could be anywhere by now. Adrian was trying to track down his boat, and the maritime police had also been informed, in case Lindqvist decided to go to sea.

Next to the bedroom was a spacious black-and-white bathroom, which looked as if it had been renovated very recently. The sink was ultramodern, an oval bowl on a stand.

Aram went back to the living room. Thomas opened the bathroom cabinet; there was a package of condoms on the top shelf.

"I've found his computer," Aram shouted.

Thomas went to join his colleague, who was standing next to a desk in front of a large window, contemplating a sophisticated desktop computer. Aram pressed a key and the screen came to life, but it was no surprise to discover that a password was required.

"We need to get this looked at as soon as possible," Aram said. "If he's got magazines like that lying around, I'd like to know what's on his computer."

The rain was still pouring down, but Thomas could see the small playground directly opposite the apartment building. Did Lindqvist sit here watching the children?

Unopened mail lay on the coffee table by the lead-gray sofa. Thomas flicked through the envelopes, but they were all bills or advertising flyers. Nothing to indicate that Lindqvist had access to another property.

They'd already been down to the basement and established that there was no one in the storage compartments. There was no attic.

Lindqvist's home was neat and clean, with a selection of potted plants that appeared to be thriving. For some reason Thomas had expected it to be grubby and messy, not this well-ordered place with its leather sofa and armchairs. Then again, it didn't matter; the guy was filth, irrespective of the decor.

There had to be a clue to where he'd hidden Benjamin.

Where?

Thomas tried to think like Lindqvist, even though he despised everything he stood for. He opened the top drawer of the desk and stared at the contents: pens and paper clips, Post-it notes in various colors, receipts.

He rummaged in the other drawers but found nothing of interest. He couldn't help looking at his watch again. Time was passing much too quickly. How long did they have before Lindqvist or one of his associates started on the boy?

And destroyed him.

Chapter 101

"I think it's time you went home," said an unfamiliar voice in his ear.

Christian Dufva looked up from the table in a daze. His arm was numb from the weight of his head.

A waitress was standing there with a worried look on her face.

"You can't sleep here," she said.

Christian glanced around. Someone laughed at the next table. There were several empty glasses in front of him, and this wasn't the first bar he'd visited. He'd drunk way too much before passing out.

Reality caught up with him.

He had to contact Ninna, but realized he'd forgotten to switch on his phone. *Fuck.*

"Sorry," he said. "I just need to call my wife, OK?"

It took him three attempts to remember the right code. The screen lit up, and Christian stared at it blankly.

Twenty-two voice-mail messages.

A dozen or so from unknown numbers, the rest from Ninna or Åsa.

How could he have forgotten to switch on his phone? He'd only intended to have one drink before he called Ninna; what the hell was wrong with him?

He certainly couldn't face listening to those messages now.

He stood up so suddenly that he knocked over his chair. The world was spinning around; he had to lean on the table for support.

"Are you OK?" the waitress asked as he staggered toward the door, but he didn't bother replying.

It was raining hard when he emerged onto the sidewalk; he needed a cab.

At that moment his phone rang: Åsa. He didn't want to answer, but felt he had to.

"Benjamin!" she yelled in his ear. "He's gone missing from the sailing camp!"

"Benjamin's gone missing?" Christian repeated. His tongue was thick and shapeless, too big for his mouth.

He was soaked to the skin in seconds, and sought shelter in a doorway.

"Where have you been all day? I don't know how many times I've called you. Why didn't you answer?"

Åsa was hysterical. He held the phone away from his ear, and a woman passing by gave him a curious look.

"The police have been trying to reach you all day as well!"

Twenty-two voice-mail messages.

"Calm down, Åsa," he ventured.

She started to cry. "He's only eleven."

Christian had heard her sobs far too many times. He knew what she looked like when the tears began to flow. Her face grew puffy and ugly, and she made him feel guilty.

All these arguments, he thought wearily. *What were they really about?*

"I've spoken to his friends, but nobody's seen him or heard from him."

Christian leaned against the wall; he was afraid his legs might give way.

"Where can he be, Christian? Where's he gone?"

A wave of nausea came surging up from his stomach, and he swallowed hard several times. Sour Cognac and bile filled his throat.

"You were the one who insisted he went to camp," Åsa went on. "He didn't want to go. Benjamin didn't want to go, but he didn't dare stand up to you. And now someone's taken him!"

She was crying so hard she could barely get the words out.

"This is your fault!"

She was right. This was all his fault.

CHAPTER 102

Aram was tackling the kitchen while Thomas went through the bedroom one more time. The clatter of cutlery told him that Aram was doing a thorough job.

Thomas threw back the bedclothes and searched beneath the mattress: nothing. He'd already checked the closet and nightstand. He went over to a dark-brown chest of drawers. Carefully folded T-shirts and sweaters, black boxer shorts from one of the big chain stores, socks. He was about to give up when something caught his attention. One of the neat piles wasn't quite symmetrical.

He took out the drawer and tipped the underwear out onto the bed. Between two pairs of men's pants he found a pale-blue pair of boys' pants. He looked at the label: nine to eleven years.

He shouted to Aram, who came at once. He stopped dead in the doorway when he saw what Thomas had found.

"Shit—what do you think has happened? Are they Benjamin's? Has he already . . . ?" He couldn't finish the sentence.

Thomas stared at the item of clothing that shouldn't have been there.

They'd been *so* close to catching Lindqvist.

"There has to be something in this apartment that will tell us where he's hidden Benjamin—even if he's moved him by now," he said. "Keep looking."

Aram sighed, then went back to the kitchen. As Thomas left the bedroom, he noticed a slim closet by the front door. He opened it to find a collection of coats and jackets for different seasons, but when he pushed aside the clothes, he discovered a well-concealed key cupboard in the same color as the closet's dark wooden paneling.

At last.

He hardly dared to breathe as he carefully teased it open. Inside was a row of keys on small brass hooks.

There was also a bunch of keys attached to a flat cork float—the same as the one Thomas used for his boat on Harö. It must belong to Lindqvist's boat, which they had yet to locate. Hopefully it meant he hadn't gone to sea.

"I think I've found Lindqvist's boat keys," he called out to Aram.

A silver key gleamed at the bottom of the cupboard; he'd almost missed it. It had a rounded top and was very flat; could it be for a safety-deposit box?

There were thousands in Stockholm, several hundred in the central station alone. It was impossible to guess where it was from without an address label.

Still, it was a possible lead—the only one so far. Thomas slipped it into his pocket. Maybe Staffan Nilsson and his team would be able to figure it out.

He felt a wave of disappointment. He'd hoped that the key cupboard would provide vital information, the keys to a storage facility or cottage. If Lindqvist had another place, then surely the keys would be here—otherwise why would he have gone to the trouble of camouflaging the cupboard?

At that moment the phone rang in the living room. He straightened up quickly and banged his head on the wall.

The key cupboard fell to the floor. It had been inserted in a small alcove, easy to lift out if you knew about it.

Thomas rubbed his head. The cupboard had landed at his feet. There was a key taped to the back. He bent down and carefully removed it. He carried it over to the light and read the word *Sureguard* on the pale-gray rubber tag.

He went into the kitchen, where Aram was rummaging around wearing latex gloves. Drawers and cupboards were open. Glasses and crockery were neatly arranged on the shelves; even the cans were lined up like soldiers on parade.

Thomas held out his hand, with the key resting on his palm. Aram stopped in mid-movement.

"Taped to the back of a key cupboard," Thomas explained.

"Wow." Aram took a closer look. "Sureguard—don't they have a place in Trångsund?"

He was right. Thomas could see the facility in his mind's eye; it was in an industrial area near the freeway. He'd passed it countless times. Trångsund was pretty close to Farsta; all you had to do was follow Nynäsvägen.

All kinds of things were hidden away in those storage units. The police had found drugs and stolen goods, even the victims of trafficking on rare occasions. The units were soundproofed and far away from residential areas, which meant there were no nosy neighbors wondering what was going on.

Thomas pulled off his gloves. His fingers were sweaty, and his knuckles felt stiff.

"Let's get over there, see what we can find."

Chapter 103

Through the windshield Thomas saw the sign advertising self-storage. Fifteen years ago there had been no need for companies like Sureguard; back then most people hadn't owned more possessions than they could accommodate in their homes. These days it was a booming industry, keeping pace with the consumer society. One of IKEA's fastest-developing business sectors was smart storage.

Apparently the value of the items stored rarely exceeded three months' rent.

Thomas got out of the car; it was still pouring. He should be tired, but the adrenaline was pumping through his body.

He was looking at an extensive area enclosed by steel fencing; there were storage units of various sizes. The gates, wide enough to let a truck through, appeared to be securely locked, but Thomas went over and gave them a shake anyway.

No chance.

The ground showed no sign of fresh tire tracks, but the weather made it impossible to tell if a vehicle or a person on foot had recently passed this way.

Aram had gone up to the reception office and was peering through the door. Thomas joined him. A notice informed them that the units could be accessed from five thirty in the morning until ten o'clock at night. Anyone wishing to visit at other times was asked to contact the manager.

"There must be a security guard who can let us in," Aram said.

Thomas looked around. The industrial complex was deserted. The nearest building was a Japanese car showroom, and farther along he could just see some kind of workshop. He assessed the height of the fence; there was no way they could climb over it without a ladder.

"We're not going to be able to get in without help," Aram went on, rubbing a hand over his wet forehead. His tone of voice revealed how exhausted he was. "The question is, are we going to achieve anything at all tonight?"

Thomas knew he was right. They were both soaked to the skin and worn out; it had been a long day, and they desperately needed rest.

However, walking away went against every instinct.

"We have no evidence that Benjamin's here. We don't even know for certain that the key you found belongs to one of these units. Sureguard has dozens of facilities all over the city."

Thomas stared at the fence, his mind racing. They had to get ahold of someone from Sureguard who could let them in, and they needed a dog team to check out the units.

That would take hours.

He checked his watch. Almost midnight. If they came back first thing in the morning, five or six hours would have passed. That was an eternity for a sick pervert like Lindqvist. He peered at the units through the rain. Were they even ventilated? How much air was in them? The smallest ones measured no more than thirty square feet. Were they heated?

He caught sight of his own reflection in the window of the office; his hair was plastered to his head, his jacket was dripping, and his jeans were sodden.

His daughter would be fast asleep in a warm bed at her grandparents' house, with her favorite dolls tucked up beside her. She wasn't cold and alone; she wasn't crying for her mommy and daddy.

Elin was safe.

"We're not leaving yet," he said.

Thomas took out his phone and called for assistance.

Chapter 104

Time slipped by as he woke up, fell asleep, woke up again. Benjamin had no idea how long he'd been locked up; he didn't even know if it was day or night anymore.

Would he ever see the sun again?

He was so cold. It had crept up on him; he didn't know when it had started, but now he was shivering all the time.

A faint noise broke the dense silence. It sounded like an engine, but different, not so close and loud as before.

Benjamin raised his head from the mattress and listened.

Maybe it wasn't too far away . . . He waited, minutes passed. Was it someone calling his name? Someone who'd come to save him?

He held his breath until he felt dizzy.

A new, terrifying thought came into his mind. It could be the kidnapper, coming back to hurt him.

Was he going to die soon?

He lay motionless, fear filling his veins.

The noise faded away.

Nobody's ever going to find me.

The realization had come gradually, but now he knew he had to get used to the idea.

I'm going to die here.

His index finger was very sore, and his hand had begun to throb. His throat felt as if it was closing up; it hurt to swallow.

The hunger had passed; he wasn't even thinking about food, and his stomach had stopped rumbling and complaining. The thirst was something else, however. He'd finished the Coke; there wasn't a drop left.

Could you drink your own piss? He glanced toward the bucket in the corner and grimaced. It must be hours since he'd used it. And it was so far away; he felt so weak he didn't know if he could get there.

The shivering increased; his pulse was racing, despite the fact that he could barely move.

He let out a dry sob. He couldn't even think about trying to escape. There was no point. It was easier to close his eyes, give in.

Sleep until he just didn't wake up anymore.

CHAPTER 105

Thomas shivered in his soaking clothes as he waited for the dog handler. Five cars were assembled in the parking lot outside Sureguard. The gates stood wide open; the manager had unlocked them as soon as he arrived, and the whole area was illuminated by headlights and blue flashing lights.

Aram had taken four uniformed officers to carry out an initial check. Thomas could hear them going from unit to unit, calling out Benjamin's name.

Finally a Volvo pulled up and Thomas hurried over to it. Not Sofia Granit and Jackson this time. He didn't recognize the colleague who introduced himself as Lasse Theorin, but he was very glad to see him. Theorin opened up the back of the car and let out a German shepherd that was whimpering eagerly.

"Over here," Thomas said.

"Do you have something belonging to the boy?"

Thomas held out an evidence bag containing the pale-blue underpants. "We think these might be his."

"OK, let's give it a try."

Theorin stroked the dog's nose. "Come on, boy."

They set off toward the nearest row of units.

Thomas shuddered. If Benjamin was in there, they had to find him. But what if he was lying on a concrete floor, drugged and unable to call for help? In that case they would be entirely reliant on the dog.

"Who has keys to these units?" Theorin asked.

"Only the people who rent them. There's no master key."

The manager had explained that this was part of Sureguard's marketing strategy. Anyone renting a unit could feel secure in the knowledge that no one else could get to their possessions.

Which didn't help Benjamin.

"But we might have Lindqvist's key, if his unit's on this site." Thomas squeezed the key in his pocket.

"So where do we start?"

"On the ground floor." Thomas assumed Lindqvist would have chosen a unit with direct access from a vehicle. If he were hidden from view by an open trunk, it wouldn't take long to transfer a little boy; it seemed unlikely that Lindqvist would have risked carrying the child to one of the upper floors, using either the stairs or the elevator. He wouldn't want that kind of exposure.

Another car turned into the parking lot behind them—hopefully the locksmith, whom they'd called in just in case he was needed.

Thomas and the dog handler set off.

"You have no idea which unit it might be?"

"I'm afraid not."

There was no Pontus Lindqvist in the manager's database, but Lindqvist probably wouldn't have used his own name; he seemed to have a systematic approach. Look at the way Benjamin had been abducted.

Thomas remembered the neatly arranged glasses in the kitchen cupboard, the folded T-shirts in the chest of drawers.

"Any CCTV cameras?" Theorin said.

"Yes, but they're run from a central location by a specialist surveillance company, and we haven't managed to contact them yet. We won't have the footage until tomorrow."

They had reached the first unit.

Lasse Theorin bent down and undid the dog's leash. "Seek, boy," he said encouragingly. "Seek!"

The raindrops sparkled on the dog's fur as he put his nose to the ground and set off.

CHAPTER 106

Wednesday, June 18

Isak opened his eyes. It was after one o'clock in the morning. He must have fallen asleep while he was waiting. He couldn't even get this right. What a loser.

The word hammered into his brain: *worthless.*

He turned his head to look at Wille's bed. He was sleeping on his back with his mouth half-open, snoring gently. Isak hadn't heard him come in.

It was time.

Isak sat up and reached for the notepad and pen on the nightstand. At first he'd planned to text his parents, but that didn't seem like a proper farewell letter. Plus text messages sometimes vanished into thin air, which wouldn't be fair to his mother.

He'd already worked out exactly what he wanted to say.

It was my fault that Benjamin went missing, no one else's.

I love you, Mom.

I'm sorry.

Isak

He wrote fast, pressing down so hard that he almost went right through the page. Then he sat there clutching the pen. Was that enough? Should he provide a more detailed explanation?

There was nothing else to say.

He tore off the sheet of paper as quietly as possible. He pushed his bag under the bed, then crept out of the door.

The storm had abated, but it was still raining hard. The water weighed down the trees, and a loud gurgling came from the gutters and drainpipe at the corner of the building.

Isak hesitated; should he go back and fetch his sailing jacket?

There was no point. What did it matter if he got wet? In a little while he wouldn't know anything about it.

Suddenly he started to laugh at himself, and had to cover his mouth with his hand. Wave after wave of hysterical giggling overwhelmed him. His stomach hurt, and tears poured down his cheeks.

He no longer knew whether he was laughing or crying. His body was shaking so hard that he couldn't stay upright.

He sank down onto the wet ground and hid his face in his hands. It was quite some time before he managed to stop shaking and get back on his feet.

He began to walk toward the sauna.

Chapter 107

Aram came to meet Thomas; his face was drawn. With exhaustion? Despair? Thomas wasn't sure.

"We've been through every floor," Aram said. "Checked every unit. We found nothing—no sign of the boy, no wet footprints outside any of the doors. I don't think Lindqvist has been here."

Thomas glanced over at the dog, working its way methodically from one unit to the next. Every time he stopped, Thomas held his breath.

"Send the uniforms back in," he said. "Tell them to check again."

Aram shook his head. "There's no point in going in without the dog. Knocking and shouting is a waste of time—we've done that."

Thomas felt overtired and groggy.

"How many ground-floor units are there?" Aram asked.

What had the manager said? "Around five hundred. This is the last row."

Aram placed a hand on Thomas's shoulder. "In that case we let the dog do its job. I need to get some sleep, and so do you. We can't carry on like this—we'll come back in the morning."

Suddenly the dog started barking. Time seemed to stop for a second, then Thomas turned and ran.

The dog took a few more steps, sniffed, and barked again.

Thomas rattled the handle of the unit. It was locked, of course, but he couldn't help trying.

The dog was still signaling, its nose pointing forward, its tail rigid with concentration.

Where the hell was the key? Oh God, it was in his hand.

"Get the locksmith over here!" he shouted. If the key didn't fit, they needed his help as quickly as possible.

He heard the sound of running feet. The locksmith opened his bag as Thomas inserted the key in the lock. Everything was happening in slow motion.

Thomas turned the key. The locksmith waited anxiously.

"Benjamin, can you hear me?"

At last, a click. Thomas grabbed the handle and the red roller door shot up with a metallic clatter.

Aram switched on his flashlight. The narrow beam of light showed a medium-size space, maybe ninety square feet. The concrete floor was gray and dusty, the air stale and unpleasant.

The height from floor to ceiling was around nine feet.

Brown cardboard boxes were piled up by the door, blocking off the rest of the unit.

Thomas moved closer. It was impossible to see if there was anyone behind the boxes. He pushed aside the nearest stack and peered into the darkness.

"Is he there?" Aram said from behind him.

CHAPTER 108

"Wake up!"

Someone was shaking David, but his body didn't want to know.

"Leave me alone," he mumbled.

"David, you have to wake up!"

A familiar voice right by his ear. Distressed.

"David, it's an emergency."

David forced his eyes open and saw Wille standing by his bed in his boxers and a T-shirt.

"It's Isak," he said, his voice rough with emotion. "I think he's planning to do something stupid."

David blinked and reached for his glasses. He always felt more stressed when he couldn't see properly. "What are you talking about?"

Wille held out a notepad, the kind that was issued to every member of the staff. "Look at this."

David stared at a blank page. "What am I supposed to be looking at?"

"Can't you see?" Wille held the pad right in front of David's nose.

David peered at it and realized there were small impressions in the paper. They formed letters, which formed words, and suddenly he understood.

It was a farewell note.

He read it again, registered the last three words.

I'm sorry.

Isak

Oh God. David pulled on his jeans. His fingers were stiff, and he fumbled with the zipper. He grabbed a T-shirt from the end of the bed.

"Do you know where he's gone?"

"No idea. Something woke me. I got up because he hadn't switched off his bedside lamp. The notepad was in the middle of the bed, it looked odd. I don't really know why I picked it up, except the letters showed up in the light." Wille stumbled over his words, his expression terrified as he stared at David. "Do you think he's serious? Do you think he's actually going to . . . ?" He couldn't say it.

David tried to think. Where would Isak have gone? "Has he mentioned this to you? Given any indication of what he was planning to do?"

Wille's cheeks flushed red, and he shook his head.

"You didn't talk before you went to bed?"

"He was already asleep when I got back from the meeting. I've kind of left him to his own devices. I didn't realize he was thinking of . . ."

David stared at the pad, trying to work out where Isak could go to make sure he had enough time.

To kill himself.

There shouldn't be many places to hide away in camp, but that wasn't the case; they'd learned that over the past few days. It had taken hours to search the island on both occasions.

Isak could be anywhere, in Heinecke's Tower, down by the marina. He might even have taken one of the escort boats and gone off to one of the skerries.

There were way too many alternatives. How could they possibly track him down before it was too late?

"How much time do we have? When did he leave the room?"

"I'm not sure." Wille shifted nervously from foot to foot. "Maybe ten, fifteen minutes ago? I came straight here when I figured out what he'd written."

How long did it take to die?

"Maja might know something," Wille suggested. "Isak often hangs out with her."

Maja. Why hadn't David thought of her right away? He was already on the move, running out the door with the notepad in his hand.

"Wake all the other instructors, Wille. And call Björn Ekholm—he's staying at the Sailors Hotel on Sandhamn. Get everyone searching—all over the island."

Maja stayed in the neighboring dormitory. David raced in and flung open the first door he came to.

"Maja!" he shouted into the darkness.

"Next room," someone mumbled sleepily.

David ran into the room next door. "Where's Maja?"

"What's the matter?"

It was Maja's voice. She sat up and switched on the bedside lamp. As soon as she saw David's ashen face, her hand flew to her mouth. "Isak?"

David nodded.

"What's happened?"

He held out the notepad and showed her the impressions. Now that he'd seen them, they were sharp and clear, like a red light flashing on the wall. He couldn't understand why he hadn't realized immediately.

"I think he's planning to take his own life," he said. "He's written a farewell note."

"No no no, he can't . . ."

"We have to find him. I don't know where he's gone."

Maja pushed back her tousled hair. "The sauna's his favorite place . . ."

Of course. That was where Isak had been earlier in the day.

Maja ran her fingertips over the page, then she got out of bed and pulled on her jeans.

"We have to stop him," she said.

Chapter 109

Isak opened the door of the sauna and felt for the light switch. The sudden brightness made him blink.

Water was dripping from his clothes, forming small puddles on the floor. He couldn't help thinking that the housekeeper wouldn't be happy.

He paused in the doorway of the first room, where the hook was. After a few seconds he went and stood directly beneath it, looking up.

It was only just over seven feet from floor to ceiling, but that would be enough.

He felt at the hook with his right hand; his finger just reached. It was secure, screwed deep into the wood.

He fetched the box and positioned it in the correct spot. Then he took the rope and made a noose with a proper knot, a bowline hitch, just as the children learned to do in their theory classes.

As he drew the end through the hole, he began to cry. For a moment he hesitated, let the rope fall to the ground.

Then he remembered the sterile hallway in the psych unit, the look on his father's face when he came to pick him up.

Worthless.

It was better this way; Mom and Dad would never need to be ashamed of him again. They would be much better off without him ruining everything he touched. So would his siblings.

He picked up the rope, stepped onto the box, and slipped the noose over his head, settling it around his neck. It scraped against his skin, making him retch involuntarily. He forced himself to stay where he was, waited until the impulse to tear off the noose had passed.

Should he have switched off the light?

No, he decided to leave it on. He didn't want anyone to bump into his body in the dark.

He'd made so many mistakes, gotten so many things wrong. At least he could try to do something right for once.

Show some consideration.

Isak balanced on the edge of the box and lifted one foot.

Now.

CHAPTER 110

It felt as if the phone had started ringing only minutes after she'd fallen asleep, but the clock on Nora's nightstand was showing one thirty. She groped for her cell and pressed it to her ear.

"Hello?"

"Hi, it's me."

"Jonas? Where are you?"

"Still in Bangkok."

She was awake in a second.

"Hang on," she said. She didn't want to disturb Julia, who was fast asleep beside her in the double bed. Nora kissed her daughter's forehead and crept out of the bedroom. Her movements were slow and heavy, reminding her of the time when Julia was a baby and it had caused Nora physical pain to be woken up after only a few hours' rest. She had been forty-two years old, and had forgotten the exhaustion that came with a newborn.

"When will you be home?" she said quietly.

"Now, don't get upset," Jonas began.

Nora closed her eyes. She knew it. She took a deep breath, then went into the living room and over to the window. She placed the palm of her hand on the ice-cold glass.

It was still pouring out there.

Part of her wanted to end the call before Jonas had the chance to say any more.

"The plane can't be fixed. They're going to have to send a new one out. They're busy trying to find a reserve aircraft."

"What does that mean?"

"In the best-case scenario, it should be here tomorrow."

"And if it's not?"

Her lips, her whole face felt stiff. They belonged to someone else, a Nora who was on the point of falling apart, but stayed in control by not moving a muscle.

"It might take a couple of days to locate a new 767 and fly it down here."

"A couple of days?"

"Forty-eight hours at the most. That's what they're saying anyway."

The time difference between Sweden and Thailand was five hours, so it was six thirty in the morning in Bangkok. Wednesday morning.

In forty-eight hours it would be Friday morning. Their wedding day. If the plane didn't arrive until then, and still had to be serviced and loaded, Jonas wouldn't be back in time.

"You promised you'd be home in time! You promised!"

"Darling, listen to me, please."

Nora stared at the vase of peonies on the table. They were her favorite flowers, and the beautiful pink buds had opened up in all their glory.

On Friday there would be peonies and lily of the valley in her bridal bouquet.

"Let's look on the bright side," Jonas continued. "With a bit of luck, the plane will be here tomorrow, and everything will be fine."

Nora couldn't speak.

"I'm just as disappointed as you are, sweetheart, but right now there's nothing I can say or do to change the situation. We just have to hope for the best."

The reception she'd been planning for months. The seating plan for all their guests. The priest and the chapel, booked for three o'clock.

Her dress, hanging up in the closet.

She would have to stand there all alone and explain that her husband-to-be wasn't coming, because he was stuck on the other side of the world.

Tears burned behind her eyelids.

After the divorce from Henrik, she had sworn that she would never marry again. It wasn't worth the pain when everything went wrong.

Jonas had made her forget her resolution, but now she remembered why she'd made it.

It was better to leave than be left.

This wedding was never meant to happen. She'd been fooling herself all along.

The words came out of her mouth by themselves.

"You might as well stay where you are," she whispered. "How could you do this to me?"

Chapter 111

David and Maja ran toward the sauna through the wet undergrowth and bushes. The branches whipped their bodies and scratched their faces. The rocks were slippery, and David could hardly see through his rain-spattered glasses. His heart was pounding; he'd never run so fast.

He should have spoken to Isak during the evening, should have realized how upset he was. He knew Isak was fragile, yet he'd chosen to leave him alone, thought it was better if Isak didn't have to deal with any more questions about what had happened.

He knew Björn Ekholm blamed Isak for Benjamin's disappearance; he had seen Ekholm rip into him.

He should have stepped in; why hadn't he done something?

The wind was still blowing hard, and the choppy white-topped waves were clearly visible, crashing against the shoreline of the island opposite Lökholmen.

The small building housing the sauna was silhouetted against the water, a faint glow shining through the square window.

There shouldn't be a light on if no one's in there.

David thought he could make out something behind the glass. The wooden decking gleamed in the rain.

He'd sat here so many times, enjoying a sauna after a long day at sea, recovering at the end of camp and after the big cleanup in the fall. The instructors would get together and relax over a beer as the sun slowly set behind Telegrafholmen.

Maja suddenly stopped dead.

"I don't dare go in there," she whispered, her eyes huge and frightened. Her lips were trembling.

David was breathing heavily. Could he see a shadow inside? Something dangling?

He straightened his shoulders, walked up to the building, grasped the handle, and opened the door.

CHAPTER 112

Nora didn't want to cry, but she couldn't stop the tears from soaking her pillow. A few days ago she'd been so happy; now there was nothing left.

A part of her brain was still working rationally, telling her that Jonas wasn't to blame for the situation. It wasn't his fault the aircraft had developed a fault in Bangkok.

Another part was drowning in disappointment.

She had warned him about the possibility of something going wrong, and yet he'd risked their wedding for the sake of his job. At least she now realized where his priorities lay, what was really important to him.

She wasn't at the top of his list.

She touched the engagement ring on her left hand. She'd worn it every day since Jonas had proposed on Sandhamn; she didn't even take it off at night.

The whole thing had been a stupid idea from the start.

She should never have agreed to marry him.

She wiped her eyes with a corner of the pillowcase. Thank goodness she owned this apartment; she had the security of knowing she wouldn't have to move if they split up.

But what about Julia? Would she end up spending alternate weeks with each parent, just as Adam and Simon had done for the past few years? That was exactly what Nora had wanted to avoid. She'd felt terrible every time the boys went to stay with Henrik; she'd never really gotten used to not having them every weekend, school break, and holiday.

Julia was barely five years old.

Fresh tears sprang to Nora's eyes. It was beginning to grow light outside. How was she going to get dressed and go to court in a few hours? She turned over onto her side and curled up in the fetal position, rocking back and forth.

The pain was unbearable.

CHAPTER 113

David let out a yell when he saw Isak's limp body hanging from the ceiling.

Time stood still.

The white rope around Isak's neck was so tight that the skin bulged over it, both above and below. Isak's mouth was half-open, his tongue protruding between bloodless lips. He seemed to be staring at the wall, and his face was almost blue.

Suddenly David was able to move again. He hurled himself forward and flung his arms around Isak's legs and hips, trying to lift the body in order to stop the noose from restricting the airway.

But Isak was so heavy.

David's face was pressed against Isak's chest; it was impossible to tell if he was still breathing.

"Help me, Maja," he groaned. "Maja!"

The lactic acid was already causing agonizing pain in the muscles in his arms. He couldn't hold on much longer.

He caught a movement in his peripheral vision. Maja was pushing a box forward; she climbed onto it and reached up to the ceiling. David looked up and saw that the rope was attached to a metal hook. He tried to move his shoulder to support Isak that way, but it didn't help. The body was like an unmanageable sandbag, threatening to slip from his grasp at any second.

David was almost in tears from a combination of fear and effort.

Maja was on tiptoe, doing her best to free the rope. David suddenly remembered why the hook was there, the idiotic game they'd played.

"I can't do it," Maja sobbed. "The rope's too tight."

With strength he didn't know he possessed, David managed to raise Isak's body a couple of inches more. Sweat was pouring down his face; his cheek slipped against Isak's stomach, where his shirt had ridden up.

Was his skin already cold?

David closed his eyes and made a huge effort.

"Try now," he gasped.

Maja tugged at the rope, and suddenly succeeded in freeing it from the hook.

David crashed to the floor with Isak on top of him. He rolled away and sat up. Isak was lying on his back, his head slumped to one side.

Maja dropped to her knees beside him, then looked up at David. "Is he still alive?"

David bent over the pale, lifeless face. Isak's chest wasn't moving.

"Isak? Can you hear me?" David blinked away the tears, fragments of his first-aid training flitting through his mind. "Can you hear me?"

Nothing.

Maja pressed a clenched fist to her lips. "No, no . . ."

She leaned forward. Pinching Isak's nose between her thumb and two fingers, she blew air into his mouth.

David placed his ear on Isak's chest, desperately hoping to hear a heartbeat, however faint.

Please.

There was a heartbeat—he was almost sure of it.

Chapter 114

Thomas's mind was filled with uneasy thoughts, snakes wriggling back and forth, apparitions of shadow and light drifting in and out of one another.

He was gasping for air.

Every time a pattern began to form, it vanished again, sank out of sight, or was erased. Everything dissolved as soon as he got too close.

Nothing made sense.

He was moving through a labyrinth of dead ends, a thick, wet fog that clung to his body.

He began to run, but couldn't find his way out.

When the phone rang at six thirty, he was awake in a second, with sorrow in his breast.

"Christian Dufva's gotten in touch," Margit informed him. "Can you come in?"

They hadn't found Benjamin at the Sureguard storage facility. The unit had revealed nothing but cardboard boxes and a few plastic bags containing Lindqvist's clothes and personal possessions. The dog must have reacted to his smell; the child's underpants had been kept in his drawer, after all.

Failure weighed heavily on Thomas's shoulders as he and Aram made their way to the interview room where Dufva was waiting. They had no idea where Benjamin was, not a single lead.

Revenge was one of the words Margit had written on the board during their most recent briefing, and it came into Thomas's mind as soon as he saw Dufva's gaunt, hollow-eyed figure.

If someone had wanted to take revenge on Benjamin's father, they had undoubtedly succeeded. His face was gray, and he was constantly licking his cracked lips.

If someone took Elin, would I look like that?

"Would you like some water?" Thomas began, pointing to the carafe on the table.

"Please."

As Thomas poured a glass, Aram switched on the tape recorder and gave the obligatory details.

Dufva's eyes were darting all over the place. The pale-green decor had been deliberately chosen to create a calming ambience, but it didn't seem to be having the desired effect on him.

"Thank you for coming in," Thomas said. "We were trying to reach you all day yesterday."

"Sorry, my phone was switched off, I had no idea . . ." His voice died away, and he fingered the shabby leather briefcase on his knee.

Thomas gave a brief rundown of the measures they'd undertaken so far, but Dufva interrupted him before he'd finished.

"You have to find him!"

"There's a major search operation going on out there," Aram said reassuringly. "We're doing all we can to track down your son, and we have officers working around the clock."

"Good, good." Dufva couldn't sit still; he was constantly changing his position.

Everything pointed to Pontus Lindqvist, but they had to consider the possibility that Benjamin's disappearance could be about something else.

"We're wondering if anyone's contacted you about Benjamin," Thomas said.

"What . . . what do you mean?"

"Has anyone been in touch—demanded a ransom payment, for example?"

"No."

The response was brittle.

"If that were to happen, you would let us know?"

"Yes, of course."

"Even if they told you not to go to the police?"

"I already said yes!" His voice broke.

Aram decided to take a slightly different approach. "How would you describe your relationship with your son?"

"Good." A heavy sigh. "It hasn't been easy for him—since the divorce, I mean. Åsa's still very angry with me, and that's affected my relationship with Benjamin. We haven't seen each other very often over the past year." He spread his hands wide. "It's difficult with my new family. I've had a lot to deal with, and unfortunately Benjamin has suffered because of that."

"According to Åsa, you were the one who insisted that Benjamin should go to sailing camp."

"She has a lot to say for herself." The tension in Dufva's face was clear. "But it's true, it was my idea. I went to sailing camp when I was his age, and I wanted my son to experience the camaraderie, the adventure." He looked away. "Åsa treats him like a baby," he said wearily. "I thought it would be good for Benjamin to make new friends instead of spending all his time with his mom."

"Do you have any enemies who might want to harm you or your family?" Thomas asked.

"I hope not."

"You haven't fallen out with anyone?"

"No."

"Are you absolutely certain?"

Dufva reached for the glass and drank deeply.

"Have you been subjected to any kind of threat recently? Any form of blackmail or extortion?"

Dufva shook his head and stared down into his glass.

Thomas had a strong feeling that Dufva didn't dare trust them.

"Has anything unusual happened in your life lately?" Aram asked.

Beads of sweat broke out on Dufva's brow. "Where the hell are you going with this?" he snapped. "Why are you asking me stupid fucking questions when you should be out there looking for my son?"

Aram refused to be diverted. "Your wife told us you were testifying in a major court case yesterday. We just wanted to make sure that there's no connection between your testimony and Benjamin's disappearance."

Christian Dufva gripped his briefcase so tightly that his knuckles whitened.

"I can't help you. Just find Benjamin, please."

CHAPTER 115

Would she take it all back if she could?

Nora's eyes were sore from the lack of sleep as she stepped into the shower. She had eventually drifted into a no-man's-land somewhere between sleep and wakefulness. When the alarm clock rang, her muscles were still tense.

She turned on the hot water.

The back of her neck was aching, and she increased the heat until it was almost unbearable. She allowed the needles of scalding water to massage her body, but didn't feel any better.

After a long time she turned off the water, reached for a towel, and rubbed herself dry until her skin was an angry red.

The apartment was quiet; Julia hadn't woken up yet. At least Nora didn't have to pretend that everything was fine.

She couldn't think about Jonas right now. Her personal problems would have to wait until tonight. If she was going to have to call around and cancel the wedding, a few hours wouldn't make any difference.

She went into the kitchen, checked her phone, and saw that she had a missed call. It had come through fifteen minutes ago, at ten to eight.

Jonas, she thought. Her heart flipped over, even though there was nothing more to say. She'd made that perfectly clear last night.

The call was from Leila Kacim.

Nora still hadn't managed to speak to Thomas, but Leila's words were ringing in her ears. She mustn't come up with fresh accusations against Niklas Winnerman out of sheer desperation brought on by Christian Dufva's U-turn.

She no longer trusted her own judgment. She couldn't go to Barbro Wikingsson without solid evidence—that much was clear in the cold light of day. If she did, she would make her own position untenable.

She called Leila, sending up a silent prayer that her colleague would have good news. The pain in her neck was spreading across her shoulders; even her coffee cup felt heavy in her hand.

Leila answered immediately, sounding excited. "The guy from the bank contacted me. He went into work early, and he thinks he's found the CCTV footage we wanted."

Finally.

"Do you want to come with me to take a look at it? He can meet us at the head office at quarter to nine. You can make it if you hurry."

Nora glanced at the clock above the kitchen doorway.

The trial was due to start at ten. She'd intended to go through some of the documents again, but if the footage contained what she was hoping for, then it may still be possible to avoid disaster.

One disaster anyway.

If she took a cab, she'd be there in thirty minutes. "I'm on my way."

Chapter 116

Margit met Thomas in the hallway on his way back from the interview with Christian Dufva.

"We've picked up Pontus Lindqvist in the Huddinge shopping mall," she informed him. "He's in room five." She gave Thomas a searching look. "Are you OK to lead?"

"Absolutely."

Margit didn't seem completely convinced, but let it pass.

"Has anyone checked Lindqvist's computer?" Thomas asked.

"They're working on it—they'll be in touch as soon as possible."

"What about the apartment and the storage unit?"

"I'm expecting a report from forensics in time for morning briefing. The background check on both of Benjamin's parents has also been completed; nothing of interest there." Margit looked at her watch. "I have to go—see you later."

Aram was by the coffee machine. Thomas poured himself a cup, too, knocked it back, and grimaced at the bitter aftertaste.

Christian Dufva had given them nothing that would lead them to Benjamin. It was just as Thomas had expected, but he'd still hoped for a breakthrough. He refilled his cup and headed for the elevators with

Aram. Just as the doors were about to open, he heard Margit calling his name.

He turned to see her hurrying along the hallway, her phone pressed to her ear. The expression on her face gave him a bad feeling.

"Something terrible has happened at the sailing camp overnight. One of the instructors tried to kill himself. He was found in the sauna with a rope around his neck."

"What's his name?" Aram asked.

"Isak Andrén."

A shiver ran down Thomas's spine. Isak. Benjamin's group leader.

"What else do we know?"

"Not much—it's not possible to speak to him yet. The senior instructor found him just in time and managed to get him down; he was taken by helicopter to Karolinska Hospital. Just like you were . . ."

Several years earlier Thomas had fallen through the ice and suffered a heart attack due to hypothermia. The body of the man he'd been chasing had never been found.

"How is he?" Aram said.

"He's still unconscious. It's possible that he's suffered permanent brain damage due to oxygen deprivation. His condition is critical." Margit bit her lower lip. "He's only nineteen."

Aram and Thomas exchanged a glance.

"We met him yesterday," Thomas explained.

Isak had obviously been stressed, pale, and strained, but Thomas hadn't thought he was so deeply affected by the situation that he didn't want to live anymore.

"He left a note saying it was all his fault. Apologized to his parents."

"Is that exactly how he expressed himself?" Thomas wanted to know.

"Yes."

They'd discussed how Lindqvist could have known where to find Benjamin, how he'd found out. There was a darker alternative: he'd had help from someone in the camp. Someone who knew exactly where each child slept.

Isak was only nineteen, but sex offenders often embarked on their activities earlier than that. There had been several cases of young pedophiles who'd been caught when they'd volunteered to help out at preschools, and had abused the children.

However, it could simply be that Benjamin's disappearance had placed too heavy a weight on a young instructor's shoulders, and that Isak had been overwhelmed by feelings of guilt.

"We need to talk to him, find out if he's involved in some way."

"You won't be able to do that for a while," Margit said, her voice subdued. "The doctors don't even know if he's going to regain consciousness."

CHAPTER 117

Pontus Lindqvist had a hell of a lot of questions to answer. When Thomas and Aram walked into the sterile interview room, he was sitting at the table with his defense lawyer.

It was clear that Lindqvist was another person who hadn't had much sleep, if any. He looked considerably better in his photograph; now he had dark shadows beneath his eyes, and a deep scratch above one eyebrow, presumably from running away through bushes and undergrowth.

I hope it hurts, Thomas thought.

Hjalmar Andersson, the lawyer, was about sixty years old. He was wearing a dark jacket without a tie. His thick mustache had turned gray, with only the odd strand of black remaining.

Thomas hadn't met him before, but there were plenty of criminal lawyers in Stockholm.

How could someone defend a sex offender? How could anyone bear to deal with a client who abused children? No doubt Andersson had been asked the same questions many times in the past, and no doubt he had formulated a response that enabled him to sleep at night.

Thomas still didn't understand.

He offered a stiff handshake, then sat down as Aram turned on the tape recorder. Thomas poured them each a glass of water from the carafe provided.

"Where's Benjamin?" No point in wasting time.

"Who?" Lindqvist stared blankly at him.

Thomas clenched his fists. He had no intention of playing cat and mouse with Lindqvist, indulging him in some game until he confessed after hours, maybe days of interrogation. He really wanted to get up and leave the room, lock this guy up for the rest of his life, and never give him another thought.

But that wouldn't help Benjamin.

Aram cleared his throat. "Do you have to make this difficult for us? That won't help your situation. Abduction is one thing, but if the boy dies, you'll be charged with homicide. You'll go down for life."

Andersson glanced sideways at his client. It was impossible to read any reaction in his neutral expression.

"And I can promise you it won't be in an easy place like Skogome," Thomas added. "I'll make sure of that."

Andersson was about to protest, but Thomas didn't let him interrupt.

"Tell us where you've hidden Benjamin. We're going to sit here until you do." He leaned forward until he was only inches from Lindqvist's face. The scratch on his face was edged with black, congealed blood.

However, Lindqvist seemed unconcerned.

"I don't know what you're talking about. I haven't abducted anyone."

Aram sighed. "So why did you run when we arrived at your apartment building yesterday? If you're innocent, you could have stopped and talked to us."

Andersson coughed discreetly. "Not surprisingly, my client was afraid when two unknown men appeared outside his front door late at night. I don't think that's difficult to understand." He gave an apologetic smile. "Given his background."

"We're police officers," Thomas said dryly.

"He thought you were intending to attack him. There are some nasty people out there, if you know what I mean. If I've understood correctly, you didn't show any ID," Andersson concluded with a charming smile.

There was no point in saying that they hadn't had the chance to produce their ID before Lindqvist took to his heels.

A heavy silence filled the room.

"Tell us where Benjamin is," Thomas said again.

Lindqvist shook his head. "As I've already said, I don't know what you're talking about. I haven't abducted anyone."

It was going to be a long morning.

CHAPTER 118

The cab dropped Nora outside the head office of Handelsbanken on Kungsträdgårdsgatan in the city center.

She closed her eyes.

Please let the CCTV footage show Winnerman.

Leila was already waiting as Nora walked in through the heavy doors. The building dated from the early 1900s, and was reminiscent of a stately home. Presumably it was cheaper to stay in these opulent surroundings rather than commissioning a modern palace in glass and steel.

A young man with shoulder-length hair came to meet them. He introduced himself as Rasmus Skoglund. They took the elevator to the floor below and entered a windowless room with a large screen on the wall and a laptop on the table.

"Thank you for doing this so quickly," Nora said. "We're in the middle of a trial that's due to finish today, which is why it's so urgent."

Rasmus produced a black cable and inserted it into a port on the computer. "No problem," he said with a smile. "We always try to cooperate with the police." He pointed to the projector on the ceiling. "I've downloaded the footage from our Hallunda branch, but I presume you don't want to see everything that went on in the bank for the whole day?"

Bertil Svensson hadn't been entirely clear about what time it had been when he met Niklas Winnerman. In the morning . . . between ten and twelve . . . possibly after lunch . . .

"If you can fast-forward, that would be really helpful," Leila said, pulling out one of the upholstered chairs. "Start when the bank opened for business."

"Of course."

Rasmus dimmed the lights and pressed a couple of keys. The interior of a bank appeared on the screen, with fittings in pale wood and Handelsbanken's signature blue color.

"OK, here we go."

The pictures whizzed by. Nora gazed intently at the screen as the minutes passed by. She had to leave by twenty to ten at the latest to be in court by ten.

It appeared to have been a quiet morning. An elderly lady with a wheeled walker shuffled in, and two men disappeared into a conference room with the manager. Then a mother with a stroller, clutching the hand of a fretful toddler.

Nora tried to maintain her concentration. The door opened again and a man in a black baseball cap appeared. He was wearing glasses and a dark-colored winter coat.

Bertil Svensson had mentioned a cap.

"Wait," Nora and Leila both said at once. "Can you stop it there?"

Rasmus pressed a key and the image froze.

"Could you rewind a few seconds, then play the footage in slow motion?" Leila's voice was shaking slightly.

Slowly, slowly the man walked in. The cap was hiding the upper part of his face; it was impossible to get a clear picture of him. He went over to one of the tables, picked up a pen and a withdrawal slip, and began to fill in the details.

Nora stood up and moved closer, but the image became too grainy. She sat down again, studying the rear view of the man. She couldn't claim to recognize the back of Niklas Winnerman's neck however hard she tried.

He went over to the counter, and this time his profile was visible. He was wearing glasses with brown frames, wasn't he?

"Those look like Winnerman's glasses," Leila whispered.

There was no sound; they watched as the cashier exchanged a few words with the man before handing over two one-thousand-kronor notes and a five hundred.

That was the exact sum Winnerman had taken out, according to Svensson.

It had to be him.

They'd checked his bank account looking for a withdrawal that matched the payment to Svensson, but had found nothing. There was no way they would have missed a withdrawal from the Hallunda branch, but now Nora realized they hadn't checked his sons' accounts— the two boys who'd been in court on the first day. They were both minors, which meant that Winnerman controlled their accounts. Had he used their names?

She already knew he was a cunning bastard.

The man turned and raised his chin a fraction; suddenly the camera caught most of his face.

"Pause!" Nora burst out.

The screen was filled with a close-up of his features. The cap was pulled all the way down over his forehead, almost completely covering his brown hair. His glasses were perched on his nose. Nora could just see a white shirt and tie beneath the thick coat, which was open at the neck.

Leila stopped chewing gum.

Nora stared at the screen.

She'd prayed for fresh evidence. And there it was.

CHAPTER 119

Christian Dufva fumbled with the keys before he eventually managed to open the door of his apartment. He stumbled into the bedroom and collapsed on the bed without even taking off his shoes.

The room was hot and stuffy, yet he was shivering. His left arm ached. He lay there with his eyes closed, wondering if he'd ever be able to get up again.

The police had told him to go home and wait by the phone in case the kidnapper got in touch. Under no circumstances must he switch off his cell again.

If he thought of anything, anything at all, he must call them.

If he was contacted by the kidnapper, he must call them.

Sweat was pouring off him.

He hadn't dared answer the questions the police had asked him, hadn't dared tell them about the threatening voice on the phone twenty-four hours earlier.

If you go to the cops, your family will suffer.

He'd done everything the man had demanded, changed his testimony, withdrawn his accusations against Niklas, even defended him in court.

Just do as we say and the kid will be back in no time.

The words reverberated around Christian's head.

Benjamin should be home now. Christian had followed the man's instructions to the letter.

But that detective, Thomas Andreasson, had said they suspected a convicted pedophile who'd been seen on Lökholmen. He'd been in Benjamin's dormitory—they even had his fingerprints.

Christian inhaled sharply.

Had they fooled him all along? Made him lie for nothing, just by making a threatening call?

He had no proof that they were telling the truth and really had kidnapped Benjamin, yet he'd been so scared that he'd blindly gone along with their demands without asking any questions. He hadn't even contacted the camp. As soon as they pulled the strings, he'd danced like a marionette.

Benjamin.

No one knew if he was dead or alive. Christian pictured his son's face and tried to slow his breathing.

After a while he turned over onto his back. There was a crack in the ceiling.

His phone rang.

He hoped it wasn't Åsa again with her bitter accusations; he couldn't cope with listening to her yet again. He sat up and took his cell out of his pocket. Ninna, thank God.

"Hello?"

"Christian, what's going on? Have they found Benjamin yet?"

He tried to find the right words, but when he heard Emil babbling in the background, he started to cry.

He couldn't tell Ninna any of it.

"Not yet," he mumbled, trying to pull himself together. "They're still searching."

His guilt was suffocating him, pressing down on his chest like a lead weight, constricting his airway.

What had he done?

CHAPTER 120

Benjamin tried to turn onto his back, but his body refused to obey him. His finger, his entire hand felt weird; the numbness was spreading upward.

It took a huge effort just to open his eyes.

Eventually he succeeded in rolling over, but couldn't find a more comfortable position. Why did his arm ache so much? He'd stopped shivering; now he was too hot. He'd pushed down his sleeping bag and was lying on the mattress.

He was very thirsty.

The skin at the corners of his mouth had cracked; it was really sore. He felt as if his lips were shrinking away to nothing, becoming narrow, sunken lines stuck to his teeth.

Swallowing was agony.

He reached out for the soda bottle with his good hand, even though he knew it was empty. He tried to drink; it still smelled of soda, but not a drop came out.

He dropped the bottle with a sob; it fell to the concrete floor and rolled away. In the darkness he couldn't see where it had gone, but it didn't matter.

Benjamin started to cry again. The physical effort had made his heart start racing. When he blinked he realized how swollen his eyes were. Even his eyelids felt sticky, yet dried out.

For a moment he thought he saw his mother's face—had she come to get him?

Then she disappeared, and everything went black again.

Chapter 121

Nora almost ran out of the bank's head office. She was still finding it difficult to process what she'd just seen, but this changed everything.

If only she'd gotten hold of the footage earlier.

She needed to call the court office and request a few hours' postponement for preparation so that the new evidence could be presented after lunch.

Leila had stayed behind to get a copy of the CCTV film. She would follow Nora as soon as possible.

It was now twenty to ten.

The first tourists of the day were strolling among the magnificent flower beds in Kungsträdgården, while a man in overalls ambled along the street with his trash cart picking up litter. The shops on Hamngatan had already put up huge signs in their windows advertising the midsummer sales.

Nora was so agitated she could hardly breathe.

She rummaged in her purse for her cell phone, scrolled down to the number of the court, and asked to speak to Barbro Wikingsson.

She listened to the rings, one after the other.

"I'm afraid there's no answer," the exchange operator said with no interest whatsoever.

"Could you please try again?"

Nora hurried toward the taxi stand, the phone pressed to her ear. Finally she heard the judge's voice.

"It's Nora Linde." She had to make a real effort not to pant.

"Yes?"

"I have new evidence that could affect the outcome of the case against Niklas Winnerman. I am therefore making a formal request for a postponement until one o'clock this afternoon."

And then she explained why.

CHAPTER 122

Several hours' questioning, and nothing that might lead them to Benjamin.

"My client needs a break and something to eat," Hjalmar Andersson said.

Thomas wasn't ready to give up yet. "Your client will just have to wait. I want to go through this one more time."

Andersson sighed loudly. Thomas couldn't have cared less.

"We know your boat was in the marina on Lökholmen while the sailing camp was on," he said to Pontus Lindqvist. "We know you were in Benjamin's dormitory looking for him. We even have a witness who saw you carrying Benjamin out of the dormitory in the early hours of the morning. So why won't you tell us where he is?"

"I don't know where he is. I've already told you. I didn't take him."

Lindqvist was starting to look exhausted. His hand shook when he reached for his glass of water.

Thomas didn't care about that either.

"Why did you leave Lökholmen so suddenly?" Aram asked.

Lindqvist glanced at his lawyer. "I heard that another child had gone missing. A group of kids came to my boat, asking if anyone had seen him." He gave a wry smile. "With my background, staying around didn't seem like such a good idea."

"Do you really expect us to believe that?"

Lindqvist shrugged. "You can believe what you like, but it's the truth."

"We're going to find Benjamin's DNA on your boat, so there's no point in denying it."

Aram kept on pressing him, despite the fact that they didn't know where the boat was moored. Lindqvist refused to tell them, and Thomas wondered if that was where he was keeping Benjamin.

There were dozens of harbors and marinas suitable for small boats in and around Stockholm; it was like searching for a needle in a haystack. Adrian was busy contacting insurance companies to see if he could find out that way.

Almost thirty hours had passed since Benjamin went missing.

If Lindqvist had handed the boy over to an accomplice, he could be miles away by now—out of the country, perhaps. If he'd acted alone and Benjamin was locked up somewhere, there was a risk that the child wouldn't have enough food or water while Lindqvist was being held at the station.

Or enough oxygen.

There were way too many alternative scenarios, each one worse than the last.

Thomas slammed his fist down on the table with such force that the carafe of water jumped. "You've already been convicted of serious sexual offenses against children. We have witnesses who saw you at the scene of the crime, and your fingerprints are everywhere. What can you possibly have to gain by prolonging this process?"

"We also found Benjamin's underpants in your apartment," Aram interjected. "You're not helping yourself."

Lindqvist blinked several times, then stared stubbornly into space. "I haven't kidnapped anyone."

"We've got more than enough to charge you," Aram continued. "You'll be arrested this afternoon; we've already spoken to the prosecutor."

Thomas turned to Andersson. "Perhaps you could inform your client that he won't be leaving here until he's confessed and told us where Benjamin is." He pushed the photograph of Benjamin across the table so that the lawyer couldn't avoid looking at it. "He's only eleven years old. Can you imagine how frightened he must be?"

Andersson glanced at Lindqvist, who was now studying his thumb. He brought it to his mouth and bit off a loose piece of skin by the nail, then spat it to one side.

"We're talking about a young boy who's been taken away from his parents," Aram said slowly. "A young boy who will probably die unless your client decides to cooperate."

Silence.

"Where is Benjamin?" Thomas asked yet again. "Tell us where you've hidden him."

"You're fucking crazy!" Lindqvist snapped. "How many times do I have to say this? I don't know where he is!"

Chapter 123

They'd sat here like this on Monday morning: Nora on the left, Winnerman and Svensson and their two defense attorneys directly opposite her.

The early-afternoon sun was shining in through the window. The trial would be over in a few hours.

A screen had been put up in the middle of the room, and a projector stood on a small table in front of it. The audio system crackled as Dennis Grönstedt leaned forward and switched on the microphone.

"The court calls Christian Dufva."

Nora had requested the opportunity to question her own witness again.

The doors were opened by a security guard, and Dufva shambled in. He was unshaven and his shirt was creased, his face ashen and lined. He looked as if he'd slept in his clothes.

Nora waited until he was seated. She could see that he was wondering why he'd been recalled.

"Thank you for coming," she began. She didn't mention his missing son; it wasn't her place to bring up the issue in court.

Dufva picked up the carafe. As he poured himself a glass, his hand was shaking so much that water went everywhere.

Nora was holding the remote control, but chose to put it down for a moment.

"I have some CCTV footage I'd like to show you and the court, then I have some follow-up questions—if that's OK by you?"

Dufva nodded, still puzzled. "Of course." He ran a hand over his shiny forehead.

Nora signaled to Grönstedt, who dimmed the lights. She picked up the remote and pressed the green button.

The only sound was the dull roar of the traffic outside the courtroom. Niklas Winnerman leaned forward to get a better view, his mouth compressed into a thin line.

Nora had asked for the film to run slightly more slowly than usual. She wanted to make sure everyone had plenty of time to take in what was happening.

The man entered the bank. His face was hidden by the black baseball cap as he walked over to the table with the withdrawal slips.

This time Nora knew what was coming.

The judge and jurors were staring intently at the screen.

The man went over to the counter; now it was possible to see his face in profile.

Winnerman let out a half-stifled cry.

Nora was completely focused on Christian Dufva. His eyes were wide open, as if he couldn't quite believe what he was seeing. His fingers kept opening and closing around his glass of water.

The cashier handed the money to the man in the cap and dark overcoat—two one-thousand-kronor notes and one five hundred, just as Bertil Svensson had said.

The man turned around.

Nora froze the image as the camera caught his face in close-up.

"That's him!" Bertil Svensson shouted. "That's the man who gave me the money!"

Christian Dufva stared out from the screen, wearing the same glasses as Niklas Winnerman.

CHAPTER 124

The plan was to break Pontus Lindqvist, but Thomas had a horrible feeling that the reverse was happening. They'd made no progress despite hours of interrogation, and in the end Hjalmar Andersson had threatened them with the Swedish Code of Judicial Procedure if they didn't take a break.

Thomas had forced down a hamburger even though he wasn't hungry at all, his brain feverishly trying to sort through the facts.

Nothing else of significance had been found in Lindqvist's apartment, and the technicians were still working on his computer. Kalle was back from Lökholmen, and he was working on the material from the storage unit with a CSI.

They still had no idea where Benjamin was being held.

Margit appeared in the doorway of his office. "Thomas—I've just had a call from the hospital. Isak Andrén has regained consciousness. He doesn't seem to have suffered any brain damage, but he's in a bad way."

Thomas knew he had to talk to Isak.

"I'll go over there right away," he said, grabbing his jacket. "Tell Aram to continue with Lindqvist on his own until I get back."

He took the elevator up to the third floor, and was informed by a nurse that Isak was in room five. The smell of disinfectant made him stop dead in the hallway.

He hated being in a hospital; he couldn't shake off the memories. His foot immediately started aching. He'd had two toes amputated after falling through the ice; many years had passed, but the phantom pains were just as strong. He had to shake his foot several times before he was able to move on.

He knew it was illogical, but he couldn't control his body's recollections.

Isak's room was at the far end of the hallway. Thomas tapped on the door and gently pushed it open.

Isak was lying on his back, with a drip attached to his right arm and a thin oxygen tube taped to his nose.

A woman about the same age as Thomas was sitting by the bed. Her eyes were red-rimmed, and she gave a start when Thomas walked in.

"I'm from the police," he said quietly. "I'm sorry to disturb you, but I really need to speak to Isak—it's very important. Are you his mother?"

The woman's eyes filled with fresh tears. She wiped her cheeks with the back of her hand.

"Ulrika Andrén. This doesn't make any sense. I'm trying to understand, but . . ." She looked at Thomas. "He was better. Why would he do this to himself, when everything was fine again?"

Thomas picked up the other chair and put it down beside her. "Do you mind if I sit down?"

Isak hadn't moved. A monitor was humming away in the background.

"I believe Isak woke up a little while ago?"

Ulrika nodded. "Yes, but then he went straight back to sleep." She reached out and stroked her son's arm. "I'm so worried that he might have done himself permanent damage," she whispered. "Brain damage.

They say that oxygen deprivation can affect the motor skills and the speech center."

Thomas gazed at Isak. Several small blood vessels in his cheeks had burst, forming a spider's web pattern on his pale skin. His sun-bleached hair was plastered limply across his forehead.

"It's really important that I speak to him," he said again. "It has to do with Benjamin Dufva, the little boy who was abducted from the camp. We still haven't found him."

Chapter 125

Nora left the frozen image on the screen even though Dennis Grönstedt had brought up the lights again.

Christian Dufva turned away.

As a prosecutor, Nora was obliged to take into account facts that might be to the advantage of the accused, and right now she was going to fulfill that obligation.

In the name of truth.

"Perhaps you could explain why you were in the Hallunda shopping mall on January 11, 2013. And why you withdrew the exact amount of cash that was paid to Bertil Svensson."

Dufva opened and closed his mouth. Not a sound emerged.

"It seems as if you've lied about a number of things during this trial," Nora continued. She waited, even though it was obvious that no explanation was forthcoming.

"OK, let me show you something else."

She pressed a button on the remote. The man's face disappeared and was replaced by a bank statement—a transfer to Åsa Dufva's account. The screen was filled with letters and numbers.

Down at the bottom, highlighted in bright yellow, was the sum of ten million kronor.

"Do you recognize this? It's a payment to your ex-wife. The money was transferred three days after the contract between Alliance Construction and Vine Holdings was signed."

You could have heard a pin drop in the courtroom.

"I'm assuming this payment was made as part of your divorce settlement?"

Without Leila, she wouldn't have been able to figure this out. The young detective had achieved miracles in the short time since they'd seen the CCTV footage at the bank's head office.

When the truth became clear.

It wasn't Niklas Winnerman who'd defrauded his company; it was his partner and cofounder, Christian Dufva. The same man who'd spent hours being interviewed by Leila, leveling accusations at Winnerman and talking about his bitter divorce, his ex-wife sitting there in her luxury apartment with no financial worries.

Leila had put two and two together and come up with the idea that Dufva must have been in desperate straits at the end of 2012, when he had to pay off his ex.

His share of Alliance Construction had been worth around thirty million kronor; Åsa Dufva was entitled to half of that amount. However, by paying her ten million in cash and signing over an apartment worth five, Dufva had managed to hold on to Alliance Construction.

"Let me ask you again," Nora said. "Did Niklas Winnerman have anything to do with the payment to Bertil Svensson?"

Annika Sandberg and Barbro Wikingsson were both listening openmouthed.

"Did he?"

"No," Dufva whispered, his voice breaking.

"Was Niklas Winnerman duped when he entered into the agreement with Vine Holdings in order to secure planning permission that was completely worthless?"

"Yes."

"Who was behind the deal with Vine Holdings?"

"It was me."

At the other table, Winnerman looked as if he'd been hit with a brick.

"How could you do that to me?" he said, loud enough for his former business partner to hear.

A faint flush stained Dufva's gray cheeks, but he kept his eyes fixed on a point on the wall.

"Tell us what happened," Nora said. She wasn't entirely sure of the details, but hoped that the shock would knock Dufva off balance. Spontaneous admissions in court were rare, but right now everything was pointing in that direction. Dufva was deeply shaken, not least by his son's disappearance. Nora felt a little guilty for exploiting the situation, but it had to be done.

When he finally spoke, his words were barely audible. Nora hoped Barbro Wikingsson wouldn't interrupt and ask him to speak up. Not now, when they were so close to a confession.

Dennis Grönstedt began typing feverishly, his eyes darting between Dufva and the keyboard.

"I was desperate. Åsa had demanded a valuation on the apartment. She was insisting on half of everything. I couldn't afford to buy her out. I couldn't let her take my shares, not after all the hard work I'd put in over the years. Plus I was expecting a baby with Ninna by then; Åsa would have destroyed my life if she'd become a part owner of Alliance Construction. I had to do something."

He cleared his throat, raised his voice slightly.

"I had no way of borrowing that kind of money. There's a clause in the co-ownership agreement between Niklas and me: I wasn't allowed to borrow money using the shares as security; otherwise I'd have to sell them to him."

He paused, his jaws working.

"The idea was to take the money out of the company and then, when I was back on my feet, to repay it somehow. I mean, it was my money—it didn't feel as if I was stealing it."

For the first time, he turned his head and made eye contact with Winnerman.

"I swear, I'd intended to fix everything."

"But that didn't happen," Nora said.

"I never imagined we'd go bankrupt, never. I panicked."

Beads of sweat had broken out on his brow.

"The official receiver uncovered the situation and reported the company to the police. He was the first to realize it was a scam, but he thought Niklas was the guilty party."

Dufva cupped his hands in front of his mouth and nose and inhaled deeply several times.

"I had to go along with it. In the end I believed my own lies."

Nora was still having trouble getting her head around all the details. "So why did you disguise yourself as Niklas when you picked out Bertil Svensson and went into the bank to withdraw money?"

The flush on Dufva's cheeks deepened. "Our relationship was toxic by then. Niklas took Åsa's side in the divorce. He said I'd behaved like a total piece of shit toward her." He grimaced. "Niklas had also gone through a divorce, and I never criticized anything he did. But when it was my turn, he got on his high horse, felt he had the right to lecture me."

Barbro Wikingsson frowned, the neutral façade cracking for the first time.

"Niklas once left a pair of glasses at my place," Dufva continued. "So I put them on and used his name when I spoke to Svensson. It felt good to hide behind his identity, just to be on the safe side."

The two men were undeniably similar in appearance; they were the same height, and had the same hair color and deep-set eyes. Now

Nora knew what had happened; she could see how easy it had been for Svensson to make a mistake.

There was no longer any doubt about what had gone on. Or who the guilty party really was.

The case against Niklas Winnerman had to be dismissed.

Nora turned to the judge. "No further questions, Your Honor."

"Wait!" Dufva yelled, stumbling to his feet. He was staring at Winnerman, his expression pleading.

"Does the witness have anything more to say?" Barbro Wikingsson inquired.

"Niklas, please!"

Winnerman merely shook his head and turned away.

Dufva sank back down on his chair.

Nora sensed rather than heard the whispered words:

"Where's Benjamin?"

CHAPTER 126

A murmur came from Isak Andrén's closed lips. Ulrika wiped a little saliva from the corner of his mouth and gently patted his arm.

"Isak, can you hear me?"

Nothing.

She tried again. "Darling, the police are here."

Slowly Isak opened his eyes.

"Are you OK to talk for a minute or two?" Thomas said quietly. "About Benjamin."

"Benjamin." Isak closed his eyes.

Please don't let him go back to sleep. Time was short.

"Isak, there are a couple of things we're wondering about."

Isak opened his eyes again; Thomas could see the despair in them. The boy was so fragile, but the question had to be asked.

"Do you know more about Benjamin's disappearance than you originally told us?"

Ulrika inhaled sharply. "What are you implying?"

Thomas placed a reassuring hand on her arm. "It's OK. Isak, did you hear me?"

"I'd like you to leave." There was no reaction from Isak, but Ulrika was on her feet. "I said I'd like you to leave."

"Don't worry, I promise I won't stay long."

"I'm going to fetch the doctor."

The door closed behind Ulrika. Thomas bent down to Isak's ear; he didn't have long.

"Benjamin's still missing," he whispered. "We're trying to find him. If you know anything, you have to tell us. It's our only chance."

How long had Isak been hanging before David found him? He had a livid blue mark around his neck, like a grotesque necklace; it was hard to understand how he'd survived. Permanent brain damage was sustained after four to five minutes of oxygen deprivation, sometimes less. Maybe it was too much to hope that Isak would be able to answer his questions.

"Someone called," Isak mumbled, his chest heaving beneath the white sheet.

"What do you mean?"

"On Monday evening. A man called . . . said he was Benjamin's dad . . . said he couldn't remember where Benjamin was sleeping."

A tear found its way from under a closed eyelid and trickled down his cheek. A vein throbbed beneath the thin skin, and his eyelashes fluttered briefly.

"It was my fault, I told him. I . . . I thought . . . it was . . . his dad."

Isak's voice was hoarse and strained; he was finding it increasingly difficult to speak.

Thomas felt only emptiness as he grasped the significance of those words. Isak had helped the kidnapper with only the best of intentions, and had then blamed himself for Benjamin's abduction.

He heard footsteps in the hallway; the door would open at any second.

"Do you remember what time it was? Did you see the number?"

If they could trace the call, it might help them to find the place where Benjamin was being held.

Thomas waited with rattled nerves.

The door flew open and a doctor marched in.

"What do you think you're doing?"

Ulrika Andrén was right behind him, with a male nurse.

"Leave him alone! I'll be reporting this to your superiors, you can be sure of that."

Thomas was already on his feet.

"Evening," Isak said faintly. He groped for Thomas's hand. "Common-room phone."

Chapter 127

Jacob Emilsson beamed as he held out his hand to Niklas Winnerman.

"Have a fantastic Midsummer weekend; I'll be in touch in a few days to discuss compensation. In the meantime, relax and have a couple of schnapps with your herring and new potatoes!"

They were standing outside the courthouse, on the top step. It was three o'clock in the afternoon. Niklas had been acquitted.

He managed a stiff smile in return. His sense of relief was already dissipating as his anger grew. "What will happen to Christian?"

"He's really messed up," Emilsson said as his cab pulled up. He waved to indicate that he was on his way. "He'll be charged with fraud and perjury, for a start. That will give the prosecutor something to sink her teeth into."

Emilsson seemed to find the situation amusing.

"He's destroyed my life," Niklas said, hearing the bitterness in his own voice. "I don't understand how he could do that to me. He was prepared to let me go to jail . . ."

"Don't think about that now. Nora Linde did a good job—you have a lot to thank her for." Emilsson glanced at his watch. "I have to go. Call me in a few days."

Winnerman watched as his attorney got into the black cab and sped away.

He was still in shock, his legs trembling.

The nightmare was over, but that gave him no satisfaction. Nor did the fact that Christian was facing a long period behind bars.

A woman cycled past, her basket piled high with grocery bags. Niklas followed her with his gaze.

He wanted to do Christian some serious damage, pay him back for everything he'd done—and then some. See him suffer, just as Niklas had suffered. This past year had been hell.

The small step he'd taken so far wasn't enough. Not by a long shot.

CHAPTER 128

Thomas put the car in first gear and traveled ten yards. Stress was pulsating through his body despite the fact that he'd contacted Aram and passed on the fresh information from Isak.

It was three forty-five, and he'd already been stuck in traffic for half an hour. He'd hit the afternoon rush; he had to go through the city to get to Nacka from the hospital in Solna, but the cars were crawling along.

His cell phone was on the passenger seat. He'd just received a text from Pernilla; her plane was due to land at midnight. Needless to say, she hadn't called back after their last quarrel.

The phone rang again; he glanced at the display and saw that it was Nora. Damn—he'd promised to get in touch when he had time. She'd sent him a text late yesterday evening, but he hadn't seen it until he got home in the middle of the night.

"Can you talk?"

Nora sounded terrible—more than exhausted. Was something wrong?

"How are you?" he said.

She responded with another question. "Have you found Benjamin Dufva yet?"

Thomas shook his head, even though she couldn't see him. "I'm afraid not, but we do have a suspect, a known pedophile. He's being questioned at the station right now; I'm on my way over there."

Nora took a deep breath. "Are you absolutely sure it's him?"

"We found his fingerprints in Benjamin's dormitory, and he had a pair of boys' underpants in a drawer in his apartment."

"OK, but . . . what if it's just a coincidence?" She hesitated, then continued: "What if there's another explanation?"

"What do you mean?"

Nora quickly summarized the afternoon's events—Christian Dufva's confession and Niklas Winnerman's acquittal.

"I tried to tell you yesterday that Dufva had unexpectedly altered his testimony. I was convinced he must have been put under pressure somehow. Only one person could be behind a U-turn like that: Niklas Winnerman."

Thomas let go of the wheel with his left hand and rested his elbow on the open window. They'd spoken to Dufva that very morning, asked him if he'd been subjected to any kind of threat, blackmail, or extortion. He'd told them nothing. He'd seemed ill at ease, but Thomas had chalked that up to anxiety over his son.

Now Nora was suggesting a different interpretation.

The car inched forward, then stopped again.

"I was going to leave it when you didn't call back yesterday evening," Nora went on. "There was no concrete evidence; I was starting to think I must be imagining things. But then Dufva said something today, right at the end of the trial."

Thomas passed a set of traffic cones. One lane became two, and suddenly the traffic was flowing smoothly.

"Go on."

"Dufva turned to Winnerman, and I'm sure he said, 'Where's Benjamin?' Why would he say that unless he thinks Winnerman is behind the kidnapping?" Nora's voice faltered. "I can't stop thinking about it."

Thomas put his foot down. He was crossing the Central Bridge at last, with the City Hall on his right. The air in the car was stifling. He turned the fan to maximum, which merely served to deliver a burst of exhaust fumes.

What Nora had said disturbed him more than he wanted to admit.

Lindqvist had to be guilty. He'd left his fingerprints in the dormitory. His history, his previous convictions—everything pointed to him.

But Nora had put her finger on a weakness. Christian Dufva, the chief witness in a trial, had dramatically altered his testimony at the last minute. What were the chances that his son would be abducted on the very day he was due to testify?

On the other hand, the most remarkable coincidences did occur in criminal investigations—the kinds of things no one would believe if they turned up in a novel.

However, Thomas didn't like the picture that was forming.

"Couldn't you at least check it out?" Nora pleaded. "For Benjamin's sake?"

CHAPTER 129

Niklas Winnerman had splurged on a cab ride home from the courthouse. When the driver stopped at a red light, Niklas saw two police officers who'd stopped a foreign-looking guy with a beard.

The sight of the forces of law and order made him uncomfortable. He turned his face away until the car started moving again.

As soon as he'd unlocked the front door, he went straight over to the liquor cabinet and poured himself a very large Cognac. He knocked back half of it before sinking down on the sofa.

It was over. He could stop putting pressure on Christian, stop sending threatening emails to the prosecutor late at night. Christian had been arrested, and would pay for what he'd done. That knowledge should have made Niklas feel better, but it wasn't enough. The bitterness grew every time he thought about Christian's betrayal.

He ought to call Albert and Natan, tell them their dad had finally been declared innocent, but he couldn't handle being drawn into a long conversation and going over every detail right now.

Christian.

Was there a risk that he would spill his guts to the cops, tell them he'd been threatened in order to make him change his testimony? It didn't really matter; Niklas was in the clear. Everything had been taken care of by Artūras's men.

Anyway, who would believe Christian now, after all his lies?

Niklas finished the Cognac and pulled the laptop toward him. The important thing now was to pay the Lithuanians what he owed them, make sure he never had anything to do with them again.

He logged in to his overseas account to transfer the money; the payment was due today. He'd intended to do it this morning, but had overslept and had to rush off to court.

He sat there with his hand on the mouse. His head was spinning. The Cognac didn't help; he felt as if he was going to faint, even though his body was as tense as a coiled spring.

He reached for the remote. He hadn't watched TV or picked up a newspaper for several days; the trial had absorbed every scrap of his energy.

He switched on Swedish Television's text news service and flicked through the pages at random.

The headline didn't make sense, however many times he read it.

Boy abducted from sailing camp.

His hand shaking, Niklas brought up the page.

The police suspect that eleven-year-old Benjamin Dufva was abducted from a sailing camp on the island of Lökholmen during the early hours of Tuesday morning, and is asking for the public's help.

The words merged into a meaningless blur before Niklas's eyes. Jesus, what had the Lithuanians done? He'd contacted them, asked them to scare Christian so that he'd change his testimony—but this?

"What do you want us to do?" Artūras had asked.

Niklas wasn't interested in hearing the details.

"Frighten the shit out of him. Threaten his family, his new wife. No, wait—tell him something terrible will happen to his son. He's at a sailing camp on Lökholmen. Benjamin's his Achilles' heel; Christian always feels guilty about the kid."

"OK, you're the one who's paying." Artūras had almost sounded amused.

"Do what you like, as long as he speaks up in my favor in court."

Nobody had mentioned abduction . . .

Niklas clutched his empty glass.

It was all Christian's fault. He was the one responsible for this ridiculous situation. All Niklas had done was defend himself against his former partner's lies. If Christian hadn't taken the money and made Niklas the scapegoat, none of this would have happened.

He stared at the TV screen, trying to stay calm.

The warmth of the computer on his lap was seeping through the fabric of his jeans. The bank's home page was still open; a few clicks and the transfer would be done.

But he needed a distraction, just for a little while. There was only one thing that could make him relax.

Last night he'd sworn never to play again, but today had been brutal, stressful beyond belief.

He fetched the bottle and poured himself another drink, gazing at the dark-golden liquid with its aroma of vanilla and oak barrels.

Just for a little while. Not long—he would soon be able to calm his overstretched nerves.

He needed that more than anything else right now.

He had no choice.

CHAPTER 130

Thomas went straight to Aram's office as soon as he'd parked the car. The desk was littered with empty coffee cups, and Aram was sitting in front of a pile of papers, reading with absolute concentration.

"How's it going?" Thomas sat down in the visitor's chair, feeling the tiredness in every fiber of his body.

"Lindqvist is still insisting he's innocent. He denies all knowledge of Benjamin and the kidnapping, but he has admitted that he was in Benjamin's dormitory." Aram shook his head. "He claims he found a T-shirt that someone had left lying around, and wanted to return it. He went to the camp, but there was no one in sight, so he put it on a bed in the nearest dormitory."

"Which just happened to be Benjamin's." Thomas could already hear Lindqvist's defense attorney explaining exactly what had happened.

Aram nodded. "The technicians have managed to get into his computer. We've got enough to charge him with serious child-pornography offenses, if nothing else."

Thomas felt a wave of nausea. "Were there any pictures of Benjamin on his computer?"

"None so far, but it's going to take time to go through everything. The hard drive is full of crap."

They heard rapid footsteps in the hallway, then Karin appeared in the doorway.

"These are the names and numbers of the people who called the landline at the camp on Monday." She put a sheet of paper on Aram's desk. "We're looking at a total of fifteen calls. The penultimate one was at seven thirty in the evening, then nothing until ten thirty-four."

Thomas studied the list. A third were 08 numbers from Stockholm; the rest started with 07, which meant they were from cell phones. All except the last one had the name of the subscriber neatly noted down by Karin.

"That must be him," Aram said, pointing to the bottom line.

"Unfortunately it's a pay-as-you-go or burner phone," Karin said. "Impossible to trace."

Thomas sighed as Nora's words came back to him.

Lindqvist had admitted that he'd been on Lökholmen at the time that call was made. He'd said he left on Tuesday, when the search for Benjamin began. There was no reason for him to contact the camp and ask where Benjamin was sleeping. Even if he had an accomplice, there was no logic to it. Lindqvist could easily have found out for himself; the camp was empty during the day.

Niklas Winnerman, on the other hand, had no idea which dormitory Benjamin was in. All the forensic evidence pointed to Pontus Lindqvist, but Nora's argument was convincing. Had Thomas become too fixated on Lindqvist because of his revulsion at the man's perverted tendencies? He got to his feet.

"We need to talk to Christian Dufva again."

Chapter 131

Niklas was lying on his bed with his arms tightly wrapped around his upper body, in spite of the pain from his broken ribs.

What had he done?

He was unable to stifle a whimper. He buried his face in the pillow to shut out the sound of his own voice.

He was breathing faster and faster.

All he'd wanted to do was settle his nerves. Relax for a little while. He'd pushed aside all his good intentions, his promise never to visit those online gambling sites again.

The game had drawn him in as it always did. He'd allowed himself to place larger and larger bets each time he lost, until he reached the point where he could no longer afford to quit. The only way out was to win back the money.

His luck had to change, he'd thought. Any minute now things would improve. Nobody could have this much bad luck.

Eventually all the numbers on the screen had flashed red. He couldn't continue without making another deposit.

It was gone, all of it, within just a few hours.

What was he going to do now?

His cell phone buzzed. The three words on the screen made him want to throw up.

Time to pay

He heard a sound from the stairwell; the elevator had stopped on his floor.

Niklas clenched his jaws until his teeth ached.

Were they here already?

As soon as they realized he couldn't pay, they would kill him.

The elevator door opened. Someone fumbled with a bunch of keys. His neighbor's door opened and closed.

Niklas was drenched in sweat.

He sat up and ran a hand over his damp hair. He couldn't stay here. This was the first place they'd look.

He had to get out of the apartment. Right now, before they figured out what was going on.

There must be somewhere he could hide out.

The summer cottage on the island of Ingarö. He could lie low there for a few days while he tried to come up with a solution.

He grabbed a bag, packed a few clothes, then picked up his car keys and left.

CHAPTER 132

Christian Dufva had been taken to the Kronoberg custody suite, only a stone's throw from the courthouse. He'd been arrested immediately after the trial.

Thomas and Aram waited in the interview room until Dufva arrived with a guard. He was wearing the regulation green custody shirt and pants. His clogs seemed too big; he was shuffling along.

"Have you found Benjamin?" he asked hoarsely as soon as he saw the two detectives.

Thomas shook his head. "I'm afraid not, but we do have a few questions for you."

Dufva sank down on the chair nearest the wall. He looked completely exhausted; his face was pale and sweaty.

Thomas and Aram sat down opposite him.

"We believe serious threats against you and your family have been made over the past few days in relation to the trial in which you were a key witness. Is that correct?"

Dufva's haggard face contorted. "Yes."

"Is that why you changed your testimony in court?"

Dufva nodded.

"Why didn't you tell us this when we asked you this morning?"

"I didn't dare. I'm sorry."

"What happened?"

"I was about to leave home yesterday morning when my cell phone rang. It was an unknown number. I don't know who he was, he didn't introduce himself. He said they'd taken Benjamin, and if I didn't retract my original statement, I'd never see him again. I had to speak up in Niklas's defense, make sure he was acquitted." He wiped under his nose with one hand. "If I did exactly as he said, Benjamin would soon be back home."

Thomas wanted to groan. Dufva wasn't the first person to have lied to the police in similar circumstances, but it was totally counterproductive. If they'd known about the threat earlier, they would have deployed their resources differently, rather than focusing exclusively on Lindqvist.

"Was the caller Winnerman?"

"No." Dufva shook his head. "I'd have recognized Niklas's voice. This was another guy, but Niklas must have been behind it. Who else?"

That was exactly what Nora had said.

Winnerman must have had an accomplice. Thomas realized he'd had exactly the same thought about Lindqvist a few hours ago. Once again he reproached himself for not having widened the scope of the investigation.

"He had an accent, by the way," Dufva added. "Swedish wasn't his mother tongue."

"Could you identify this accent?" Aram asked. "Any idea where he came from?"

"I'm not sure—it sounded kind of Slavic, but not quite. It all happened so fast."

"Did he say anything else?"

"He told me not to go to the police if I wanted to protect my family. He said that more than once." His shoulders slumped. "Benjamin was supposed to be back by now. They promised. I did exactly what they told me to do."

"A major search is underway," Aram assured him.

Thomas's phone buzzed in his pocket. He took it out and read the text message from Margit:

No one home at Winnerman's apartment

They'd sent a patrol to bring him in when they left for Kronoberg.

"We're trying to get ahold of Winnerman, but he doesn't seem to be home," he said. "Is there anywhere else he might be?"

Dufva shifted uncomfortably on his chair. "I'm not sure. I don't think . . . He doesn't really use it . . . He might have gone to Ingarö."

His expression was tormented; he clutched his left arm.

"He and his sister used to have a summer cottage over there. They might have sold it though—I don't know."

He rubbed his chest. Sweat was pouring down his face, which had taken on a grayish hue.

"You have to find Benjamin," he whispered.

Christian Dufva groped for something to hold onto, then he slid off the chair.

There was a thud as his body hit the floor.

Chapter 133

Niklas Winnerman increased his speed to eighty miles per hour. He put his foot down, leaning forward to the point where the seat belt was cutting into his ribs.

The pain was a reminder of the Lithuanians' brutality. His fingers tightened on the steering wheel. They would never leave him alone. He had no choice; if he couldn't come up with the money, he would have to leave the country.

There was very little traffic, but he caught up with a red Honda that refused to move. He kept his hand on the horn until it switched to the inside lane. As he shot past, so close that the cars were almost touching, he saw the other driver's horrified expression.

Fuck it. Maybe a car crash would be best for everyone. If he died, the situation would be resolved.

Albert and Natan.

Niklas saw the faces of his sons, and groaned out loud. This was all Christian's fault. He'd had a good life before the company collapsed. It was Christian's deception that had made him lose control. Christian was to blame for his spiraling gambling debts.

On the passenger seat lay a half-full bottle of vodka that he'd taken out of the freezer. He grabbed it with sweaty fingers, unscrewed the cap with one hand, and took a swig.

It did nothing to allay his fears.

His head was all over the place. Where was he going to get ahold of that much money—several million? There was no one who could help him now. He had nowhere to turn.

To be on the safe side, he'd tucked a small, sharp kitchen knife into his back pocket. He had no intention of being unprepared this time if they found him.

His hand found its way to his ribs. He reached into his pocket for the blister pack of painkillers and washed down two pills with another swig of vodka.

The road narrowed; one lane was closed off due to road construction. Last night's heavy rain had been replaced by brilliant sunshine, and the surface water had dried up.

The exit for Ingarö was coming up, but Niklas didn't bother slowing down. He turned left onto Ingarövägen, ignoring the stop sign. He drove without paying any real attention to his surroundings; after all these years, he could find his way with his eyes closed.

The last stretch was a dusty, winding dirt track through the forest. The car bounced along until it skidded to a halt in front of the cottage, gravel spraying up around the wheels.

Niklas switched off the engine.

The property was the last one along this little track, hidden away behind tall lilac bushes. He peered through the windshield, checking the place out just to be on the safe side. The blinds were pulled down, the door closed. The gate was ajar, but otherwise everything looked the same as usual.

He could stay here for a few days, think things through. Try to come up with a way out.

This was the first time he'd been here since last summer. He'd been too restless, with the trial hanging over him. Katrin lived abroad; she and her family wouldn't be over until the end of July.

Niklas took a few more slugs of vodka, still thinking about Christian, who had destroyed his life. After a while he took out his cell and read the message again, even though he already knew what it said. He knew those three words by heart.

A faint whimper forced its way across his lips.

CHAPTER 134

The unmarked patrol car sped along the freeway, overtaking one vehicle after another.

"Careful!" Thomas admonished Aram as the back wheels lurched toward the shoulder.

His phone rang: Margit. He switched to speakerphone.

"We've put out a call for Niklas Winnerman. I have more information about the summer cottage: it's registered in the name of Katrin Dupont. She's his sister, and she lives in Brussels. I managed to get ahold of her a few minutes ago; she has no idea where her brother could be. Says she hasn't spoken to him for a long time."

They left the freeway, following the sign for Ingarö.

"However, when I explained the situation, she said she's suspected for a while that Niklas has gambling debts. He's tried to borrow money from her on several occasions, but refused to say why. He's also been trying to persuade her to sell the summer cottage. She thought he was sounding increasingly agitated, almost panic-stricken."

Nora had mentioned the threatening emails; she was convinced they'd come from Winnerman. She'd referred to him as a criminal, despite the fact that he'd just been acquitted in court.

The picture of Niklas Winnerman was becoming increasingly alarming.

"He drives a black Audi," Margit added before ending the call.

They reached a T-junction. Aram consulted the map and turned left. The dirt track narrowed. They passed one house, then another. Nearly there.

Thomas imagined Benjamin's frightened eyes.

The warm evening sun painted the meadows golden yellow. White fluffy clouds drifted across the sky.

Aram slowed down for the last few yards.

"Look," he said.

A black car was parked on the drive.

CHAPTER 135

He didn't want to open his eyes, but the noise beyond the thick wall brought Benjamin out of his semiconscious state.

It sounded like a car, the roar of an engine slicing through the dark silence surrounding him.

Suddenly it stopped.

Someone was here. His body was shaking uncontrollably—was it fear, or a fever? His muscles ached, and from time to time he suffered cramps, painful spasms in his arms and legs.

More noises above his head. Heavy footsteps, creaking floorboards, a door slamming shut.

I don't want to die.

Benjamin started to cry yet again. He couldn't hear properly, couldn't even lift his head any longer, but he tried to curl up on the mattress and pull the sleeping bag over him with his good arm so that he wouldn't be seen. When he caught his sore arm by mistake, it hurt so much that he almost let out a scream.

If he lay perfectly still, maybe no one would find him.

This is pointless, a little voice whispered. It was the kidnapper who'd locked him up, so why bother hiding?

Benjamin breathed as quietly as possible, but the air around his face grew hot in less than a minute. He felt as if he were suffocating beneath the slippery fabric.

His heart was racing faster than ever.

Footsteps again—coming downstairs? There must be a staircase outside the locked door. Was he in a cellar?

Someone fumbled with the lock, and Benjamin heard a key turning. *Please, God,* he prayed. *Please save me.*

CHAPTER 136

Niklas Winnerman had staggered down the stairs. He'd finished the vodka, but there ought to be a bottle of schnapps in the cellar, left over from last summer's crayfish party.

The more he drank, the more his bitterness grew.

The thought of Christian made his head pound. He was the one who had started all this; it was his fault that Niklas had to hide away out here in the middle of nowhere instead of celebrating his acquittal with his family.

The key was stiff; he had no recollection of having locked up the last time he was here. When he eventually managed to turn the key, the door flew open with such force that it banged against the wall.

The stench of urine and fetid air made him recoil. It smelled as if an animal had died in there.

He groped for the light switch, but nothing happened. The bulb must have blown; nothing was going his way today.

He squinted his eyes and peered into the room. The light from the stairs wasn't much help, but eventually he spotted the bottle of schnapps on the top shelf. He grabbed it with a sigh of relief and turned to leave.

Why did the cellar smell of piss?

He caught sight of something out of the corner of his eye as he was about to close the door. A mattress over by the wall, with some kind of bundle on top of it. He was pretty sure he'd never seen it before.

He felt a surge of fear as he thought of the Lithuanians. Had they somehow located the cottage, found a new way of making life difficult?

Better check.

Niklas put down the bottle. He still had the kitchen knife in his back pocket. He took it out and moved closer to the mattress. His eyes had grown accustomed to the darkness; at least he could see his hand in front of him now.

The smell was getting worse.

Suddenly the bundle made a whimpering noise.

Niklas gripped the knife more tightly, ready to strike if necessary.

Now he could see a dusty, torn sleeping bag. He leaned forward and yanked back the fabric.

A white, tear-stained face met his gaze.

Benjamin.

Niklas stared at the boy as the truth dawned on him. Those fucking Lithuanians had abducted Benjamin and hidden him in Niklas's cottage.

They'd set him up.

Jesus.

If anyone found Benjamin here, Niklas would be in deep shit. The police would hunt him down; he'd never get out of this mess, even if he managed to pay off his debt.

He was still clutching the knife.

He'd spent the last few hours fantasizing about revenge, about destroying Christian's life just as Christian had destroyed his.

A darkness rose within him, poisonous and unstoppable. It took over, pushing everything else aside.

He looked at the child he'd known for so many years. Benjamin's face was dirty, his eyes sunken.

Hatred blinded Niklas, obliterating the boy's features and filling him with burning lava.

All he could see was Christian's face.

A pulse throbbed at his temple.

He raised the knife, the shaft catching the light from the stairs.

Benjamin opened his mouth, but Niklas didn't hear him scream.

Chapter 137

Aram parked the car behind a tall lilac. Thomas drew his gun before getting out. Aram ran forward, stooping as he pushed open the gate.

Thomas placed a hand on the hood of the Audi: still warm.

"He must be in there," he said quietly, trying to spot any sign of movement through the window.

Nothing.

"I'll go round the back."

Aram disappeared as Thomas continued toward the front door, his senses on full alert. He moved slowly, holding the gun with a straight arm. He tried the door with his left hand; it wasn't locked.

He pushed it open and peeped inside. There was a musty smell, as if no one had been there for a long time.

He stood perfectly still, listening for sounds or voices, but heard nothing.

Winnerman had to be in there somewhere, but if he'd seen their car, he could be lying in wait.

Thomas kept going, constantly looking around with jerky head movements.

The hallway led to a country-style kitchen. There was an empty vodka bottle on the draining board. It was cold to the touch, which suggested Winnerman had put it there fairly recently.

Thomas listened again.

He thought he heard a clinking sound, but couldn't tell where it was coming from.

A door at the far end of the kitchen was ajar. When Thomas got closer, he could see a flight of stairs, presumably leading to a cellar. The light was on, but the angle of the stairs meant he couldn't see what was down there.

Should he wait for Aram, or check it out himself?

He heard something again, and this time he was pretty sure it was coming from the cellar. He looked out the window, but there was no sign of his colleague.

Silently he began to edge downward, avoiding the mouse droppings.

The stairs ended at a dark wooden door. It was half-open. Gray cobwebs dangled from the ceiling.

Thomas paused and flicked off the gun's safety. Took one more step, then another, and pushed the door with his foot.

He could see a male figure with its back to him, crouching down over by the far wall. What was he doing?

"Police!" Thomas roared. "Come out with your hands up!"

Slowly the man turned around. It was Niklas Winnerman.

"Don't shoot!"

Behind him Thomas saw a child who appeared to be semiconscious. *Benjamin!*

"Don't shoot!" Winnerman yelled again. Something glinted on the floor beside him—a knife?

Thomas was breathing heavily. He was gripping the gun so tightly that his hand was shaking. He couldn't take any chances with Benjamin's life.

"On your feet! Walk toward me with your hands above your head!"

Suddenly he heard Aram's footsteps on the stairs.

"Benjamin's here!" Thomas called out over his shoulder, keeping his eyes fixed on Winnerman. "Move away from Benjamin! I'll shoot if you don't raise your hands right now!"

Winnerman half turned.

"If you touch the boy, I'll shoot!" Sweat was pouring down Thomas's face.

After a few seconds Winnerman slowly got to his feet. He raised his hands in the air and walked toward Thomas.

"I just found him," he stuttered. "Someone had locked him in here—it wasn't me. I think there's something wrong with him."

Aram was already securing Winnerman's wrists behind his back with a pair of handcuffs.

Thomas rushed over to Benjamin. His breathing was rapid and shallow, his face streaked with dirt, his lips cracked.

"You don't need to be frightened anymore," Thomas said gently. "I'm a police officer, and we're going to look after you. Everything's going to be fine."

Benjamin's eyes rolled back.

Thomas picked him up, just as he'd picked up Elin countless times. Registered how little the boy weighed, even though he was twice her age. His body was worryingly limp. He placed the palm of his hand on Benjamin's forehead; it was red hot.

"Call an ambulance," he said to Aram.

Chapter 138

The smell of cooking met Nora as she opened the door of the apartment. Adam must be fixing something to eat for his girlfriend.

Thank goodness—Nora was both late and exhausted. Her body felt as heavy as lead.

This had been one of the strangest days in her entire working life. The charges against Niklas Winnerman had been dropped, and the verdict on Bertil Svensson would be delivered next week. Looking at the jurors' faces, she had no doubt he would be convicted of aiding and abetting.

Christian Dufva had been arrested, but was now in the hospital after suffering a major heart attack. He was in critical condition; a large part of the cardiac muscle had been damaged.

She had passed his case on to a colleague and exchanged a few words with her boss. Officially she was on vacation as of tomorrow. Right now she couldn't even think about the deputy district chief prosecutor's post.

Her priority was to postpone the wedding. Contact all the guests and explain the situation.

The very thought brought tears to her eyes again.

With a weary sigh, she kicked off her dark-blue pumps and slipped off her jacket.

There was an enormous vase of pink and white orchids on the table in the hallway. Nora reached out and touched the beautiful flowers. The petals were fresh.

Jonas had brought back boxes of orchids on other occasions when he'd flown to Bangkok. They were sold prepacked at the airport. You could buy a dozen in Asia for the same amount that a single bloom cost in Sweden.

Someone had left a black airline bag on the floor.

"Hello?" she called out, barely able to speak. She was so fragile she didn't dare believe what she was seeing.

A few seconds passed. She could hear the kitchen fan, the sound of the oven door closing.

"Hello?"

The tears began to fall.

"Don't cry, sweetheart!"

Jonas emerged from the kitchen with a dishtowel over his shoulder. He was at her side in no time. He drew her close and stroked her cheek.

"Are you really home?" Nora whispered.

"I told you everything would be fine."

"You did."

Nora rested her forehead against his, closed her eyes. She'd let it all get to her. It wasn't Jonas's fault he'd been delayed.

Things could have been much worse.

She hadn't heard from Thomas; little Benjamin was still missing. She couldn't begin to imagine how his mother was feeling.

It didn't matter if she and Jonas got married on Friday or Saturday or some other day. The important thing was that they had each other, that the two of them and the children were safe and well.

"What happened?" she murmured after a long time.

"They fixed the fault, got the passengers on board, then we flew home."

He made it sound like nothing.

"I'm so sorry for all those things I said," she whispered in his ear. "Thank you for coming back."

"I had to come back. We're getting married on Friday."

CHAPTER 139

There were times when Thomas remembered why he'd chosen to become a police officer. This was one of those moments, as Åsa Dufva raced into the hospital where Benjamin had been brought by ambulance.

Her jacket flapped around her as she ran down the hallway, almost cannoning into a nurse who was pushing along an IV stand.

Thomas was about to return to Nacka for an initial interview with Winnerman. Aram had already gone straight to the station, while Thomas had chosen to check on Benjamin first.

"Thank you so much for finding my son," Åsa said, squeezing his hands. "I'll never forget it."

Benjamin was in stable condition, his frail little body receiving intravenous antibiotics and nutrients. Thomas hoped his recovery wouldn't prove too tough. The effects of the kidnapping would require a great deal of therapy and love, and his father was in intensive care.

But that was all in the future. Right now it was a matter of dealing with serious blood poisoning. The doctors had sounded optimistic. A few more hours and it would have been a different story.

Thomas gently freed himself from Åsa's grip. "I'm just so glad we found him in time."

There would be many interviews with Niklas Winnerman. Margit had offered to step in, but Thomas had refused. He wanted to meet the man face-to-face, understand what had happened.

Aram was waiting outside room five.

"How's Benjamin?" he said as soon as the green elevator doors opened.

"The doctors are hopeful, but it's too early to say for sure. His mother refuses to let him out of her sight."

"What a mess."

Thomas nodded and led the way into the interview room. He immediately recognized the lawyer standing by the window with his phone pressed to his ear: it was Jacob Emilsson, one of the best-known defense attorneys in Stockholm.

Damn. Thomas knew how Emilsson worked; everything was going to take longer than necessary.

Winnerman looked up as the two officers entered the room. His bloodshot eyes widened.

Thomas was unable to summon up any sympathy whatsoever. Winnerman had had a child abducted in order to save his own skin. He was just as much a piece of shit as his former business partner.

Winnerman's expression was a mixture of fear and confusion. "It wasn't me," he burst out, just as he'd done in the cellar. "You have to believe me. I'll tell you everything."

Emilsson quickly placed a hand on his client's shoulder. "You don't have to say anything. No one can force you."

"I'm not a criminal, I'm not!"

Thomas wondered how many times he'd heard those words in this room. Right now he was too tired to listen to that kind of crap.

"It's been a nightmare," Winnerman continued. "I knew Christian was lying, that there was no truth in his allegations against me. I just didn't understand why."

His eyes were bulging, and his shirt was filthy with dust from the cellar.

"Dufva's admission came as a total surprise to everyone in the courtroom," Emilsson interjected.

Winnerman stared at his attorney for a long time. "I kept on telling you, but you didn't believe me."

Thomas had expected Emilsson to show some kind of embarrassment or remorse, but his face didn't change.

"You were the one who said that Christian would finish me. You said I'd go down if he didn't change his testimony." Winnerman scratched his throat; when he raised his arm, the faint smell of body odor reached Thomas's nostrils.

"I had to do something to stop him—I had no choice. Christian forced my hand. I couldn't go to jail, I knew what was waiting for me in there. I wouldn't survive."

"So you put pressure on him by kidnapping his son?" Aram said.

"No, no! You've got it all wrong!"

"Perhaps you'd like to explain," Thomas said icily.

Contradictory emotions passed over Winnerman's face.

"I had contacts," he mumbled eventually. "From Lithuania."

Emilsson placed a cautionary hand on his client's arm, but Winnerman shook it off. He seemed to have made a decision.

"I have gambling debts. Over the past twelve months, I've lost huge sums of money. In the end the situation became untenable. I'd taken out loans using the apartment as security, and sold everything there was to sell."

His sister had been right in her suspicions.

"Someone put me in touch with a guy from Lithuania, who lent me the money." Winnerman clutched his ribs with a grimace. "This happened last Sunday. Two broken ribs. I was late making a payment. They came calling, told me it was my final warning. That was what gave me the idea. If they could threaten me and beat me up, then maybe they could help me with Christian."

His cheeks flushed red.

"I realize now how stupid that was," Winnerman continued, "but I didn't know what else to do. I contacted them, asked if they could make him change his testimony."

Aram folded his arms. "And they agreed, just like that?"

"I had to pay. They added ten percent on to my debt—several hundred thousand—but I had no choice. I was prepared to do anything to avoid going to jail."

Thomas was finding it hard to buy his story.

"I never asked them to kidnap Benjamin," Winnerman insisted. "I just wanted to get Christian to withdraw his allegations. I know him, he's not a brave man; I thought a threat against him and his family would do the trick. Or maybe they'd give him a beating, just like they did to me."

"Is that how you expressed yourself?" Thomas said.

"I asked them to make sure Christian didn't testify against me."

It was going to be a challenge for Jacob Emilsson to defend his client this time around.

"How come Benjamin was abducted from the sailing camp?"

"I've no idea."

"How did they know he was there?"

Winnerman looked down at the table. "I told them."

"Who went over there and took Benjamin?"

"Once again, I've no idea."

Aram sighed.

"I know how it sounds, but that's what happened. I swear—all I did was ask them to put pressure on Christian and his family. I did mention Benjamin, but I never thought they'd actually kidnap him."

Aram leaned forward. "If we assume you're right, and these Baltic mafia guys decided to give you value for your money, then why hide Benjamin in your cellar?"

"I've discussed this with my client," Emilsson said. "I think they wanted to make sure he was in the frame if there were any problems. The whole thing wouldn't have taken more than a few hours—in, out, a quick job that made them a lot of money. And it was risk-free—if they were caught, the blame could be squarely placed on my client's shoulders."

Thomas wasn't convinced. "But what about Benjamin? Were they intending to leave him to die down there?"

Emilsson exchanged a glance with Winnerman. "The debt was due to be repaid today. Our guess is that the Lithuanians were planning to reveal Benjamin's whereabouts once they'd received their money. Using Niklas's summer cottage gave them extra insurance. And maybe something to hold over him in the future."

Thomas couldn't help wondering if they'd ever track down the real kidnapper. Emilsson's take on what had happened to Benjamin sounded so unlikely that it could well be true.

"My client did not deliberately incite anyone to kidnap the child," Emilsson added. "He denies all involvement."

"Well, he's going to be charged," Aram said. "And he can expect to spend a long time in jail."

CHAPTER 140

It was almost ten thirty by the time Aram and Thomas returned to the third floor. Margit was still in her office. She called out to them as soon as she heard their footsteps.

Thomas sat down in one of the visitor's chairs, while Aram remained standing with his back to the wall.

Margit was shivering even though she was wearing a thick sweater. "So how did it go?" she asked.

Aram gave her a short summary of the interview with Winnerman.

"Sounds like revisionist history to me," Margit said sourly.

Thomas wanted nothing more than to agree, but he could still hear Emilsson defending Winnerman's version.

"There is a certain logic to it," he said reluctantly. "We'll see what forensics have to say." He rubbed his forehead; his eyelids were heavy.

Whatever the outcome, Winnerman was facing a significant jail sentence. The courts didn't look kindly on those who blackmailed a witness. Interfering in a judicial matter, to use the technical term.

"They might find the kidnapper's DNA on the sleeping bag," Aram said. "Or something else to support Winnerman's story."

"The main thing is that Benjamin's been found," Margit said. "I called the hospital a little while ago, and he's responding well to treatment."

"Any news on Isak Andrén?" Thomas asked, thinking of the livid mark around Isak's neck, and his mother's despair.

"He doesn't appear to have suffered any serious neurological damage, thank goodness. However, Christian Dufva is in a bad way. He still hasn't regained consciousness." Margit pushed several sheets of paper across the desk. "You remember Pontus Lindqvist's last conviction? It was based on a video where he was abusing a young boy, and he was found guilty even though they never managed to track down the child."

Pontus Lindqvist.

Thomas had forgotten about him over the past few hours; now the man's face came into his mind again.

Not for one second did he buy Lindqvist's explanation as to why he'd been in Benjamin's dormitory. There was something creepy about the fingerprints in there, even if he wasn't the one who'd actually taken Benjamin in the end.

Lindqvist must have had evil intentions.

Margit pointed to the papers. "I've just spoken to a colleague in Gothenburg."

The detention cell was small. Niklas was perched on the bed, staring at the wall. Everything was gray in here. The floor, the walls, the ceiling. Everything except the yellowish ring around the toilet.

The alcohol had left his body. His chest felt tight and he was shivering. The thin blanket around his shoulders wasn't helping at all.

He felt as if somebody was repeatedly hitting him over the head with a hammer. He was trying not to groan out loud.

He had turned into a monster. How was he going to live with the memory of Benjamin's terrified face as he raised the knife?

Now, when he was sober, he couldn't understand how he could have acted that way. He had almost been prepared to murder a little boy in order to punish his father. He had seen red; the rage boiling in his blood had taken over.

He had stopped at the very last second, pulled back his hand and dropped the knife.

He had been like a different person.

Albert and Natan would never forgive him when they found out what he'd done. There was nothing he could say that would fix this.

He'd lost everything—his business and his family. He would end up in jail; he might be murdered in there, purely as a result of his own actions.

The Lithuanians would show him no mercy.

For the first time, dying didn't seem like the worst option.

Chapter 141

When Thomas and Aram entered the interview room, Pontus Lindqvist was slumped on a chair next to his lawyer. He looked dazed, as if he'd just been woken up.

Hjalmar Andersson was not impressed.

"Is it really necessary to question my client again at this hour? Couldn't it have waited until tomorrow?"

Thomas gave him an icy glare. "We've found Benjamin Dufva. Your client is no longer suspected of abduction."

Lindqvist sat up a little straighter. "I told you I didn't do it." A smug smile spread across his face.

Andersson reached for his briefcase. "So we're free to leave?"

Thomas ignored him and spoke directly to Lindqvist. "There was a bag of clothes in your Sureguard storage unit."

Kalle had gone through everything they'd found, with meticulous attention to detail.

"Among other things, there were items of clothing that appeared to belong to a boy aged about ten, the same little boy who owned the underpants you couldn't help tucking away in your apartment."

The police dog had done its job well; they just hadn't realized this was about another child, not Benjamin.

Lindqvist looked away. The thin skin beneath his eyes had a bluish tinge.

"The clothes were neatly folded along with a map of an area outside Gothenburg. A place where your parents used to own a summer cottage."

Aram folded his arms. "The Gothenburg police have been out there this evening with a dog team."

"They found the grave where a small boy was buried," Thomas said. "Or rather what was left of him."

Hjalmar Andersson inhaled sharply.

"The DNA from the body will be compared with DNA from the clothing we found in your possession. The age of the child seems to match the boy you abused when you were convicted of child rape some years ago. The abuse you filmed. We'll soon know the identity of the victim."

"You will be arrested first thing tomorrow morning," Aram informed him. "You can expect to be charged with homicide. That means life imprisonment."

Every scrap of color had drained from Lindqvist's face. He looked ten years older.

Thomas felt a bitter satisfaction. They'd managed to nail him after all, but exhaustion was making his head pound.

He glanced at his watch. Pernilla's flight was due to land in an hour. Time to go home.

CHAPTER 142

Thursday, June 19

A key turned in the lock. The sound didn't make Thomas's heart leap. He'd dozed off on the sofa, but wondered if it was a good idea to have waited up for Pernilla.

Maybe there wasn't much to talk about anymore?

It was after one. The night sky was still dark blue. He was both mentally and physically exhausted after the past twenty-four hours, but at the same time he was jumpy and restless. The brief nap hadn't helped him to relax.

He couldn't stop thinking about what Margit had told him in the elevator before they left the station. The restructuring. It looked as if Karin Ek would be surplus to requirements, and Staffan Nilsson would be forced to retire.

What good could that possibly do?

The front door opened, creating a cross draft from the balcony. Thomas heard the faint rumble of a wheeled suitcase, the rattle of a coat hanger.

Pernilla appeared in the doorway. "You're still up."

"I was waiting for you." Thomas made a small gesture, beckoning her into the room. Pernilla bit her lower lip, but remained where she was.

"This isn't working," Thomas said, knowing the words were true. "If you're going to keep traveling so much, then it's best if Elin and I live on our own."

If they had to go their separate ways, then so be it; he couldn't live like this. He hated the thought of Elin not growing up with both parents together, but she wouldn't be the first child it had happened to. Half of all marriages in Sweden ended in divorce; surely he and Pernilla could take a civilized approach to a split.

Pernilla wrapped her arms around her body. "Oh, Thomas . . ."

There was nothing to add. He'd never been good at analyzing his emotions. He'd said what he had to say; they might as well go to bed now, try to get a few hours' sleep.

There would be more interviews to get through in the morning.

He was too exhausted to discuss the practicalities at this point. He was about to get to his feet when Pernilla stopped him.

"Wait."

Her eyes were shining with unshed tears.

"I was too hard on you on the phone the other day. I'm sorry. I felt so guilty that I attacked you instead. I know I've been working a lot lately, but you don't understand what it's like."

No, he didn't. All he knew was that his partner would rather focus on her career than on him and their daughter.

"I love you and Elin—this isn't about the two of you," Pernilla went on quietly.

Thomas was no longer annoyed and frustrated; he was simply tired of it all. Tired of being the one who had to deal with Elin's disappointment every time Pernilla wasn't there for dinner or to put her to bed. Tired of the fact that they were never together these days. He sank back on the sofa.

"So tell me what it is about."

There were new lines around Pernilla's eyes. Her hair was caught up in a barrette from which a few stray tendrils had escaped.

"I don't know if I can fix this either," she said. "I'm always so tired and irritable, always in a hurry. I realize I'm not spending enough time with you and Elin."

She made a shuddering sound, somewhere between a sigh and a sob. She rubbed one temple, as she always did when she was upset.

"Of course I've noticed things aren't great between us. It's . . . there's so much to do. It's like a spring tide that never stops. When I go to bed at night, I've just about gotten through my emails. When I wake up the next morning, a hundred more have arrived."

Thomas wasn't sure what to say. His job was also demanding, and sometimes he, too, felt as if he were drowning, but he didn't want to sit here arguing about who had the most to do. It was undignified.

This wasn't some kind of duel.

"I don't know how to handle everything," Pernilla continued. "The constant phone calls, meetings, budget forecasts, staff interviews . . . There's not enough of me to go around."

There was a cold draft from the balcony. Thomas got up and closed the door.

"Why don't you come and sit down?" he suggested.

Pernilla perched on the armchair opposite the sofa. "I feel guilty every evening when I'm away, or when I sit up late with my laptop. You might not believe me, but I do realize how irritated you get. I know exactly how you're going to react each time I ask you to pick up Elin even though it's my turn."

Elin was still with her grandparents. The last question she'd asked before falling asleep was when Mommy would be home.

"Why do you think I send text messages instead of calling? I can't face fighting with you when I'm so stressed."

Thomas had to admit that he sometimes overreacted. He, too, had allowed work to take over on more than one occasion.

Pernilla leaned across the coffee table and took his hand cautiously, as if she expected him to pull away.

"As I said, this isn't about you. I'm exhausted. I promise I'll try to sort it out. If the worse comes to the worst, I'll have to find another job."

She took out the barrette. As her hair fell to her shoulders, Thomas saw the Pernilla he had married fourteen years earlier in Djurö church. The Pernilla who had left him after Emily's death, then come looking for him again.

Something inside him began to thaw.

"I really want this to work," she whispered.

Could they find their way back to each other? One more time?

Thomas stood up and opened his arms. Brushed her forehead with his lips when she came to him.

"Me, too," he murmured in her ear, although he didn't know how that was going to happen.

How he was going to summon up the energy.

But there were two of them in this relationship; she wasn't the only one to blame if things had gone wrong.

"Let's go to bed," he said. "We can talk more in the morning."

The warmth of her body reached his. In spite of his weariness, the desire began to awaken.

As it always did.

CHAPTER 143

Nora felt the cool dew beneath her bare feet as she wandered out onto the jetty. It was after eleven. The sun had gone down half an hour earlier, but the sky was still pink over Harö, where the last rays had disappeared behind the pine trees.

Tomorrow they were getting married.

She turned and looked up at the dark façade of the Brand villa.

Jonas was asleep; the jet lag had caught up with him. Just as well— it was better if he was rested for the next day. The first guests were coming over on the morning boat, which was due at nine.

A sailboat showing its navigation lights passed by on its way to Sandhamn. The white hull was reflected in the shining surface of the water, and a small rubber dinghy bobbed along behind the stern.

Nora inhaled the smell of the sea and seaweed, feeling the calmness that always came when she gazed out at the peaceful inlet, the lighthouses that had started flashing in the distance, guiding seafarers to safety.

After a while she went back and sat down on one of the seats by the table.

Was she doing the right thing?

A week ago she'd been sure she wanted to marry Jonas; the day before yesterday she'd been equally sure that it wasn't going to happen.

Twenty-one years had passed since her first marriage. She'd been convinced that she was going to spend the rest of her life with Henrik.

Nora shivered.

All those terrible things they'd said to each other. All the tears, the disappointment. The pain when she found out Henrik had been unfaithful.

It had taken them many years to realize that the marriage was over, and even longer before they were able to talk to each other again like civilized people.

But without Henrik, she wouldn't have Adam and Simon. Nora smiled when she thought of her sons. They were both out with friends on this summer night; Simon was supposed to be back by midnight. They were looking forward to the wedding; they both liked Jonas very much, and they adored their little sister.

She couldn't regret her marriage to Henrik, only what had become of it in the end.

Nora pulled her cardigan more tightly around her body.

She loved Jonas, and he loved her. But the warm glow of happiness she had felt a week ago had been diluted with doubts that hadn't been there before. The memory of the terrible night when she told him to forget the whole thing wouldn't leave her. There was a crack in the security she'd taken for granted.

She picked up a handful of gravel and let it trickle through her fingers.

It was too late to change her mind now. Tomorrow they were getting married, and it was going to be a wonderful day. They loved each other, she reminded herself once more.

Please let it work out this time.

CHAPTER 144

Friday, June 20

The doorway of the chapel on Sandhamn was decorated with branches of pale-green birch as Thomas and Pernilla made their way up the hill. This was one of the highest points on the island, with a truly beautiful view. From here you could look out across the archipelago in all directions.

Thomas could see Harö through the sun haze.

A steady stream of boats was on the way into Sandhamn to celebrate Midsummer. One after the other passed by with the Swedish flag fluttering proudly in the stern.

He gazed toward Lökholmen and thought about the past twenty-four hours. This morning he'd heard that Benjamin was able to sit up, and had laughed during a conversation with his mother. She hadn't yet told him that his father had passed away on Thursday as a result of his heart attack.

"Shall we go in?" Pernilla said, smiling at the friendly churchwarden who was handing out copies of the order of service.

Pernilla looked beautiful in her turquoise summer dress. They went and sat in one of the pews at the front on the left-hand side, directly behind Nora's parents. Adam and Simon were already waiting at the altar. Thomas gave the boys the thumbs-up; they didn't look entirely comfortable in their dark-blue suits, white shirts, and dark-blue ties. Simon gave his godfather an embarrassed grin and stuck his index finger inside his collar in an exaggerated gesture.

The chancel was adorned with vases filled with midsummer flowers—daisies, buttercups, and cornflowers. The organ began to play; time to stand up.

Thomas turned and saw Nora and Jonas walking up the aisle hand in hand, preceded by Elin and Julia, each carrying a woven basket filled with rose petals. Elin was slightly behind Julia, keeping a close eye on her friend.

Thomas couldn't help smiling proudly as his daughter passed by.

The bride and groom were followed by their bridesmaid—Jonas's daughter Wilma, who was carrying a bouquet in the same colors as Nora's.

They'd been through a lot, but now they were standing here, Nora and Jonas. She couldn't have found a better man.

She was sparkling today.

The music faded away, and the pastor stepped forward with an expectant smile. Soon Nora and Jonas would exchange their vows.

Thomas reached out and took Pernilla's hand.

Last night she'd sat up in bed with her laptop yet again, despite everything they'd talked about the previous evening. He had felt the inevitable stab of anger and frustration, but had managed not to say anything. Elin had been thrilled when she came home from staying with her grandparents and found Mommy there.

Thomas really wanted things to work between them. He brought Pernilla's hand to his lips and gently kissed it.

I love you, he thought. *Isn't that enough?*

ACKNOWLEDGMENTS

In the Name of Truth gave me the opportunity to combine two scenarios I've been toying with for a long time: partly the story of a child who goes missing from Lökholmen, where both I and my children have attended sailing camps, and partly the idea of writing a courtroom drama where everything isn't as it first seems. One day the plot simply came into my mind, and it has been a real pleasure to write this novel.

A pleasure I hope my readers will share.

I have taken certain liberties—with the routines in camp, with the information that is held in the marina office on Lökholmen, and with airline procedures when it comes to the deployment of crews. I have also dramatized court proceedings to some extent. As far as the characters go, any resemblance to persons living or dead is entirely coincidental, and I take full responsibility for any possible errors.

Many kind people have helped with this book, and I would like to thank them all:

District judge Cecilia Klerbro, my good friend and fellow student, went through every detail of the trial and showed great patience with a former business lawyer who hasn't set foot in a courtroom for many years. The author Jens Lapidus helped me to understand the role of the defense attorney, and gave me many helpful tips.

The Royal Swedish Yacht Club allowed me to visit their sailing camp on Lökholmen and generously shared information about this annual activity.

Filip Bäckström, an instructor on Lökholmen, was an absolute rock who clarified many concepts during my stay.

Camp leaders Nisse Wikland and Axel Eklund answered a thousand questions and took me out to sea with their students.

Deputy Chief Prosecutors Anna Remse and Anna Karin Hansen, together with District Prosecutor Michael Målqvist, all with the Economic Crimes Authority, provided facts and information about the work of the Authority.

As always, Detective Inspector Rolf Hansson has been a great help with various aspects of police work. Janne Tannlund, a senior pilot with SAS, supplied all the details about his profession and the airline's routines. Senior consultant Nils Kuylenstierna explained the possible causes and onset of blood poisoning.

Friends, family members, and Sandhamn neighbors who have read and commented on the manuscript along the way are Anette Björklund Brifalk, Helen Duphorn, and Gunilla Pettersson, plus of course Lennart and Camilla Sten. Camilla is a student of psychology, and her knowledge of young people suffering with mental health issues was enormously helpful.

Karin Linge Nordh, my fantastic publisher, you just keep getting better and better.

John Häggblom—I'd like to nominate you for the title of Sweden's best editor.

Sara Lindegren and everyone else at Forum—it's an absolute joy to work with you!

Karin, Annika, Therese, and everyone at Bindefeld—thank you for all the work you've put in.

Anna Frankl, Joakim Hansson, and the whole team at Nordin Agency—your commitment means so much. Together we are conquering the world!

Last but not least, my darling family: Lennart, Camilla, Alexander, and Leo. Thank you for being there. You mean everything to me.

Sandhamn, September 30, 2015
Viveca Sten

ABOUT THE AUTHOR

Photo © 2016

Since 2008 Swedish writer Viveca Sten has sold more than 4.5 million copies of her Sandhamn Murders series, which includes *In the Name of Truth*, *In the Shadow of Power*, *In Harm's Way*, *In the Heat of the Moment*, *Tonight You're Dead*, *Guiltless*, *Closed Circles*, and *Still Waters*. The novels have established her as one of Sweden's most popular authors. Set on the island of Sandhamn, the bestselling novels have been adapted into a Swedish-language TV series, shot on location, and seen by seventy million viewers around the world. Sten lives in Stockholm with her husband and three children, yet she prefers spending her time on Sandhamn Island, where she writes and vacations with her family. Follow her at www.vivecasten.com.

About the Translator

Marlaine Delargy lives in Shropshire in the United Kingdom. She studied Swedish and German at the University of Wales, Aberystwyth, and taught German for almost twenty years. She has translated novels by many authors, including Kristina Ohlsson, Helene Tursten, John Ajvide Lindqvist, Therese Bohman, Theodor Kallifatides, Johan Theorin, with whom she won the Crime Writers' Association International Dagger in 2010, and Henning Mankell, with whom she won the Crime Writers' Association International Dagger in 2018. Marlaine has also translated *Guiltless, Tonight You're Dead, In the Heat of the Moment, In Harm's Way*, and *In the Shadow of Power* in Viveca Sten's Sandhamn Murders series.